SLEEPING DOGS

S. A. BAKER

SLEEPING DOGS
S. A. BAKER

WICKED TALES

HTTPS://WICKEDTALES.CA
A division of DAOwen Publications

Sleeping Dogs / S. A. Baker

ISBN 978-1-998029-19-8
EISBN 978-1-998029-20-4

Cover Art by MMT Productions

10 9 8 7 6 5 4 3 2 1

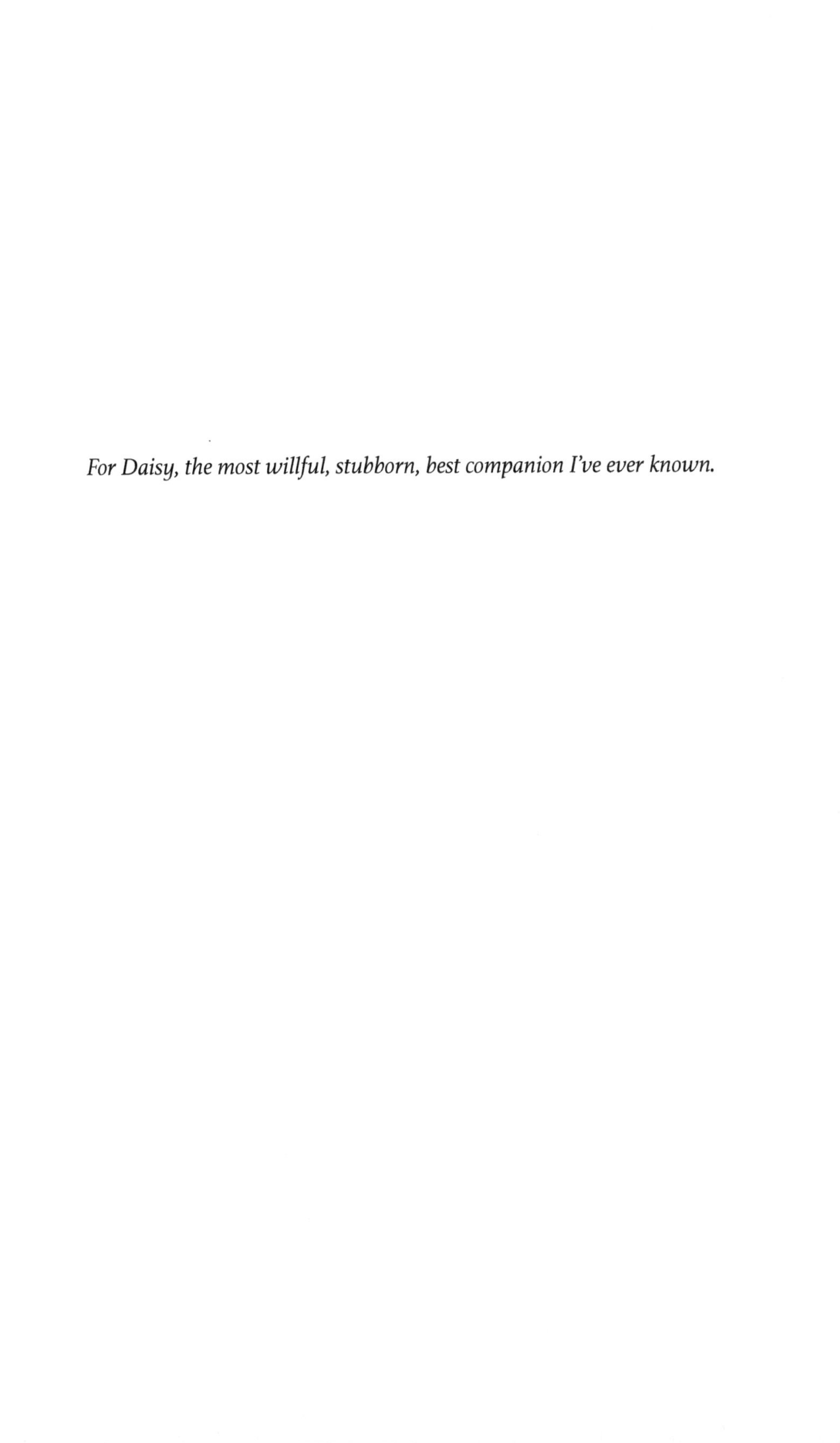

For Daisy, the most willful, stubborn, best companion I've ever known.

Outside of a dog, a book is man's best friend. Inside a dog, it's to dark to read.

    - Groucho Marx, 1954

1

He sat in his Bronco watching the sun crest over the tops of the bungalows on Grandview Avenue, heralding another day in suburban Winterbourne. The man looked at his wristwatch. 7:45. He glanced at the middle-aged Asian man dragging trash bags from his garage to the curb in a steady rhythm of panicky grab, drag, and flop it into place beside the last one, cursing all the while. The man in the Bronco stared at the school kids bouncing out of the front doors of all the cookie-cutter houses. They came in drips and drabs at first, becoming a steady flow as the minutes moved closer to school time. The children giggled and gaggled and walked, almost as a single mass of hands and feet, and all of them heading toward the public school four blocks away.

They held his attention briefly, but hand in hand, arm in arm, they practically moved as a single, giant ball of children. They carried on up the street, fearless – clueless. He'd taken that road before. They were too easy and didn't interest him. No, the man was always looking for a challenge, and it walked out of the front door of 29 Grandview Avenue, wearing a backpack too big for him and red sneakers – one of which was untied. He looked at his watch again, more of a nervous impulse than a need to know the time. 8:04.

The kid was young, the man thought. Young, but not too young. He figured the kid in the red sneakers to be around 13. Just about to start high school. He had no proof of this, no reason to believe he was right about any of it, but he knew people, and was a decent judge of age. "Thirteen," he said. "Thirteen if he's a day. If he's an hour older, I'll eat my shit." He chuckled and put the Bronco in gear. He played a little game with himself. If the kid in the red sneakers went left, it was to go to the grade school and couldn't be older than 13, unless he was one of those weird January kids who was always a year ahead of everybody. If he went right, he was likely bound for Winterbourne High School and was fourteen or older. The man steered the Bronco to a set of lights at the end of Grandview Avenue and pulled over next to Mason's bakery. From here, the kid could only go left or right. He watched. He inhaled. He waited.

The red sneakers stood on the corner for too long, the man thought. The boy danced along the edge of a razor. It was after eight already. If he went left, he'd have to hurry to get to the public school on time. If he went right, he'd have to run to get to the school on time. The boy stepped to the crosswalk and stopped.

"What the fuck?" The man sighed. "Really?"

The kid stopped dead, took off his backpack, and knelt on the sidewalk while he tied the laces of the undone red sneaker. He rose slowly and set off again.

"C'mon," the Bronco man said. "C'mon."

The boy in the red sneakers stepped to the curb and pushed the crosswalk button on the stop-light pole. The red hand disappeared, replaced by the bright white walking figure and the red sneakers headed left.

"I fucking knew it!" the man said.

He pulled away from the curb and headed toward Grandview public, driving quickly but not speeding. Not fast enough to draw attention to himself, just enough to get ahead of the boy in the red sneakers. He checked his driver's side mirror, and the kid came up next to him. His heart pounded. He looked at the passenger seat and decided he was as ready as he'd ever be.

"Hey kid," he said and pulled alongside red sneakers. "You want to make some money?"

"Fuck off, mister," the boy in the red sneakers said.

"What?"

"I'm not touching your prick. I don't care how much candy you have."

The man in the bronco laughed and flashed a smile at the boy. "Is that what you think this is?"

"Isn't it?" Red sneakers said with a scowl.

"No," the man said. "I need help to look for my dog, but if you're not interested in making fifty dollars, then I'll go find somebody else."

"Wait," red sneakers said. "What do you need me to do?"

The bait hung there in front of the boy's face like a dew worm in a trout pond.

"Hold on and I'll show you." The man pulled the Bronco over. "You'll trip if you're not careful." He pointed at the boy's untied red sneaker.

"God dammit it," the boy said. His shoe had come undone again. He knelt and tied it. As he stood, the man was nearly on top of him. "Oh, hi." He took a couple of steps backward.

The man towered over him, which might not have been saying much. Slim, but not skinny, like he worked construction for a living. Like his dad, only without the beer gut. His hair was brown except for little bits of silver here and there and had a forehead that the boy and his friends would have laughed at and called a five head. He wore jeans and sneakers and a black shirt under a grey, members only jacket. But the thing that really stuck out was the cane. The man from the Bronco walked with a serious limp and had a dark wooden cane in his hand.

"So, I could use a little help to try and find my dog. I can't get around so well right now, and my dog is really little and really fast. If you find him and catch him for me, I'll give you fifty bucks. Deal?" He extended a hand toward the kid in the red sneakers. The kid took this hand and shook it. "This is what she looks like." He produced a photo from the pocket of his jacket of a smallish, fluffy brown and white dog. "Her name is Flower, you know, like the skunk from Bambi? Anyway, I call her Flo and we were out walking near Vic Park. She saw a squirrel that she figured she could get a hold of, and she bolted. Jerked the leash right out of my hand, she disappeared in the bushes. I tried looking for her and calling her, but with this bum leg, I couldn't do much. That's where you come in."

"Do you think she made it this far over?" the boy said.

"No." The man laughed. "No, I think she's probably still around the park. She thinks she's a brave hunter, but she's really a complete coward. Probably cowering under a bush somewhere. We'll head over to the park, and you can have a look I the places I can't get to because of my leg. I'll look in the places I can and hopefully we'll find her, and you'll be fifty dollars richer." The man headed back to the Bronco and climbed inside, smiling at the boy in the red sneakers. "You coming?"

The boy looked up and down Grandview Ave and walked around to the passenger side of the Bronco, pulled off his backpack, and got in.

"Alright," the man said. "My girl will be back with me in no time, I'm sure of it. She loves kids and will probably come to you if you just call her name. Speaking of which, my name is Michael. What's yours?"

"Billy," red sneakers said.

"Well, glad to know you, Billy. Thanks for your help."

"Oh no problem," Billy said. "I didn't much feel like going to school this morning, anyway."

"Does anybody really want to go to school?" The man laughed. "Say, what are you going to spend your fifty on?"

"There's this new game I want," Billy said. "Frankenstein's Castle 2. It just came out and I'm dying to play it. It costs forty-five ninety-nine plus tax."

Michael smiled, wide and warm. "Well, you'll be able to get it now, no problem."

"Hey, isn't Victoria Park the other way?"

"It is." Michael smiled another thousand-watt smile. "I just realized I don't have Flo's leash and harness. If we find her, I'll need them. I can't very well carry her and try to walk with this cane."

"Oh, that makes sense," Billy said.

"I think so," Michael said. "We'll just buzz by my place. I'll get the leash, and we'll head to the park."

Billy Anglin leaned back in the passenger seat of the Bronco and closed his eyes.

"Not too far now," Michael said, and the Bronco gave a little shudder as it dropped into a lower gear. He steered the truck away from Grandview Ave, heading past downtown and near the faded townhomes and tract houses of Grey Hollow Road. He pulled into the driveway of a squat, greyed war house and threw the Bronco into park. "Here we are."

Billy opened his eyes and looked around. "You live by the old cemetery?"

"Yeah," Michael said. "For a while now."

"That's so cool. Like if you were ever going to be like Frankenstein, you'd have a supply of fresh bodies right next door?"

Michael laughed, big and bright and warm. "Something like that."

The two of them walked through the front door. Michael insisted the guest should always be the first into the house. It brought good luck. He suggested Billy could watch a little TV while he looked for the dog's leash. The room the TV sat in was as washed out as the outside of the house. Panelling that had been the colour of ancient oak and California redwood in its heyday, was now sun bleached to a shade of beige that looked more like ripples and billows in the desert sands, than the walls of a rustic cabin in the woods. The wall-to-wall carpet was the colour of congealed oatmeal and was nearly as interesting, save for the burgundy lava lamp shapes scattered randomly across it.

"You don't know where your dog's leash is?"

"Well, after she disappeared, I didn't know what to do. So, I came back here and sort of fell apart. I didn't quite know where to start. I called everybody I could think of to help me find her, but nobody could. I threw her leash somewhere and now I can't remember where I threw it. Stress'll make you do some crazy ass things, am I right?" Michael said.

"It must," Billy said. "My parents lose their shit all the time. Oops, sorry I swore."

"Swear all you want," Michael said. "This is a safe space, no parents allowed. Say whatever you want. I might be a bit yet. Why don't you try to find something on the TV?"

It was after nine, practically ten, really.

"There isn't a lot on right now. I know when mom lets me stay home sick, I usually take a shower around now. All the cartoons are over and there's nothing on but talk shows until Price is Right starts," the boy said.

"Hah, I bet you Bob Barker isn't even out of bed yet!" Michael said.

The boy smiled at him nervously.

"I'm sure you'll find something on that TV. I've got cable."

Billy rushed toward the TV and switched it on. The images that appeared on the screen weren't cartoons and, unless The Price is Right had changed a lot since the last time he had the flu, neither were they Bob Barker and his beauties.

"Well, would you look at that? I've seen that one before. That muscular guy has come over to fix that lady's TV, but she doesn't have any money to pay him," Michael said.

"I should probably get to school," Billy said. "My parents will be mad if they find out I skipped another day."

"What?" Michael said loudly from the other room. "I can't quite hear you."

"I... I said I should get going. To school, you know?" A note of panic rang through the boy's words.

"So... no fifty bucks? No help? Poor old Flo, just left to wither and die, lost in the park?"

"I really want to help, mister, really, but I just don't want to get into trouble."

"Fifty dollars is a lot of money, Bill. You could get your new game. What was it called, Frankenstein's castle?"

"Two."

"What?"

"Frankenstein's castle two. I know I could get the game and everything. I'm just worried about what my parents will say."

"I understand," Michael said. "Just let me change my shirt, and I'll take you to school."

Billy heaved a sigh. "Okay."

"Are you ready?" Michael whispered.

Billy felt a pressure just above his chest. An odd feeling in the divot of his ribcage, just where it meets the neck. It wasn't pain, not exactly. Rather, it felt like he had swallowed a couple of cold pills dry and now they were hovering at the top of his neck, threatening to stay there unless he threw a glass of water in there on top of them. He stood motionless, unsure of what he should do. Billy Anglin knew something had happened. Something was terribly wrong. But he couldn't, for the life of him, think of what he should do next. Michael answered for him.

"You're stabbed, Bill, and you are going to die. In about three to five minutes, I'd say," Michael said, glancing at his watch.

He watched the tears roll down the Billy's cheeks like fat summer raindrops. The boy had wanted to go to school. He wanted to go home. He wanted to be anywhere but here. And now was about to die. The thought of it alone was enough to cause Michael's hands to tremble with excitement.

"Hey! Wanna know an interesting fact? If you stab someone, almost anywhere, and assuming you haven't ruptured a major artery, and you don't pull the knife out, you have more time than you think before they die. For example, one of the first in the group you are about to join lasted for twenty full minutes before I pulled the knife out. He was really the litmus test. I learned so much from him I could never possibly thank him for being such a wonderful teacher. Where to stab, how to put the knife in and not hit anything too vital, and how to make a minimal mess to clean up after the fact. Of course, he's dead, so I couldn't really thank him anyway, but you get the point." Michael said.

Michael pushed Billy toward a plain, metal, and vinyl chair that seemed out of place in the living room. It was a chair you'd find around a kitchen table. Function over form. It had four legs and a seat that was covered in plastic. It was stain proof and easy to clean. He then spread a series of black garbage bags and dark coloured tarps over the floor in front of the TV. He helped Billy to stand and positioned the chair and the boy in the middle of the floor coverings.

"I'm going to take the knife out now, Bill," Michael said. "And then things are going to move quickly. You're going to feel hotter than you've ever felt before, like you've got a sunburn inside your body, and then you're going to get sleepy. So very sleepy. And then you'll just drift off."

The boy's gaze met his, full of fear and so many questions he could no longer ask.

"I know," Michael said. "You're scared. Of course you're scared, and you're worried it's going to hurt. I can tell you not to worry, though that almost never helps. I know, from the others, that it doesn't hurt at all. It's like slipping under a nice warm blanket with a cup of hot chocolate before you fall asleep."

Billy's gaze darted around the room in a panic.

"Ready?" Michael jerked the knife from the boy's throat. "See, the skin forms a seal around the knife. It's your body trying to stop the bleeding and keep you alive. Isn't that amazing? I mean, who knew that a body will always try to preserve itself? I sure didn't."

The blood gushed from the wound in Billy Anglin's neck like a burst garden hose. He tried to fight it. But he might just as well put the knife back in the hole in the throat in hopes of stopping the bleeding, for all the good it'd do. And his eyes slid shut.

"Get it, Jack!" Danny Nesbitt yelled and threw the ratty teddy bear as hard as he could.

He was four days shy of his fourteenth birthday and had lived in Winterbourne his whole life. They say a person can't remember anything from before they were seven, a piece in their brain hasn't formed or hasn't finished growing or something. He read it in a fat science book that an equally fat teacher assigned him chapters to read. But Danny remembered a lot. He remembered a Christmas when he was three. His mother and father bought him a tricycle and left it under the tree, wrapped in a red bow bigger than he was. It took him the better part of a month to get it to go, mostly from lack of strength and coordination and not really understanding how the damned thing worked.

At six, he saw his first live musical. A snappy little thing about an ugly duckling that every first-grade class in Winterbourne, three school's worth, attended en masse. It was childish – even for a room full of first graders and about forty-five minutes too long. At eight, his parents gave him an impossibly small, incredibly dirty little dog that he called Jack without thinking. Five minutes later, they told him they were going to move away from Winterbourne.

At eight and three quarters, the police came to his front door at 11:23 pm and scared the holy hell out of his babysitter and her mostly pantless boyfriend, while Danny sat unnoticed at the top of the stairs. A tall cop explained there had been a pileup on the highway and his parents had died in the middle of it. At nine, they labelled him a ward of the court. It was him and Jack against the world until he was told there was no way he could go into the foster care system with the dog, the odds of finding a family that would take a nine-year-old boy and a dog were astronomical. It was only when the tall cop agreed to pay for whatever damage the boy or the dog caused that he could keep Jack.

After that, it was foster home after shitty foster home. Danny grew up and grew resentful of a system that bounced him from house to house and didn't give a shit about him, biding its time until he was old enough to age out and become someone else's problem. At eleven, he thought of ways to get away from Winterbourne, somewhere he and Jack could go. Someday they'd go where they counted for something more than an extra check at the end of the month. It wouldn't be today.

Jack dropped the teddy bear at Danny's feet and sat, waiting. The boy never could figure what kind of dog he was. He was small and muscular and lean like a Jack Russell, but broad at the chest and short in the face like a bulldog. And then there was his hair. It was short and tight to his body, from his feet and midway up. From there, it was a wiry, coarse collection of twisty spikes and clumps of hair that looked like a dirty white fright wig, flecked with red-brown splotches. If you judged Jack on his hair alone, you'd think someone who only had a vague idea of what a dog should look like designed him. But he was loyal and tenacious to a fault. God help the foster parent, or one of their bratty kids, that came to Danny's bedroom with shitty intentions. Jack was small but could crush a man's hand with a single bite – a skill he would gladly show to anyone who got too close to the boy with the wrong idea.

They spent their days roaming the streets of Winterbourne, downtown mostly, just the two of them, with the whole town for their playground. Past the shops on Parker Street, especially the alleyway behind Wiedersens's Groceteria. Mr. Wiedersen would always give them something, a half of a loaf of French bread that wasn't too stale and a handful of fat smoked sausages or an overstuffed bag of day-old donuts, if Danny offered to help bring in the bread racks from the bakery trucks. He always did. They strolled through Victoria Park and ran across the back lot of Winterbourne Home, stopping often to let the residents pet Jack, who would sit still for strokes from aging, arthritic hands until the old ones drifted off to sleep in the warm air.

Occasionally, they ran past Seonagh's woods. Too scared of what everyone thought lived in those trees to stay too long. No matter the route, their destination was always Millar's field. The Millars had been dead and gone from Winterbourne for years, and they could play the whole day away and nobody would care what they were up to. They were happy. They were safe. They were miles away from foster homes. Miles away from Winterbourne.

"Get it, Jack!" Danny threw the doll's head again and the little dog took off after it. It was after a handful of minutes that Jack didn't return before he thought anything was wrong.

"Jack?"

It felt like an eternity now and the little dog still hadn't come back and after a lifetime's more worry and frenzied name calling, panic grabbed him.

"Jack!"

He'd never run off before, not without returning the teddy bear or dead bird or squirrel clenched firmly in his teeth.

"Jack!" he hollered again, and the fear gained a foothold. Awful scenarios of the little dog fighting and failing against all kinds of terrible things crawled across his brain. Millar's field was the go-to spot for opportunistic deer hunters and fox trappers and Danny's mind forced itself into images of the Jack mangled in the jaws of a steel trap, trying to gnaw away at a crushed leg.

"Jack!" he screamed. "Shit. Fuck shit, shitty shit. Where are you?"

And then he heard it. A bark, but it wasn't near. He started walking, hurrying to a trot. Running forward made sense to him, though he couldn't say the noise came from that direction. Another bark. It sounded closer now, maybe coming from the right of him. He turned and jogged toward the noise until a flash of his dog barking at a hunter levelling a shotgun at him shoved itself into his head and he took off in a run toward the yipping.

The mid-summer grass in Millar's field was long, nearly waist high in some spots, left fallow when the Millar's son died, and nobody bothered much about it after the parents went their separate ways. Finding Jack in it would be next to impossible, but so long as the dog kept yowling, Danny figured he could zero in on him if he listened hard enough. The dog didn't disappoint and kept whining and growling. After a few more minutes of running, the boy could see a grubby white tail poking out from the long grass.

"C'mere, Jack!"

Jack continued growling and barking, not paying attention to Danny's voice.

"Jack!"

The little dog reversed itself, pushing back through the long grass, until Danny could see its haunches, but he refused to come any further or stop barking until the boy came up beside him.

It was a foot. A foot in a red tennis shoe, white laces flecked with blood and untied. Danny walked slowly past his howling dog.

"Easy," Danny said, and touched a hand along the dog's back.

Jack let loose a long, low, guttural growl and stiffened. Danny jerked back his hand, surprised by the little dog's reaction.

"Jack, it's me," he said and stroked cautiously along the dog's back.

The dog backed all the way out and turned. He stared at Danny, raised an eyebrow and growled at him, baring his teeth, and backing into the long grass.

"Jack!"

The moment passed, and the dog jumped at him, licking and barking and wiggling his back end, pushing him backward.

"Hi, Jack," Danny said. "Hi, Jack."

The reunion was short lived. Danny pushed the dog off and continued forward into the grass to get a look at the person attached to the shoe. He tugged at a few handfuls of the longer grass that surrounded the legs. The grass that deer hadn't already flattened was beneath the owner of the red sneakers. He pushed the grass aside and crept forward.

It was a boy, and he was dead. He was on his back, his hands grasping at his neck, like he was adjusting the knot of a tie, but there wasn't a tie. Only a huge wound across his throat and a circle of blood soaked into the ground that was as wide as he was tall. Danny felt vomit rise in his throat and turned away from the dead kid. He sucked in a long and deep breath, but the air tasted different, tasted wrong, and made him more nauseous. All he wanted to do was grab his dog and get away from this awful place. And then he looked back down at the body in the red shoes.

It was the colour. It was wrong. Blue-grey lips and dull, unnatural yellow skin that said he couldn't be anything but dead. Billy Anglin was his name, and Danny knew who he was. He lived on the other end of Winterbourne, the money end, the *nobody ever came to school with a black eye because the old man had a bit too much at Butler's last night and wasn't interested in helping anybody with their goddam homework*, end of town. He lived up near the new subdivision, past Grandview Heights.

As far as Danny knew, the kid wasn't a star athlete or a math whiz or even the winner of the local spelling bee. He hadn't done a single thing that would make him stand out. Anglin could have been any of the kids he knew from school or hanging around downtown. He stepped a little closer, never taking his eyes off the dead boy's face. The eyes were milky, vacant, and Danny wanted to give them an explanation for why he ended up like this, wanted to help him, but just the same, there was something else. Something stirred inside Danny. It was dark, and it was awful, and it wanted to touch Billy Anglin. Wanted to rub his dead face and look into those milky eyes as he probed the wound on his neck with a finger.

Danny Nesbitt stepped toward the dead boy, hand outstretched, leaning in close, his fingertips just grazing the cold blue skin when he felt a tug at the back of his jeans. He pushed forward but felt the tug again, followed by a loud bark and a small nip to his heel, assuring the message wasn't misunderstood.

"Ow! God dammit, Jack! That hurt."

The little dog barked and jumped at him, dropping the ratty bear at his feet and waiting patiently for him to throw it.

"Well, now what?" he said to the dog.

Jack nudged the bear toward him and sat in anticipation.

"That's not what I mean. I mean, what do we do about him? I should tell somebody that we found him, but if I tell somebody, they'll know we were up here. And you know as well as I do, we're not supposed to be up here anymore."

The dog looked at him and cocked his head to the left.

"But if I don't say anything – shit, I would want somebody to say something if it was me up here. C'mon, Jack."

He picked up the doll head and threw it high and far and the dog disappeared after it, down the field, toward Parker St. and away from Billy Anglin.

"I would want somebody to say something." Danny turned back to look at Billy Anglin one more time, then took off after Jack.

The dog had the stuffed thing firmly in its mouth and continued forward, stopping and turning occasionally.

"Alright, fine. I'll say something when we get home."

They walked together across Parker St. until they could see the lights from the city turn on as the sun began its slow creep beneath the horizon. Danny saw headlights, and they were turning into the entrance of Millar's field. Likely a couple of high school kids on their way into the long grass to drink and fool around before it was back to school tomorrow.

"Or I could just let them find him," he said, and Jack dropped the bear in front of him. "Aww shit." He picked up the head and threw it again. "Monday."

2

———

Bob Miflin shouted at his roommate and pushed back from the table in a snit. "Fuck you, Don Pierce!"

Donald Pierce remained silent.

"Fuck you. Fuck you, fuck you, and fuck you too!" he yelled at Don again and jabbed an arthritic finger at the other two men at his table for good measure.

He turned away from the table quickly, at least as quick as a man in his later years could while using a walker with a dodgy front wheel, and headed out of the dining room, muttering under his breath as he went.

It was a small thing. A crust of bread, maybe, or a crumpled napkin that dropped to the floor unnoticed and got kicked by feet in too much of a hurry to stop and pick it up. Whatever it was, to Bob Mifflin's cataract clouded eyes and rampant OCD, it was a mess. It was filth, a heaping helping of laziness, no doubt left by one of an entire world full of people that just didn't get it. A clean and orderly world was a safe world.

"I'll just pick this up then, shall I?"

He bent at the hip, clung to the handle of his walker, and stretched out with the other hand, feeling the tips of his fingers graze across the rolled-up bit of gauze. An air of smug satisfaction chugged through him like the buzz of cheap package store wine, seconds before his hip gave out with a loud crack that sent him to the floor screaming in agony.

"Don't send me out, don't send me out!" he hollered as the orderlies and nurses crowded around him.

"Wait, wait!" he said, begging the young nurse. "I have a few hundred dollars stashed in my room. It's all yours if you treat me here."

"Mr. Miflin, we have to send you out. I'm pretty sure your hip is broken. You really need an x-ray and probably need to have it set, maybe even surgery. We can't do any of that here. I'm sorry."

"No, no, no! You ignorant bitch! That's just what you want. Get another old man out of here, right? What's one less to you goddam people?" He swatted at the nurse.

The words hung in the air like a foul smell. The nurse and her orderlies moved on him, proceeding more cautiously the closer they got to him, but he wasn't much more than an inconvenience now. One of them noticed the paramedics entering the ward and stayed beside the old man lying prone on the floor. There were other people in the dining room, people who needed help with their evening meal. People who weren't leaving. The paramedics pushed past the orderlies and flung the old man on to a gurney like a sack of wet laundry. By now, the seriousness of the situation had spread through the dining room and a crowd of the able-bodied had gathered where he fell.

Don Pierce muscled his way through the throng of morbidly fascinated seniors as they wheeled his friend to the door.

"Aww shit," he said.

"Don, don't let them do it. Don't let them send me out. Stop them, Don. You gotta help me!" Bob said, pleading.

Don Pierce knew... hell, all of them in Winterbourne Home knew what being sent out meant. It meant your injury was serious enough for examination by actual skilled medical professionals, not the overtired, overworked, and underpaid staff of an old age home. It meant being strapped to a bed for the slightest hint of a forceful personality. Worst of all, it meant drugs, a shit ton of them. Pills to make you crap, I.V. drugs to make you piss more, make you piss less or make you stop pissing altogether, and hourly injections to keep you just this side of comatose. Combine all that with a physical insult as massive as a broken hip to an already aging body and you could say goodbye to your remaining golden years and hello to fading away gradually in a wheelchair. That is, if you came out of the hospital at all. If living in a nursing home was a life sentence, being sent to Winterbourne General with a broken hip was the electric chair.

"Aww shit, no," Don said again as they wheeled his friend out the locked front door.

It was a full week before they wheeled Bob Miflin back in through the door of the room he shared with Don. He was back in body, at least. They had crushed his spirit under a haze of narcotics and an apathetic nursing staff. The old man remained in his bed, despite Don's urging to get up and walk with him.

"C'mon you old bastard, there's a new nurse on the ward and she looks just as good from the front as she does from the back. Know what I mean? Get up, we can go check her out."

"Maybe later," Bob said.

And an unseen clock began ticking down. It would be a matter of a few days, maybe a week. If his heart was strong, he might even last another couple of months. You were never completely sure when the end would come. You just knew it was sooner rather than later. Keeping track of time in a place like Winterbourne was about as much use as counting new grey hairs. When you knew the outcome, why would you torture yourself watching the hours tick away? He sat with his friend all that day and into the next. Sometimes he held his hand and told him what a good man he was. Sometimes Don just listened while the other man unburdened his soul and hoped there really was redemption for everyone. Mostly, he sat quietly so at least his friend wouldn't be alone, sleeping in the chair while Bob slept in the bed.

"I'm cold, Don," Bob said after laying still so long, the other man thought he'd already passed.

And then, with no fanfare, no coughing or retching or clutching at his chest, Bob Miflin died and Donald Pierce, his one remaining friend, was alone.

"I'm gonna rifle through your stuff and mess it all up, you asshole," Don said, choking back a sob.

He was halfway serious. Don knew the very idea of anyone going through his things would have driven the old bugger to cardiac arrest if he wasn't already dead. And Bob Miflin was dead. There was no mistaking that. And with no family to mourn him or come around to collect his things, Pierce guessed a day or two would pass before the Winterbourne staff came in and took all his roommate's earthly possessions away for donation. Don couldn't see the harm in taking a couple of the recent deceased's shirts and a handful of cotton underpants, to make up for the deficits in his own closet.

There were a couple of Acapulco shirts he always had his eye on and two or three thick tartan flannels he envied on the winter nights when the boiler downstairs was less than co-operative. He stuffed them in his own closet, fearing the staff might burst through the door at any moment and haul all of it away. After the closet, he looked at the dressers and nightstand and found most of the socks and underpants to be full of holes. Satisfied there were no more creature comforts to be had, Don thought of those things that were a littler more obscure.

Bob Miflin didn't have two-hundred dollars stashed in his room. Or any other amount of money beyond a couple of bucks to spend at the tuck shop when he had a mind to. Cash, even a rumour of it, did strange things to people in this place and there would have been no end of people – staff and residents alike – wandering in and out of the dead man's room, looking for treasure. There wasn't any, never was that Don knew about. There was a wristwatch, and he thought they should bury his friend with it, and his good cufflinks and matching tie bar. All the things that said Robert A Mifflin had worked faithfully for Winterbourne G and E for 40 years and all he had to show for it was a gold-coloured Timex. There was also a photo album, yellowed and worn, but full of pictures of happier times. A wife and a child, and then later, a grandchild. The wife died some years before Bob. Lung cancer from second-hand smoke. She'd been a waitress and never raised a cigarette to her lips. The world was a shitty place with an even shittier sense of humour when you got right down to it. A year later, his daughter, her husband, and his grandchild died in a car wreck on I-95, and it left him with nobody. Shortly after, he moved in here with Don.

The pictures made the old man sad. Bob had a family, a life that meant something. Even if it was all gone, Bob mattered. Don had a wife that hated him for most of their married life but stayed with him for the convenience of a second paycheck. Bob mattered. Bob was loved. People humoured Don. Tolerated him at best.

As he flipped the back cover of the photo album closed, his eyes darted to the gleam of a metal label on the cover of a scrapbook in the drawer's bottom. Don lifted the book out of the drawer and opened the front cover. There were a few pictures inside, but mostly it was clippings and newspaper articles from the Winterbourne Gazette. *Jesus, some people will collect anything,* he thought. Stamps, wildflowers, and even newspaper clippings. But it was the subject of the clippings that was odd, and he realized for the two years he had lived beside him, speaking with him day after day about his fears and what few dreams he had left, that he knew absolutely nothing about Bob Mifflin.

The front of the Winterbourne Gazette, showed a nearly full-page photo of police crowded around the body of a dead child and in the background, looking as though he was hoping not to be noticed, but sticking out like a hooker in church, was his roommate, Bob Mifflin.

"What the fuck were you up to?"

3

The clock radio blared to life. *Good morning campers!* Floyd Guthrie refused to open his eyes. It was 5:15, and he'd been awake for the better part of an hour. Still, the glaring blue light from the clock radio at his bedside felt like it was boring a hole in his brain, even through closed eyelids. There was no fighting it. The time to get up had come, whether he wanted it to or not. For the record, he did not. He rolled himself out of bed to a chorus of moans and groans from a body that spent the best years of its life clomping along the sidewalks and alleyways of downtown Winterbourne. Two years ago, nearly to the day, the powers that be saw fit to bring him into the fold as a junior detective. An advancement that many would see as a high compliment. Guthrie was well into his middle fifties and viewed anything that applied to him with the word "junior" in it as an insult. And it was, it was little more than lip service for an aging cop they had little use for.

The junior detectives of the Winterbourne PD were awful to a man. Any of them would have gladly driven a knife in to the back of the junior detective closest to them if it meant even a slight chance of a promotion. Floyd Guthrie wasn't conniving enough to get out of the junior pool like that. But being a detective, even a junior one, afforded him better priced whiskies on the weekends and a healthier retirement package when he finally left the force.

He was good at the job, despite the laughter and derision of the kids with badges. Maybe because of it. Floyd could walk a crime scene or examine a handful of photographs and, in a matter of hours, arrive at a minimum of three solutions to the crime. Two of which were plausible, and one was the truth. When they plopped a fat banker's box of unsolved cases on his desk a year ago, they all figured it would be years before the aging junior detective tied up all the loose ends that had dogged the department since God knows when. Guthrie, who never could explain why he could do the things he could, thought it would be a breeze. Sewing up the loose ends, bringing the guilty of Winterbourne to justice, and bringing closure to the wronged parties so many years ago.

And mostly, he made quick work of it. The Cavendishs got back the stereo that somebody pinched out of their car three months beforehand – the next-door neighbour's smack-head son had boosted it out of the car in the middle of the night and pawned it to get high. The Maitland's Garden tools had wandered across the street into a back shed, seemingly of their own volition, until Guthrie leaned on the elderly man across the street who swore they were his. Mrs. Meyers believed, without any doubt in the world, that Mrs. Meara hadn't stolen her cat. He was, in fact, dead and gone. But his luck ended there. One folder remained in the box, and it had stymied every detective assigned to it. Even Floyd Guthrie.

They were kids, five of them. All dead and found ten years apart, nearly to the day, and all of them brutalized. Des Anderson, 13 years old, was the first. Found in 1947, just inside the front gate of the graveyard on Grey Hollow Road. The city was closing the place in favour of the new, bigger cemetery on the other end of town. The sextant found him on his last rounds, about 6 am. His throat was a gaping, jagged wound and his insides ripped out. The evidence suggested the mutilations were post-mortem and could well have resulted from an animal, but Guthrie didn't buy it. 1957, Michael Martin 15. The killer stuffed him behind a dumpster in the alleyway between Butler's bar and what was the Lyric theatre. His injuries were identical to Des Anderson – throat cut, and organs ripped out. Coyotes or stray dogs were blamed, even the thought of a person capable of doing that to a child was positively unthinkable. Alice Fitzgerald 1967, 13. She was laid spreadeagle on the back property of the Winterbourne Asylum with the same wounds as the other two. This was a huge break in the case. Who else but a maniac could do something so awful to a child? And there he was, leaving the evidence on his front doorstep. But there hadn't been a single inmate escape in the asylum's history, and that huge break died after three days of inspection and questioning. 1977 brought Keith Johnston, 11. A wiry kid whose parents Guthrie had known casually. A group of kids found him. They'd been looking for a place to finish the cans of Red Cap they swiped from somebody's old man's beer fridge. They were just about drunk enough to head into Seonagh's woods when they saw the boy's body laying along the tree line. It was one of Guthrie's first cases on the job and it nearly broke him to show up at the Johnston's doorstep on a warm Saturday night in July and tell them their only child was dead.

The summer months of 1987 came and went and by September and it looked like they might make it without losing another kid, but one of the rivermen, working along the banks of the Nyegard, found a body stuffed inside a drainage culvert he was leaning against while having a smoke. From the state of her, Angela Eichner had been in there since mid-June. Somebody cut her throat with a jagged edged knife, same as the others, but, and this is the hill Guthrie was well willing to die on, there was no evidence of her being anywhere but the drainage culvert post-mortem. The temperature and insect evidence backed that up. If that was true, then the injuries to her abdomen couldn't have been inflicted by anything other than the person who killed her. There was no dog, or coyote, or even Lon Chaney Jr munching on her insides in that narrow drainpipe. If the crimes were being committed by the same person who inflicted all the injuries, and maybe they were in their twenties when the crimes began, that would put them into their seventies now. The decade mark was any day and there hadn't been a new dead kid. Guthrie had his doubts there would be a new one. What seventy-year-old can still stomp around killing kids and still be careful enough not to get caught? He stared at the three words scrawled across the bottom of the last photo, willing them to give him some inspiration or clue to bring him closer to the truth. But they didn't. They remained as empty and hopeless as the day he first wrote them. *The Bicycle Man.*

He was an old man now. Hell, looked like an old man when Guthrie was a young beat cop. He didn't live in a house of his own or rent a bed at one of the flophouses that used to dot the back end of Parker Street. Occasionally, they'd chase him from under the new overpass or wake him up while he dozed in an alleyway, but mostly, people saw him wandering around Winterbourne, hair cut like Moe Howard and wearing everything he owned all covered by an ankle length, black raincoat. What he couldn't wear, he attached to a wreck of a bicycle with almost no paint left on it and a bent front end and wheeled it around town, stuffed animals, colourful scraps of wallpaper, several pairs of tennis shoes and... The Bicycle Man. He was an easy target, a convenient scapegoat, for anything that went wrong in the town. Garden tools missing from your shed? Arrest the Bicycle Man. Prize chickens missing? Arrest the Bicycle Man.

When people realized they weren't noticing him around anymore, he went from scapegoat to boogeyman in a heartbeat. Eat your vegetables or the bicycle man will get you. Children teased each other in his name and teens all over town spray painted bicycles on every unguarded surface as a warning to mind your business, because Hell had an obvious emissary in Winterbourne, and he wore a long black raincoat. There were rumours, of course, that he was a lunatic, out for revenge against someone in town that had wronged him. Or that he was a distant relative to H. H. Winterbourne. Or, even better, that he was old man Winterbourne himself, gone mad and in hiding to save himself from punishment for 86ing his whole family.

Floyd met him once. Well, sort of met him. Guthrie was getting breakfast in the Pharaoh diner when he saw the Bicycle Man hovering over a cup of coffee and a plate of eggs. He finished his own meal and made his way to the cash register just about the same time as the Bicycle Man. Guthrie was feeling generous, and a little self righteous, and offered to pay for the other man's meal. But before he could offer, a grubby hand emerged from beneath the raincoat, holding a wad of money big enough to choke a horse. The Bicycle Man peeled off two twenties and set them on the counter without a word. Guthrie looked back at his table and saw a half-eaten plate of eggs and two pieces of uneaten toast. Floyd guessed the coffee cup was empty, and the bacon was all gone, if there ever was any.

He was weird. He was weird, and he was dirty and smelly, and apparently, he was rich. And because the people of Winterbourne didn't like him, he became the first and greatest suspect when the dead kids showed up. There wasn't any motive, there wasn't any reason or anything to gain by his committing the murders and the only reason Floyd hadn't dismissed him entirely jumped out at him every time he flipped through the photos of the five dead kids. There in the background, behind the cops, trying to hold back the people who wanted to crowd around the bodies, trying to remain inconspicuous, but not out of sight, he was. Guthrie went back over the photos dozens of times to be sure he wasn't imaging it. He wasn't, and he wrote the words on the bottom of the last photo, as a constant reminder there was something else to him. *The Bicycle Man.*

Floyd pushed back from the table, where he'd spread the contents of the murder file the night before, rubbed the sleep from his eyes and headed into the kitchen to make himself a cup of coffee. He trudged into the bathroom from there, still a little bleary-eyed but headed into the neighbourhood of awake and ready to face the day people. After the shower, he was awake, cup in hand, and feeling defeated that the answer to the who's and whys weren't any closer than they were yesterday or the day before that or the year before that. After dressing and running a comb through his still wet hair, he gathered up the contents of the file and headed out the door.

"Shit." He jammed the keys into the ignition of his ancient Ford Escort. "It's Monday."

Mondays were case load days, when his superiors would expect a verbal report of progress on ongoing cases. And they expected results. Results made people feel safe, gave them faith their police force was providing safety in their streets, which translated to continued votes for the current administration, including the chief of police. Guthrie was lowest on the list of junior detectives and, otherworldly success rate or not, they gave him the banker's box and told not to expect anything new until he'd put all of them to bed. They did it to all the lowest detectives. It was a way of thinning the herd of all the Dirty Harries who'd rather shoot first, second, and third and then worry about pesky details like guilt or innocence. As an added bonus, it also got rid of the ones who couldn't cut it. Detectives might have been all guts and glory in the movies, but cops in the real world spent more time with a pencil in their hand than a pistol. A lot of young cops didn't like it and quit after a week. But Guthrie was far too stubborn for that.

In detecting terms, being assigned the Ripper file was like being handed the keys to the dead letter office. He only made detective because they didn't know what else to do with him, too young to retire and too old to keep being a beat cop, so give him something he'd never find his way out of. No matter how good he was, they saw him as only slightly above useless. What better way to keep the old fool out of the way of the real detectives than giving him a case he could never hope to solve? And, if by some miracle, Floyd cracked the case, they'd all say they knew it all along and it was their faith and support that helped him solve it. The senior junior detective. Shit, even the drug-sniffing dogs got a better deal out of being a cop than he did.

If he played his cards right, avoided the break room on his way in and kept his head down while he walked, he might make it to the back corner, and to his desk, avoiding the whispers and barely contained laughter. He could appear to be hard at work until at least lunchtime, by then it would be too late to talk to the chief and the council members or, better yet, the younger dicks would be too busy crowing about how well their own cases were going to worry about grandpa Serpico and his unsolved murder box.

The kids *were* in the break room, he could hear them, gathered around the coffee machine, bragging how easy it had been for them to get laid and how few drinks they'd had to buy before the badges came out and the clothes hit the floor. They sugar-coated the truth, one upping each other for at least the next hour, before they stood in front of the department and talked about the greatness of their own exploits. By then, Floyd would be chin deep in looking occupied by something important and deeply detective like. Which was more difficult than it looked in a town where the worst thing used to be drunken high school kids bending street signs or snapping signal knobs off unlocked sports car steering wheels. But that wasn't the worst thing anymore, not by a long shot.

Now and then, Floyd would get to feeling pretty good about himself. Okay, so he hadn't been able to keep a wife happy much beyond either of his trips down the aisle and his kids viewed him as something of a necessary embarrassment, as long as he kept footing the bill for their education. He was a decent person. He probably drank too much for his own good, but he never hurt anyone that didn't already have it coming. In twenty-five years behind the badge, he'd only drawn his gun once and even then, he shot the man in the leg. Enough to slow him down, but not to cause actual harm. He could look at himself in the mirror and sleep with a clear conscience most nights. Until the five of them came out of that goddamned box.

They were always on his mind, from the first time he saw them, to the day he realized there would be no simple answer to any of this. When he spread their pictures out over his bed at night and then again across his kitchen table in the morning, they were with him. There wasn't a moment of satisfaction Floyd Guthrie could feel for himself that those five sets of dead eyes wouldn't crush their way through and reinforce what kind of failure he really was.

The detective sergeant stuck his head out and called to him. "Guthrie!"

"Fuck," Floyd said.

"Guthrie! Get in here, please," the sergeant said.

Floyd rose silently and headed to the big back office, knowing he was about to receive a verbal scalping for not having produced anything new on the Ripper case for far too long.

"Aww shit," Floyd said.

"What?" the detective at the desk across from his said. "You worried about what he's gonna say? Can't be anything new? You're in there once every couple of weeks about this time, no?"

"No, it's not that. It's Monday. Danny will be waiting for me."

4

Danny Nesbit hated Mondays. He was a ward of the court, placed into the foster care system after his parents died, and that meant money to the people he lived with. They all got cash to care for him, tax free and in ample supply, so long as he continued to live within their walls and attended school – until the day he aged out and became another one of the unwashed masses. After that, it was sink or swim in a world that had little use for him to begin with. Nobody cared much about what he did, so long as it wasn't anything that stopped the flow of cash.

Danny lived with a couple who'd been appointed by the court to care for him. They weren't his parents, of course, and, after living with them as long as he had, couldn't see them being parents to anyone. They reminded him regularly he was a guest in their house, and he should conduct himself by their rules or hit the bricks. "Friday afternoon at 4:00 to Monday morning at 9:00. I don't give a shit what you do." And they didn't. Danny would wander the town and surrounding fields until well past dark, all weekend, and nobody said a word to him. But miss a day of school and put the house's extra income in jeopardy and all manner of hell would rain down on him. "9:00 Monday morning to 4:00 Friday afternoon, your ass had better be in that school minding your p's and q's or I'll take that goddam dog out back and shoot it myself."

It was the one threat they could use. Jack was the only thing Danny had that was his, the only thing that he really cared about. And Jack was the only thing that gave a shit about Danny and what happened to him. He didn't get it when he was younger, but Danny figured out that the Foster's money depended on him. No Danny, no money. It occurred to him recently that if they had done something as stupid as harm his dog, there'd be nothing to prevent him from running far away from the pair of them. Sometimes, most times, he thought he might just do it, anyway.

"Nesbitt!" the teacher yelled and sent a chalkboard eraser careening toward him.

"What? Ah... what... where were we again?"

"The declaration, yes? Of independence, yes? You were about to regale us with the vast repository that is your knowledge of the founding fathers?"

Danny lied. "Oh, right."

He walked to the front of the classroom, mind working overtime, hoping to grab hold of a nugget of information about something he couldn't remember ever learning. He turned and faced the class.

"There was a group of fathers, fifteen or twenty of them from a long time ago, who burst forth upon our soggy shores and got lost. They wandered around, still really lost, not knowing what the hell to do and then, lo-and-behold, somebody found them. And to this day, every fourth of July, we celebrate the founding of the fathers."

The class exploded into laughter, and he lapped it up. He'd been invisible this morning. He was invisible every day, from the first shitty step he took into this shitty school and every day since, but now, right now, he made a joke, and it was killing them, and he didn't care about the consequences. Right now, they loved him.

"Office, Nesbitt. Now!" the history teacher said and threw a glare at him that would stop traffic. Danny stood and headed to the classroom door, the laughter of his classmates still ringing in his ears. They would find him the same odd little freak again tomorrow, but it didn't matter. Today he won. He turned back to the class and took a deep bow. The laughter started again, and he made it through the door just as another chalkboard eraser disappeared in a cloud of dust as it bounced off the wall beside him.

He knew the walk to the principal's office well. He could probably walk it blindfolded for all the time he'd spent walking there. But he wasn't afraid. The result of this visit would be the same as it had always been. The principal, the Reverend Dr. Laurel Koch, a sweaty, jelly salad of a man who was a Methodist preacher on the weekends, believed that God, above all others, was the ultimate judge and we would all answer to him in the great hereafter. Therefore, no punishment he could hand out would ease the torment that awaited the guilty as their ultimate reward. His advice was to go home and contemplate the road you are currently on. Turn back to God before it is too late. Come to St. Gertrude's on Sunday and ask almighty God for his own sweet mercy.

Danny would look as guilty as he could, knowing full well that punishment doled out by the lord at the end of all time and no punishment at all, were practically the same thing. He picked up his step. He'd be in and out of Koch's office in a matter of a few minutes, and then it was just counting down the time until the end of the day. Then it was home to play with Jack and keep his head down until the fosters passed out or forgot he was there. Maybe this Monday wouldn't be so bad after all.

"Have a seat, Danny," the secretary said. "Mr. McCabe will be right with you."

"Wait, what? Where's Dr. Koch?"

"On a sabbatical," she said, and Danny swore a smile crept across her mouth like a cat stalking a mouse.

"What's a sabbatical?"

"It means he ain't here. Until further notice," she said.

The boy sighed. Elias McCabe was the vice-principal of Winterbourne High School and one of the strictest adults Danny had ever met. He was also the sole reason the boy and his dog couldn't go tromping through Millar's field for the next two weeks. Well,

McCabe, a handful of broken radiator fins at the back of Danny's English class and a less than serious attitude about the whole thing.

"You can go in now," she said, replacing the phone handset.

Danny walked in and took a seat on the other side of the large, Formica topped desk. McCabe sat across from him, leafing through a file folder. The vice principal flipped page after page, muttering to himself and licking his lips periodically, as though he'd found little bits of breakfast left in the corners of his mouth. He pulled a calendar off the wall and examined the current month.

"Three-day suspension," he said without looking up.

"Wait??" Danny said in a voice that was dangerously close to yelling.

"You're a habitual offender. You clearly can't stop yourself from taking the easy way out, time and time again. I'm sure it's only a matter of time before I testify at the first of many of your court hearings."

"How can you just–"

"I've told that policeman friend of yours about of all this as well. He'll meet you out front shortly."

"Wait, the three days start today?"

"No. Your suspension begins tomorrow. You are being dismissed immediately as a favour to you, young man. To spare you the humiliation of finishing out the rest of the day with your classmates who undoubtedly know what you're being suspended for. You'll thank me for this later."

"What am I being suspended for?"

"My good God, boy, you are an insubordinate, disruptive menace to everyone who has the misfortune of being infected with your company. You think only of yourself and getting your own kicks. After you, everyone else comes first, right?" McCabe said, looking Danny in the face.

"No! That's not it at–"

"All I can say, Nesbitt, is it's a good thing your parents are already dead, because they would likely die of shame with a child that turned out the way you have."

The bottom dropped out of Danny's stomach, and he felt queasy, sick enough that he worried he might throw up on the floor of McCabe's office. He breathed his way through it until the nausea left him.

"Yes sir, you're right. I'm sorry. May I go now?" he said.

"You are free to go, young man, I would say that I hope this finally helps you to straighten out and learn to make something of yourself, but I fear the only thing you're likely to make in the future is license plates." The vice-principal said.

The minutes scraped by as Danny sat by the big glass doors inside the foyer of the school, trying to make himself invisible, waiting for Floyd Guthrie to come and get him.

"Bullshit." He exhaled and tried to suck back the tears running down his face.

Strictly speaking, not that he didn't like Guthrie. He liked Floyd well enough. Hell, he might even have liked the cop as much as he liked Jack. It was just that Floyd was old, and he had old ideas about how the world worked, about how people treated one another and how a boy his age should be behaving. It was hard at the best of times. At the worst, it was practically medieval. Danny remembered the first time the cop gave him a lecture about moving around in the world.

"You're not a kid anymore. So, keep your fingers out of your nose and start looking people in the eye. They'll think you're up to something otherwise," Floyd said.

He would pick him up faithfully every Monday and take him across town to Dandy's, an ancient drive-in restaurant that advertised the best cheeseburgers for 200 miles. They would sit in silence, broken occasionally by Floyd asking how Danny's day had gone. They didn't talk about much else – certainly not what either of them *wanted* to talk about. Dany wanted to know about his parents, everything the old man had learned about them the night they died. Floyd wanted nothing more than to tell the boy everything he knew.

It dawned on Danny just then that, if he would not be at school for the next three days, he'd better take whatever books he needed to stay caught up on the homework. The three-day vacation was going to cause enough of a shitstorm around his house as it was. More detention or suspensions for unfinished work were out of the question. He headed back to his locker and began throwing books into his backpack.

"Hey, creep," a familiar voice said, and a hand pushed the door of his locker closed.

"Jesus!" Danny instinctively raised his hands. He rolled his eyes and frowned at her, but that faded quickly into half a smile. "Cripes, Raisin, you scared the shit out of me."

Raisin Chan was the closest thing Danny had to a best friend. They met in the first grade, shortly after her family moved from China. She spoke very little English back then and he barely spoke. Her name was Wei Hsien, which he never could pronounce. Raisin was about as close as his six-year-old mouth could get to it, and she liked the sound of it. Danny liked having a friend and so the name stuck. They had been close and fallen out and been close again, more times than either could remember. Like Jack, she was a constant he sorely needed after the accident.

"You've got a little time before you gotta get back to motel Hell, wanna go down by the river and watch the barges come in? It's Monday. That's when the containers come from overseas."

Danny sighed. "I can't. I just got a three-day suspension, starting today."

"Really? How'd you get so lucky?"

"Lucky? Shit, it gets even better. Guthrie's on his way, too."

"Damn, that sucks. Catch up tomorrow?"

"Sure, whatever." He headed back toward the glass doors to wait for his ride.

It was dismissive, and he meant it to be, though he felt a little bad about it. Today was Monday, and he hated Mondays. If Raisin Chan still didn't get that after all the years they'd known each other, how was that his problem?

The Ford Escort rolled up in front of the school in a wheezing, coughing, cloud of blue smoke and gasoline vapor. Danny hurried down the stairs, hoping to avoid anyone seeing him getting into the belching rust bucket that Floyd still called a car. Knowing full well the entire school was aware of the gruesome thing out front.

"Hop in," the old man said.

Danny dove into the front seat and squashed himself downward, attempting to remain as out of sight as possible until they were well out of view of anyone he knew.

"Hungry?" Guthrie said.

Danny sighed. "No."

"Good," Floyd said, ignoring the boy's answer. "Sounds like you need a good burger. Yes, sir, a thick and juicy burger. Just the thing to fill a body up."

"It isn't a good burger, and the only thing juicy about it is the grease at the bottom of the bag."

"So, you'll have something to start a fire with if you get lost in the woods later."

They spoke very little after that. Exchanging awkward small talk followed by even more awkward silences as they pulled into the empty driveway of the drive-in restaurant. Guthrie got out of the car and returned with a paper bag that was nearly translucent with grease. He handed Danny a paper wrapped burger and a cardboard tray of fries that reeked of the ghosts of fast-food past. And, after a few mouthfuls of a burger that was both greasy and painfully dry, choked back with ample helpings of ketchup and gulps of lukewarm milk shake, Danny had screwed up his nerve enough to ask the cop about how his parents had died.

"What do you know about–"

The radio in his car snapped and crackled suddenly to life, cutting Danny off mid-sentence and giving them both a momentary fright.

"This is Guthrie. Go ahead central," he said, speaking into the handset. He looked at Danny and raised a finger to his lips.

"Floyd, is that you?" a lady's voice said in a chirp over the radio.

"Of course, it's me, Janice. You called me."

"Oh, right."

"What is it?"

"Floyd, the chief wanted me to track you down right away."

"Oh?"

"Yes."

Guthrie sighed. "Did he mention why?" He threw a sideways look at Danny and crossed his eyes, bringing a much-needed smile to both of their faces.

"Oh yes," Janice said. "He said to track you down because there's been another one."

"Wait, what? Say again, central?"

"There's been another one. Another one for your case file. Somebody found a body in Millar's field about an hour and a half ago."

5

I t wasn't anything special. It was a scrapbook. The kind you might find in a five and dime in almost any beach town. Each page was heavy black construction paper with built-in corner brackets to hold photos of the wild and exotic places you were going to tell people where you'd been, whether or not you actually had. But this scrap book didn't contain holiday photos. At least not the kind you'd share with the neighbours when they came over for cook out burgers and G and Ts.

It was the history of Winterbourne, sort of. A written account of incidents throughout the town. Mostly newspaper clippings with photos of livestock mauled and ripped up, dating back to before the first world war. Cows and sheep and goats. Hogs and dogs and cats, all chewed and gutted and all with no actual answer to what was responsible. The farmers thought it was the work of coyotes or stray dogs, but nobody could ever confirm that. The livestock remained healthy and happy and very much alive from the spring of 1917 until near the fall of 1919.

But it didn't stop for good. By August of '19, one of the Danvers found a prize Guernseys gutted and the whole town whispered. It was clean, deliberate, and probably killed by someone with a great deal of time and a very sharp knife. The killings continued with regularity, one or two large animals every couple of months, and when they stopped in the winter of '41, folks thought it couldn't be an animal. At least, not the kind that walked on four legs. Maybe one of those crazy bastards from up at the institution escaped to ransack the livestock and then disappeared into Seonagh's woods or slipped back inside Winterbourne Asylum unnoticed. The whispers turned to rumours and spread through the town like pubic lice at the whorehouse. Until the summer of '47. The summer of Des Anderson.

They found the boy stuffed behind a growth of bushes near one of the main gates of the cemetery on Grey Hollow Road. They immediately suspected the man who found him of the crime. He knew the kid and didn't seem upset enough when he found the body. Coupled with his doing a stretch in Embro Penitentiary, never mind that he went away for kiting checks before landing the job tending the lawn, the finger of blame pointed squarely at him. The boy's injuries, however, told the story of someone, something attacking with a ferocity that could only come from madness. If the groundskeeper was responsible, he hid his depravity well. If he were any calmer when the cops interviewed him, he'd have fallen asleep halfway through the questioning.

The dead boy's injuries were horrific. Even the most hardened of Winterbourne's finest were blowing chunks of breakfast all over Grey Hollow Road. Des Anderson's spine was snapped. An awful, jagged gash remained where his throat used to be, and he was ripped open from below the ribcage to just above his crotch. The organs were present, though chunks appeared to be chewed out of them, likely eaten by something hungry and opportunistic. The cops turned to the asylum. Who else but a lunatic could do something that awful to a child? When they discovered that Winterbourne Asylum hadn't lost a single inmate from opening day to the present, the case stalled. Frustrated cops filled out forms and stuffed them in fat manilla envelopes and tucked them away safely in boxes, hoping to get back to them when more evidence presented itself. The crime was all but forgotten. Eventually, even the newspaper articles about the case stopped. The whole town let out a sigh of relief. Nothing like that poor boy's murder would ever happen again. Not until 1957. And 1967 and '77 and '87. It was just long enough between bodies for people to forget, before another murdered kid showed up.

Donald Pierce read. He flipped through the scrapbook. Bob Mifflin had written comments in the margins and on the clippings from the newspaper. Notes and comments on each article, starting from the cattle mutilations and other livestock deaths to which he wrote, *Really, livestock?* However, words written in a frantic hand that surrounded the articles concerning the children were more cryptic. Starting in 1947 with a young Des Anderson. *Mad man. Mad man!* 1957 *Michael Martin. Found behind the Lyric theatre. Killed elsewhere. No blood at the scene. Dumped.* 1967 *Alyce Fitzgerald Back property of Winterbourne Asylum. Deflecting the blame? Inmate blamed?* 1977 *Keith Johnson. Why aren't they seeing this?* 1987 *Angela Eichner. MOLOCH is here.* Then there was a hand drawn picture of something Don thought looked like a handful of crosses and lines that made little sense.

He turned the last page of the scrapbook and found a yellowed envelope taped to the back cover. Don carefully pulled it off and opened it. Inside was a handful of pictures and a folded letter.

"What the fuck?"

They were images of the five dead children. His hands trembled as he opened the letter and read. Bob Miflin dated it the week before he fell in the dining room. His eyes glanced down at the hand-written words, and he decided it was too important to just skim over. He opened the drawer on his nightstand and searched it for his reading glasses.

"Ready for lunch, Mr. Pierce?" the orderly said.

"Wait, what? Lunch, oh, shit. Right, lunch, yeah, I guess." He tucked the scrapbook under a stack of clothing on the top shelf of his closet.

Don made his way to his seat at the table, his two tablemates already seated, and Bob Mifflin's seat was conspicuously empty.

"Shame about old Mifflin," Margaret-Mary Castle said.

"Shame I didn't get to the two hundred bucks before Pierce did," Dave Bulger said.

"There was no money," Don whispered.

"You keep telling us that and see how far it gets you," Dave said.

"If Bob Mifflin had that kinda scratch lying around here, do you think he'd be eating this kinda shit every day? Or been sober every day?"

"Can I borrow ten?" Margaret-Mary said.

"Ten what?"

"Ten dollars. From Bobby's two hundred. That would still leave you with more than enough."

"Margaret-Mary, there was no money," Don said.

"You be that way, Don Pierce. But the lord helps them what does unto others. Charity begins in a home. That's right there, your good book," she said, snorting and pushing back from the table.

"But there was something," Don whispered.

"Is it gold? Maybe it was jewellery? Gold jewellery, maybe?"

"No, nothing like that. Well, there was some jewelry, but it came to him by way of WG & E, so I doubt it was anything more than gold painted tin."

"What was it then? What did you find? I know you already rifled through his drawers and closets," Dave said.

"What makes you think that?"

"Because it's what any of us would've done. No sense the staff donating the goddamn stuff to the winos downtown."

"No, it wasn't the clothes, either. I found... a scrapbook," Don said, and his voice took on an air of seriousness.

"What!" Margaret-Mary said. "A fucking scrapbook?"

"Shhh. Yeah," Don said.

"My grandkids, hell, my great grandkids do scrapbooks."

"Not like this scrapbook they don't. This book is different."

"Different how? Has it got pictures in it? You know... *pictures*?" Dave said.

"It's got pictures in it, but not the kind you would want to spend too much time looking at."

"Pfft, this is the stupidest thing I've ever heard. Scrapbook, the idea of it." She hobbled her way out of the dining room and away from the two old men.

"So, it's got dirty pictures, right? You just said it didn't to get the old gal outta here, right? You said you wouldn't want to look at them much. Jesus, they're not... recent pictures, are they?"

"No, it's not that. Nothing like it at all. I wasn't kidding. The book is full of all sorts of weird shit," Don said.

"Such as?"

"Drawings and... that's not the worst of it. There were newspaper clippings and... polaroids."

"I thought you said there weren't any pictures like that?" Dave said, trying to lighten the suddenly very dark mood.

"Do you remember the kids?"

"What k - oh, do you mean, *those* kids?"

"Yeah, *those* kids. He had pictures of them, polaroids. Awful, *awful* polaroids and newspaper clippings were about all of them, with stuff written around them. Weird stuff, crazy stuff. Dangerous stuff."

"Jesus, you don't think Bob..."

"Do I think Bob, what?"

"Do you think he did it? Do you think Bob could've been the ripper?"

"Don't be stupid. Bob Mifflin wasn't tough enough to hurt anyone. He was a wrinkled up old man," Don said, spitting while he talked.

"But he wasn't always," Dave said.

"What?"

"He wasn't always a harmless, wrinkly old man. None of us were. He was young and strong and maybe behind the shining family man face he showed the world. Maybe he was crazy as a shithouse rat."

"No, no, he wasn't. Bob Mifflin was a good man. He was a man who loved his family. He worked for the gas company long enough that they gave him cufflinks and a cheap watch. His family was all dead, but they loved him until the end. He was no murderer, he was my roommate, he was my friend."

"Show me this book," Dave said.

"No way."

"You can't let the cat halfway out of the bag and then just try to stuff it back in there. You told me about the damn thing, told me what was in it. Now you want me to just forget about it because I said something you didn't think of, something you don't want to hear?"

"You don't understand," Don said, and a sadness crept through his voice.

"I do, I really do. You think if we find out something about Bobby Mifflin. Something awful. It rubs a shit stain all over your friendship with him because it might be the one thing he never told you about himself, right? Only It doesn't. Whatever the two of you had will remain safely locked in your brain and in the minds of everyone that ever saw the two of you together. Now let's have a look. I was a cop, you know. I can probably sort this out quick enough."

"You were never a cop. Your cousin Berniece was a meter maid. You told me that three years ago."

"Fine, right. Whatever. Just get the goddam book."

6

____

He was hungry. There was always hunger, but not like this. It was a gnawing deep inside. A hole in the middle of him he could never fill. Like a narcotic, the ache scraped through his veins on unseen fishhooks and rooted itself down deep inside, refusing to budge until it got what it wanted. And that alone was enough to push him on, drive him forward toward another hit. Just one more to hold him over. He liked the feeling of it, the satisfaction of it. There was no pretending he didn't. It was raw. It was overwhelming. It was power. And it set him apart, made him feared, respected, above reproach. But he'd felt the hunger for so long. He was old now and his bones ached without end most mornings and seeing the world, even in the eye that wasn't clouded over with age and scar tissue, was like staring out a dirty window. He looked grubby. And tired. Self-doubt and failing strength hung over him like the bad smell of cheap cologne.

He'd been walking since before first light and was cold and tired before he left. Now, some two hours later, he was positively spent. Tendrils of gold and coral had pushed their way through voids in the low-hanging branches along the horizon, but the approach of the sun didn't make him feel better. The only guarantee he had for the day was he would be warm. He'd gone past the high, marbled gates of the new cemetery, out past Grandview heights, and down toward the dairy farms to the northwest of Winterbourne. He knew if someone found him out here, looking the way he did, they would make quick work of him with a barrel or two full of buckshot.

A light on his right suddenly burst to life and cast him in an electric yellow glow, revealing just how exposed he was. He hunkered down, pushing his chest into the dew-soaked grass and the cold went straight through him, chilling him near to the bone. Still, he pushed lower to the ground, hoping the low light would help camouflage him in the mixed hues of the still rising sun. A second light flared into existence, and then a third and fourth in steady succession. But, to his relief, the lights illuminated, moving further away from him and toward a large, dark building away from the main house. And then something struck him. Something brilliant and, altogether, satisfying. This was a farm... a dairy farm, and that meant cows. Big, dumb, nearly defenseless milk sacks that were practically fricassee on four legs. The hunger hit him again, chewing at him from deep in the pit of his stomach, so hard he felt like he was being eaten from the inside out.

The lights stopped coming, and he moved off slowly, keeping low to the ground and glancing cautiously side to side frequently to make certain he wasn't noticed until he came to a copse of bushes that afforded him a view of the entire field. He tucked in and sat. And waited. The cows came out, one by one. A handful bounded out, as if happy to be free of their cramped stalls. Some came walking slowly, cautiously, scanning the horizon for signs of danger with every new sound. The remaining few strolled out, obviously with no more thought to it than that. He watched them carefully, gauging which was the best prospect for his purposes, which of them would go down the quickest without alerting the others in the paddock or the man who chased them in there.

And then the moment arrived. An older heifer, straggling near the back of the herd. Visibly walking stiffly, nearly as stiffly as he had earlier, moving much slower than the rest. The old cow was awkward and slow. Weak. She was vulnerable. He pushed back on his haunches, contracting them like a coiled spring and, when he was certain the perfect moment was right in front of him, he released the spring and bolted toward the old cow like a freight train. He caught up and chomped a jaw, as tight as a bear trap, around her back leg. The pain caused the cow to call out long and loud, which sent a wave of moos through the rest of the herd. It was all the chance he needed, and he struck.

He struck clean through the cow's Achilles tendon, which dropped it to the ground, unable to stand. From there, he moved quickly and crushed the old girl's throat, preventing any air from entering and silencing her from any further cries. A few more minutes and a few hundred pounds of pressure around the big dumb thing's neck and the cow was silent and still. He had to work fast now, dragging a dead cow by himself wouldn't be easy, but if he wanted it, wanted all of it, he'd have to get her back as far as the bushes until it was safe enough for him to eat.

The heifer was massive, but between pulling on her back leg and by the scruff of the neck and with immeasurable effort, he finally got her carcass into the bushes, and lay down beside it, exhausted. Soon sleep took him, and his mind wandered. Far from here, far from the dairy fields of Winterbourne, to a grassy meadow that felt familiar, but he didn't quite recognize. The sun was high, and a fragrant breeze blew across his face. His muscles didn't ache, and he was warm and young and strong. Ahead of him, near to the horizon, a small lamb bleated out a dejected cry. It looked lost and afraid. It looked ripe for the picking. He crouched low and crept toward it, trying to stay downwind until it was too late, and the little thing became a hot lunch.

The lamb called out again, panicky. Frightened. But he would silence it soon. He could see it now, practically hear its heartbeat thudding. Lub-dub. Lub-dub. A gulp of air passed through his lips silently and he headed for the long grass. Lub-dub. Lub-dub. Walking slowly, barely moving, he crept toward it. Lub-dub. Lub-dub. It bleated again, and he leapt from the long grass. Lub-dub. Lub-dub. In a heartbeat, he was on the lam. Lub-dub. Lub-dub. Lub-dub. Teeth clamped onto hindquarters and shook back and forth with the force of a Mack truck. Lub-dub. Lub-dub. Lub-dub. Lub-dub. Stopping just short of shaking it until its neck snapped. Lub-dub. Lub-dub. Lub-dub. Lub-dub. Lub-dub. The thing's head came into view. It was a lamb, for all intents, white, wiry curls of hair surrounding it. But where there should have been two large, doughy brown eyes divided by a light fur covered snout, there was a face. A human face. Lub-dub. Barely developed, nearly devoid of features, but unmistakably human. Lub-dub. It bleated a noise at him that sounded like a scream, and he released it. Lub...d...ub. The lamb stood upright and shook the blood from its hind end, its powder puff tail wiggling the pooling blood and shooting it everywhere. It flecked across his muzzle and snapped him back to consciousness. Lub... dub... And it was gone.

The meat from the cow was still warm and felt firm against his teeth when he rolled over and ate. The dream shook him but did little to slow the hunger. He tore into the carcass with rattle boned abandon. Maybe he had never eaten this well. He sunk his teeth deep into the cow, tearing and gulping chunk after chunk of the warm, salty flesh. Lapping the blood, crushing bone between powerful jaws, and sucking the marrow within.

Full. Stuffed beyond full, he lay down again beside the carcass. His mind wandered again, not to ghastly places or awful things. There were men here. Not men in orange with their infernal guns. Men of old with spears and torches. Men who feared the dark. Men that feared him.

7

———————

"Stay in the car," Guthrie said.

"Really? I'm not a kid anymore, Floyd. You just said it yourself."

The old man raised a thick finger and pointed directly at the boy's face. The lines across his face seemed to gather and sag downward in a unanimous frown.

"Stay. In. The. Car. Danny."

He sighed, leaned back in his seat, and closed his eyes. "Fine. Whatever."

They parked the car near the bottom of Grey Hollow Road. Guthrie started the trek up to where Winterbourne's finest milled around. It wasn't a hill, but more of a thick sloping pile of decades' worth of illegally dumped garbage. Occasionally, the township would hack the grass down almost to bare earth to keep it from becoming a total jungle, but that hadn't happened in years.

"Afternoon, Barney. What we got here?"

"Hey Floyd. It's a kid. Up there in the long grass." The other cop looked pale and fragile, like a wrung-out bedsheet. Floyd thought the man might burst into flame or barf if he made eye contact with him.

Guthrie walked the short distance from where the patrolman

stood and crested the berm. There were other detectives here, juniors like himself, and though he half expected them to be examining the crime scene looking for clues or anything resembling police work, he couldn't say he was surprised to see them all standing around the expanse of waist high grass, drinking coffee and not doing a God-damned thing. The forensics team was up here too, being equally useless.

"What's the holdup, fellas?" Guthrie said to himself.

"We weren't really sure where to start," one of the younger detectives offered.

"And you?" Floyd motioned to the forensics team.

"We can't begin anything until you boys clear it first."

"Oh, f–. Fine. Just gimme a minute."

He walked slowly, carefully, into the long grass where it was disturbed, trying not to compromise the scene. Seeing nothing close up, it wasn't hard to tell something had been in it, maybe deer or two bedding down for the night or a young couple up here drinking beer and playing grab ass, but something had flattened the grass. He saw it then, a red sneaker with blood-stained white laces poking out of the vegetation. Guthrie's mind switched into a different gear, and he saw everything that had happened in this area.

"Nobody comes up here 'til I say so, Barney!" He made sure his voice was loud enough for the cop could hear.

"You got it, Floyd."

Floyd wanted to go back to the car to retrieve the toolbox full of the things he'd normally use in a case like this – a flashlight, measuring tape, evidence markers and his camera – but forensics had equipment far superior to his to do just that. It left him free to just take it all in. Without moving further into the grass, he could tell that there were three distinct sets of tracks. Four if you counted the tracks of the red tennis shoe. One set, obviously human, as it bore the markings of a sneaker. Converse Chuck Taylor. The other two weren't human. They were canine, one large and heavy. A coyote, or maybe a wolf, though Guthrie was pretty sure there hadn't been a wolf anywhere near Winterbourne since the stone age.

Ignoring the second set of animal prints for the time being, Guthrie instructed the forensics team to document the scene before he moved the grass and began mentally dismantling the whole place so he could put it back together bit by bit. Someone had moved most of the tall weeds around the body. He could tell that from the way the thick stocks bent inward and someone, or something, had torn away the long grass and piled it all on top of the kid's body, making the whole thing look like a wild and overgrown funeral mound. He pulled a portion of the grass back and saw what he knew he wasn't the first to see.

The boy was dead and laying on his stomach. Experience taught the old man what the stages of decomposition looked like, and by his estimation, the body had laid here for about three days. Today was Monday, which meant somebody had a hell of a kickoff to their weekend early on Friday night. Guthrie pulled back the rest of the grass and weeds and took a pair of rubber gloves from his pocket and put them on. After a few dozen shutter snaps from the forensics cameras, he turned the boy right way round. A sickening knot twisted itself around the bottom of his gut and sweat beaded up on his forehead and soaked into the back of his shirt. He wasn't surprised by what he saw, nor did it frighten him. He'd seen his share of bodies twisted and ruined by car wrecks and construction accidents or mangled by boyfriends and lovers who were jealous types or just sick of the other's shit.

"Pull up his left sleeve for me, can you?" Floyd said to the forensics officer and felt his shoulders tighten up.

"What?"

"Lift the left sleeve of his jacket. Do you see anything?"

"No, I don't see anything, maybe some superficial scratches."

Guthrie's shoulders relaxed.

"Oh wait, there is something. Looks like letters. A word, maybe. Not sure. You wanna look?"

"I don't need to look. I know what it is," Floyd said with a sigh.

He looked up at the cop. "Should we call this in?"

Floyd wasn't angry. Hell, he wasn't even sad. But he was

disappointed. Disappointed that whatever leads he thought he had, whatever ideas of who was responsible for five dead children, just vanished along the blood-stained laces of a red tennis shoe.

"Should we call this in?" the forensics officer said. "Are we going to need more help?"

"Yeah," Guthrie said. "Call it in."

"Yes, sir," the other cop said and walked back to his truck.

Floyd sighed. "Fuck."

DANNY JERKED FORWARD in his seat as an awful thought wormed its way into his head. *He'll know. He'll see everything that was up there, and he'll know I was up there too. He always knows.* Fear crept through him like morning fog rolling in off a lake, slowly, ominously, and swallowing everything it touched.

He sighed. "Shit."

He was now precisely in the spot that Floyd Guthrie said he would find himself countless times in his life. This was a crossroads. That's what this was. A decision had to be made. It wouldn't be easy and likely. It would be the least appealing thing to cross his mind.

"You're between a bastard and a sonofabitch," Floyd would tell him. "The right answer is always the thing you don't want to do. Always. Follow your gut and then follow your nose."

He opened the car door and looked across Millar's field toward the flashing lights that crowded the northwest corner. A crowd gathering near the car and handfuls of people filed past, heading up toward the cruisers. Middle-aged mostly, mom and pop types and he wondered how the news of it had spread so quickly through the town. Danny shifted in beside a group of them as they pushed on toward the scene. The group made it as far as the first pair of squad cars when they were stopped dead by a young uniformed officer practicing her police procedure.

"Nothing to see here, folks," she said forcefully.

"Really, then what in the hell is going on back there?" a man said, pointing up at the cops milling around the long grass at the top of the berm.

"Hunting accident or something. Nothing to get worked up about. Go on home."

"Easy for you to say," a woman said in a loud voice.

The buzz of the crowd increased. They didn't. They stayed, and their guesses and worry rose to fever pitch and spread through their ranks and to Parker Avenue. Soon there seemed to be a hundred frightened people standing on the other side of the twin cruisers.

The boy ducked in and out of the assembled crowd and eventually made his way up alongside the police car on the right. As the young cop exchanged pleasantries with the crowd that continued to tell her where she could put those pleasantries, Danny crouched his way around the car and headed the fifty more feet up the berm where the rest of the cops were working. Barney Douglas stood here, stone-faced and blocking the entrance to the crime scene. Danny knew him. He knew most of the old guard of the Winterbourne PD through Guthrie. He also knew that Barney had a soft spot for him as he was one of the first cops on the scene the night his folks died.

Danny smiled at the cop. "Hiya Barney."

"Nope, nope, nope," Barney said firmly.

"What?"

"No way, Danny. You ain't going up there."

"C'mon Barney, what's the harm?"

"This ain't like when Hagedorn's shop got broken into or when the bakery burnt down. This is serious."

"I know, I've already seen it," Danny said, trying an entirely new angle.

"Bullshit," Barney said. "Nobody's been up there but cops."

"It's a boy, right? Dead and all chewed up? I bet he's wearing red tennis shoes."

"How'd you– Y'know what? I don't want to know. But look, Floyd told me nobody up there without his say so."

"He'll never even know I was there," Danny said.

"I am going to the other side of my cruiser," Barney said. "Y'know, to take a piss. Since I can't witness what I am not here to see, just about anything could happen. While I was all the way over here. Pissing."

Danny moved quickly and quietly and crouched just out of sight of everybody up there. Things were still just about the way he left them. The grass pushed aside, but the red tennis shoe faced the other direction. One of the forensics men wearing a head-to-toe white jump suit stepped aside, and Danny got another look at the face and the milky white eyes. They pleaded to him for help, and he felt compelled to move forward toward the cops, toward Floyd.

"Do we have an ID yet? Anybody recognize this kid?" Guthrie said to the assembled cops.

"His name was Billy Anglin," Danny said.

8

____

He practically tiptoed through the town. It was still early morning when the cow became a hot lunch. It'd taken so much longer than it used to eat and hide the remains to come back to later. He had to stop for a break too many times and slept at least twice that he could remember. The sun would make its way to the horizon before long. A whole day wasted, and he had accomplished nothing. He found an alleyway between two grey, faded brick buildings that looked quiet enough. Just the same, he crept down to it, his eyes constantly searching for threats.

"Hey, boy. Whattsa matter? You lost?" the grubby, middle-aged man pissing on the side of the building said.

Hey, boy? He wondered. *Boy? Like I'm a dog?* The big thing looked at his paws and had to admit, there was a slight resemblance to man's best friend, but he was twice the size of any dog he'd ever encountered, and his fur was matted and spiky in patches and the scar across his face gave him the appearance of an animal that had seen the worst the world offered and came out the other side. He growled at the dirty man who quickly zipped his pants despite not having finished relieving himself and hurried into the back-room Butler's tavern. The not dog began scratching behind his right ear, grumbling to himself over how much like a dog he wasn't. His back-leg stroked and dug, becoming more forceful until a small fissure erupted between the ear and the skull. It turned to its paws, gnawing and chewing on them until blood trickled. He lay on all fours and stretched forward as long and as far as he could make his body, front legs extending well beyond normal proportions. As the immense paws ruptured and gave way, two perfectly formed human hands made their way forward through them. The fur retracted and folded inward and under itself, a human form that lurked beneath the animal the whole time. He opened his mouth wide, yawped, and placed his new hands inside it. From top and bottom jaw, he took hold and pulled in opposite directions. The beginning was always the worst. The jaw cracked, and the blood pulsed its way down his chest, but he'd pulled hard and far enough that the top of a head emerged between the two rows of jagged teeth, wet and bloody as though it pushed its way out from a shredded womb.

"What the f-?" The man peeing against the building, quickly zipped his pants and ran back into the doorway he came out of.

As the head cleared the jaws, the hands continued to pull downward, twisting them sideways to accommodate the width of the shoulders. From there it was a few grunts and forceful wiggles, and his hips were free. Two more short tugs with his feet pushing down from his knees, and he was free of the pelt completely. It lay in a small bloody bundle on the ground beside him. He dripped with streaks of blood and bits of errant flesh, which he licked away furiously. He took up the pelt and tucked it into the dumpster, between black trash bags and a handful of empty pizzas boxes.

A barman stood in the doorway, looking up and down the alleyway. "Hey, buddy, you seen a big dog out here?"

"It wasn't a dog," the pee-stained man interjected from behind the barman. "It couldn't have been a dog. Way too big for a dog. What I saw was a goddam wolf."

"A wolf in downtown Winterbourne?" the naked man standing in the alleyway asked.

The gathering crowd of drunks howled with laughter, jeering and pointing at the man for even suggesting something so foolish.

"On the other hand," the naked man suggested, and the crowd grew quickly silent. "There is a dog called a Scottish deerhound. Huge they are, and some are as grey as ash, while others still are black as midnight. What did this wolf of yours look like?"

"It was grey and shaggy, and the bastard was huge," pee-pants said. "His shoulder was taller than my waist."

"The very fellow then, I should think," the stranger agreed.

"I told you it wasn't anything worth worrying about, McCabe. You're an idiot," someone from the crowd said.

"Surely, there must be a house or two where the folks make enough money to afford such a fine, expensive dog," the stranger wondered.

"Oh yeah, there's a bunch of folks with that kinda money. Outta town folks with outta town money. Most of them live up around Grandview heights and the new subdivisions up there."

"There you have it then. Say, it looks rather like rain. Why don't we step back inside for a drink or two? Maybe even three. It's the weekend, after all."

"It's Monday morning, and the bar ain't open," a balding man in the dirty apron said.

"And yet, here you all are, most of you worse for the drink, am I right?"

"Private after-hours club," the drunk blurted. "Members only."

"Ah, and I suppose you're all members, are you? Well, maybe just the one." The stranger winked and flashed a knowing smile. "Just the one drink and we'll make sure the police never catch wind of these members-only clubs."

They began the walk back into the dark of Butlers when one of the crowd noticed the man was not following them into the bar.

"Er, aren't you coming in for a drink, pal?"

"Me? No, never touch the stuff."

"Oh, well, there's that, then."

"Oh, for Christ's sake," McCabe said. "Am I the only one who can see?"

"What the hell are you talking about? He seems perfectly fine to me." One of the gathered patrons said.

They headed back into Butler's. All of them were content to leave him standing naked in the middle of the alley, none of them even remotely interested in who he was or what he was doing naked in the alley behind their local bar. But one of them inexplicably felt the need to turn back to him and noticed a thick bead of crimson ooze trailing down the stranger's forehead, headed for his top lip.

"What the hell is that?"

"What?" the stranger said.

"Your head is bleeding."

"Oh, that." The stranger grinned and produced a black comb from his pocket, running it through his hair, resulting in a near perfect part to the ride side of his head. He returned the comb to his pocket, but not before running a finger along its teeth, removing the trail of blood.

"For fuck's sake, Harris," pee-pants said again. "He's got no fucking clothes on!"

"So, no time for a quick one inside?" Harris turned to McCabe. "How much have you had? Of course, he's got clothes on. Jesus."

"Sorry fellas, I really must be off," the stranger said, and most of the crowd turned and headed back inside.

Pee-pants remained near the back of the crowd, heading back inside Butlers. Most of them were drunk enough to not notice or not see what he did next, but he saw all of it. The stranger took the finger full of bloody glop and jammed it quickly into his mouth, licking it with relish until the gore disappeared. The naked man looked directly at McCabe and his eyes flashed a deep crimson and he smiled before stopping and allowing McCabe into the bar first.

He stopped just inside the doorway and looked like he might turn and walk back out. "I'm embarrassed to say I'm new in town and haven't started my job yet. I haven't any money just now."

"Oh, is that all?" Harris said. "If that's the only thing stopping you from having a drink with us, then come on in. The water's fine. We got your back and then some."

"Left your wallet in your other suit?" McCabe said.

He followed them in and took a seat at the bar beside the man with the moistened trousers, who turned to him.

"What'll you have?"

"Oh, whatever he's having." The stranger motioned to McCabe. "I've never been much of a drinker, goes straight to my head."

Pee-pants smiled. "Two double Chivas, Jeanine."

"Shee-vaas?"

"An excellent scotch, if you know nothing about scotch. It'll get you there without feeling like a wino."

The glasses arrived in front of them, filled nearly to the top with the amber liquid. McCabe pushed a glass toward the stranger, who clutched it tightly, waiting for a cue to drink. He took his own glass and hoisted it to his lips.

"Over the teeth and through the gums, I might be an alcoholic and that's why I'm having trouble holding on to a fulfilling relationship," McCabe said and downed the glass in one monumental gulp and slammed the empty glass on the bar top.

He looked over at the naked man, who was now wearing matching tan work pants and shirt, the kind of outfit a janitor would wear.

"What the fuck?" he mumbled.

McCabe held up a solitary hand and stared at it. It seemed solid enough and attached, so there was that. He'd never drunk himself into a hallucination before, but here he was, drinking cheap liquor and seeing naked men in an alleyway behind the bar that over served him with the cheap liquor as long as his money held out. It wasn't too far of a leap from blackout drunk to his seeing things that were and weren't there.

The stranger followed suit and poured the large shot down his throat. He sputtered and coughed as the liquid burned its way down to his stomach.

"It's an acquired taste." Pee-pants chuckled and extended a lily-white hand. "Alan McCabe, vice-principal at Winterbourne high."

The stranger returned the shake, never taking his eyes off the now considerably drunken man and choked down the last swallows of his whisky.

"What brings you to our little town?" McCabe said.

"Children," the stranger said in answer.

9

Guthrie grabbed Danny around the wrist and practically jerked him out of his shoes and away from the crime scene and back down the berm and to the nasty Ford. They walked in thick silence the entire way, broken only by the creaking moan of the car door.

"Get in there," Floyd said, and slammed the door after the boy sat.

He walked back toward the scene when a thought occurred to him, and he stomped back and opened the car door.

"Stay in the car," he said and drilled the door of the ford shut hard enough that it might as well have been the door of a dump truck. Sprinkles of rust from the door fell like snowflakes, leaving a small pile of desiccated steel under it.

Floyd chugged his way back up the hill and remained there for a lifetime, leaving Danny in the car with nothing to do but think of what he'd done and what he'd seen. He thought of coming clean with the old man and telling him all of it. Being up this way, despite being told not to. Coming across Billy Anglin's stiff body. And then his mind became crowded with the awful thoughts that dig their claws in when fear shoves reason out of the way.

What if Guthrie wasn't mad because I got out of the car? What if he was so mad because he thinks I was involved in all of this? Oh god, did I move anything? Apart from the grass? Shit, the grass! I moved the grass. But I put it back over him. Nobody would know any different. It looked just the same when I left as it did when I found him. Guthrie will know. Guthrie always knew. It was scary. He could practically tell the time on the watches of the last three people to touch the fridge door in his apartment. *Jesus, did I touch him? Did I touch Billy Anglin?*

He was cold. Freezing. His teeth threatened to rattle out of his skull from the shivers writhing through him. It was fear. Fear he would wind up in more trouble than he was already in, or worse. Guthrie would give him a look that said I trusted you and you blew it. Fear they would all find out what they'd suspected all along. The fosters, the school, the whole god-damned town. All of them would know that he really *was* a fuck up and it would have been so much simpler if he would've died in the car with his parents.

"Tell me what you know about this and no bullshit," Guthrie said as he got back into the car.

A light rain fell and beaded up on the window, flashing from diamond, to sapphire, to ruby, in time with the spinning of the squad car lights.

"Ah, fuck." Guthrie sighed and got back out of the car. "Wait here."

Back up the hill he went, where the forensics team was already pulling blue plastic tarps and tent pegs from the back of their truck.

"Barney, make sure they tarp it at least fifteen feet out in all directions around the body. I don't want to lose anything if this weather picks up."

"You got it, Floyd," Barney called back.

Floyd headed back down to the car again, nearly out of breath and completely out of patience by the time he opened the door and sat back down.

"I should kick your ass just for making me walk this much."

Floyd meant it as a joke, but it missed the mark on Danny. The look on his face said he was wrestling with something more awful than a joke could relieve.

"I didn't do it," he said.

"Wait, what?" Floyd choked and nearly spat a mouthful of warm, melted milkshake on the steering wheel.

"I didn't do it Floyd. I didn't kill Billy Anglin."

"Is that what you think this is about?"

"Well, you know I was up there."

"You didn't make it too difficult. Your shoe prints are everywhere."

"How do you know they're my shoe prints?"

"Because I bought you the God- damned shoes. I'm sure there are other kids around your age and approximate weight that have the same shoe, but I doubt if any of them went tromping around in Millar's field with a doll's head and a dog that shed's hair like he's got a skin condition."

"You should be on TV. It's creepy what you do," Danny said.

"It's not creepy, it's just the truth. The truth is always there, it just gets buried. If you can look past all the other crap, filter it out. The truth is what's left. Always."

The boy eyed the old man with an innocent awe, like he was a movie star or a magician who'd just pulled the greatest trick he'd ever seen.

"Now tell me what the hell happened here?"

Danny explained he and Jack spent Sunday wandering the town, throwing the doll's head, eating day old's from Wiederson's and wound up in Millar's field by accident or maybe by habit. It was the dog that found the body and growled at him, trying to keep him away. He said Jack seemed confused and upset by the whole thing and only calmed down when he moved up and stroked the dog, convincing him everything was alright.

"I didn't say anything because I didn't want to get in any trouble with the fosters. I didn't want them doing anything to Jack."

"Jesus, Danny." Floyd sighed after a few tense moments of silence. "You really should have said something. You could have, at least, called me and given me a warning about what was up here. Everybody knows I look after you on the side. If they find out it was you who discovered this kid and didn't say anything about it, they're going to ask questions."

Danny lowered his head. The truth of his discovering the boy was out and Guthrie didn't seem angry about it. He looked at Floyd. It was the one thing Guthrie valued above all other things. A man had his word. Without that, he had nothing. And now Danny had nothing.

"I'm really fucking mad at you right now. You know that, right?"

A sigh escaped Danny, like the knot coming out of a balloon. Air hissed out quickly over nervously clenched teeth. Floyd was pissed, raging maybe, and the angrier he got, the more likely he was to punish Danny further. But if he said nothing, or worse, driven him back to the foster's straight away and been cool and distant, the boy would know he'd really hurt the old man's feelings. Anger always felt a bit like a slap meant to get your attention. There was a kind of caring in the delivery. A *this will hurt you more than me*. He'd be hot and angry and full of emotion. Silence was cold. It was abandonment and apathy, and it was awfully hard to find your way back from there.

"Your three-day suspension starts tomorrow, right?"

"Yeah," Danny whispered.

"Good, then so does your sentence."

"Wait, what?"

"Because you couldn't keep your shit together long enough to keep away from Millar's field when you knew you weren't supposed to go up there, I'm going to make sure you're nowhere near it for the next seven days."

"What do you mean?"

"For the next three days, you will report at 9:00 a.m. and you will finish at 4:00 p.m. When you're back in school, you will report at 4:00 P.M. and you will finish at 8:00 p.m. Your foster parents will be told about it and, much to their relief, there won't be an interruption of funds because of all this."

"But Jack, what about Jack? I won't leave him alone with those assholes, not for a whole week," Danny said.

"That's the best part," Guthrie said. "Since your Jack is so well behaved, I've arranged it so he can tag along with you. He might even like it."

Danny grew quiet.

"This is bullshit Guthrie," Danny said under his breath.

"So was not doing what you should have done."

"But I found him, I found Billy Anglin. Shouldn't that count for something?"

"It should, but you didn't tell anybody about it. Now it doesn't count for shit. As far as anybody knows, a couple of vagrants looking for a place to bed down for the night found him." Guthrie opened the door. "I've got to get back up there. One of the uniforms will take you home. I'll pick you up around 8:30 tomorrow morning."

"Fine," Danny said. "Whatever. You didn't tell me what I'm doing or where I'm going."

Guthrie smiled. "Starting tomorrow, you and Jack are volunteering at Winterbourne Home."

10

There was no dinner waiting for him when he got home, not that he expected there would be. Danny made himself a sandwich – ham and cheese with grainy mustard and grabbed a plate from the cupboard. There were only dinner plates and so, before grabbing a can of coke from the pantry, the boy took a bag of Doritos from the shelf above the coke and buried the sandwich beneath a mountain of deep-fried corn and processed cheese powder. He headed upstairs. Jack followed close behind. Most of the sandwich stayed uneaten, though if Jack had his way, it would have all been gone. It had been a day. The sandwich wasn't very good, and the Doritos were stale. Danny kicked off his shoes and crawled under the sheets, fully clothed.

The brain is a wonderful thing. 3 million years of evolution, the most complex organ of anything on the planet. Capable of precise calculations in a split second. Able to think and reason and speak and absolutely guaranteed to switch into overdrive when all you really want to do is sleep. There was just too much going on in there to rest now. There were two sets of eyes that kept coming back to him, eyes that beckoned and nagged, and tried to bore a hole through his skull and out the other side. Guthrie's eyes. Red ringed and heavy and a little sad too. He couldn't hear the old man's voice, but he didn't need to. The eyes said enough. But even they weren't enough to keep Danny from sleeping. He'd felt guilt from Floyd before and knew in a day or two, especially after doing whatever he was supposed to do at Winterbourne, things would be back to normal. But the other eyes, Billy Anglin's eyes, weren't saying anything.

There wasn't any guilt in them. No sorrow or longing, nor begging or pleading. There was no love or hate in them. There wasn't anything in them, and there never would be again. The kid was not hurt. There was no way he was just walking this one off. The kid was dead. Danny barely knew him and couldn't have cared less about him when he was alive. He knew his face to see him in the hallway. He knew his old man drank too much, and in the fourth grade, he came to school with a broken arm and a black eye that didn't come from falling down the stairs. But he wasn't the only kid who had parents that knocked them around. So why couldn't he get the kid out of his mind now? What did he want?

It was dark in his room. Dark enough that he couldn't see his alarm clock. Puzzling about the dead boy gave way to exhaustion and sleep crawled across his face, and his eyes felt like he walked through cobwebs. They slid shut. The alarm screeched out and jarred him out of bed. It was 8:23 and Guthrie's driver would be sitting at the end of the driveway waiting for him.

"C'mon, Jack."

At least he could doze on the way to Winterbourne.

11

"Are you Floyd's friend?" the nurse said.

"I wouldn't exactly call us friends, but I guess that's me, yeah," Danny said.

"This way."

She led him from the main entrance, where the cop dropped him off, through a set of double doors and to a single door with a thick pane of safety glass in the middle of it. The nurse pulled a nylon lanyard with an ungodly collection of keys on it from her neck and, after a few minutes of flipping keys, unlocked the door.

"You keep it locked?" Danny said nervously.

He knew Guthrie was mad at him. For lying to him, for Millar's field, and for ditching school. But mostly, Floyd was mad at him for Billy Anglin. He might have even hated him a little for it. But he didn't think the old man was mad enough to put him in a room full of people that needed to be locked in.

"Good lord, yes," the nurse said quickly. "You can't imagine the buckets full of sloppy hell that would rain down on this place if we didn't keep this God-damned door locked."

She was young. Older than he was, of course, but Danny thought she looked to be in her early twenties. She was prettier than anyone he'd ever seen before. Her skin was a coppery brown that seemed to glow when the light hit it just right. It might have been sweat, but Danny wanted to believe her skin was that beautiful. The sheen on her cheeks highlighted a small and impossibly cute, upturned nose. Her eyes were a deep-set mocha and flashed with a seriousness that left Danny wondering just what in the hell he'd gotten himself into.

"Really? Like what?" Danny swallowed hard, not wanting to know the answer.

The young nurse sighed and lowered her head, like the weight of what she was about to say was so intense, it forced her head downward under the burden of it. Slowly, her head came back up and a playful smile danced its way along her lips. A laugh bubbled out from deep within her belly that soon doubled her over in a fit.

She laughed. "Floyd said to give you a little red ass for all the shit you've been up to. Sorry, honey."

Danny felt lightheaded, like he might faint. The tension and worry had built up practically to fever pitch, and now the adrenaline ran away from him like a scalded dog. He put his hands on his knees and bent forward a little, sucking in gasps of breath. When his heart rate had calmed, he looked back up at the pretty nurse.

"So why do you really keep the people locked up?"

"We have some folks who like to wander. Wander out their front door, wander into open spaces, wander into traffic. We keep the doors locked so the worst they can do is to wander into somebody else's room. It keeps them safe. It keeps them out of trouble. I know it kinda makes them seem like prisoners, but there isn't much else we can do apart from drugging them back to the stone age. And nobody wants that."

"No," Danny said. "That wouldn't be very good."

"Don't worry, sweetie. There isn't anybody scary in there. Nobody is going to hurt you, despite what you might think. In fact, they're all going to love you. Go in, be yourself, and have fun. They will."

She pulled the door open for him and waited until he stepped all the way in. The door slammed closed behind him with a metallic clang and he turned to look at the pretty young nurse. She pointed to the desk behind him, the hub of the ward, and wiggled her fingers at him in a playful goodbye. She called him sweetie. He was pretty sure he was in love with her. In his mind, he was already planning their wedding.

"Are you the new volunteer?" the nurse behind the desk said.

"Ah, yes. I guess so..." Danny said.

"Good. Head into the dining room. They'll let you know where to go and who to sit with. You've done this before?"

"Of course," he said, lying through his teeth.

The staff directed Danny to a table with four elderly people seated at it and told he was to help feed them.

"How do I... uh..."

"Didn't I just hear you tell the nurse you'd done this before?" the kitchen lady said.

"I... um... I thought she meant something else." The embarrassment scorched across his cheeks and rushed up to his forehead like a fever.

The kitchen lady, a smallish, greasy-haired gnome of a woman, sighed and stomped toward Danny. She grabbed a spoon from the placemat, scooped an unholy amount of the mush from the blue plate, and jammed it into the old woman's face until most of it ran down her chin.

"Have you ever fed a child?"

"Oh... ah... once, maybe," Danny said.

"Same idea. Here." She turned the spoon toward him, handle first, and pushed it at his face.

It was brown, and there were two large globs of it on the thick plastic plate. Beside the two brown puddles, a smaller unnaturally yellow one spread and oozed toward the others, threatening to envelop them both. All three had begun the day as food, possibly even edible. Breakfast, Danny guessed, but to say that they remained food by the time they hit the plate he was scooping it off would have been an insult to edible things all over the world. It was closer to pudding than it was to the bacon, eggs, and fried potatoes it was supposed to be. He scraped a little from the first brown puddle and held it gingerly toward the mouth of the woman to his right.

"Nobody's gonna get fed that way," the kitchen lady sounded annoyed. "Just shovel it in. Like this."

She took the spoon from him, gathered as much off the plate as she could in one go, and pushed against the mouth of the woman Danny had tried feeding. The elderly woman opened her mouth, almost automatically, and the breakfast pudding went in. Most of it trailed out of her mouth and down her chin.

"Get as much as you can in and move on to the next one. You should be able to feed two people at a time. Her and her." She motioned to the two women sitting on either side of him. Danny inched his stool toward the middle of them and took up the spoon again. He scooped up a hellacious amount of brown and yellow and jammed it toward the face of the woman not choking on a mouthful of food too large to deal with. The calm wouldn't last. They both spat and gagged and choked and coughed, trying to dislodge the awful breakfast slurry. Afraid the kitchen lady would scowl at him again; Danny jammed another unhealthy glob at both of them. Neither of the old women were ready. For every spoonful running down the chins of the two old ladies he fed, two more scoops of it ran down his arm. It went on like this until the plates were empty, and both ladies, and Danny, were dripping in the brown glop.

"Where are you going?" the kitchen boss lady asked as he stood from the table and crossed the dining room.

"Uh, everybody looks to be done, so I guess I am. I was just gonna go downstairs and wait for Guthrie to pick me up again," he said.

The kitchen lady laughed, and laughed, and laughed. If a laugh were words, hers would have extolled the stupidity of the kid who thought work time concluded 45 minutes after entering the ward.

"Done? There is no done around here, just the time between shifts. Get in the elevator, back by where you came in, and head downstairs. I'm sure they can use a hand in laundry. Then you can make your way back here and help at lunchtime."

THE PRETTY YOUNG nurse was behind the desk now, and he waved to her as she buzzed him through the locked door. The prospect of being stuck in this place all day seemed brighter now, knowing at least he'd get to see her a few more times before he had to go home. He tried the door, and to his surprise, it was locked. Danny looked back to the nurse, who no longer smiled at him, and waved her hands, trying to communicate the idea of pulling on the door when she pushed the big red button beside her desk. He got it the second time and walked through, refusing to look back at her, even though he was dying to.

Danny stepped off the elevator into the dank humidity of the basement of Winterbourne Home. To his right and left, darkened hallways that sent icy fingers tickling up the back of his neck just looking down at him. He wasn't sure where he needed to be, but he hoped like hell it wasn't down to either of them. Straight ahead of him, another hallway stretched out. One with awful lighting, but the noises coming from it and the mingling of the perfumery odour of laundry soap, and the sour burn of bleach made him feel a little better. By the sounds of it, there were people down there, and that was better than nothing. He headed toward the light and popped his head in the doorway when he got to the end of the hall.

The room was big. For as dull as the light in the corridor was, this room was well lit and bright. It also looked spotless, despite the awful smells coming from around it. A man stood near the far wall with his back to the doorway. Danny cleared his throat for fear of startling him.

The man turned around and smiled. "And you must be the lazy volunteer."

He was tall and wide and had a broad, friendly face framed by a shock of black hair that refused to stay off his forehead, despite his repeated attempts to keep it that way. He stuck a meaty hand toward the boy.

"John Thomas," he said.

"Wait, what?" Danny sputtered, barely containing a laugh. "John Thomas like..."

"Nah, just seeing if you're paying attention. It's Evan." He laughed and slapped a big hand on Danny's back.

Danny felt a weight lift from his shoulders and a sigh whistled through his lips like steam from a broken radiator. He even returned the smile. It was fair to say that Danny liked Evan right away.

"They sent you down here to help, I take it?" Evan said.

"Yeah, that's what the lady in the dining room said."

"Ah, Lorenza." The laundry man smiled. "Pleasant ray of sunshine, ain't she?"

A laugh bubbled across Danny's lips, and he raised his hand to cover his mouth, thinking this was a test and the big man would report him if he wasn't careful.

"It's okay to laugh. Nobody ever comes down here, not this far in any way. And she is an awful woman. Okay, it's good you're here. I can always use the help. It stinks down here. I'm not gonna lie. It smells like shit, and it smells like bleach, and it smells like a wet dog, like always, but it looks like you might be used to that." He pointed to Jack, who'd already begun nesting in a pile of clean towels. "Like I said, nobody comes down here. We're pretty much on our own."

Danny stood up a little straighter. He liked the idea of nobody bothering him and the best part of it all was, it was *laundry*. He'd being doing his own laundry, sorting, washing, bleaching, when necessary, drying, folding, and even ironing, for years now. How much more difficult could it be here? Sure, there was a ton more of it and it smelled completely vile, but the operation was still to put things in one machine, wait, and them put them in another. Simple.

"Put these on," Evan said and handed Danny a dull yellow apron and a pair of blue-green rubber gloves.

Danny put them on and found the apron extended from just above his chest and reached down to the tops of his shoes, and the gloves fit well past his elbows.

"They're a little on the big side," Danny said.

"In a few minutes, you're gonna wish they were bigger. Come on."

They walked through an archway in the big clean room and entered a larger room overrun with laundry bags. So full, in fact, there almost wasn't enough room for the two immense washing machines.

"Simple day today." He smiled. "We'll get all this stuff cleaned and dried and then you can go with the girls from housekeeping and get it put back into the rooms."

Evan opened the first bag, carried it to the first of the industrial washers, and dumped its contents into the hopper, motioning for Danny to do the same. The boy opened the neck of the laundry bag and a smell snarled up at him, nearly knocking him over. It was a wet smell, a musty smell. A day's worth of soap and water-soaked clothes that clean residents who'd soiled themselves and their clothes thrown into the laundry bag. There they sat, festering and fermenting the whole day, and that was bad enough. But it was only the beginning.

Shit stinks. Danny knew this. Anybody who's ever had to clean up after a dog knows this, but the stink of shit that percolated with stale urine in a nylon bag that allows for almost no airflow creates an assault on the senses that few people have ever had to experience. It slapped his nostrils and stuck there like a glue trap, and then it was all he could smell. He backed away further, hoping the distance would help the smell dissipate, but it seemed to follow him wherever he turned.

"Best to pick it up and dump it in the machine as quick as you can," Evan said.

Danny grabbed the bag near the bottom and gripped it tightly as he stood, which forced a burst of air to puff up through it and drove the awful smell that much closer to his face. The sweat beaded up on his forehead and the heat of the room bit at his cheeks and the back of his neck. The surrounding air was thick with ammonia and bleach. His nostrils flared, hoping for fresh air, but they only sucked more of the funk into his lungs. His head swam, and he turned around, looking for a direction. *Any* direction that might get him away from it. The dizziness spun through him like a top and settled in his stomach, where it continued to twirl and churn in an off-rhythm dance. His knees left him and soon he was hurtling toward the floor like a sack of wet, shitty laundry. What little breakfast he'd had pulsed out of him in frothy pools.

Evan let go a full, warm belly laugh. Danny burned with the heat of embarrassment and anger at the big man's laughter but found a smile creeping its way onto the corners of his mouth and soon the laughter, not the nausea, kept him doubled over.

"You lasted longer than I did." Evan laughed. "I didn't get the bag off the ground before I blew chunks. You should be proud of yourself."

"How can you stand it? Smelling that all day?"

"In the beginning, that's all I could smell anywhere I was. I lost thirty pounds because everything I tried to eat smelled like shit. After a while, though, I could smell other things along with it. Little by little. Mostly potent stuff, garlic shit, onion shit, hot pepper shit. Then, one day, I couldn't smell it all anymore. Don't even phase me now. Stick around, you'll get used to it too."

"I'm hoping not to," Danny said.

He tried again, huffing and gagging, and eventually got the contents of the bag into the washing machine. The two of them carried on like that for the rest of the morning, the awful smell lessening by degrees with each bag Danny chucked into the hopper. Before long, the washing finished, and it was time to dry the immense amount of wet laundry. The dryer was huge. Big enough to fit five bags of washing at a time. Danny stuffed in as much as the giant, electric maw would hold and closed the door to switch it on. In short order, the heat in the room skyrocketed to only slightly cooler than temperature inside the sun. The upside of it was nearly every stitch of laundry had been dried to within an inch of its life in a little under two hours. The two of them joked and laughed. Evan joked for the most part, for the entire part, really. Danny didn't know any jokes, not any that he thought somebody as funny as Evan would ever laugh at, but he felt a warmth that didn't come from the dryers. Just being with Evan and listening to him talk to him like an equal made Danny feel better than he had in a long time.

The dryers buzzed one after another as the loads of laundry finished drying.

"Break time," Evan said. "The break room is this way. If you get your appetite back, be sure you wash your hands first."

The thought of eating brought back the thought of vomiting, which fuelled memories of the smell that had made him puke. In a minute, the odour of the BM came racing back to him and then it was *all* he could smell. The nausea danced around the back of his throat and threatened to show him the true meaning of a dry heave. Danny wandered absently toward a seat in the break room and lowered himself onto it slowly. Lowering his head on the cool Formica tabletop, sucking huge breaths of fresh air into his face, he hoped the nausea would pass quickly. He hoped no one would see him like this. He hoped one day of this shit was enough to make Guthrie happy. His eyes slid shut and exhaustion pressed in on him like a lead sleeping bag.

Danny snapped his head up, awake now, but only just. He was alone and standing in the middle of Millar's field. Though, the large box elder tree to his right said that maybe it wasn't the abandoned farmer's field at all. It was hot here, and the air was muggy and thick like the laundry room, but it wasn't stale and there wasn't a whiff of feces. Here it smelled clean and hot, and it clipped at his nostrils like the time he took a sauna at the Y with Guthrie and half a dozen of the oldest, sweatiest men he'd ever seen. That they all kept securely in their towels was the only thing that kept it from being a permanently traumatic memory. He closed his eyes and turned into the breeze that came up out of the east, enjoying the clean scent of it. *Lilacs,* he thought. *Lilacs and maybe a little mint.* It reminded him of someone's breath blowing against him after they'd just brushed their teeth and suddenly, he was nervous.

The fear prickled at him, crawling up his back and teased up his back like the hairy legs of a spider, crawling toward the softness of his neck. He needed to run. He was sure of it, though he couldn't be certain why. There was nothing around him. He leapt forward and took off. The fear became monstrous and overwhelming, and it drove him onward, pushing him to run beyond exhaustion. For all the running he did, he couldn't seem to make it beyond the big box elder, like he was running complete circles around it. Danny collapsed in front of the tree, puffing and panting and wondering just what it was he'd done to get here and what he could do to get away from it.

"Funny thing about travelling. You have to begin with a single step," a voice behind him said.

"What the f–" Danny moved closer to the tree and rapped his hand against it. "Did you just say that?" he said to the big box elder.

"You ever heard of a talking tree?" the voice answered from beside him now.

"What the f... what are you? Where are you?"

"I am," the voice said. "And that's all I can tell you just now. And, for the record, I am just over the small ridge to the west."

"My west?" Puzzlement engulfed Danny. "Your west?" He'd been to two and a half boy scout meetings in his nearly 14 years and, as much as he tried to get a handle on it, compasses and directions completely eluded him.

"Stand up and move to your left," the voice said. "And take slow and steady steps toward the top of the hill."

Danny stood and took a handful of small, stuttered steps until he felt like he was moving forward. It wasn't long before he crested the hill then and saw them standing at the top of it. Two figures, clear enough from where he stood to tell what they were. A dog, maybe the largest one he'd ever seen, shaggy like a golden retriever, but as big as a Great Dane and as black as coal. Next to the dog, very bloody but very much upright, was Billy Anglin.

12

"Detective Sergeant William Kemmler," the man said and held a spindly hand toward Guthrie.

He was tall and thin. His clothes looked expensive, though they were too short for him. The grey suit hung around his frame like a trash bag on a giraffe. He wore his hair closely cropped along the sides of his head, parted severely on the right and pasted in place like the style favoured by neo-Nazis and other dangerously nostalgic conservatives. The man's face was as thin as the rest of him. His dark, narrow-set eyes were set too close to the long tapering nose that made him look like an enormous rat. A fact reinforced by a nervous tick that made him twitch and wipe at his nose constantly. It convinced Guthrie that the man had a serious drug habit or recently got rid of one. Despite his looks, there was an arrogance to him that was so forceful it almost arrived ten minutes before he did.

"Floyd Guthrie," he said, and extended his own hand.

The handshake felt cold and as limp as a bag of grease. Guthrie's gaze never once moving from the younger man's eyes.

"What brings you to Winterbourne, Detective Kemmler?"

"You," he said. "That is, your inability to figure out the identity of someone killing children for longer than most of us have been alive."

"Wait, what? Who sent you here?"

"CID sent me."

"What?"

"The CID. It stands for Criminal Investigation Division," the younger man said. "It's a unit of the police. CID has jurisdiction over everything police related in the whole state. We police the police, you might say."

"I know what the CID is," Guthrie said. "What I meant was, why is a slick outfit like the CID interested in a handful of murders in our little town? There must be bigger cases upstate somewhere that need your attention, detective? Didn't I read in the paper the other day that somebody has been ripping the guts out of prostitutes up around Eagle's Glen? Taking pieces of them as souvenirs and sending letters out with each new bit? I'd think that would command a little more attention than a handful of dead kids?"

"You would think. However, Superintendent Markham has taken a particular interest in this case and will give you the benefit of the doubt for the time being. We've heard of you in the city, the cop who solves it all, right? The senior junior detective who can do no wrong. No clue goes unexamined, and no criminal goes unpunished. When it came out that they gave you the Winterbourne Ripper case, we all assumed you'd tie it all up with a neat little bow in a matter of days. Weeks at the most. But here we are, almost a full two years, and you're still no closer to the end than you were when you got it, right? When the news reached upstate about this latest boy here, the child of a niece or nephew of Superintendent Markham herself, well, you can imagine what a ripple that sent through the head office. The superintendent sent me down here to get to the bottom of it all and bring the guilty party or parties to justice, quickly and quietly."

Guthrie knew the man was lying to him, but Floyd had no interest in the grief that would follow if he said anything about it. So, he smiled, looked inquisitive when he needed to, laughed when he should, and carried right on lying back to Kemmler, every chance he got.

"Huh," he said. "Is that a fact? Well, I sure welcome the help. This case has got me stymied."

"I'm fairly certain I can sort this out quickly," Kemmler said matter-of-factly.

"I look forward to your input," Floyd said, insincerity dripping off his tongue like too much spit. "Now, what can I do to help you help me? What do you need from me?"

"I need nothing from you specifically, but it would be best if I could examine the body and then the crime scene. I assume the Anglin boy is not still lying on the ground up there?"

"No, we moved him to the morgue yesterday, but the scene is still being processed by forensics," Guthrie said. "Which do you want to see first?"

"I'm guessing the morgue is in the basement of the local hospital?"

"Yes, right down there. Underground and everything."

"And where is this hospital?"

"About ten minutes from here," Guthrie said.

"And the crime scene?" Kemmler said.

"Millar's field? About three blocks west of here."

"The crime scene then. That's probably the best place to start. I don't imagine your forensic team picked up nearly all the evidence," Kemmler said.

THE RAIN FELL like an early morning mist, but it was enough to soak them as they walked to Millar's field. They crested the berm in silence and continued that way as the younger man walked circles around where the body of Billy Anglin had been. Kemmler would stop randomly, crouch low, get closer to the dirt and mutter to himself as he went along. Guthrie couldn't be sure, but it looked like the young detective was sniffing the ground where the corpse had been.

"Umm, you alright?" Guthrie said.

"Shh," Kemmler said.

The younger man moved his face toward the blood that stained the ground and lingered there for too long, as far as Guthrie was concerned. Until he stopped and dropped to all fours and began scuttling like a cockroach crawling along the baseboards of an abandoned house.

"Hey!" Floyd bellowed. "You're gonna destroy evidence pissing around like that. Look, just why in the hell are you here, really?"

Kemmler ignored him and continued around the bloody impression that had been the last resting place of Billy Anglin's body. The younger detective sat back on his haunches and removed a small silver tape measure from his jacket pocket, stretching it across what would have been Billy Anglin's neck. It slid closed again quickly and Kemmler produced a polka dotted notebook from his other pocket, writing the measurements as he went. He flipped over a handful of pages, stopping briefly to examine what he wrote on it, and moved on to the next. After what seemed a lifetime of mewling and muttering to himself, Kemmler turned to Guthrie and spoke.

"What are your thoughts, Detective?"

"What?" Floyd sputtered, surprised to suddenly be called back into the game. "Theories about?"

"Motive for one," Kemmler said flatly. "What were the weapon or weapons used? Were there multiple killers or a single perpetrator? You know, detective things."

"A knife, approximately six to eight inches long, with a serrated edge. Like a bread knife or a carving knife."

"So far so good, but what about the other wounds, and the near total evisceration of the children?"

"I think it was probably done intentionally. But not by the killer. The consensus around here points to animal predation. Fox or coyote, something like that."

"Ah," Kemmler said. "But what *kind* of animal?" The tone of his voice was a little on the mocking side, like a teacher holding out on the answer, just to watch a student struggle.

"I was thinking a coyote, maybe a dog? I have known dogs to

snack on the bodies of deceased owners after a couple of days with no food. Feral dogs are probably pretty opportunistic."

"No," Kemmler said. "The bite radius is much too small for a coyote or dog, and the wounds are far too jagged. Look near the top there, the ribs are cracked and splintered away, but the breaks are singular. No coyote, no family dog, stray or otherwise, has the strength to inflict that kind of damage with a single bite."

"So, what then?"

"A bear, perhaps, but more than likely a wolf. And an exceptionally large one at that," Kemmler said.

The rain fell heavier, making Kemmler's hair look even more slick than it was. Every time he glanced up at the other cop, the wet and the questioning looks got on Floyd's nerves. He wasn't happy coming here in the mist, he hated being here in the rain.

Guthrie stared at the man; certain his mouth was hanging open in disbelief.

"A wolf? A fucking wolf! In Winterbourne?"

"Yes," Kemmler said. "Why not? Or perhaps something wolf-like."

"Why not? Because it's ridiculous. There hasn't been anything like a wolf around this part here for hundreds, maybe thousands, of years. The idea something that big and powerful has been stomping around here for better than fifty years completely unnoticed. It's as laughable as my chances of making senior detective before I retire. And wolf-like? What the fuck does that even mean?"

"Tell me, detective, what is a more logical explanation? What do you think is responsible?"

Guthrie sat silently for a time. Logic didn't walk the same path as this case and chasing after it hadn't gotten him any closer to solve it now than it ever had. "Well, it was a man that killed him, that much is certain," he said finally.

"How certain?"

"Very," Guthrie said, slamming the door on that line of distraction. "A human being killed these kids. I don't doubt there was animal predation postmortem, but the fact remains that all these murders happened almost the same day every ten years? Even the fucking coyote from Saturday morning cartoons isn't that clever. No, this was something else. The body dumps are too clean. There was blood underneath them all, but not arterial, and not in the amounts there should have been if he killed them where we found them. Even if most of it had soaked in the ground. He killed these kids somewhere else and dumped in out of the way places. On purpose. The killer, I say that like I know there was just one, could have been more than one for all I know. Two working together? Copycats? But the killer meant the bodies to be found. It was a message. They were all messages to... somebody."

"Interesting choice of words, Detective. How much do you know about this town and Winterbourne Home? Do you know what it was before it became an institution?"

"About as much as the next guy, I suppose. Old man Winterbourne bullied and bought his way into this town, built a big house up on the hill, went nuts. Killed his wife and kids before burning the house down around himself. What he left of it became the nut house and then, after the state closed that, it became the nursing home it is now. Creepy place if you ask me."

"That's surprisingly detailed, but it's not entirely accurate. A.H. Winterbourne used his wealth and power to build the biggest house anyone had ever seen, but he also used his considerable influence to get several other buildings put up around here. The Masonic Hall on Edgar Avenue, the catholic church St. Gertrude's, and Winterbourne high school."

"So, he was generous before he lost his marbles. Andrew Carnegie built scores of libraries and gave away millions, to soothe the guilt of having shit all over his fellow man trying to get to the top. What's that got to do with dead kids and wolves?" Guthrie chuckled.

"Nothing, probably nothing to do with it at all. What if I told you that A.H. Winterbourne wanted, desperately, to join a very secretive fraternal order?"

"The Masons?" Guthrie said. "So what? My old man was a Mason and his old man before him. Stupid handshakes and funny little aprons? A little comic maybe, but certainly not the type of group that goes around killing kids."

"No, not the Masons, Detective Guthrie. Not the Masons or the Elks or the Beneficent Order of Water Buffaloes. Or any sort of organization anyone around here has ever seen before. This was a secret society that begun simply enough, a men's club of a kind, but somewhere along the line, things turned from too much drinking and cheating on their wives with passing around prostitutes to the worst sorts of things. From *Do what thou Wilt*, to *If a God is for us, who can stand against us?*" Kemmler said.

Guthrie stared at the other man in silence, feeling a little like he was being taken in by a man at a carnival trying to get him to toss a few rings. Every town had its secrets and, in his experience, the smaller the town, the bigger the secrets. There were always whispers about the wealthy folks of Winterbourne and what they got up to, but it wasn't anything more than them feeding their dogs from the kitchens while they forced their servants to eat out of the trash. Silly shit like that got passed around the schoolyards so often nobody knew the truth anymore. But it wasn't true, at least not in the way everybody thought. The idea of a sinister organization operating under the noses of everyone in Winterbourne since before World War 2 was laughable.

Thunder crackled in the sky, and it burst like a water balloon, pouring rain on Kemmler and soaking any ounce of humour Floyd Guthrie had left.

"Enough," Guthrie said and turned to leave. "I've heard enough. You're talking about the Hellfire club. The fucking Hellfire club. Do you think this is England? In the seventeenth fucking century? There was never anything like the Hellfire club in this shitty little town. Winterbourne is full of busybody rivermen and nosy housewives. There isn't a chance in hell that a fraternity could go on killing kids for fifty-odd years without a single person knowing about it. Not in this town. Jesus Christ, my wife cheated on me once and I knew about it before she got home for supper that night.

"Here's what I think, detective Kemmler. I think they sent you down here from upstate to get you out of the office. I'm betting you might have been hot shit up there for a while, but then your brain broke, and you started peddling this evil conspiracy bullshit and they sent you down here to get you away from the real detectives. 'Hey guys, Ol' Billy's gone off the deep end. Let's send him to Winterbourne and stick him in the dead letter office with Guthrie. Kill two birds, one old cock up and a loon, with one fucking stone.'" The rain streamed down Guthrie's face and down his nose as he stomped off down the hill.

"You don't believe me?" Kemmler called after him.

"Gee, whatever gave you that idea?" Guthrie said in a mocking tome.

"What could I do to convince you otherwise?"

"Maybe some evidence. A little fucking proof there was even a nugget of truth in all this Weird Tales magazine bullshit. How about a fucking photo of Lon Chaney Jr gnawing on Des Anderson's innards? That would be a great fucking start," Guthrie said. "Otherwise, you could fuck off and try to sell your snake oil someplace else."

"Detective Guthrie, we are the same, you and me. We have a knack for seeing beyond the immediate situation and getting to what's there. If I show you something, a clue common to all the victims, a clue you've missed perhaps, would you listen to what I have to say, then?"

"Sure, I'll play along, sonny. But I've been over the evidence every day since they gave it to me. There isn't anything about these kids I don't know."

"Except who killed them," Kemmler said. "What if I could tell you something you think nobody else knows?"

Floyd wiped the rain from his face. He may have been a whiz at solving the little crimes that happened around Winterbourne but for something as big as the Ripper case, he was fumbling in the dark as much as the rest of the Winterbourne PD. He just didn't have the strength to admit the case had beaten him. Pride stung, but the ghosts of six dead children tugged at him, pleaded with the old man to just shut up and listen.

"I'd say you were full of shit," Guthrie said. Cheap liquor does much to silence nagging ghosts.

"Oh..." Kemmler stammered. "Oh, okay. Never mind then. I'll just ask for a desk at your precinct and carry out my investigation alone. I won't bother you any further."

The younger detective turned up the collar of his coat and walked down the berm toward his car.

Good riddance, Guthrie thought. *Fucking nut job trying to push this evil world order shit on me.* But then something struck him. The motto of the club. He wasn't the religious type, but his mother was practically fanatical, and he recognized the words. "Wait," he called out. "Detective, wait a minute."

Kemmler turned back to him.

"The sayings you mentioned, are they real? Did this secret bunch of yours really use them as mottos?"

"It looks that way," Kemmler said. His voice changed. It was softer, less formal, and less nervous. It was tired. "I've seen some official documents, things on the society letterhead intended for members only that had the first saying and then changed to the second one shortly after the killings began."

"But why would they use a bible passage? Romans 8:31 is about an army that marches in the lord's righteousness has no fear from any enemy. It's not about something evil, it's about the love and power of God to protect his followers."

"That's not quite what it means," Kemmler said. "But I didn't say God, I said *A God.*"

"What?" Guthrie said. "I don't see–"

"Detective Guthrie, do you *really* want me to keep going?" He turned his head to the sky and closed his eyes. The rainwater poured over his face. It felt cool and fresh against his skin, and he stood there, letting the water hit him and run down the back of his neck. He reached up and wiped the water off before turning back and meeting Floyd's gaze.

"I don't. I *really* don't. But I think you probably need to."

"I said *a* god, detective, not *the* God. As in, not the lord of hosts, not the father and the son and the holy ghost, and not Mary's baby daddy. *A god as in a thing a group of men a very long time ago thought... believed they could call up whenever they wanted to and get it to do whatever they wanted for a small price as far as they were concerned. The blood of one child every ten years."*

"Do you know how fucking crazy that sounds?"

"Completely crazy. But I'm telling you, it's the truth. I've been following this case for years. Much longer than you have. I've seen pieces of letters, snippets of notes and read transcriptions of phone calls between members. None of the evidence actually comes out and says it, but it all hints at it. A group of Winterbourne's richest citizens have been killing a single child every ten years."

"But why? What do they get out of it?" Guthrie said.

"I don't know. There isn't much to go on for motive. I thought maybe they were just doing it to get their jollies, maybe even some kind of sexual thing, but that didn't add up. There was no evidence of anything sexual in any of the victims."

Guthrie was now soaked, his clothes and his mood, and he could hear the rain pounding off his coat as he walked past the younger man and headed for the rusted-out Ford. He was tempted to look back at the other cop, but resisted and quickened his pace toward his car.

"This isn't a lot to go on. You haven't really said anything that makes me think you're anything but a loon from upstate. I'm sorry, but maybe it's better if you get your own desk and do what you need to do until you go back home."

"Guthrie!" Kemmler called out.

The older man kept walking.

"Guthrie," Kemmler called out again. "Have you looked at the autopsy photos of the Anglin boy?"

Floyd turned and faced the other man.

"There was a burn on his left forearm, right? An upside down cross above two proper ones and some letters beside it, right?"

"It's not a burn!" Guthrie raised his voice to make it uphill to the other man.

"What?" Kemmler said, raising his own voice.

Floyd trudged back up the hill and looked at the other detective. "It's not a burn, it's carved in all of them. Likely with a different knife than the one that cut their throats."

"It's a carving," Kemmler said, doing little to contain his excitement at a new piece of information.

"Right," Guthrie said. "A carving."

"But, burned or carved, how would I know about it?"

13

D anny made his way to the top of the berm and started down the other side. A stark, white structure jutted up out of the landscape to his left like new molar erupting through gums. A girl, about Danny's age, sat on a thick iron grate that covered a drain culvert. She was swinging her leg back and forth, tapping it off the cement. At the end of her leg, a thick manacle with a length of chain trailed down and jangled like the bells of a carriage horse every time she swung her leg.

She was pretty, at least she had been. Her hair was blonde and, though half of it was pasted to the side of her head by long dried blood, the rest of it blew in the breeze. Danny thought her eyes had been blue, though he couldn't say why he thought that. Now they were little more than blanched and awful things staring out from blackened sockets. Pale, ghastly skin covered her face and had an unmistakeably blue tint that said, without a doubt, the girl was no longer a going concern. Flecks of ancient, splattered blood, black and viscous looking, stained the ragged gash that stretched nearly ear to ear across her throat enough that it might be mistaken for a high collar stretched nearly from ear to ear, reaching down almost to the spinal cord and the black blood caked around her throat and the bottom of her chin. A ratty, grey hospital gown soiled all across the front with the same awful blackened ooze hung on her boney shoulders.

A smile teased its way onto the corners of the withered blue lips and white eyes narrowed at him. Fear twist and turn and knot itself deep inside his guts, wadding into a ball that threatened to leave if he didn't get away from the source before long.

"Jesus!" Danny jumped as he felt the icy touch of Billy Anglin's hand on his shoulder.

With his other hand, the dead boy pointed further down the field and walked. Danny followed quickly, keeping his eyes to the ground, glad to be away from the dead girl on the culvert.

His surroundings changed the further along the two of them walked. What started out as the dried out grassy plain of Millar's field, warm and sunny, cooled and darkened. Soon they walked past a grove of trees that blocked out more and more sunlight the closer they got to it. It was Seonagh's woods. Rumours and ghost stories hung around this place thicker than the Spanish moss on the surrounding trees, and he didn't know anyone brave enough to get any closer to it than he was now. His stomach tightened, and his shoulders hunched over. If walking past the place was enough to make him feel this uneasy, he could only imagine what it would feel like to actually go into it. Billy Anglin pointed past Seonagh's woods and continued walking away from it. *Thank God,* Danny thought.

They carried on further, putting enough of the forest behind them for Danny to relax a little. Though, when he looked up and discovered where they had travelled, the fear stiffened his shoulders again. Grey Hollow Road was one of the original roads in and out of Winterbourne, long ago cut off from the rest of town when the old sections became less desirable, and more farmlands became available to developers. Winterbourne Cemetery, once the high-water mark of burials in town, was now an abandoned and grown over mess of bracken and stinging nettles. Nearly impassable to anyone who wanted to keep any exposed flesh intact. Danny figured that's where the two of them headed. So, it came as no surprise when the blood caked arm of Billy Anglin pointed beyond the gate. It took less to get the heavy gate open than Danny figured it would, and he followed the dead boy in.

They walked for a time, and Danny tried to understand why they were here. Headstones crowded the place, most worn down by years of weather and barely readable. The two boys crossed the length of the cemetery and came to a huge marble building that was brand new compared to the grave markers they'd passed on the way. Billy Stopped and pointed at the monumental structure.

"Are you nuts? I'm not going in there," Danny said.

Billy Anglin's corpse continued to point at it. Danny stepped toward the heavy tarnished door of the mausoleum, certain it was locked. He grabbed hold of one of the iron rings and pulled. The door swung open.

"I don't care how easy that was. I'm not going in there."

The dead boy continued to point. And he couldn't be certain, but Danny he thought he saw a faint smile play across the dead boy's mouth.

"Really?" Danny said. "Really, I *need* to go in here? How am I going to see inside this goddam thing?"

He pulled the door wide enough for the two of them to go in side by side. Danny stepped through the door and proceeded into the room, but stopped. Something didn't feel right. He turned back to see Billy Anglin still on the other side of the door.

"Wait, what? Not coming with me?"

Billy said nothing. His blank eyes blinked slowly as he turned to leave.

"Fine, God-dammit, just leave! Who the hell needs you, anyway? I'll just crawl around in the dark by myself."

Billy remained silent as he had the whole time and strolled down toward the cemetery gate. He turned back to the boy and gave a last point in the mausoleum's direction. Danny sighed and stepped inside the door.

The air smelled old and stale. It was well lit with candles and tapers that hissed out greasy black smoke. Danny squinted, but found the flickering and sputtering flames bright enough to make his way safely around without tripping or bumping into anything he couldn't see first. He moved slowly, quietly for a handful of steps before he chuckled to himself and picked up the pace. If dead people were able to speak, he had serious doubts that they'd want the living to keep quiet around them. A monstrous screech ripped the air behind him, and he whipped around just in time to see the door swing shut with a loud clang. When he turned back, a boy stood beside him. A different boy, smaller than he was. Smaller than Billy Anglin, too. He was gaunt, and the same washed-out colour of Billy and the girl. Standing in the quivering candlelight shadows, he looked lost and sad.

"Who are you?"

The small boy stepped forward into the light, where Danny could see him more clearly. His hair was dark and close cropped. His neck bore the same ragged gash as the others, and he wore the same bloodstained hospital gown as the blonde-haired girl had. Around his leg, a shackle and chain jingled as he walked. And he walked toward Danny.

"Wait," Danny said, anxiety rising in his voice.

The dead boy ignored him and continued to advance, moving on a few feet past him to a small set of stairs heading downward. He pointed down the stairs and beckoned to Danny with his other hand. The boy showed no hesitation and walked down the steps. To his left and right were stacks of coffins, small ones, large ones, and everything in-between. Some were ornate and expensive looking, others looking like well-meaning orange crates. Ahead, lay another small staircase which the dead boy had already gone down.

Danny made it this far with no harm, apart from a little nervous nausea, and continued following the other boy downward through more rooms. Some were nearly in total blackness, and others lit up like high mass, until they came to a small door in the middle of the far wall. The dead boy pointed at the door and stared back at him. He gave Danny a look that he couldn't understand. It wasn't sadness, though there was a trace of it, tinted with anger and guilt. If they pressed him for an answer, Danny thought the boy's look said he was forced to bring him this far. He wanted to hate the boy for dragging him further into this nightmare, but he was sure that, if given the choice, the little dead boy would have chased him far away from here. Danny made his way through the door, thinking just how easy it had been getting to all these places. A door slammed behind him, with the dead boy on the other side of it.

The new room was bigger than where he had just come from. It was cavernous in here and it smelled musty, cool and damp, like a root cellar. After his eyes adjusted to his surroundings, he knew exactly where he was. The fosters forced him to be an altar boy, and as a result, he knew the layout of St. Gertrude's from top to bottom. He felt for the light switch to his right. It wasn't there. Guessing he was along the far wall, though he couldn't remember ever seeing a door there, he felt his way in the dark until he made it to the other side. His hands groped for the switch and hit pay dirt. He flicked it and the fluorescent lights flickered and buzzed to life.

"Jesus Murphy!"

In front of him stood another boy, reedy and tall, taller than the other three kids, but not any less dead. His skin was the same awful colour as theirs. The same ugly gash stretched across his neck, and Danny wondered if this was the reason all his guides had been silent. He wore the same blood-stained ratty gown though, because he was so much taller than the others, it barely came past his waist. It left him constantly tugging at the bottom, trying desperately to conceal the grimy, white, y-fronts beneath.

The tall boy raised his arms to point, and immediately lowered them again, embarrassed and trying to cover himself. Danny imagined the kid's cheeks would have flushed bright red if there was still blood flowing through them. It went on like that for several minutes until he realized where the tall corpse had intended for him to go. The scene should have been comical, if it weren't for how absolutely miserable. He felt for this dead kid. As if what happened to him wasn't bad enough, now he had to spend the afterlife in a gown that was eight inches too short for him and showed his underpants to anyone who happened across him. For all eternity.

Danny moved through the door beside the light switch, knowing there would be a set of stairs on the other side of it. He was pretty sure that's where the tall boy was motioning for him to go.

At the top of the stairs was another door, one he knew well. It led to a small hallway with a door on either side of it. One opened into the vestry, small anteroom behind St. Gertrude's altar, the other led to the altar itself. The vestry held robes and the other priestly vestments. The cups used for the sacrament and, more importantly, it was where the priest kept the communion wine. Danny, strictly speaking, was not one of those kids. He wasn't one to sneak drinks when the adults weren't looking. He knew a few people like that in his class, boys mostly, who would get goofy on a bottle of dad's beer or even something stronger, the second their folks' backs were turned. But he'd tasted the sacramental wine once or twice. Before the first services he helped with, when his nerves were rattling his jaws so much, he thought his teeth would come loose. Father Cunningham told him it would help calm him. To the old man's credit, it did. And now, what with being led on an adventure by three or four, clearly dead children and all, Danny figured he could use as much calming as he could get. He knelt and took the bottle from the cupboard the priest had shown him.

He took a healthy pull off the decorative silver bottle, and it went to his head immediately. Thankfully, the good congregation of St. Gertrude's had never been very generous when the collection plate came around, so the wine was little more than grape juice with a bad temper. His head cleared, and he got up off his knees. Through the door on the other side of the vestry was the altar, and from there, it was forty or fifty feet down the aisle and out the front door. He'd be back home in no time and away from whatever the hell all of this was.

Danny pulled on the small wooden door and found it wouldn't open. It was the first real obstacle he'd come across, and it stymied him. *What now?* He circled the room for no other reason than he hoped that walking around might jar something loose in his brain and the answer would just pop up.

"Sonofabitch!"

He realized mid-circle that Father Cunningham was always forgetting the keys to the church at the rectory, so he kept a set of spares in a drawer in the vestry. He struggled to remember which drawer they were in but was relieved to find there were only four available in the entire room, three of which were on the small desk along the far side. The keys were in the middle drawer and in seconds, the door was open.

He stepped through the door with relief, only to find it soured like old milk. It was an altar, yes, but it was not St. Gertrude's by a long shot. The room was dark and hot. The moisture hung heavy in the air and the walls narrowed on either side of him. Danny felt like a snake had swallowed him and with each step he took, its throat flexed and moved him closer to oblivion. He could see a staircase in the distance, maybe fifty feet from where he stood, and decided that his best plan for getting away from this place was at the top of them. He started toward the steps when a blast of heat hit him, nearly pushing him back, and suddenly the room was aglow in flickering crimson and coral light, giving life to the shadows that surrounded him. An acrid, dirty smell rose through the air. And it became clear where he was. There was only one place, one location in the whole of Winterbourne, so under-funded it forced them to continue burning coal when everywhere else in town had long ago switched to gas or electric. He was in the boiler room of Winterbourne High School.

The furnace belched out another blast of heat wreathed in the glow of inefficient combustion, and Danny set out toward the stairs. The basement was a narrow series of hallways that seemed to go nowhere, yet all led, in a roundabout way, to the central staircase and the upper levels of the school. But as he walked, he discovered this was not the basement he'd been to before. To his right, in the heat's direction, stood the altar, a huge granite thing with large sandstone pillars, topped with pyramids on either side of it. Around the altar stood a group of men. He didn't know any of them, didn't recognize any of their faces, but they looked well fed, mostly clean shaven and clean well-groomed hair and clothing. From behind the altar stepped the girl and the three boys he'd seen on his way here. They held out a filthy hospital gown to him and a shackle for his leg.

Danny backed away, but a squat, balding, older man holding a long, serrated knife blocked his path.

"You should just lie down, son," the old man said.

The boy pushed back and turned, trying to avoid the old man grabbing him, only to be surrounded by the dead kids. They grabbed his arm and leg and waist and hoisted him onto the altar.

"Stop!" Danny screamed.

But they kept at it, tearing his clothes away, pulling the nasty gown onto him, locking the thick iron shackle around his leg, and fastening the chain to a large iron ring at the base of the altar.

"No!" he screamed franticly.

A figure emerged from the darkness, younger than the man who was trying to keep Danny on the stone slab, and flashed the wicked looking knife at the boy. He raised it and turned to the assembled men.

"It is by the spilling of blood that I atone for that which is given me."

He considered Danny for what seemed like hours. A grin played at the corners of his mouth, threatening to become a full smile, but the second his gaze met Danny's, the smile vanished. Replaced by the cruelest eyes the boy had ever seen.

"No!" Danny screamed, but the arms of the dead children pull at him, holding him down.

"Danny," the voice said quietly above him.

He searched the crowd of men and dead children, desperately looking for the owner of the voice.

"Danny!" the voice commanded.

He pulled back against the iron grip of the dead groping hands, fought to sit up to escape their grasp, but failed. Hope left him there on the cold stone slab and Danny Nesbitt resigned himself to the few minutes he had left before they cut his throat and exposed his guts to the fresh air, and he too would wear a massive stain on the front of his filthy hospital gown.

"Danny!"

"No!" Danny screamed as Evan's thick, meaty hands continued to shake him, trying to bring him back to reality.

"Jesus kid," the big laundry man said. "You were out like a light. Break time's over. Go help the ladies put away the laundry."

14

———————

on Pierce's eyes rolled open. His eyelids felt heavy, sticky, almost as if filled with grade school white paste. He didn't feel out of sorts or druggy, not sedated, so much as entirely overwhelmed by the thought of another day at Winterbourne Home. Another day like yesterday and the day before that. And the day before that and, in fact, every other day since he set foot in the place. The awful food they called breakfast would be the same. Cold, rubbery eggs, cold, leathery, overcooked, reduced salt bacon, warm orange juice, cold coffee and, if he was still in the mood for more, Winterbourne Home's famous oatmeal. The colour of wood ash, thick enough to stop traffic, and chock full of inedible, teeth shattering raisins. The conversations with his tablemates, each of them as demented as cross-eyed barn cat, and each one saying exactly what they had said at the breakfast table the day before.

He had been a high school librarian in a small town downstate somewhere, and he loved what he did. He didn't shape the minds of tomorrow's leaders, not the way a history or English teacher could, but he was an endless source of information and a trusted confidant and shoulder to cry on for even the hardest nuts at his school. Problems at home? Go talk to Don, the librarian. Late assignment?

Go to the library. No idea when Alexander conquered the known world? Don knows. He got the job straight out of college and stayed with it, not wanting for anything else, no dreams of anything bigger than what he already had. He married, raised a family, and continued maintaining the library until the day his wife left him for another woman. After that, the rift between his son and him that had been sizeable to begin with broadened to irreparable. He stopped going to work until they threatened his pension, but he was just going through the motions, counting down the days until he could leave it for good. His drinking increased, while his personal hygiene fell away and, at sixty-two, rheumatoid arthritis made his body attack itself and the aches and pains that plagued him daily made him angry all the time and rendered him all but useless to anybody at the high school.

Don lived with his son for a full week before the younger man had his fill and trundled him off to Winterbourne Home. That was seven years ago. Four spent with Bob Mifflin, just about the best friend he'd ever had, though from all outward glances, you would have thought they cared little for each other by the way they spoke to one another. Now, two weeks later, the old bastard was gone, and Don Pierce was alone. Sure, his son came to visit him but, what started as weekly half hour or forty-five-minute chats in one of the coffee shops on Parker Street, became ten-minute obligatory pop ins once every month or two, which Don was pretty sure his son only did to find out if he was dead or not.

"Good morning, honey," the ginger haired girl said. "Your eyes are open. Do we want to get up?"

"Yes, we do," Don said. "But I don't need any help to do that, thank you. I'm old, I'm not stupid."

"Of course you're not," the redhead said.

He was never sure about it, but the old man thought he heard a note of condescension in her voice every morning when she came into his room, like a teacher talks to an unruly child. *Mind your Ps and Qs, Donny, or there'll be no Otter Pops for you at recess.* She represented everything he hated about this place, about himself. And he despised her for it. The woman was probably a lovely girl when she wasn't dragging him out of bed at ungodly hours, and he bore her no real hard feelings, but she was everything now that he had been and would never see again. She was young and pretty and clever and had clean breath and neatly combed, fiery red hair. She didn't droop anywhere, not like the old farts who lived in here with him. They drooped everywhere. The red head laughed at people's jokes, even if they weren't funny and did more things than not to put people at their ease whenever she could. The girl was absolutely at the head of the line and her whole life stretched out before her like a row of steam trays in an all you can eat buffet, where she could pick and choose and had enough time ahead of her to go back for something different if she didn't care for the first plateful and still not regret a single decision. Not like Don, who found himself at the back of the line now, with all the other poor buggers. Too old and too slow to get more than the scraps left by a world too hungry and too fast to spare more than a crumb or two for the ones who'd gone before.

"Suit yourself." She smiled. "But you don't say I didn't offer."

The redhead shot him a smile that made him feel better, though he shot her back a look that said he didn't, and left his room, pulling the door closed behind her. The old man lay in his bed, in near total darkness. Don shut his eyes, knowing sleep would come nowhere near him now. Despite that, he rolled away from the door and shut his eyes hard enough to see stars dancing behind them.

"Shit," he said and sat up slowly.

The old man fumbled for the large, easy grip lamp switch and clicked it on. He slid his legs forward, off the bed, and stretched his feet toward the ugly, freezing cold linoleum floor. Don was awake, mostly, and just about ready to face another day of mindless tedium at Winterbourne Home. Breakfast, newspaper, nap. Lunch, TV, nap. Unless it was Wednesday, which today wasn't. Wednesday was bath day, and he'd do his best to get the bath lady to give him a grope. Then it was supper, TV, jammies, bed. Rinse. Repeat. For ever and ever. Amen. Until the day he would die. Sooner rather than later, he hoped. There were ways to opt out. Methods to hasten your exit from the home and the crazies inside it, but they weren't quick and they damn sure weren't pleasant.

Most of the ones that did it just stopped eating. Farmers and such that were used to huge portions of meat and potatoes and bread with every meal found themselves unable to swallow any of those things very well anymore and ended up on a pureed diet. A kind of warm food pudding. They refused the insult of it and then refused to eat altogether. It wasn't long before there was an empty spot at the table. There were also a few who took more drastic measures. Sliding down their beds until they could wedge their heads between the mattress and the bed rail and then pushing the rest of their body off the bed. It was a makeshift noose that killed them quick, but Don bet they suffered immeasurably in the few minutes before they blacked out and shit their pyjamas. He heard there were a few who broke mirrors and slashed wrists or throats, but nothing that gruesome had ever happened since he moved into Winterbourne.

"Jesus!" Don said. The shock of the cold floor shooting up through his feet and well into his legs nearly made him slide them back up the bed and under the blankets. Instead, he walked his feet into a pair of slippers, and padded off toward the bathroom.

The water coming out of the bathroom hot water faucet was cold. It was always cold. Don turned the handle until the slightest stream of frigid water trickled onto the palms of his hands. He rubbed them together vigorously, hoping to bring some warmth to the water, but ended up splashing most of it out of his hands and into the sink. In the end, the old man rubbed his damp hands against his face and hoped it would be enough to wake him fully. *Thank God I don't need a shave*, he thought. A cup sat beside the sink. Flat, turquoise, and plastic, containing his toothbrush, a tube of toothpaste, and a roomful of anxiety. He had crippling stiffness and pain in his hands and his fingers were curled under like he was making shadow puppets. It made doing something as simple as cleaning his teeth difficult at best. The fact the water took the better part of five minutes to warm and bring some relief to his hands made it downright herculean. His left hand was in worse shape than his right, thankfully, and he jammed the toothbrush into the solidly balled up fist. The toothpaste, his old nemesis. It sat on the side of the sink, practically mocking him. His hands hadn't worked properly in decades and the fine motor skills he needed to open a tube of toothpaste and then put it on the damned brush frustrated him on a good day. On a day like today, it didn't happen at all. Don grabbed the bottle of mouthwash from its spot beside the toothpaste. He twisted the cap off in his teeth and spit it as hard as he could toward the sink. He swished a few mouthfuls around his mouth and called it a day. As he spit the last into the sink, he felt the splash of the water from the still running tap, finally approaching the warmer side of tepid.

Don left the bathroom and limped toward his closet. He slowly opened the door. These days he did everything slowly, and it was not lost on him. Perhaps, when he was younger and in his prime, there might have been some merit in doing things more slowly. Now it was a nuisance and a completely bloody inconvenience. The old man stared blankly at the neatly pressed shirts and pants hanging in front of him. He had four flannel shirts of various tartans to choose from and several pairs of nicely faded blue jeans. Or there were the two pairs of Sans-A-Belt slacks that he could pair with the three stylish, though years out-of-date pastel dress shirts. However, his insistence on being alone to dress himself and the lack of hot water had allowed the arthritis to render his hands almost useless to button a shirt or pull the fly on a pair of trousers, even the kind that didn't need a belt.

The old man pushed out a defeated sigh and reached for a pair of thick cotton sweatpants and a complimentary cotton pullover. Something struck him, and he threw the clothes on the bed before shuffling off to the bathroom. Don sat on the toilet and removed the thick, padded undergarment graciously supplied by the good folks at Winterbourne Home, to all poor bastards like himself who couldn't hold it beyond a glass or two of watery orange juice. He prayed for some good news to brighten this already cheerless day. There was none. He hadn't soaked through the incontinence underwear, but it hadn't been an entirely dry night either. Don pulled the soiled disposable underpants off and threw them into the trash. Satisfied he was completely empty, he rose from the toilet and took a dry pair from the closet above the sink and headed back to the bedroom.

He pulled the soft, warm cotton over his cold, aching bones and stared at the two pairs of shoes on the floor of his closet. He wanted desperately to grab the gloss black Florsheim oxfords, but the throbbing of his hands won out and he grabbed the thick, rubber soled walking shoes with the Velcro straps.

Don sighed. "Fuck."

The old man headed out of his room, bound for the dining area and the nearly edible meal he would receive there. He pulled the door but turned back to the room before closing it, staring at the wooden cane that hung from the foot of his bed. *Not today.* Don Pierce wouldn't use the damnable thing today. He would walk on his own, entirely under his own steam, to the dining hall, and he would be all the better for it. At least he'd feel better about it.

It began well, with squared shoulders and head held high. He rose from the bed and put one foot in front of the other, like any other normal person. However, twenty feet from his room, Don's right hip decided his best days were behind him, and a life of pain and stiffness was all he knew from now on. And to reinforce this, it sent a burst of dull, throbbing pain across his back and deep into his hip. Short, sharp jolts of misery rocketed down his legs, threatening to drop him to the floor in a heap.

He reached out to steady himself on the wooden rail that ran the entire perimeter of the ward but misjudged the distance, and in doing so, made a half-hearted leap for it. The pain ripped through him again and he clung to the railing like he was adrift at sea, and it was a chunk of flotsam.

"You really should walk with your cane, Mr. Pierce."

He could see the nurse staring at him. That she noticed he was teetering earthward and sent an orderly scurrying after him. The big man helped Don get back on solid ground and then disappeared into the old man's room, reappearing moments later, carrying the hated piece of wood.

"Here you go, chief," the big orderly said. "Try to use this. It'll help you stay upright."

"Yeah, yeah. I know," Don said in a grumble.

He hobbled his way to the dining room, cane in poorly functioning hand, and tried to ignore the constant reminders that his brain might still be sharp as a tack, his body was now paying the price for a lifetime worth of apathy and bad decisions. *Exercise is for people that have nothing better to do and I've always got something better to do.* It had been a rallying cry for his generation. Work hard until you retire and then sit and smoke and drink and doing as close to nothing as you could get away with. You've earned it. One day we're all gonna die anyway, so why go out healthy? Eat it, drink it, smoke it, screw it. Use a body up, you can't take it with you. He crossed the threshold into the dining hall and took a seat at his table with the people he'd been sitting with for the entire time he'd lived in Winterbourne Home.

Margaret-Mary Castle sat directly across from him. She was a thin, frail, wispy thing whose hair was the only thing about her that had any strength at all. It was grey, white in some spots, and packed into a bun so high and thick and tight that it looked more like a grey helmet than it did the hair of a woman well into her nineties. She was pleasant, if not a little overbearing, and always had a kind word for Don except on days like this one. Arthritis had twisted and contorted her body so badly that her feet resembled the gnarled roots of an ancient tree. Withered, blue, and venous things that scared him a little just to see them. They ached and drove the old girl a little mad on the days when the nurses came around to trim toenails. Today was such a day, and she was in no mood for pleasantries.

"You don't need to be here," she hissed at him. "You can just go home."

"Okay, right after I eat."

"They must have given it to her good today. She didn't even bring her shoes."

John Bolger, Don's tall and thick tablemate, had the meaty hands of a man that spent his whole life earning a living with them. He'd been a welder or steam fitter or some other well paid industrial cog that Don never could quite remember. He was a good man, a little too crude and too quick to laugh, but now that Bob Mifflin had passed, he was the nearest thing to a friend he had. Across from Don stood a space once occupied by the man he would readily call a friend. No one had moved into his room yet, so it stood to reason no one had moved to his table either.

To say the dining room was loud was to admit you lacked the vocabulary to describe it any better. It was loud beyond volume, deafening and overwhelming. It induced panic inducing in the timid and caused unreasonable anger in even the most patient. It was noisy, awful, chaotic, and uproarious. The clink of plates being unstacked, followed by the chank-chank-splunk of dirty plates being scraped before being dropped in a basin of tepid, soapy water. And the shouting, sometimes screaming, of residents who were terminally unhappy and willing to let anyone within earshot know it. Even if earshot meant loud enough to be heard across town.

Some yelled their refusals for help, some yelled for more assistance. Others shouted they were being ignored while their tablemates insisted they only wanted to be left alone. Others screamed and screamed for no reason at all, apart from their eyes being open and it seemed the thing to do given the current situation. The clamour was suffocating and made the old man feel the entire world might close in on him.

"Which one would you like for breakfast, Don?" the head kitchen lady said.

She held two plates wrapped in cling film and shoved them under his nose and stood waiting for a response with a look that said she'd rather be knitting or learning Jai Alai than asking this old fool what he wanted for breakfast. The first plate held a generous helping of fluffy, yellow scrambled eggs, two well cooked rashers of bacon, and a slice of bread, toasted golden brown and smeared with butter. The second contained a fat lump of beige oatmeal with black flecks of raisins throughout it, a scoop of home fried potatoes, and an assortment of fresh fruit slices. Don pointed silently to the plate of eggs and bacon, knowing she would never hear him over the cacophony of the room, no matter how loudly he spoke.

The old man felt suddenly nostalgic. Remembering many servings of bacon and eggs and fresh juice, coffee as he got older, shared with his father when it had just been the two of them. The old fellow made it a point to pick him up every Sunday morning while he was in college and take him to the same awful smelling diner. He claimed it was so he could be sure Don had at least one decent meal in him a week, but Don liked to think it was because his father missed him and genuinely enjoyed the company. As time pressed on, a lifetime of too much work and too little leisure outside the moist dank of Butler's bar, took Don's father and withered him like a dried flower, the son took up the Sunday ritual as the only unhealthy indulgence he would allow his father.

They would talk. In the beginning, they would always talk. Sometimes well past the point of cold food. Politics, religion, sex, weather, television, movies. Nothing was sacred, nothing was safe. They jawed over it all. Later, when the old man's strength declined, sharply, Don would wolf down his bacon and eggs, hoping it would inspire the old man to eat as well. He mostly abstained and sat with his son in knowing, ominous silence. Some months after, his time ran out, and the younger man lost his taste for bacon and eggs. But today, for no good reason, he would eat them again. He would eat bacon and eggs, and he would remember all those times when his father and he were together, and the world was only the two of them caught up in this moment.

"Here you are, Don. Fresh bacon and eggs with a side of toast."

But it wasn't. It wasn't even fucking close.

The eggs were fine enough, though a closer inspection proved them to be closer to grey than they were to the bright yellow, fluffy well-cooked eggs they had shown him. What came next could only be thought of as food by a dog or perhaps an imbecile in some shitty old institution. The bacon and the toast both were reduced to two medium-sized lumpy brown puddles. There was nothing bacon like or toasty about either, nor did continuing to look at them, never mind trying to eat them, make Don feel nauseated to the point of wanting to forget breakfast altogether.

"What the hell is this?"

"Bacon and eggs," the kitchen lady said. "And toast."

"Those may be eggs," he said. "But that is not toast and *that* sure as shit is not bacon."

He was agitated and disappointed, and the tension warbled in his voice as he spoke.

"You know you can't eat regular bacon anymore, Don. On account of you not swallowing too good anymore. We chopped it all up for you, makes it easier to swallow. Just put a little ketchup on it and it'll be fine."

"There's nothing the matter with the way I swallow. Never has been. Now just you go back and get me some proper bacon and some new, hot toast."

"I'm afraid I can't do that, Don. Why don't you just eat this, and we can see what we can do about getting you something new for lunch?"

"Lunch? I haven't had breakfast yet, for Christ's sake. Why are you people always trying to push us around? Haven't we done enough already? We've paid our taxes. We fought the wars and goddamned won them, but it still isn't enough for you. Not enough to stop treating us like children. I don't want lunch. I want breakfast and I want bacon and eggs."

His anxiety and the volume of his voice spread through the dining room like wildfire. It was palpable and soon they were all yelling and wanting new, better things for breakfast. Screaming their demands above the roar of the others demanding the same.

"You have bacon and eggs, honey. They're just a little different, that's all," she said.

"No, it's not. It's not just a little different. It's all different, all so fucking different!"

Don could hear himself yelling. His temper rose, voice becoming thin and strained, but he'd gone too far now to rein it back in. A mania took hold of him, and now he stood at a precipice. One sharp jolt and he would plummet, far beyond the point of recovery. His head swam, and his world became relentless, twisted and wrong. His guts were a mix of blind rage and delirious fear.

"Don," she said. "Come sit down and eat your breakfast."

"No!" He breathed, doing his best to contain the venom that pooled inside him as she continued to call the slop breakfast.

"It's okay, really. Just let's sit down and eat some bacon and eggs."

That was the last straw. He straightened his legs abruptly, the motion of which and his proximity to it sent the chair he was standing in front of crashing to the floor.

"No! No, no, no, no!" He pounded his cane on the table and, when it broke, he turned his wrath and his hand on himself and pounded his withered, knotted fist against his face.

"Calm down please, Don. Just have a seat."

Two thick orderlies moved toward him, one on either side. Don gripped the broken piece of his cane as tightly as his hands would allow and raised it up like a weapon. The two took a step closer and the old man raised it higher to swing at them.

"Get back, God-damn it."

"Don, sit down, please. I don't want you to fall," the kitchen lady said, trying to soothe him.

The orderly to his left called out to him.

"Mr. Pierce, why don't we just sit down and eat our breakfast?"

"No!" he screamed and swung the broken cane for all he was worth.

He connected with the side of the orderly's face. It was the opportunity the second beefy man was looking for, and he reached out to wrap his arms around the older man. Don screamed and struggled and swore and cursed like it was being made illegal tomorrow, but the younger man's grip was iron and showed no signs of faltering soon.

"Did you want to give him something?" the orderly asked the duty nurse who, until now, had stood in stunned silence.

"No," she said. "He'll calm down. Just help him to his room."

"Come on, Don. I'll take you to your room."

The big orderly hoisted the old man up and carried him out of the dining room, heading for his room.

"Put me down, you big ape!" Don squirmed. "I know where my goddam room is."

The big man maintained his grip. The older man seemed calmer. Time, exhaustion, and a measure of rationality had seeped back into his brain and, as his temper cooled and the noise of the dining room faded, he grew quieter. But the orderly's grip didn't even shift a little. More than once, he'd let his guard down around a resident who seemed calm and lucid, only to have them lunge at him with angry, vicious hands, and ragged, clawed fingernails caked in filth and days old shit, when his guard was down.

"Not a chance," the orderly said.

"Really," Don said. "I'm fine now. I just want to go back to my room."

"That's where we're going, old fella. I'm just helping you along. You should be thankful I took you out of there. A few more minutes, and they would have drugged you back to your childhood."

"You can put me down now. I'm fine to go from here."

"I'd just as soon not."

Don shouted. "David! Put me down, please. I would like to go by myself. Please."

David lowered the old man to the ground and eyed him suspiciously.

"Are you sure you're okay? It's my head on the block if you go off the deep end again."

"I'm fine." Don lowered his head and sighed. "I got upset because I... I got a little upset, and I couldn't find my way back. But I'm okay now, really Dave."

"What the hell got you so riled?"

"Ask me about it again sometime," Don said quietly.

"Keep your secrets." Dave smiled and headed back to the dining room.

Don stood alone in the hallway. The heat of all his anger and frustration, coupled with the wild swinging of his cane, left him covered with a thick layer of sweat under his clothes. Now, that enormous rush of adrenaline had also faded and gone. The old man was wet and cold and a little sick to his stomach. All he wanted now was to lie down and forget. He moped back to his room, the sting of disappointment still gnawing at him, but knowing he had no way to change any of it, blunted disappointment's teeth considerably.

The old man laid on his bed and closed his eyes, hoping sleep would take him far away from Winterbourne Home. If only for the duration of his nap. Maybe he'd be lucky, and sleep would take him and not bring him back. Maybe the exertion of using a broken cane like a sword was enough to earn a heart attack while you slept. No pain, no fuss, just a series of bizarro nightmares and then hello oblivion. The prospect became more and more entertaining to him. Don wondered if it was possible to will yourself to die, hoping the food was better wherever death took him.

He'd just drifted off when he heard the handle click and the door to his room swing open.

"Sorry, I didn't know there was anybody in here."

"Who the hell are you?" Don barked, tinges of fear rippling through his words.

"I'm from downstairs. I'm here to put your laundry away," Danny said.

15

———

"You want to what?" Don said, a little closer to sleep than he was to fully awake.

"Um... sir... I'm here to put your laundry away," Danny said again.

"I can do that myself. You don't need to help me. There is no reason for you to be here. You can just go," Don said. "Jesus, I sound like Margaret-Mary."

"What?"

"Never mind. Anyway, really, you don't need to be here. I can put away my laundry."

He eyed the kid suspiciously, though he had no real reason to. It might have been the way he looked. Danny stood on the short end of average and there was a lankiness to him that made him look like he should have been a head taller than he was, and his complexion was wan and tired looking. It did little to dissuade from the slightly sinister look his coal black hair portrayed. His nose was straight and thin and above it sat two dark, intense eyes, nearly always ringed with a sadness near to tears. Not like he'd recently been crying, but more like he'd shed a lifetime's worth of tears already and wore the redness like a scar.

"I'm sure you can," Danny said. "But if the ladies downstairs find out I didn't do exactly what they told me to do, I'm not sure they'll let me help anymore."

"That doesn't sound like such a bad thing, not putting away somebody else's clothes. What's the harm in that?"

"No. No, you're right. It sounds great. The only problem is the cop who volunteered me for all this fun might not see it the same way. And then my life would really get complicated."

"Cop? Oh, you some kind of criminal? Do I need to check your pockets before you leave? Or should I just hang around and wait to see if your pockets jingle?"

"I'm no goddam thief!" Danny said. All he needed was Guthrie to find out he'd been shouting at seniors, and his chances of being defended by the cop ever again would vanish like a fart in a cyclone.

"Sorry, Mr. Luciano. I did not know you were so sensitive," Don said, the corners of his mouth forming half a smile.

"Mr. Who?"

"Luciano. Lucky Luciano? Head of the New York crime syndicate? One of the most famous gangsters who ever lived?"

Danny stared blankly at the old man.

"Okay, how about Mr. Lansky?"

"Don't know him," Danny said.

"John Gotti?"

"Nope."

"Pretty Boy Floyd?"

"I know a Floyd, but he isn't very pretty." Danny chuckled. "Is it that important?"

"Jesus, I don't know." Don sighed. He didn't know why it seemed important that this kid understand what he was talking about, but something gnawed away at him to find a reference Danny would understand. Maybe it was a need to make a connection, or the desire to prove himself still relevant enough to talk with people who lived beyond the walls of this meat-pudding mad house. Whatever the reason, he needed to find it. "Al God-damned Capone. How about that?"

"I know that one!"

"What?"

"Al Capone, I know who that is. I did a project on him last year. Well, on prohibition, but he was a big part of that."

"There, was that so hard?" Don smiled. "So, Al, what are you in for? What got you here? Smoking cigarettes in the boy's room? In the girl's room?"

"No," Danny said. "Nothing like that."

"Worse maybe? Smoking reefer? You weren't smoking reefer, were you, son?"

Danny sighed. "No."

"That's a relief, son. Jazz lettuce? That's a one-way ticket to juvenile hall and a life of crime. Puff. puff and next thing you're hooked and lying in a gutter somewhere begging to do awful things for folks to get your next fix. It's no life for a young man."

"No, nothing like that."

"What then?" Don said.

"I told a joke in class," Danny said.

"And?"

"And that's it."

"Really?" Don said. He'd spent most of his life around children of varying ages and knew that sometimes, a bit of a squeeze would inspire enough guilt to force a confession from them. Danny was no exception, and he used a tone that said he knew bullshit when he heard it.

"Well, I made a bunch of jokes in class. Okay, I make jokes all the time in class. And I might have punched a kid in gym class and broke his nose. And I might have also hit the gym teacher when he tried to pull me off him and knocked out one of his teeth, but I'm not a machine, I can only take so much you know?" Anger echoed through the boy's words, edged with shame and self loathing. None of which was lost on the older man.

"So angry."

Danny snapped his head toward the old man. "What?"

"Why are you so angry? Not getting your way at home? Mom and Dad not letting you stay out late?"

"Look, can we talk about something else?"

Danny stood near to seething.

"You know what, mister? You're right. It's possible to put your own laundry away. You know? I just need to go now, you know? Out of here. I need to get out of here and go see Jack?"

"Is that your dad? Jack, is he your father?" Don said quietly.

"Can you stop talking now? Can you not mention my fucking parents anymore, please?" The boy cried, trying desperately to staunch the flow of tears.

Don sat on the edge of his bed watching the boy fall apart, a tidal wave of guilt crashing over him for taking the kid where he clearly didn't want to go. He stood and walked over to Danny. He stretched out a nervous hand and placed it gently on Danny's shoulder. To his surprise, the boy turned into him and grabbed hold of him around the waist, shuddering as the sobs wracked his body. The old man knew then that everything this child loved was ripped away from him at some point and he'd never known genuine love since.

"So, who is Jack?" Don said.

The old man didn't know this boy from Adam. He could be here putting away old people's laundry out of the goodness of his heart, or he could be here as a punishment for being a reprehensible little shit who flung smaller kids into puddles of muck and terrorized pensioners for sport. He instantly regretted asking him about Jack. It could set him off on a explosive rampage and Don was currently in the heart of ground zero. "My dog," Danny said. "Jack is my dog."

"Is that right?" Don smiled at him. "I had a dog named Jack too."

The old man sighed in relief. He might not know this kid, but he did know kids. A lifetime of being a school librarian gives a certain insight into the mind of kids. It struck him that the boy probably wasn't a lunatic, so much as he was lonely and more than a little sad.

"You're just trying to make me feel better, so I'll get out of your room," Danny said, and pushed away from him.

"No, really," Don said. "I got him when I was about ten and he was with me almost until I went to college. For as long as I've lived, I have never had a friend that meant as much to me as Jack did, and that's the truth." There was an unmistakable sincerity in the man's voice.

"Jack is the only friend I've got," Danny said solemnly.

"Then you should consider yourself lucky to have him," Don said, and patted the boy on the back. "Now, how's about we get this laundry put away?"

They picked the clothes off the big laundry rack outside the old man's room and moved them to the closet, virtually in silence. Broken only by awkward run-ins with each other trying to get past. Suddenly, the old man stopped.

"Are you okay?"

"Yeah," Don said. "Just running out of steam. I guess maybe I'm not capable of putting my laundry away."

He sat back down on his bed, where the exchange between the two had begun in the first place, and raised his aching legs up on to the bed.

"Oh, don't let me stop you." Don smiled at the boy. "I wouldn't want the ladies downstairs to think you weren't doing your very best."

"You're a regular Milton Boil."

"Berle," Don said.

"What?"

"Milton Berle was a famous comedian from when I was a kid. Milton Boil is a guy downtown that will-never mind. Tell me more about Jack. Is he a fast runner?"

"I can barely keep hold of him sometimes. Once, he caught sight of a squirrel when I wasn't really paying attention. He broke loose from my hands and was onto that thing before I had time to think about it."

"Did he catch it?"

Danny blushed. "He caught it and shook it to death in three shakes. There wasn't any blood or anything, but the squirrel was deader than dog shit. Oh, sorry. I shouldn't have said that."

Don laughed. It was full and from deep in his belly and brought a release he hadn't felt in years. Despite what this kid had done, maybe because of it, he liked him.

"I've been around young people for years and if I've noticed anything, it's that you all think swearing belongs to you. That nobody ever said dirty words before the moment they left your lips. Honestly, it's like trying to claim ownership of sex. Do you think your parents got here by pixie dust? Oh, shit. Sorry, I shouldn't have said that. Forgive me," Don said.

Danny smiled and he let go a laugh.

"You wear all this? None of this stuff looks very comfortable," Danny said, hanging several pairs of nylon Sans-a-belt slacks in Don's closet.

"It's not comfortable," Don said. "But what is comfortable makes me feel like I'm in pyjamas all god-damned day. I'm not sick, I'm old. I don't need to be in pyjamas."

"Where do you want these?" Danny held up a handful of knotted socks.

"Top shelf, just throw them up there. It's what I do."

Danny stood on his tiptoes but lost his footing before long and grabbed hold of the closet shelf. Its contents spilled out onto the floor in front of him. Mostly, it was socks and undershirts and a belt and a pair of black suspenders. A large book, a photo album or scrapbook landed on top of the socks and undershirts with a thud. He flipped the cover open.

Danny gasped. "What the fuck?"

Don sat up on the bed. "What's the matter?"

"Why?"

"What, what why?"

"Why, why, why?" Danny droned, anger and sorrow mixing freely in his words.

"What? What's wrong?"

Danny held up the book to the old man the first image on the very first page of a book in this old man's closet, was of an old man he'd never seen before standing arm in arm with his father, while they stood beside his mother, holding him in her arms.

"Why in the fuck do you have a photo album with pictures of my parents in it?"

16

"Is there somewhere we can get a drink and talk?" Kemmler said.

"Yeah," Floyd said. "I know a place."

They walked over the berm and down to the car in silence and continued that way nearly the entire drive to their destination. Floyd knew who Kemmler was, maybe not by name, but any police officer within a hundred miles of the state capital had heard of the creepy cop from head division. There was something otherworldly about him, something spooky that bordered on mental illness. It was his methods. Anyone who saw him at work said he could practically smell clues and, from what Floyd had seen, it wasn't far from the truth. Until a half a day ago, Guthrie was the only cop in town the others whispered about whenever he came onto a crime scene. Now there was another one, younger, more successful, with methods weirder than his own, relieved him. But just the same, it made him dislike the other cop that much more.

"This is it," Guthrie said, and pulled into one of the angled parking spots out front of Butler's.

The front parking was in prime position to get to and from the bar. The real trouble began after a handful of rounds bought and paid for inside. By the time the owner of the car came out, he was too drunk to negotiate the angle he'd parked at or lacked the patience to wait out the near constant flow of traffic down Parker St. Or both.

"Not much to look at, is it?" Kemmler said.

"It's no screaming hell on the outside but it's got it on the inside, where it counts."

Floyd held the door for the younger man to enter the bar first. The cloud of cigarette smoke that hung in the air like mist surrounding a harbour practically slapped them as soon as they crossed the threshold. It mingled with the natural pungency of stale urine and even staler beer and became the enchanting aroma that was the inside of Butler's. The smell nearly dropped the man to his knees.

"Jesus," Kemmler said and clamped a hand across his nose and mouth.

"After a while, you don't smell it anymore," Guthrie said. "Even when it's all through your clothes.

They walked into the dark of the bar and headed for a booth across from the beer taps. Guthrie could feel the eyes of everyone inside the place boring holes in the other man's back, and it made him a little uneasy, but not enough to suggest some place else to talk.

"Is this the best place to chat? These people clearly know we're the police. Is this going to be a problem?"

"Nobody gives a shit that we're cops," Guthrie said. "Anybody care about two cops coming in here for a drink?"

The noise level in the bar stayed at a constant beehive hum of clinking glasses and raised drunken voices.

"No, the problem here is that they don't know you and folks inside this bar go a little funny when strangers come in here. It's a workingman's bar, full of men who have nothing else. They drink to forget how shitty their life is, knowing that their life might not be any better than the fellow they're drinking with, but it sure ain't any worse. You come in here wearing expensive looking clothes, with a clean shave and a slicked down haircut, and they all know that bad news is going to follow you like a kick me sign."

"Get you gentlemen something?" the waitress said as she stood in front of the booth. "Hey, nice to see you again. After last time, I didn't think you'd be back so soon."

"Excuse me?" Kemmler said.

"Excuse you," she said. "You were in her about four hours ago and pretty worse for wear, too. Hey, how'd you sober up so quick?"

"You're mistaken, miss. I've never been in here before in my life."

"Funny, that's what you said four hours ago. You also said you'd never taken a drink before today. Might explain all the shit you did after a while."

"You're mistaken," he said, and a tone settled in his voice that made the woman uneasy. "As I said, I've never been to this town of yours, let alone inside this... establishment before," Kemmler said again.

"Well, you were hanging off the glass racks like some kind of goddam monkey and crawling around on all fours like an animal. You even started howling. After that, you said you could whip the ass off any man in the bar. And you almost did too. Quite a few challengers stepped up. But then you offered to buy a round for the bar, and nobody dared put you on your ass then, not one. Nobody's done that in forever, bought the place a round. The boys were loving you," she said. "Of course, it all turned out to be bullshit. You knocked on the bar and said drinks for everybody and, in all the excitement, you slipped out the front goddam door and stiffed me for all the drinks on a Friday night. I'm out of pocket for almost three hundred bucks. You owe me a lot of goddam money and I would appreciate you settling up before the two of you leave."

"Look," Kemmler said, and the annoyance thickened his voice like early April fog, dropping low and sounding harsh. "I can only say this so many times. I have never been to Winterbourne or inside the walls of this shitty little toilet you call a tavern, so if there was somebody here acting like an idiot and breaking the stemware, it wasn't me. If somebody stripped off all his clothes and danced a merengue on the bar, it wasn't me. If somebody whispered sweet nothings at you until your pink panties were ringing, it wasn't me. Now, can you get me a fucking drink, please?"

She stood staring at him, mouth agape and flushed with a mix of embarrassment and rage.

"What would you like, sir?" she said through gritted teeth.

"Lagavulin 18, neat," Kemmler said.

"Umm... what *is* that?"

"This isn't one of those kind of bars. You're not going to find anything close to that here. Nobody could afford to drink it." Floyd said.

"Whatever then. Get what you'd like," Kemmler said.

"Bring us two doubles of the top shelf scotch, Jeanine."

She frowned at the older cop and looked toward his table mate with contempt and loathing.

"It'll be okay. Get us some drinks, please and thank you. Everything will be fine. Okay?"

She sucked in a handful of deep breaths before she answered.

"I'll be right back, fellas," she said through partially gritted teeth and headed to the bar.

She returned after a time and set the drinks in front of the two.

Guthrie waved her off, anticipating more trouble between her and the younger detective. "We'll likely have another round."

Jeanine snorted her derision and headed back toward the bar.

"Never been in here before?" Guthrie said.

"Never," Kemmler said. "I've never been this far downstate before, let alone in this shitty little town or this shitty little hick bar."

"You might want to watch the shitty little bar talk. People around here don't cotton to strangers. Especially ones who run down the only place they have ever lived and the only joint in town where they can drink enough to stop them from burning the whole fucking town to ash and still have a little left over for rent or groceries."

"I would expect nothing less down here." He sighed. "Could we just drink these and get out of here?"

"Sure. We can go whenever you think you're ready to run the gauntlet," Floyd said.

"What? Run the gauntlet? What does that even mean?"

"It means that the three esteemed gentlemen at the bar, the ones who have been clocking us since we entered this public house, might take umbrage to our attempts to bid a hasty retreat from the establishment they are currently occupying. Clear enough for you?" Guthrie said.

Kemmler glanced toward the bar and saw the three men, all of them larger than he was, probably larger than he *and* Guthrie, staring at the two of them. The largest of the three sported a fresh, angry looking black left eye and an equally unpleasant blood filled right one. He seemed to zero in on the man from out of town, sizing him up as though he were a pig ready for slaughter and he was holding the knife.

"All the more reason for us to be on our way," Kemmler said and tipped the whisky into his mouth.

Kemmler sputtered and coughed. "Jesus! That's the best they've got in this place? It tastes like kerosene."

"No, it's not the best in the place, but it's the best we'll get for now."

The older man waved the waitress over to them.

"Same again, Jeanine."

"Wait, what?" Kemmler said. "What the hell for? We should just be getting out of here and on to someplace where we could discuss the details of this case and stop anymore children from being gutted and dumped."

"It will soften the blow and, strictly speaking, we might take care to wait several moments before attempting to take our leave," Guthrie said.

"Do you always talk like that?" Kemmler said.

"What way?"

"Like a character from a Wodehouse novel?"

"Who?" Guthrie said.

"You sound like a butler," Kemmler said.

"I just figured you being from upstate, and all might appreciate the refined conversation, not like the awful butchery of the English language you'd get from all us hayseeds down here."

"If that's your idea of refined conversation, it leaves a good deal to be desired. I'm from upstate, not turn of the century London for Christ's sake. And I'm quite certain I don't need any more of that paraffin you call whisky. I'm leaving here, with you or without you. It makes no difference to me. It does, however, make a world of difference to the people who sent me here. You know they could make things awfully uncomfortable for you if they chose to. There is a personal interest in this case, after all. You wouldn't want to see your career thrown away over something as simple as refusal to accept the help that was given to you, if you catch my meaning?"

"You're absolutely right," Guthrie said. "Those three men have been watching us since we came in. They *really* started watching us after your exchange with Jeanine. As soon as we get up to go, they are going to try to stop us. To stop you. And they will not ask nicely, but if you feel you can get past them, you go on ahead. I'll be right here waiting for your report."

"We could just arrest them. We are the law for God's sake," Kemmler said.

"Yes, well, that's fine for you. Arrest the three of them if that'll make you feel better. On what grounds, I'm not sure but bust them and then toddle off on your way back upstate. Go right ahead. You don't live here Kemmler, and you'll get on just fine after you've gone. There'll be no fallout upstate, and you won't spend the next month looking over your shoulder, hoping one of them isn't waiting for you with a straight razor while you're out walking the goddam dog."

The older man shouted now, his frustration rising to a full boil. Frustration over this weird, young asshole being sent down to *help* him solve a case he'd been unable to. Frustration that the brilliant detective from the big city had showed up to steal the torch from the aging Prometheus. He was bitter about his own shortcomings, kept at the forefront of his mind by the ghosts of five, now six, mangled children, whose bloody faces came to him and robbed him of sleep he needed to make sense of it all and just maybe find their killer. But if there was one thing, one sliver of doubt that grew daily and threatened to cover him like a shroud, it was this. His mind wasn't what it once was, it wasn't as sharp or fast as it used to be. Floyd struggled sometimes for the simplest of answers, like the location of his car keys, and it made him feel sad and beaten down. And a little fragile. Guthrie felt old.

"Well, I'm sorry for that. We don't have those kinds of problems in the city. But we really should get out of here and go someplace to figure this out. Someplace without so much distraction. Someplace that isn't so... here," the younger cop said.

He stood and gulped down both drinks in rapid succession, gagging as they clawed their way down his throat and into his stomach, and stood.

"Wait," Guthrie said, grabbing hold of the younger man's arm.

From outward appearances, William Kemmler, detective from upstate, was tall and spindly and a little on the scrawny side, but the arm that Floyd took a hold of now, was anything but. It felt firm and steely, taught, and muscular.

"What?" Kemmler said.

"If you're going through the front door, leave your gun on the table."

"Really?" Sarcasm dripped from his voice.

"Really."

The older man shot him a look that said it wasn't a joke, it was a demand. Kemmler pulled the revolver and holster from off his belt and set it on the table, but as he turned away from Guthrie and made his way to the door, three mountainous mill workers took up residence in front of him.

"Good evening, gentlemen, if you wouldn't mind? It's about time I was going."

Pete Jackson, the biggest of the three, stepped forward and spoke. "You got a lot of goddam nerve coming back in here."

Floyd sensed the chaos about to erupt and stood, moving alongside the younger cop.

"Look fellas, why don't you just head back to the bar, and junior here will buy the next round?"

"Why don't you mind your own goddam business, Floyd? This ain't got nothing to do with you," Tom Eichler said and pushed his way past the other two, closer to Kemmler.

"Is this going to be a thing, Tom? Is this going to be a thing where you and Pete and Mike start in on this guy, getting a little rough with him, pushing him around until he does something stupid and then you set in on him like a pack of wolves?" He raised the right side of his jacket, revealing the pistol tucked neatly into its holster beneath his arm.

"If you'd seen what this asshole did in here, you'd be lining up to smack him too," Tom said. "This sonofabitch drank his weight in the best in the house, smacked me and Mike and Pete around like we were toys, and he was some kinda goddam cat and then..." He choked for a second and Guthrie swore he saw tears welling in the corner of the big man's eyes. "And then, to make up for it, no hard feelings and all that, he buys a round for the bar and then skips out on it. Poor Jeanine was in goddam tears by closing time, wondering where all that money was coming from except her goddam pocket. Sonofabitch is lucky I don't carve another goddam scar in his face to go with the one he's already got."

"As I mentioned to the young lady, I've never–" Kemmler stopped. "Scar? Well, there you go. This is a simple mistake. You say the person who was in here last night had a scar?"

"Yeah," Tom said. "He–"

"He had a big bastard of a scar across his face," Mike said. "Looked like somebody dragged a big ass knife from his forehead clear to his chin. Said he was in a nasty fucking car wreck when he was a teenager. Said that was why he didn't drink no more, on account of the driver being blind drunk when they wrecked. Made him lose his taste for it. But he sure got his taste for it back last night. Didn't he, Pete?"

"Floyd, I swear, little prick was trying to poison himself or drink the whole goddam place dry."

Guthrie sized up the three of them. They were big and dumb and drunk. Normally, he'd just move aside and let rough justice take its course. There wasn't much worse than somebody stiffing the waitress in a small-town bar, except maybe buying the entire bar a round and then stiffing the waitress. He stepped to the three of them, arms out, hoping to diffuse the situation. Hell, he'd even buy them a round if it meant saving the ratty little bastard from getting his head kicked in, he nearly made it before the cooler prevailing heads, started to roast in an oven already on the broil of insult and too much cheap liquor.

Tom bolted forward and landed a series of rapid blows on Kemmler.

Guthrie reached for his gun. "Stop it!"

Pete and Mike crowded around the older cop, grabbing his arms and holding them at his sides. Not threating him with any kind of violence but not letting him move either.

"Nothing personal, Floyd," Mike said. "We just wanna make sure your friend gets what's coming to him."

"Fuck you Mike," Guthrie said. "Let go of him, Tom, and get out of here before you do something really stupid. He's from upstate. You know what that means?"

"It means I'm gonna show him how things get done in the country."

The fist landed soundly across Kemmler's nose. To his credit, the younger man didn't flinch, even as the blood poured.

"What the f–"

Tom raised the other arm. Kemmler caught it and held both, firmly, in front of his chest. The bigger man struggled against the cop's hold, like a coyote stuck helplessly in a leg trap, staring down the inevitable. Either starve or gnaw off the trapped bits and hope you didn't bleed to death along the way. The young cop locked eyes on the bigger man, the expression never changing. His cold, pale, nearly lifeless blue eyes didn't stray from the disinterested stare they when he entered the bar.

The pressure was slow and steady at the wrist as Kemmler squeezed and pushed upward from the underside of Tom's captive arms. It increased ever so slightly, and the young detective focused on the one blackened eye. Seeing that he had the man's full attention, seeing the terror that swam in the blood-streaked iris, he squeezed a little harder now and that black eye winced and Tom blew out air through pursed lips. He half expected the young cop to say something clever and tough sounding before - ultimately releasing his hands and sending him on his way. At best, with a warning. At worst, a fine and slightly achy wrist. But the other man remained silent. His gaze was unflinching. Piercing.

"Okay, okay," Tom said, worry flowing through the words like a venom. "I get it, sir. I'm sorry for the misunderstanding. It wasn't you that was in here last night. It just couldn't have been. Could you let go of my arms now? Please?"

Kemmler's eyes locked onto Tom's.

"Please," Tom said. "Please stop!"

Kemmler's face was stone, and his grip was an iron vice. A sound escaped his lips, low and vicious. Somewhere between a groan and a growl and he continued to squeeze Tom Eichler's wrists now without stopping. The bigger man struggled to get away from the pain, but there was no escaping this. He stared into the other man's eyes. There was no mercy. Not in the eyes. Not in the man. The cop continued to wrench on Tom Eichler's wrists until the bones shattered with a nauseating crack and three blanched twigs shredded their way through the bigger man's skin. He followed that up by doing the same to the left arm, with equally sickening results.

The young detective released the man and grabbed a handful of paper napkins from the table he'd been sitting at. Using them to wipe away the smears of the other man's blood, he hummed a stale little tune and clean his hands meticulously.

"If you'd like to keep the use of those arms" –he glanced down at the man with the black eye and now, two shattered wrists– "I would suggest you get your friends here to get you to the nearest hospital as quickly as possible."

He turned back to Guthrie, who stood nearer the other two men, silent and as stunned as they were at having just witnessed whatever the hell that just was.

"So, somewhere to talk that is a little less... busy?"

Floyd remained silent, trancelike. Kemmler snapped his fingers so close to the older man's face, that he could practically feel the wind coming off his them.

"Wait, what? Oh, yeah. Yeah, I know a place. What time is it? I gotta do something first," Guthrie said.

17

———

Don stared at Danny, his mouth agape. "What?"

"Why do you have all these pictures of my parents?" Danny said. "Are you some kind of stalker?"

"Wait, what? A what, some kind of what?"

"How long were you following them - me?"

He paced anxiously in the space between the old man's closet and the empty closet next to it. Danny was upset now, thoughts of his parents leaving him and this man having something to do with it peppered into a seething cauldron of loathing and crippling self doubt. That he traipsed back and forth in a space of only twenty feet, instead of walking far enough to disappear from this awful place like he wanted to, only pissed him off more.

"Wait a minute, this isn't even my book," Don said.

"No? Let me guess, you just found it on the sidewalk on one of your daily walks into town, right? What gives you the right to go through other people's stuff and take photo albums of people you don't even know?" Danny said, sarcasm ringing at every word.

"Now that's enough!" Don said. "You know perfectly well I couldn't get out of this shithole if I tried. I didn't steal the book. It was in the drawer with Bob's belongings. I took it after he died. And some shirts and a handful of pairs of underwear, too. It wasn't like he was going to need them where he was going. I'm no goddam thief and I would give all that shit back, all of it, for one more day with my pal, but I can't have that. There's nothing for me in this place now. So, if you want to come stomping around in here talking about right, I say take the goddam book and piss off, leave me to my time. It's all I've got left anymore and nothing but it until I die."

Danny stopped and looked at the old man, who had by now sat back down on his bed and turned to the window.

"Why did your friend have this book?"

"The people in the picture are his kids. He told me about them endlessly. I guess that would make him your grandfather. You never met him?"

"No," Danny whispered. "My parents never mentioned a grandfather. Was he my mother or my father's father?"

"I don't know. Your father's father, I think. Doesn't make much difference now that they're all gone, does it?"

"I guess not," Danny said.

"Bob told me they had a falling out. They had been close. I remember them coming to visit all the time and after a while, they brought a baby with them too. But then something changed, and they visited less and less. Eventually they stopped coming all together."

Danny sat for a minute, remaining quiet, nearly motionless, trying desperately to make sense of the thoughts that rattled around in his head like stray cats trying to corner a mouse. He wanted to scream at the old fool for having had the pictures all along and failing to tell him of that fact and completely missing the recognition of him as the child they once brought here. But it wasn't the old man who he was angry with, and he knew it. Somehow, he'd always known a moment like this would come, one that would force all the anger and resentment and the mountains of guilt, crawling up to the surface and he'd have to face them all at once.

He was angry, raging at them both. Angry for their splitting up in the first place and for being so forward thinking that they could remain in the same house while going through the misery of a divorce. Angry that calm discussions about the mundane probably devolved into arguments about what each of them thought was best for Danny - which parent he should spend most of his time - and trying not poisoning the well of his relationship with the other and, if possible, making sure he didn't come out the other side with any permanent psychological damage. He felt like a well-worn piece of furniture. Not desired in the strictest sense, but held on to out of some sense of obligation or lingering nostalgia and ultimately unwanted by either party.

The boy was angry that the two of them were still civil and environmentally minded enough to carpool to the divorce lawyer, if they'd have been shitty to one another, like the reams of divorcing parents he's heard about at school, shitty enough to take separate cars, he'd have at least one of them left. He was angry that he didn't know them better, either of them. Angry that they left him without so much as a goodbye. But they left him, permanently, and they would never share another thing with him for as long as he lived. Not another birthday with him, or Christmas or Thanksgiving. There'd be no more school plays or any of the other million milestone things that everybody else had parents to share with. Danny's parents were dead, and they were never coming back and for that, he almost hated them.

Danny stared at the picture in his hand. It was an image of his mother holding him. She was young and beautiful. Fiery red hair fell lazily across her forehead and framed her face perfectly. Green eyes, almost too wide, glittered across a thin, straight nose that turned up at the end, and gave her an almost otherworldly appearance but not an unattractive one. A broad, raucous smile completed her face. He was in her arms, chubby and apple cheeked with a tangled mop of strawberry-blonde hair that nearly obscured the green eyes that shone with the same intensity as the woman's. Beside his mother, crouched down to remain in the picture's frame and, from his expression, laughing wildly at the absurdity of it, was his father. He had a thin face and a narrow nose between dark, nearly almond shaped, serious eyes that still seemed warm and genuine. His hair was dark and the way it hung in his face, mirroring the woman's and the baby's hair, Danny guessed there had been a breeze during the photo.

And then it came to him, suddenly, the hazy recollection of that day. They say babies can not remember these things, but Danny could remember it. Images of it anyway. A flash of blue sky and the smell of the salt air. They had gone to a beach somewhere, and it had taken most of the day to get there. It had been hot. Annoyingly hot, and Danny remembered wandering down to the shore and wading in the water, feeling the coolness moving up his ankles and to his knees, rocking waves against him that soon moved up to his waist. The breeze was soothing here and the sun, though still teasing its bite at the tops of his shoulders, was held at bay by the gentleness of the summer air.

Without warning, water was everywhere, surrounding him, overtaking him, and in seconds, he was underneath it. A pair of blue denim legs stood over him, and two huge hands reached in to haul him out ungraciously, choking and sputtering the liquid from deep in his lungs, fighting for fresh air. He remembered the woman - his mother - hugging him too tight as she dried him off. Suddenly, it felt alien to call her that. Had it been so long that neither felt like his parents anymore? Danny wondered if people stopped being your parents after they were dead. Despite that being exactly what they were. He remembered what that day felt like, even after he went into the water. It was warm, and they were happy, the three of them. He remembered what love was like. It had been so long, it seemed, since he'd felt that kind of warmth from the sun... or anything... except maybe Jack.

There had always been Jack. The night the two of them died, he bawled and held the dog so tightly he groaned and grumbled at the boy, but he never moved. When the tears became overwhelming and threatened to soak his fur, the little dog licked the boy's face until he surrendered to sleep. The more he thought about it, about the two of them, the more Danny just wanted to be away from here, away from this old man and the ghost of a grandfather he never knew too, away from the nauseating smells coming from the basement and the equally nauseating way the people who couldn't feed themselves anymore ate. He wanted to get out of this room, take his dog, and go for a very long walk. The tears welled in the corners of his eyes, and he felt ashamed of himself for it. The boy gathered the pictures off the floor and stuffed them in the photo album. A quiet sniffle from across the room drew his attention back to the old man who had since turned away from the screeching teenager and went back to looking out his window.

"Why don't you take those? They'll mean more to you than they will me anyway," Don said quietly.

There was a sadness in his voice and Danny heard it loud and clear, but the anger at the old man's reluctance to mention the damned thing and his own selfishness told him it was his right to have it. They were *his* parents, weren't they? He turned silently and left the room, indignation burning its way through him as he started walking away from the front door.

"Hey, you're going the wrong way," Dave the orderly said.

Danny turned to the man and wiped the snot and thick stinging tears onto his sleeve. "Wrong way for what?"

"Didn't they tell you? Your ride's here. It's this way. I'll let you out."

Danny pulled the big photo album against his chest and followed the big man toward the front door. He stopped and turned back to the old man's room, suddenly overwhelmed with a nausea that only came knocking when he was guilty of something awful, like screaming at an old man who was trying to be friendly to him.

"What a minute," Danny said, and hurried back to the room.

Don still sat on his bed, facing away from the open door, looking at a window whose louvered blinds were still closed. Slivers of gold and orange of a sun beginning its descent into night pushed their way in through spaces between the slats. It gave the room a nearly aquatic feel, as the light shimmered around the room and gave the old man a striped, tropical fish appearance. Danny walked into the room and set the photo album beside him austerely.

"Um... I'll be back tomorrow. Well, actually, I'll be here all week.

Maybe we could go through the pictures together and you could tell me about your roommate?"

"I'd like that," Don said.

Danny couldn't be certain, but though he saw the traces of a smile dance at the corners of the old man's mouth.

"You want to talk in an old folks' home?" Kemmler said.

Guthrie sighed. "No. I told you I had to do something first. This is it."

"Have to visit your grandmother?"

"Yes, and here she comes now."

A boy appeared at the top of the stairs and looked around casually. He was larger than a child, but slight enough that he might still be mistaken for one. Following closely behind him was a grubby little dog who looked like it hadn't seen the inside of a tub full of water since the Nixon administration. Danny walked down the steps slowly but, as he caught sight of the familiar primer grey and rust pocked Ford that belonged to Floyd Guthrie, he quickened his pace and hit the bottom of the steps in no time. Danny instinctively grabbed the handle on the to the passenger side but gave a start as the image of the man in the front seat came into view.

"Hop in back," Floyd said, and shot an anxious look at the boy.

"Boy," the man in the front seat remarked. "This country air sure is fresh. Just makes you want to take in lungfuls of it."

Guthrie turned to the man with a look of bewilderment.

"Oh... yeah, right. We have such lovely air down here. You won't get air like that in the big city."

Guthrie turned full around to face Danny with a look that said he had no idea what the hell was going on just then and hoped the boy had been paying at least a touch more attention than he had been. He hadn't, and Danny returned a near identical, befuddled look.

He *was* sniffing. The man in the seat in front of Danny sniffed at the air, and he was sure of it now. Kemmler moved closer to the window and took in a few quick puffs of breath, leaned back into the seat and took a few more. The younger cop turned slightly right and then slightly left and took a group of sharp breaths in. And then he raised his head fully. Nose in the air and forehead pointed at the headliner of the old Ford. After that, there was no mistake. He took in huge gulping breaths of air, almost tasting it as each massive breath entered him. And then it hit him. Jack, not one to miss out on a good sniff, crawled across Danny's lap and jammed his snout out the window, snorting in the air for all he was worth. Whatever the man in the front seat was smelling, Jack didn't share his enthusiasm and sneezed twice before returning to the other seat and promptly closing his eyes.

Floyd glanced in the rear-view mirror and observed that Danny had his eyes closed, but he looked anything but relaxed. His eyes were clamped shut, and he was gripping his head like it might burst if he didn't hold on to it. "Hey," Floyd said, his voiced ringing with genuine concern. "Hey Danny, you, okay?"

"Home," he said with a groan. "I need to get home."

Danny's voice was not his own, and it took Guthrie by surprise. It was coarse and garbled like he had a mouthful of rocks. It was low, angry, and impatient.

"Now!"

Guthrie stepped on the gas.

"Where are you going?" Kemmler said.

"Something is the matter with Danny. I need to find out what it is. I'm not a doctor, so I'm going to take him to one."

"There is nothing the matter with this boy that a nap won't fix. I've seen this before, a few too many nips at Grandad's cough medicine, and suddenly, he doesn't feel so well. He just came away from the nursing home. I imagine the staff has a ton of booze hidden around the place to deal with the stress of it all. He clearly found it and now he's paying the price for his curiosity."

Danny rolled and groaned in the back seat.

"Are you fucking kidding me? Listen to him. Does that sound like someone who needs a nap?" Guthrie said.

"Home," Danny said.

"Look, don't fuck with me on this," Floyd said, nearly shouting. "Something is the matter with him and I'm not waiting around until it's too late to fid out what it is."

"I would be willing to bet that he will be fine in a matter of moments," Kemmler said.

"Yeah, he will. And in a few minutes, I'm gonna hit the lottery and I can afford to take all of us away from this."

"My fucking skull is coming apart!" Danny said.

"Nap, huh? Don't fucking tell me my business again," Floyd said to Kemmler.

"Oh my god, Floyd, help me!" Danny said and gripped the sides of his head.

Guthrie reached under the radio and pulled up the red plastic light with the magnetic bottom and stuck it on the roof just above the driver's side window. He flicked a switch on the console and his siren blared as he sped up and weaved his way in and out of the cars.

The traffic on Parker Street was thick, it was rush-hour and everyone had their own definition of importance and of how critical time was at that moment and it had little or nothing to do with a fourteen-year-old boy having some kind of seizure in the back seat of Floyd Guthrie's beat up old Ford. He turned up the volume of the siren, anticipating the crowd of motorists would open up like a shucked oyster and let him pass. When they didn't, he thrust the gearshift into park and got out of the car. The older man paced aimlessly and debated drawing his weapon and firing it in the air to frighten the crowd but thought better of it when the headline of **Wacko cop goes wild and fires gun downtown** flashed across his mind. Maybe if he called in a fire alarm, fire trucks would barrel into the street, and they'd all do their best to get out of their way of the Winterbourne FD. Who would want to be the person responsible for another person burning to death?

"Aiigghh!" Danny said.

"That's it!" Guthrie grabbed the boy from the back seat.

It had been a very long time since he held Danny in his arms and the boy had gained a considerable amount of weight since then, despite his slight frame. He nearly buckled under the weight and felt his back groan and threaten to give out as he hauled him up to his chest.

Danny winced and gripped his head tighter. "Uggnnnhhh!"

Guthrie tried to run, but between his age and the reckless lifestyle he continued living - and the unexpected weight of the teenaged boy he was carrying - the best he could manage was an eager sort of shuffling limp. A few steps of this awkward momentum, and he was already exhausted, praying he could make it to a bench on the sidewalk before his knees gave out and he dropped the writhing boy on to the pavement. His head swam. Flop sweat beaded across his forehead and flowed freely into his eyes. He bounced off a taxicab on his way across the street and the cab driver immediately blew his horn. The blast shook Guthrie, who started and dropped to one knee, nearly letting the boy onto the pavement headfirst. He could feel his temperature rising, and Guthrie knew that if couldn't set the boy down soon and get some air into his lungs, he'd drop the boy like a rock and pass out himself. Another horn blared, further away than the cab, quieter almost, and now there was a voice to go along with it.

"Dumbass!"

Guthrie looked around for the dumbass, sweat pouring from him, soaking his shirt and the back of his pants and covering his hair in a thick layer of wet.

"Dumbass!" the voice called out again.

There was a familiarity in the voice. He didn't know it, didn't really know the owner of the voice, but was familiar enough with it to recognize it among the hundreds of stranded motorists yelling at each other in the late August heat. Guthrie Wheeled around, turning in the direction he thought the voice had come from and heard it calling to him from everywhere. Above him, below and to either side of him. It overwhelmed him and nearly sent his brain screaming. Until he saw a lone, familiar face standing just outside of the passenger side of a beat-up old Ford.

"Hey dumbass! Bring the kid. The traffic is moving."

The man attached to the voice pointed toward the sea of automobiles ahead of it and, indeed, the cars were moving. Floyd hoisted Danny back upward as best he could and limped his way back to the car. Cars honking now, because he had become the reason the traffic had ceased. He made it back and deposited the boy unceremoniously into the back seat and got back into the driver's seat.

"Unnggh," Danny said.

The sweat poured over the older detective like a hot rain, soaking his clothes through. In a few minutes, the traffic cleared, and they moved. Slowly at first and then gradually picking up speed until there was no longer a need for the siren. They made it to the hospital in short order and Guthrie hopped out of the car, rushing to get Danny into the emergency ward as soon as he could.

"What?" Danny said.

"You're okay?".

"What do you mean, Floyd? Of course, I am."

"A minute ago, you'd have thought you were coming apart, with the amount of screaming you were doing."

"You see?" Kemmler said. "Nothing at all to be concerned with."

"Who the hell is this?" Danny yelped.

The younger detective turned around to face the boy in the backseat.

"Detective sergeant William Kemmler. What a pleasure to meet you, Danny," he said.

18

***

The dark-haired man was starving. The whisky swirling in his guts, courtesy of his new friends from Butler's, made him lightheaded enough to forget all about eating. But now that it was wearing off and his head was clearing, his appetite returned with a vengeance. He thought about going back to the cow, having had nothing since he'd gorged himself earlier, and shedding his skin sucked all that from him - it always did. Now the tank was empty. The liquor his new friends insisted on pouring down his throat repeatedly, left his stomach raw, but the buzz from it distracted him from the emptiness gnawing at him. Now the booze was wearing off, leaving emptiness and a blinding headache in its wake. He was hungry again. And irritated. The thought of crawling through the muck and the underbrush to get to the hunks of meat festering in the full heat of the sun, praying it would finally satisfy the hunger deep inside him, tightened the growing knot in his stomach and chased the moisture away from his mouth. He needed to eat, that much was true, but he needed to be careful about it.

He cursed himself for not taking advantage of the drunks at Butler's when he had the chance. Most of them took trips to the alleyway out back to piss when the toilets were full. It wouldn't have taken any time, and nobody would have questioned him following another man into the alley. He could have done it and hidden what he didn't use before anyone had noticed either of them was gone. "Oh, Cliff? He said he had to go. Something about work." But the booze had clouded his wits, slowed his reflexes and slowed the hunger. Now it came roaring back and demanding he do something about it.

The man walked further down the street, his pace quickening slightly, hoping to hasten the alcohol's exit from his body. His head cleared, and his sense was returning to him slowly, though his appetite hadn't diminished in the slightest. He'd have to get something into his belly soon or there'd be no keeping himself in check. Not for long, anyway. If he changed now, they'd lock him up in some god awful zoo somewhere and there he'd sit until he found time and seclusion enough to change back or until the hunger overtook him and he started gnawing away at his feet.

The Aztec diner was a small greasy spoon that sat at the northwest corners of Parker and Berwick Streets, that had been a Winterbourne landmark since the late summer of 1932. The ownership had changed hands at least a dozen times since then, though the menu had changed little. There was a generous crowd of regulars that filled the place daily. It was within walking distance of Winterbourne high school and students had supplied most of its daytime income for almost as long as the place had been open.

Around about 1952, the Aztec got its first jukebox, and it suddenly blossomed as a hangout for the younger population of Winterbourne. It never changed. Bored kids with nothing to do and appetites without end kept the place crowded and noisy. From 11:30 am, the first groups of them would trickle in the front door, ordering coffee and fries and the occasional burger until they left, en masse at 4:30, just before for the dinner crowd of working men and their families swarmed the place. Parents saw it as more of a treat than the kids ever did.

The diner was small - a single row of five booths across the back wall and six stools spread along a short counter. The kitchen, prep and grill area took up all the remaining room except for two small bathrooms tucked neatly away in the furthest back corner. Frugal designers laid it out square and even and left little room for the actual paying customers. Full was a good look for the place, and one it wore often, though the slow turnover rate made the management consider a time limit inside the place for the sake of more hands entering pockets and more money going into their coffers but gave in when the entire student body threatened to boycott the place if they ever tried it.

The man walked into the diner and was ushered by the first waitress that met his gaze to the remaining free seat in the place. A booth, as luck would have it.

"Coffee?" the chubby blonde waitress said.

Coffee? he thought. *Coffee? Would I like coffee?*

He scanned the table and grabbed the first thing that seemed able to suit his purposes. He moved blindingly quickly and jabbed the dinner fork into her neck again and again, just below the jawline. The blood pushed its way past the ragged wound in copious, bubbling spurts, coursing out in rhythm to her panicked heartbeat. He grabbed her, roughly and firmly around the shoulders and pulled her in, wrapping his mouth around the gaping hole, letting the blood fill his mouth and run lazily down his chin as his tongue darted in and out serpent like - lapping at the blood and flicking bits of shredded and torn flesh.

It was good. It was very good, maybe even exquisite, and the more he drank from the pudgy blonde, the more the yearning hunger slowed and died away. She squirmed a little, no doubt in the throes of dying prey. A sound escaped her lips. Small at first, but insistent. She made it a second time and then a third and, if he didn't know better, he would have sworn that she was speaking to him through the vice of his jaws around her throat.

"Carghlblee," she said.

"What? What?" He relinquished the steady pressure from her neck. "What did you just say?"

"Did you want some coffee or not, honey? I got other tables to get to." The waitress replied.

"Coffee! Yes, coffee. For the love of God, bring me some coffee," he said, the spell broken.

He recalled the hot black liquid, how he loved it, worshipped it in the times before now. The times when he'd known sensations other than hunger. The times before the change. He also remembered that coffee would often give the illusion of a full stomach or make a body care less about not having food if enough of it were drunk. He glanced at the well-thumbed menu the waitress tossed in front of him, knowing that anything she brought him would only waylay his hunger without ever satiating it. Eventually, he'd be forced to really feed and if he wasn't careful about it, it might be the last decent meal he ever ate.

"Awright sweetie." She sighed at him. "I've really gotta get moving. What would you like?"

There was a lilt in her voice, a happiness that grated against him like sandpaper. On any other day, it was a voice that might have been mildly annoying, like the whine of a mosquito in your ear when all you really wanted was sleep. But not today. Today, between the thunderous headache of the hangover, waiting for the first opportunity to bore into his skull, and the insatiable hunger that corroded its way through his veins, her words were seeds of rage.

"What can I get you?" the chubby blonde repeated.

"Steak," he said. "And eggs."

"How do you want those eggs?"

"Over easy."

"Fried in butter and not too greasy," she said. "And the steak? How do you want it?"

"Rare," he said with a growl.

～

HUGHIE KOCH, principal of Winterbourne high, walked through the door of The Aztec, hoping for a quick bite before heading home. Not that he was in any hurry to get home. His apartment was cramped and smelled like a wet dog that smoked too much. Things had been so much different in the city, better in the beginning, but even as things had gone off the rails, it was different. He walked in certain circles where he made an impression, and they thought him a decent and valuable member of the community. For a while anyway. But here, he was almost non-existent. There was no room for intellect or even mild cleverness in a town peopled by blue collar troglodytes and the mates they pulled around by the hair. There was a certain benefit to anonymity, but nobody told you that loneliness almost always came along with it.

He'd been an English professor at a prestigious university somewhere upstate and was within inches of tenure until a handful of nasty rumours circled around him. Whispers of coerced rendezvous with a handful of his male students - impressionable and innocent young men who looked to their teachers for guidance, not groping. These stories inevitably circled around him like buzzards on fresh roadkill at most of the schools where he found himself teaching and hovered around him like flies on a bloated corpse. There had always been tales of the fairy English teacher and what he got up to outside the ivy-covered walls of nearly every school on the eastern seaboard. But his own arrogance made him believe he was living a charmed life. He'd fallen into shit like this any number of times before and always managed to come up smelling like a rose.

Hughie had been involved with the Dean of the university since his days as an undergrad. There was nothing opportunistic about it for either of them. He was a young student, trying to find himself in a seething cauldron of self loathing and a lifestyle he'd had to keep entirely hidden up to now. The Dean was a handsome, older man with the perfect ratio of dark to grey hair, a firm, muscular physique, who wore his sexuality like a blazing sun medallion around his neck. He was gay, and he was completely at peace with it. If somebody was uncomfortable with it, that was their problem, and they'd better get used to it or find somewhere to go where he wasn't. It was fair to say that Hughie was smitten with him from the minute they first spoke, and after a year of being with him, was as in love as he felt he could ever be with another human being.

He was bright, exceptionally so, and had made a name for himself throughout the whole of his academic career. After enrolling in university two years early and being awarded virtually every scholarship he'd qualified for, Hughie became the latest academic wunderkind and his celebrity grew. Several schools tried to outbid each other to get him to attend. The Dean had a charming smile and a way about him that Hughie found tantalising, even more so with every successive cocktail the head of the school offered him. In exchange for attending his university, the older man promised him big things. After the third time they'd slept together, he delivered and gave Hughie a job as a teacher's aide. Within the year, they moved him to a full-time professor, and he seemed headed for the chair of the English department. All of this was before he'd even graduated himself. When he finished his thesis and earned his PhD, the offers rolled in. They were mostly from smaller colleges and universities, looking for someone that had a rock star reputation that new students would fall over each other trying to get a class with. There wasn't much prestige and there certainly wasn't much money in attending any of those schools, let alone working at one. He told the Dean he would stay where he was for as long as the older man would have him. But staying in the face of mediocrity is easy. Staying when the sirens of fame and possession call to you is an altogether different matter.

When Yale and Harvard both sent letters requesting him to join their faculty, and Princeton offered to rent him a house close to the campus, he thought that perhaps there were greener pastures he might move on to. He was young and decent looking and smart enough to keep his mouth shut and get along in nearly every sort of setting one could think of without outing himself until he was certain he was safe to do so. When he announced his intentions to the Dean, predictably he didn't take it well but admitted life at this University would carry on pretty much as it had - ad nauseam - until one of them retired, figuring he could sleep with the younger man and, in the throes of passion, convince him to stay. He couldn't, and the relationship soured and rotted away.

The laughter of new love quieted, replaced by long bouts of angry silence and chilly nights in the same bed, with miles between them. The old man begged, pleaded and promised him tenure and the department head in a year or two if only he would stay. But if six years with the man had taught Hughie anything, it was that the Dean was selfish and spoiled and preferred holding court, keeping everyone at arm's length, rather than getting to know anyone beyond a superficial level. Even the ones he said he loved. Things were great while he was happy, but the happiness never seemed to make it longer than a month or two. The cool silences would boil over with more and more. Where before there were words of love and pet names whispered from the heart, freely and frequently, now venom spat from the older man's lips over such serious transgressions as leaving wet dishes in the kitchen sink too long or the horror of crunching potato chips too loudly.

By the following spring, Hughie decided he needed out and told the Dean that he'd be leaving at the end of the first semester. The future had been on the phone for him for years now and it felt about time he answered it. The state of his life with the older man told him that nothing could be any worse than what he was currently living, anyway. Leaving - even to complete failure - at least presented the opportunity to get away from a situation that would eventually kill his soul. The Dean, to his credit, took it well and decided that being dumped by the younger more talented man, was about as shitty as he'd ever felt and vowed that Hughie would soon feel just as awful as he did, only he'd never get over it.

Two phone calls. That's all it took. The first, to the Dean of NYU, who was a friend of his from teacher college. He spread the news to the faculty at Harvard, who passed it on to Yale and from there it spread like leaf blight through the ivy leagues. He made a second call, as an anonymous tip to the newspaper and local television stations both. The Dean also had four football players in his back pocket. Four loud drunken assholes who'd taken too many liberties with too many female party guests in their time at the university. Two of the girls were calling it rape and contacting their lawyers. He told the jocks he could make it all go away, but it was going to cost them. He'd had designs of several midnight meetings over drinks and rough sex with all of them. Together and separately, but this was even better.

They would say Professor Koch had groped them, one and all on too many occasions to mention, they had laughed it off as just good-natured familiarity between teacher and pupil, but when coupled with the lewd suggestions that flowed out of him like river water, it could only be a threat of the highest order to their youth and virility. Once it hit the news, the ivy league schools shunned him like a leper and word spread through the academic community about the pervert English teacher. He went from rockstar to pariah in a handful of lies and phone calls.

After the dust had settled, he drifted from job to job as a substitute math teacher, gym teacher and even a part time ESL instructor at some community college two hours away from the apartment he moved into. It always wound up the same, there were the inevitable titters from the student body and the whispers and isolation in the staff room and, eventually, the head of the school would call him in and explain that he was doing an exemplary job, but it just wasn't working out the way they'd all hoped it would and they would have to let him go. Hughie had considered leaving academia and teaching altogether, when, out of the blue, a letter came to him from Winterbourne High, a backward high school in a Podunk little town down state. They offered him the principal's chair from a half-assed application he'd sent months before and forgotten all about by the time it arrived. They didn't care about what he'd done before they offered him the job, so long as he showed up on time and got the students to do as they were told.

An apartment came with the job. Small and dank, but free. It had a fridge and a stove and a sofa that looked as though it had lived through both world wars before finding its way to Winterbourne. Occasionally, he would buy groceries to put into the fridge, though they would, mostly, end up thrown out. For all the knowledge Hughie Koch had gained over a lifetime of schooling, the ability to prepare any food beyond opening a box and shoving it into a microwave escaped him. He became a regular at the Aztec and the fat blonde waitress flirted with him shamelessly from the first day he walked through the diner's door.

He didn't mind the attention. In fact, he was a little flattered by it because he was fairly certain she knew he was gay, but continued flirting with him, anyway. Maybe she thought she could make him less gay? It also reminded him he hadn't gotten laid in more than a year. He'd been so desperate for company one night after too many over the counter at Butler's, that he offered a blowjob in the alley out back to the drunk sitting next to him, who willingly obliged and waited til he got off before proceeding to kick the holy shit out of him for being a fairy. At least that's what he kept shouting as he was stomping on Hughie's face. From then on, he kept his head down and his mouth shut and did his best to satisfy his urges in the shower.

The Aztec was bursting. Hughie glanced around and couldn't see an inch of real estate that wasn't full of straggling students he knew, parents he'd met briefly, fussing over their younger children while trying to stuff handfuls of fried food into their faces, and the working folk who just wanted somebody else to make the meat and potatoes meals they ate every day. Without the prospect of a place to sit, he debated turning around and heading around the block to Butler's. They had a fryer, full of century's old grease, but the food that came out of it was practically edible. More so if he choked down a few generous whiskies beforehand. From the corner of his eye, he glimpsed a man. Young and dark haired, with skin so sallow, it nearly glowed. His eyes were as dark as his hair and his mouth was playing in the neighbourhood of a grin without actually committing enough to be called a smile. He stared, taken in by his handsomeness, to the point of distraction.

And then the man waved at him. Hughie blinked his eyes and shook his head. He had to be dreaming. Nobody this good looking ever came to Winterbourne, and if they did, they certainly wouldn't be waving at him. He looked around the diner and behind him toward the door. Looking for whomever it was the impossibly handsome man was waving to.

"Go ahead, honey," the chubby blonde waitress said.

"Wait, what?"

"He's waving you over to sit with him. He's got room at his booth."

"Good lord, is he really?" Hughie said.

"No, really," she said. "He told me to come and get you. Saw you standing by the door and told me to tell you to come and sit with him."

The man continued to wave at him until he was certain Hughie got the message and walked toward the booth.

"You're not waiting for anyone, are you? I don't think there's enough room for more than just you and I," the man said.

"No," Hughie said in answer. "Not meeting anybody. Just me."

"Excellent! In that case, won't you join me?" the man said.

"Hughie Koch," he said. "I don't believer I've ever seen you before."

"You say that as though you'd seen everyone in this town."

"It's a small enough town, I likely have. I don't know most of them, only the people I've come across at work, but I'm pretty sure I've seen most of the people who live in this town. And likely all of them in here.

"Michael Dietrich." The man smiled and extended a hand toward the high school principal. "And unless you were standing by the welcome sign out by the highway, you are unlikely to have seen me before. I just got to town today."

"Oh? What brings you to the rectum of the free world?"

"Ritual murder mostly," Michael said.

Hughie sat stunned. Uncertain what to reply to the bizarre statement.

"Oh... ah... I."

Michael grinned. "It was a joke. Clearly, I need to work on my delivery."

Hughie smiled back at him, and a tingle ran up the back of his neck that he hadn't felt since the night he met the Dean at the recruitment mixer. He could feel a tremor in the pit of his stomach. It was a flutter of nervousness that bordered on nausea. Excited, yes, but terrified just the same. The sweat beaded up on the back of his neck and his hands trembled like he had a righteous hangover. He flipped over page after page of the menu without having looked at any of them. He felt himself dwelling on the few words he'd already spoken to the beautiful man. Were they the right things to say? Did he sound like an educated man, or was he babbling like a fucking idiot? Was Michael clever enough to know the difference? Of course, he had to be. He wasn't certain how he knew, but he knew that this man, this handsome dark-haired stranger, was as intelligent as he was handsome, and that Michael would change his life forever. And with that, Hughie Koch was in love. Or deeply in lust, at the absolute least.

"So, what really brings you to Winterbourne?" Hughie said.

"History, you might say," Michael said. "Many years ago, a secret society existed in this town that, they say, did some really unspeakable things. I'm researching a book on this society and felt the best way to find out about it was to get it from the source. Get to the heart of the matter like the old saying goes."

"I can't imagine anything like that ever happening here. Nothing ever happens in this town," Hughie said.

"Have you decided, Hughie?" the waitress said.

"Oh," Hughie said. "Oh, umm, yeah. I'll have my usual."

"Meatloaf and fries, extra gravy on the side and a double helping of the veg of the day?"

"That's it, Darlene. That's it exactly. Did you want anything?"

"No," Michael said, and looked up at the waitress. "I've already ordered, thank-you."

She hovered around the table.

"Did you need something else, Darlene?" Michael said.

"Wait... what? No... no, sorry... I'll go put your order in."

They carried on chatting over the meal, Hughie nervously fluttering through words he worried might sound like he was trying too hard. At the same time being unable to maintain eye contact with him. It resulted in him speaking more to the tabletop beneath him and sneaking the odd glance of the other man sitting across from him. Michael, for his part, never took his eyes off Hughie. Mouthful after mouthful of eggs and every bloody morsel of steak, his eyes never moved from the other man's face. He never once glanced at the plate below him and never failed to get the food into its intended target. If he meant to intimidate the other man, he succeeded.

The fat blonde waitress brought the check to the table and wished the two men a pleasant evening.

Nosy cow, Hughie thought. *Who does she think she is giving me that look? It's not like I was going to go home with her - ever.* And it suddenly dawned on him that now the meal was over, likely so was his time with Michael. It wasn't as though the man would just up and come home with him. He wasn't even sure he was interested in him. He had kept everything close to the vest the entire meal, letting very little of himself out into the open. Hughie prattled on endlessly, nervously, telling Michael virtually everything but the number of his bank account. He decided then that he would go home, get in the shower, and work out his frustrations while picturing this specimen of a man as many times as it took to get him through the night.

Hughie stood and extended his hand to the man across the table.

"It was a pleasure to meet you and thanks for the seat."

Michael grabbed his hand firmly and pulled Hughie into him, bringing his face alongside the principal's ear.

"Let's get out of here," he whispered and nipped at his ear.

19

––––––––––

Danny got out of the car, almost before Guthrie brought it to a stop, and rushed toward the front door without another word to the cop.

"I'll pick you up the same time tomorrow," Floyd called to him from the car.

The boy didn't look back. Instead, for the first time since his parents died, he rushed into his house, wanting to be far away from Floyd Guthrie and the creepy, short-haired man in the front seat of the car. It didn't take long for Jack to come running behind him and he bent low to pick him up. The little dog was a blur of wagging tail and lolling tongue and spastic limbs, trying to get close enough to Danny to nearly be inside him.

"Alright, Jack." Danny giggled, and the stress of the day eased. "Gimme a minute and we'll go for a walk.

The dog barked and ran circles around the boy's feet. "Okay, okay," he said soothingly.

"Why in the hell did you name that dog Jack? You shoulda called him jerk for the all the times he pisses in this house. He's lucky I don't whip the skin off his bastard hide," Randy Hewlett, Danny's Randy said.

From the look of him, he'd been drinking. From the smell coming off him, it had been for a while now and was in no mood for back talk from some bratty kid who didn't belong to him beyond the pay cheque he brought in.

"I'm just going to take him for his walk now. I'm sure you could use a break from him now," Danny said quietly, and tried to walk past the man.

Randy grabbed Danny around the arm and held him firm, whispering his gin-soaked breath into the boy's ear. "You think you're so fucking smart? You and your fucking dog. I know what goes on around my house. And your goddam cop buddy, too. Let him take care of you and this fucking mutt."

He pushed the boy, while still clinging to his arm, and nearly knocked him backward. Jack growled at the man and stood his ground between the boy's legs.

"Shut the fuck up, Toto. Or maybe I might have to go get my shotgun."

"I can tell you're tired," Danny said in quiet, measured tones. "Why don't you go fix yourself a drink and Jack and I will get out of your hair."

The man swayed, trying to remain upright, still holding onto Danny's arm. The dog growled low and long and sent a message that Danny heard loud and clear.

"If you can just let me by, I could get Jack's leash and we could be out of here in no time."

He dropped his hand from Danny's arm but stood in place, swaying a little, continuing to prevent the boy from getting past him. A greasy, obscene smile slithered its way across his lips, and he moved slowly and deliberately out of the way of the teenaged boy. Jack hurried by and turned to watch as the boy came past the foster father. Without warning, the older man let a hand fly and clapped it across the back of Danny's head with force to jerk his head forward in a whiplash snap. The little dog moved toward the man, teeth barred and growling low and deep. Danny waved him away and continued his path to the back door of the house.

"Pick up the goddam dog shit in the backyard before you go."

Randy threw a knotted-up plastic bag in the boy's direction, which fell short of its target and descended leisurely earthward. Danny choked back a laugh, knowing that if he let it past his lips, the side of his face with meet up with the back of the man's hand the second the laughter hit his ears. He bent down to retrieve the plastic bag and stood up quickly, fishing for his back pocket to stuff the bag into. He crept past the man, who still partially blocked his way.

"Um, excuse me please," Danny said cordially.

"Oh, wanting to get by? Of course, your majesty."

Danny moved past the drunk man. However, it wasn't fast enough, and he felt a sweaty, ham sized hand connect with the back of his head. The ringing in his ears started almost immediately and the plastic bag made its way to the floor again, though the blow from the drunken man wasn't sufficient to do anything apart from getting his attention. And it did. The boy could feel the tears and the shame bite at the corners of his eyes and the heat of pent-up rage burn up the back of his neck and spread across his reddening face. His heart wanted to ball up his fists and savagely lay into the old man, raining blows on his gin-soaked face until he stopped being such an insufferable prick - or stopped moving altogether. He didn't care which came first. His head told him this wasn't the first assault he'd received from the man, nor was it by any means the worst. It was also not likely to be the last, especially if he were to do something as stupid as take a swing at him. Especially when he was as worse for the drink as he was now.

Jack growled and took up a position between Danny's legs, leaning his hindquarters against the boy in anticipation of pushing off quickly like a coiled spring. The boy squeezed his shins together to get the dog to stop. He knew from experience the dog would not let up if he felt the boy was being threatened. But the angrier Jack got, the more indignant the Foster Father got. Especially when he drank.

"You better shut that goddam mutt up if you want him to keep living in this goddam house," he said with a snarl.

Jack inched forward, grumbling low and atavistic, his eyes never moving from the grubby drunken man.

"Shut up, Jack," Danny said, yanking on the dog's collar.

He bent down to pick up the plastic bag, his own eyes never moving from the man who flashed a greasy, perverse smile at the boy that said *I own you.*

"If I find a single piece of shit in that backyard, you and that fucking dog'll be sorry."

The Foster father weaved his way into the living room like he was on the deck of a ship in high seas, narrowly avoiding a collision with the China cabinet. Danny had visions of the man stumbling into it and sending the top-heavy wooden monstrosity crashing to the earth, destroying everything within it. It would be his fault. Even if the foster father was as sober as the Pope, which he seldom was, it would be Danny's fault. It always was. If there was a bright centre to the universe and the Foster Father had taken his place among the clouds, he wouldn't have been able to ascend to his reward because of the court appointed albatross around his neck.

The hooks on the back of the bathroom door bent. It was because Danny's wet towel presented just that much more weight on them. The grout around the kitchen sink, a feat that he had prided himself on some time ago, was now cracking and falling out in chunks. It was, naturally, a result of the extra dishes from the boy, which amounted to more water from more washing of dishes. And then there was his dog. Jesus, don't get him started on that goddamned dog. Shit from one end of their six-by-six patch of land to the other. Eating them out of house and home and wanting nothing to do with anybody but the boy. The goddamned thing was a menace and, if it wasn't for that nosey asshole of a cop, he would have put the little bastard down the first time he growled at him or his overbearing wife.

The cabinet remained upright, and Danny hightailed it out of the hallway, making his way through the kitchen to the back door. Jack in tow.

"Well," Danny said to the little dog. "Take me to it."

Jack barked excitedly and moved in circles, waiting for Danny to open the door to the fenced-in backyard.

The kitchen door swung open, and the little dog ran straight for the smallish pile he'd left earlier in the day. Danny had always sworn that no matter how many piles Jack had left, he could lead him to them one by one and would wait dutifully while Danny picked them up. No matter how long they'd been away from the backyard.

The boy moved in beside the dog and picked up the small pile with the plastic bag. He tied it in a loose knot and flipped the package into the green garbage bin beside the back door.

"Anywhere else?" Danny said, unsure what he would do if the dog led him to another pile.

Jack stayed put and the boy quietly laid his leash on the back porch, knowing, from this point, he wouldn't be needing it. The dog was capable of a lot of things but likely to just run off, was not high on the list. Danny swung the gate of the chain-link fence opened and it groaned out a rusty protest. They hit the street and headed away from the house. The two of them made it a block and a half away from the foster's house before Danny took a seat on the curb and the tears he'd been holding back since the drunk man clouted him up the back of the head, found him and he couldn't keep them in check anymore. The little dog wheeled around to investigate why the boy was no longer keeping pace with him. He ran back and barraged Danny with wet, sloppy licks and pawed at his hands, trying to get them away from the boys - trying to keep them off his face and more on him.

Danny choked out a moistened protest. "Stop."

Undaunted, Jack continued licking away the salty tears as quickly as they ran down the boy's chin.

"Stop," he said again, slightly more forcefully.

And again, the little dog ignored Danny, carrying on as though stop translated to *come lick me more* in whatever language dogs speak fluently.

"God-damn it Jack, stop!" Danny pushed Jack off.

The dog whimpered and backed away, a hurt, confused look in his eyes.

"Aw shit Jack, you know I don't mean it." Danny sighed. "C'mere."

Jack yipped and rushed for the boy, leaping as he got close enough to him. He hit Danny mid-chest and bowled him over, rubbing, licking and twisting round in a way that the boy thought the dog might try to get inside him.

"Alright, sit down." The dog dutifully took a seat. "Where to?"

Danny stood and instinctively started walking toward Millar's field. It was their usual walking spot and, despite what they had discovered there the day before, he saw no reason that they shouldn't go there again today. The little dog, however, had other ideas and took a firm hold of his leg around the ankle, not firmly enough to cause a wound, but unyielding enough to get the point across that they weren't going into that field today.

"Ow, Jack!" It didn't hurt, not really, but the thought of arguing with the dog about holding onto him and trying to find the words that would express the discomfort and aggravation real pain caused, seemed excessive and a little stupid. And Jack was a dog. He might just as well have shown him a card trick for all the good either would have done. Danny suddenly faced the memory of Billy Anglin's mangled body. His guts, what remained of them, hanging out of a gargantuan wound in his abdomen. Just then, he agreed with the dog and wanted to be as far away from Millar's field as he could get.

"You're probably right. Not the best idea to go there. Probably still full of cops anyway, and we both know how you feel about cops."

He and most of the other lower middle-class families lived on Mitre Street, where the poor were not poor in the strictest sense of the word. They were average, blue-collar people. Not poor enough to live in the row houses on Grey Hollow Road, but a few too many nights in Butler's or enough sick days in a row to risk against your job, and that's just where they'd end up. They crossed Parker Street and headed uptown, away from the storefronts and excitement, and headed toward the high school. From there, it was a left onto Boulle Avenue for a block until they came to the steel truss bridge that crossed the Nygard river. They walked carefully beneath the bridge and down the banks until the ground was nearly level again. From there, they walked away from Winterbourne. Ten minutes' worth of walking with the current of the river - which was full and running quickly until it came to a small clearing near to their destination.

The depth of the river, and the speed it moved, dropped away abruptly here, caused mostly by the culverts on either side of it used to divert the flow to the hydro-electric dam half a mile away down river that powered several towns in the area, including Winterbourne. It made a great place for Danny to sit and dangle his feet in the water and not have to think about anything, apart from how nice it was in here. The fact Jack loved to splosh nearly shoulder high in the water and bite at the minnows that filled the shallows made it just about the most perfect spot. They didn't come here often. Danny always felt that a spot like this, a spot this perfect, had a shelf life, and if you visited too often, somebody'd get wind of what you were up to and the next thing you know, the whole goddamned town was showing up with coolers full of beer and inner tubes, floating around and pissing in the shallows and leaving garbage everywhere.

Jack wasted no time. The shallows loomed just ahead of them, and he tore through the underbrush to get into the water like it was the first time he'd ever seen it. Danny wasn't impressed by the slow-moving, shallow river and walked to the edge of the bank as though moving any quicker might exact some price he couldn't pay. It was a quiet place, a still and reflective place, and he walked up to it accordingly. The dog held no reverence for this place and was already sopping wet and mud covered and loving every second. He barked and snapped at fish he would never catch and moved in jerky movements as his feet touched things. He moved, jumped and splashed in the water and then stopped, suddenly.

The little dog moved forward cautiously toward one of the diversion culverts, just out of sight of where Danny was sitting.

"Stay there Jack," he yelled to the little dog who, clearly, had no intention of stopping or staying or doing anything apart from investigating whatever grabbed his attention.

A low, anxious growl, staccato in rhythm and surprising in timber, erupted out of the dog as his eyes fixed on something around the bend in the river.

"C'mere Jack," Danny said.

The little dog remained fixed to the spot and let go another atavistic, throaty rumble.

"Jack!. Get back here now!"

But the dog ignored him and remained where he stood.

"Goddamn it." Danny sighed and began taking off his shoes and socks. He rolled his pant legs to his knees and stepped into the slow-moving water of the Nygard river.

The water was icy. Even knee high, it was frigid enough to catch his breath and make him wish he'd stayed on the shore. The bottom was primarily silt, and felt a little like walking through a bed of chilled snot. Danny squidged his way through the awful stuff, leaving billowing clouds of muck blooming in his wake, and made it up just behind his dog. Jack was still standing and still growling viciously at whatever had piqued his attention around the bend. He sloughed on a little farther, and bent down to pat Jack, trying to calm the little dog somewhat. The dog, when he realized Danny was now beside him, inched up beside the boy and continued to growl with increasing ferocity, bordering on barking with each successive breath.

They continued to inch forward, Danny keeping a constant hand on the back of the dog for fear of him running forward in a frenzy of rage and panic. He trudged through the muck for a few feet and it gave way to small flat stones just around the two culverts. Without the awful mire to slow their progress, the two of them rounded the bend and Danny glimpsed what the little dog had been so upset about. A warm, cheerful smile oozed its way across his face. In a widened stretch of the shallows, just ahead of where he and Jack were standing, was an ample posterior staring right back at them. Also, it was a backside he recognized.

"Raisin?" he called out to his friend.

She lost her balance. "Jesus Christ!"

"What the fuck?"

Jack rushed to her and began barking and licking at her face excitedly, in random bursts of joyfulness.

"Call him off, Danny." She giggled. "Call off your goddam dog!"

"Leave her be, Jack."

Raisin Chow stood fully up in the water. Half of her was completely sopping and the rest practically steaming from the anger burning across her face.

"What the hell are you doing, Danny?"

"Jack and I come up here once in a while," Danny said. "When things get a little hairy with the fosters." Danny's situation with the Fosters was no secret. Especially not to Raisin Chan.

"Oh shit, sorry Danny," she said.

"I know," he said. "Don't worry about it. It's nothing now. I'll live. He'll be passed out by the time Jack and I get home, anyway. If we're quiet enough, he'll stay that way."

"That's good. But it's still a shitty deal, and I wish you didn't have to live with it."

"Hey, what are you doing here?" Danny said, trying to steer the conversation away from his home life. "You weren't..."

"Weren't what?" Raisin said.

"About to, you know..." he said shyly.

"What, take a leak?"

His face flushed crimson and the heat of embarrassment pushed across it like he was leaning over a boiling kettle.

"Something like that, yes," he said to the ground.

"No. God no. Who does that? Do people do that? Like really do that? Here?"

"Some people, I guess," he said, not really certain if people were in the habit of peeing in shallow creeks or not.

"God, that's disgusting." She recoiled and jerked her hands out of the water quickly, wiping them on her pants.

"It's a moving stream," Danny whispered.

"What?" she said, the word caked solid in revulsion.

"It's a moving stream. Even if you just peed in it a second ago, it's long gone downstream by now. Kinda nature's toilet. Anyway, what *are* you doing here?"

"Looking for mudbugs," she said.

"For what?"

"Mudbugs. You know, crawfish? Crayfish?"

"Oh, okay. What the hell for?"

Danny was familiar with the tiny crustaceans that lived under rocks in the shallowest parts of the Nyegard. Water roaches were a little closer to what they deserved to be called.

"You eat them," she said. "We lived down south before we moved here - when I was really young. My dad used to wander around the creek near our house looking for them. He likes to reminisce about those days and how good the crawfish were. I started coming down here a few years ago to look for some and to think."

"Any luck?"

"I've gotten just about enough to fill up one of my pockets." She laughed.

"Today?"

"Ever."

Just at the fringes of his peripheral vision, Danny could see Jack who, until now, had been happily splashing in the river and biting and drinking and rolling in the water, not caring in the slightest if there was a whole toilet bowl full of urine within it. It likely would have made the experience even more enjoyable for the little dog. But he stopped dead and his head snapped up, focused on the copse of trees to the right of where Danny and the girl stood, and a sound came from deep inside him, coarse and deep and unlike anything the boy had heard come out of his dog before. He felt the fear crawl up his back like a greasy centipede, winding and squirming its way past his shoulders and settling at the base of his skull. He reached over to take Raisin's hand.

"What the hell?" she said.

"Shh!" Danny pointed to the little dog. "He's on to something."

Jack let go another savage, rattling growl and moved slightly forward toward the trees. His gaze never shifting from the glade.

Danny reached down to quiet his dog, and to let him know that he'd done well, that he and Raisin were just fine. The little dog snapped at his hand and turned back to the wood, growling as fiercely as ever.

"Jack!"

Raisin shifted uneasily and moved closer to Danny.

"What the hell is going on?"

"There's something in there, in those trees," Danny whispered.

"Are you sure?"

"Something big, I think. Could be a bear."

"You saw it? Wait, what a bear? In Winterbourne? Is this some kind of weird come on to get me to move in closer to you?"

"No," he said almost automatically and after a minute or two passed and some of his sense had returned. "No, nothing like that. I didn't see anything, but I just got a feeling like there's something big in there. Something enormous. A bear was just the first thing that came to mind."

"I seriously doubt it's–"

"Shh! Did you hear that?"

"Hear what? I hear nothing and I'm getting a little sick of standing in this icy goddam river while you try to scare the shit out of me," she said.

"Shut up," he said, his voice barely above a whisper but as close to a yell as he dared to get. "There, do you hear that?"

Her expression faded.

Low and still sounding far off, there was a rustling, a crunching of dried underbrush and the snapping of low-hanging branches. It was big, whatever it was. Even at a distance, the sounds coming from the wood gave the impression that whatever was clomping through was big. And moving directly toward them. Twigs snapped as the sound moved closer to them and then it seemed larger branches and young saplings cracked and fell noisily by the wayside. Danny moved closer to her, trying to calm her. Trying to quiet her enough to stop whatever was on the trees from zeroing right in on them.

The tremor that ran through the branches moved closer, and that was enough for Jack. The little dog took off at a run and disappeared beneath the brush, leaving Danny and Raisin alone, seemingly defenseless. Images of his dog being eviscerated by a bear or cougar or whatever the hell it was, setting themselves firmly in his brain and refusing to budge.

"Shit!" He took off after the little dog.

Danny could hear Jack barking and, from the sound of it, he was still very much on the move. He ran after him as fast as he was able. Ducking low-hanging branches and leaping with surprising precision over fallen logs, and he thought if he could keep up this pace, he might actually catch up to the little bastard. What he would do after he got there, particularly if Jack found whatever it was coming through the trees at them, he didn't know.

"Jesus Christ!" His hopes of catching his dog crumbled and fell like an abandoned building.

A spasm rocked across his head, fierce and focused and accurate. Needling into his brain like a laser guided steam hammer, and it dropped him to his knees.

"Jesus Christ!" he screamed again and tried to stand, tried to force his way past the pain.

Danny got to a knee before another jolt shot through his skull and pushed him back earthward. His hands groped upward, pulling at his hair, slapping at the sides of his head, rubbing at his eyes, trying anything to get the torment to cease. It didn't. Another searing wave of agony levelled him, and he lay fetal on the piles of leaves and broken branches, praying it would pass before whatever was out there caught up to him.

"Danny, Oh my god!" Raisin said, the panic rising in her voice.

He could barely hear her. Pain became everything he knew. It was crushing in its enormity, like a radio that couldn't tune in. His ears buzzed with static and muffled voices. But he could hear it. It was loud, nearly deafening in clarity. It sounded huge and angry, and it sounded like it was moving. Moving with a purpose. Moving toward them. Heavy footfalls thudding against the damp earth, picking up speed as it got closer to him and Raisin. She continued to mouth words at him, panic written on her face. And it moved closer. She moved into him, grabbing at his shirt, pulling for all she was worth, trying to get him to stand, knowing that they would not survive whatever was about to come through the brush at them. And it moved closer still.

It was close enough to them that Danny could hear its breath now and imagined it slavering over them both before it moved in for the kill. Massive strings of saliva drooling from its mouth. Hot, rank breath steaming across their faces. Soon it would be on them and the pain in his head would pale compared to the agony of being devoured by the massive predator this obviously was. He thought of calling out to Jack, thinking the little dog might do something, anything to stop this thing from making him and Raisin a hot lunch but the message to call out got lost in the TV static that hissed around in his brain and he lay his head down, waiting for the inevitable, or the next bolt of pain, whichever came first. And then it was here.

A foot came out of the trees first, huge and black and canine, followed closely by a leg and shoulder and soon the head appeared. It was long and lanky, like the muzzle of a wolf, but stretched forward and slightly downward. Its eyes were narrow and brown and bore the look of an apex predator, zeroed in on prey, weak and defenseless. Its fur was coarse and black and flocked with bits of white, giving it the appearance of something old and angry. It stopped short of running up on them, preferring instead to take its time and idle up beside them. The pain rocketed through Danny, sharp and severe, and he thought his skull would crack before the feeling stopped.

It turned to Raisin, moving alongside her and, even through the agony in his head, Danny could see the enormous thing, its shoulders standing well past her waist. It sniffed at her, and without warning, jumped forward, knocking her to the dirt.

"Danny!" she screamed, but he was still writhing on the floor, helpless.

The thing moved back away from the prostrate girl, and back to the boy. It appeared to give a satisfied smile at having the two of them right where it wanted. It growled, and in that growl, he swore he heard the words.

"She's first."

20

The two of them walked out of the Aztec and headed toward the high school. Hughie's mind was a jangle of fear and anticipation and questions. Who was this guy, really? Did he offer to have Hughie show him around the town out of sincerity, or was this an excuse to get him alone somewhere and kick the shit out of him? He was gorgeous, for a start, and that didn't help matters any. Hughie was smart. Smarter than most. Hell, he was usually the smartest person in most rooms he found himself in. Especially in a town like Winterbourne. But smart would only get you so far if it all seemed to disappear the second a good-looking man happened by. And it always did.

Hughie used to think of himself as just waiting for the right man to come along. Someone to share the rest of his days with, while they sipped champagne together, watching tear-worthy sunsets in the south of France. Or maybe somebody a little less refined, somebody who liked cheap whisky and boxing, that he could mould and refine and introduce to the beauty of the written word and single malt scotch. When nobody came along after the first year in Winterbourne, he just figured fate would bring his other when it was damn good and ready. By his second year, he'd get recklessly drunk and try to convince himself to not go wandering downtown and offer hand-jobs to the patrons of Butler's. He was at the point now, so desperate for physical contact, that he might seriously fuck a pile of stones if he thought there might be a snake in it.

But then here was this man. This impossibly handsome, almost annoyingly clever and impossible charming man. This specimen, Michael. And he wanted Hughie. Even if he didn't, even if all he wanted was a little adult entertainment before he split, Hughie didn't care. He was a man who was interested in doing things with him and, right now, that was enough to knock the rust off Hughie's libido. Michael insisted on paying for Hughie's meal. He'd only had soup and a ham sandwich and suddenly wished he'd eaten more. If it was going to be free, he might as well get his money's worth, right? But as the check arrived, Michael dug through the pockets of his pants and shirt and announced that his wallet was missing, promising that if Hughie flipped the bill just now, he'd treat him to the best meal he'd ever eaten - plus maybe a little something he hadn't planned on - the next time they met up.

Hughie pulled his wallet out and laid a handful of bills on the table, enough for the bill plus the tip and then some. A sudden tickle of suspicion crawled up the back of his neck. He looked over at Michael, who met his eyes and flashed him a sly little smile. He could feel those baby blue eyes boring a hole straight through his own and he would have given the other man every cent he had on him. Hughie was in love from the second he sat down.

"Let's get out of here," Michael said and took Hughie's hand so fast, he barely had time to worry whether anybody had seen it. "Take me somewhere. Show me your town."

"I'll show you whatever you want," Hughie said. "But this town isn't exactly friendly to... well, you know... to people like me. We should go back to my place. It'll be safer there, so long as nobody sees us go there together."

"We will," Michael said. "Don't worry, we will go back to your place. But for now, I want to see a little of this town. Surely there must be somewhere quiet and out of the way we could talk?"

Hughie sat silently for a while, staring into Michael's eyes, wracking his brain, tried to think of somewhere he could take the other man. The park at the bottom end of Parker Ave was out, too many drunks from Butler's ended up there after hours, drinking carry out beers and screwing the dancers from Winterbourne's only strip club. Either of the two cemeteries were also out of the question. Local kids hung around them at all hours, looking for quiet places to drink their parents' stolen liquor and play grab ass away from anyone who'd tell them they should do otherwise. And then he realized. The woods behind the high school were private and, since they had built the new dams, offered a few truly beautiful places where the two of them could be alone.

"I know a place we could go," Hughie whispered.

"Oh?"

"Yeah, not too far from here. It's quiet and mostly secluded. There might be a few kids drinking in there, but they'll stay hidden as soon as they hear adult voices."

"Kids?" Michael said.

"Yeah," Hughie said. "Kids from the high school. Sometimes, I've come down here and found a few younger kids from the grade schools up here playing in the water, but it's mostly my students coming in here to horse around and drink."

"Kids," Michael said. He turned back to Hughie and grabbed his hand. "It's practically inviting us."

Hughie wanted Michael to let go of his hand. Something about it felt wrong. He was pulling him, rushing him almost toward the treeline. It felt impatient, but not like a lover, eager to get on with things, more like a parent would drag who just wanted a stuffed bear, away from a carnival. It was forceful and rough, and Hughie didn't think it would do him any good to tell the other man to let him go. Just the same, another person was holding his hand. Michael was holding his hand! He could have wanted to eat the kids in the forest for all Hughie cared.

They walked in silence for a time, Michael still gripping him around the wrist, and led the way into the trees. The ground inside the glade was dark and cool, mottled with a patchwork of sunlight beaming in through the corona of leaves overhead. The sun was still blazing overhead, and, with a jacket, shirt and tie, it felt good to slip into the shadows of all those trees. They walked until Hughie thought they'd gone far enough in and stopped walking. Michael turned back to him with a confused look on his face.

"Why are we stopping?"

"Oh," Hughie said, not expecting the question. "Oh, ah... I know this spot; I've been here before. I think it's a good place to... stop."

"And it is," Michael said.

He pulled Hughie into him, kissed him full and deep.

DON THUMBED through the pages of the photo album, looking at the captions around the pictures, and realized he knew practically nothing about the man he'd shared a room with. A man he thought was intimate enough with to call a friend, he now understood he knew next to nothing about. The pictures, most of them, were of a family he barely spoke of and seldom visited. Not an uncommon thing here. They were all living with a constant reminder of the world moving faster into the passing lane, while they remained hopelessly stuck in second gear. Canes and walkers and wheelchairs and slow, painful shuffling steps and families whose lives moved far too quickly to visit more often than the big holidays, all illustrating that the elderly here weren't out of the race entirely, but they all understood there was no hope of accomplishing anything beyond finishing. If old age was a testament to inevitability, Winterbourne Home was a shrine to the broken down. A Taj Mahal of misery housed entirely by the forsaken and the misunderstood.

But the clippings, so carefully cut from newspapers over the years. The obsessive collection of every miniscule crumb of information about a lifetime of murdered children. And the pictures – the awful pictures. They were certainly not the things one saw in the newspaper back then. Even now they'd black out the photos, but here they were, in all their glory. Dead children ripped and mutilated in the most horrific ways and his *friend* had them in a photo album alongside pictures of his family. People were funny, and they collected damn near anything from dryer lint sculptures to burnt toast that looked like the face of Christ, and Don knew that in spades, but this was downright creepy. It was not the man that Don thought he knew, not the grouchy old bastard that he shared a room with. Not the man that he'd cried to and shared his deepest secrets and fears with. This was not something his friend would do. And yet, here it was and now nothing in his world made sense. He stared out the window from his now private bedroom and watched the world go by without noticing him. The old man felt suddenly frail and very alone.

"Are you coming to dinner, Don?" the care worker said, breaking the spell.

"What?"

"Are you coming down to dinner?"

She was a larger woman, broad at the shoulders and hips. Not unattractive, but there was a harshness about her face and an annoyed quality to her disposition. When you were with her, Don always thought, she gave the impression that she'd rather be picking up fresh, steaming glops of horse shit than to be here with him.

"Oh, no. No thank-you, dear. I'm not feeling very hungry just now."

"Oh, but you need to eat, my friend. You need to keep your strength up, right?"

"Thanks for your concern, but I'm really not hungry," Don said again.

"But it'll be delicious," she said cheerfully. "I believe we're having steak tonight. And home fries and mushrooms. Who doesn't like that?"

"Steak?" Don said suspiciously.

He'd learnt in the time that he'd been here, that nothing was ever as it seemed. If they said bacon and eggs for breakfast, it was pre-cooked bacon and powdered eggs. Deli days at lunch meant packaged luncheon meat on wonder bread. The mere thought of having a steak again made his mouth water, but experience told him it would be anything *but* steak and fries.

"Steak?" he said.

"Yes," she said. "Delicious Salisbury steak."

"No, thank-you." He wrinkled his nose and turned back to the photo album.

It wasn't the answer she wanted, nor was it the one she was going to just accept and move on. She crossed the floor quickly and took hold of the book.

"Why don't we put away our picture book and come on down to the dining hall for something to eat and a little fellowship with our fellow residents? We don't want to stay in this room all by ourselves, do we?" she said. There was a firmness in her words that bordered on sinister.

The sickly condescension returning to her voice. "Would you like me to call Dave or one of the other orderlies to help you to the dining room?"

Don remembered Dave the orderly manhandling him back to his room earlier and couldn't imagine the rest of the white shirts being any gentler than he was. He jerked his arm away from her and stood up straight and proud.

"I can walk there on my own, thank you."

She grabbed hold of his arm and pulled him back down easily, close enough to whisper in his ear.

"You'll lose that fire, old man," she said.

"What?" Don gasped and tried to pull his arm back.

"You'll lose that fire and all that fight - and much sooner than you think," she said matter-of-factly. "Your brain is going to run down and, before you know it, all that piss and vinegar in your guts is going to flicker out and fade away like a dying tea light. Then... then you'll really know how things run around here, but you won't really know it, will you?"

A smug satisfaction crawled across her face in a viperous smile, and she tightened her grip on his arm, squeezing him painfully enough but finally releasing well before she left a mark.

"You just keep your goddam hands off me," Don said. "Or I'll call somebody and tell them just what the hell you're up to."

She sneered at the old man. "Who's gonna believe you?"

"What do you mean? Why wouldn't anyone believe me?"

"You think this is a hotel, Pops?"

"Of course not, but I don't see what that has to do with–"

"You have dementia." She spat. "Your brain is going soft. Why the hell do you think you wound up in here with the rest of this bunch?"

"What?" Don said. His attention completely turned to the chubby woman's words. "I don't have dementia. After my wife died, I moved here. I was having a little trouble taking care of everything on my own. Bills and grocery shopping and laundry and whatnot. I'm here because I was having trouble looking after myself, not because I was losing my mind."

"Your wife isn't dead, Don." The words fell carelessly from her lips, and she watched them linger and turn around in his head, waiting for them to go off like a live grenade.

"Of course, Jean is dead. I wouldn't be here otherwise. I'd be at home with her."

"Really Don? You sure about that? Because I'm pretty sure your wife put you I here. She put you in here because she was afraid of you."

"Nonsense. What are you playing at?"

"You attacked her, hurt her pretty bad, I hear. She was so scared, she locked herself in the bathroom and called the police."

"You're lying!"

"Am I? How was the funeral? What did you say in your eulogy? What type of flowers were on the casket? Was it open or closed?"

"That was a very long time ago, nearly ten years ago now. I don't remember any of those things."

"Really?" She smirked. "You'd think something like that, an event so huge as the death of your true love, might stick around a while. I know if I lost my one and only, I'd remember every... single... detail."

She stared into the old man's face and that awful, satisfied smile dragged its way across her face again.

"I remember the funeral. I remember the man at the funeral... the funeral person had an..."

"Yes? The funeral person had a what?"

Don suddenly felt tiny, frail, and helpless, and a darkness crept through his brain that, up till now, the disease had mercifully allowed him to forget. It grew until it blossomed into a memory he'd repressed, hidden away deep. Too awful to relive and too shameful to recall with anything but crystal clarity.

They were having dinner, he and Jean, at the kitchen table the way they had for most of their married life. It was quieter these days. The kids were both grown and gone and the level of conversation between them after 43 years of marriage had waned. There was no reason to ask how each other's day was, for they were both retired. Every day was the same as the last. The love between them hadn't changed, hadn't dissipated. They had simply run out of things to talk about as the windows of their experience moved closer to closing with the years moving on.

It was fish and chips - one of his favourites. It was out of a box and the sauce from the jar didn't have quite the zing of the place they used to frequent downtown when it was still open, but he appreciated her trying. He'd just picked up the last French fry off his plate and looked at her as he popped it into his mouth, leaving a blob of ketchup on the corner of his mouth. She smiled at him, but it faded quickly. There was fear in her eyes, the terror of a wounded animal who'd just backed itself into a corner and now was desperate and prepared to do anything to get loose. But she couldn't.

The onset of the disease had been slow, insidious, and meticulous, like a rat in his brain. Gnawing little bits away and disappearing before anyone noticed the damage done until there was no repairing it. He would forget little things mostly, like how to put socks on both of his feet instead of both on one foot, and how to brush his teeth, but it would always come back to him.

He would wander throughout the night, as though he were sleepwalking, and he would end up in the front yard or the garage with no memory of how he got there. When she mentioned it to him, told him how worried she was that one day he might stroll onto a busy street and get killed in traffic, he laughed it off as just a spell of insomnia, one symptom the doctor explained to them were completely normal in the disease's progress. When she suggested putting locks on the inside of the house, just as a precaution to keep him safe, he wouldn't hear of it. Telling her he would not be a prisoner in his own house. But all these things, even as scary as the wandering could be, were manageable.

Don saw things, mild hallucinations being another in the ever-growing list of symptoms that came along with his diagnosis. He'd have in-depth conversations with people that weren't there that would often fall into arguments. Jean could never be certain if the hallucination had ended or if Don was too angry with the person, real or not, to continue speaking to them. He fed pigeons and squirrels that nobody could see but him, with birdseed that just appeared in his pockets. It seemed to make him happy, and didn't cause any harm, so she did not try to dissuade him from doing it. But it changed, and the world soured for him.

He became withdrawn and paranoid, whispering about the people hiding in the shadows, spying on him, threatening to take her away from him. He had visions of awful things, monstrous things lurking around corners, waiting to tear him apart and feast on the marrow of his bones. His wife would offer him wine with his dinner most nights, nights where he had trouble seeing what was real and not. Wine, he was fairly certain, with something in it to make him sleep. Nights like tonight.

"Would you like another piece of fish, dear?" she said cautiously. "How about some wine with dinner? I have a nice bottle of white that would go well with the fish."

The silence that came back was a warning that he was already too far gone for wine and sleeping pills.

The words rolled around in Don's head, echoing and losing all sense and reason until they became little more than the low, guttural noises of some awful thing intending to do him harm and he'd be damned if he was just going to sit there and let it happen.

"No, you don't!" he screamed.

He shot up from the table and, in doing so, the back of his leg caught the seat of his chair and sent it flying. The noise startled him and plunged him deeper into the nightmare that was consuming him.

"No, no, no you don't!"

The thing at the table stood with its back to him and began making angry noises at him. Appalling, low rumbling noises belched out in a staccato rhythm that soon became an incessant hum of a thousand angry yellow jackets heading toward him.

Where is Jean?

It turned toward him now, and he could see it in all its obscene glory. The skin was grey and waxy, like the skin of a corpse sloughed off in huge chunks, revealing the withered lifeless musculature beneath it. Its head was large and cumbersome, with bony protrusions erupting from the left side of it sitting atop a neck that seemed entirely too slim and wiry to support the weight of the huge, misshapen thing. Monstrous arms, long and wiry, the fingertips reaching well below its knees and, from where it stood now, could easily reach Don without having to move toward him. The thing's body was wan and emaciated, as though it had known nothing but cruel, never-ending hunger. Rotted, moribund flesh hung off its belly like pendulous bunting streamers. Its legs were equally thin and impossibly long, and yet it seemed no taller than a person.

Where is Jean?

Panic gripped him now, and he searched the room, desperately looking for a way out, away from this thing, before it moved on him. Nothing seemed familiar. It was all dark and twisted and terribly wrong. This was not his kitchen, not his home. This was something else - somewhere else, and all he wanted right now was to get out of it. He took a step backward, and the thing moved forward to grab him.

"Wagabo!" it said in its impossibly low voice, and he felt the room shake.

"No!" he screamed and took another step back.

"Wagabo!"

"Jean!" he called. "Jean! What have you done with her, you sonofabitch?"

Fear ripped through him like a lightning bolt and ignited a fire in him. Fear smoldered and smoked to anger and burst into the flame of rage.

"Jean!" he called and grabbed the first thing his hand met – his dinner plate – and hurled it toward the grey corpse thing in front of him.

It struck the grey obscenity in the middle of its head, and it let go a shrieking howl but continued moving toward him.

"Zoan, wagabo," it breathed in its hideous language and reached its spindly arms toward him.

He snatched a butter knife off the table and brandished at the thing who slunk away, never taking its eyes off of him. Don heard a door close and presumed that, for the moment anyway, he was safe from the awful thing. And now, all that remained was to get out of this place and away from it. He saw nothing he recognized, no familiar things to point the way. He fumbled forward, into another, larger room and saw several large, filth covered benches. As the surge of the adrenalin wore off, exhaustion gripped him, and he thought, *if I just sit for a minute, just rest, I'll think a little more clearly and get out of here.* He took a seat, surprised to find it was considerably more comfortable than it looked.

He fought valiantly to stay awake and upright, but he was so tired, and the bench was so comfortable. His eyelids felt leaded and slid further over his eyes with every blink. The old man thought of slapping himself, maybe getting up for a brisk trot around the room to get his blood flowing, but the eyes won out and closed. Don drifted off and was snoring happily in no time. The handcuffs were being snapped around his wrists when he woke up.

"What the hell?" he shouted, still barely awake.

The cop stood him up roughly and spun him around to get his hands behind his back and clapped the other manacle on him.

"They're tight. They're so tight!" Don said.

"Don't hurt him! You said you wouldn't hurt him!" Jean said.

"Jean, what's going on? Why are they taking me out of here?"

"I'm sorry Don, so, so sorry. Just go with them, please? Just go with them for me," she said, trying to choke back the sobs.

The cop practically dragged Don out of the house and led him to a waiting ambulance, where a dour looking woman sat inside, waiting for him. She produced a large needle and jammed it into his backside before helping the cop to get the old man to lie on a gurney.

"It won't take too long," she said, and tightened straps around both of his ankles. "Can you sit up for me, sir?"

Don found himself unable to resist her commands. He tried, and his brain even made a note of the refusal, but he dutifully sat up.

"You can take those now. He'll be asleep shortly."

He felt the cop take the handcuffs off of him to his great relief and, without further prompt, he lay back on the gurney. The lady in the ambulance tightened straps around both of his wrists now and spoke gently to him.

"I won't put the big strap across your chest if I don't have to, so no trouble from here on out, okay?"

He was no longer capable of answering her. The shot had rendered him liquid. At least it felt that way, and he was presently melting into the mattress of this very comfortable bed in the back of a truck. When he came out of it, he was calm and was no longer in the ambulance. He was in a room with another man laying down on another bed.

"Hey," Don called out.

"Hey yourself," the man said.

"Where am I?"

"Winterbourne Home for the Elderly, or as we here like to call it, the tenth circle of Hell. This place is so shitty, even Dante was afraid to write about it."

He sat up and looked out the window. The lawn was manicured and there were others, his age and older, walking around freely. The one thing there wasn't was Jean. And he meant to remedy that.

"I don't care where it is or what it is, I'm not staying here. I promise you that."

"Ah, a fighter," the man in the other bed said. "You'll lose that fight."

Don gasped. "What did you say?"

"You'll lose that fight," the woman said again. "And sooner than you think. Do you need help to the dining room?"

"No," Don said, his voice barely above a whisper.

He plodded into the dining hall and took his place at the table where he'd eaten every meal for the last five years. The chaos of the dining room rang out and thundered in his ears, the madness and confusion and the people he shared space with, who were all so desperately lost in their own worlds. He lowered his head, looking for all intents like he was saying grace before his meal, and he felt a tear roll down his cheek. And in that moment, Donald Pierce knew that, before long, he would be every bit as lost as these people were. He vowed he would not lose his mind in this place. He thought about Danny suddenly, and an idea took root in his head.

21

———————

Guthrie put the car into drive and eased away from Danny's house.

"Where to?" he said to the younger man.

Kemmler remained silent for an uncomfortable length of time before finally speaking.

"I've just remembered there is something very important I need to do, and it is time critical. We can discuss the case further in the morning. When we both have fresh eyes and clear heads. If you could just drop me off."

"Oh," Guthrie said, confusion and a touch of hurt ringing through his words. "Sure, where are you staying?"

"I'm at the Moonwinks Motor Court on Belmont Avenue, out by the highway."

"Oh, the Onwin, yeah I know it," Guthrie said.

The Moonwinks Motor Court, like most of old Winterbourne, had seen its prime come and go and now was nothing more than a monument to the stubbornness of an old town. Layers of paint on the outside of the building, once a deep ocean blue, flecked with white to look like all the stars in a galaxy of promise, was now cracked and faded grey and peeling off in huge strips like chunks of blanched skin sloughing off a necrotic wound. The building was like a tic, dug in deep and refusing to die to make way for the future – Motel 6 or Howard Johnson's with clean sheets and working telephones. The neon sign out front of the place, once a beacon of hope and respite for miles around on even the darkest of nights, was now a shadow of its former glory – only the bottom portion of the winking crescent moon remained lit with enough letters to spell out *ON WIN*. It had gone from a port in a storm for families and weary travellers to a no tell motel for transient hookers and the truck drivers who paid for them.

The rooms themselves reeked of ancient cigarette smoke that practically hung from the walls like cheap art. A pair of twin beds, stained brown by a decade's worth of hourly rates and wholesale love, sat beside each other against the room's far wall. Ancient, well-worn carpets that were a chicken flavoured Rice-a-Roni coloured shag that hadn't seen the working end of a vacuum in years. Floyd had enjoyed the hospitality of the Moonwinks for several weeks after the wife kicked him out and still had a nausea inducing aversion to instant rice because of it. The place was a shithole and the whole town knew it but, for the duration of the building of the new, luxurious Ramada in up near Grandview Heights, it was the only game in town.

"Herb didn't put you in room 12, did he?" Guthrie said, and a sly smile played at the corner of his mouth.

"No," Kemmler said. "Why?"

"A homeless guy broke into 12 in the middle of the night about a year ago. He was quiet and came and went at nighttime. Nobody even knew he was in there. At some point, near as anybody can figure, he had a heart attack and died. It was three weeks before anybody found him. They still can't get the smell out of that room."

"Fascinating," Kemmler said flatly. "I can't imagine anything smelling any worse than the rooms already do."

"Herb likes to put people in there he doesn't know, tells them it's haunted."

"What a charming and jocular little community you all have here.

Perhaps when this case is all sewn up, I may move myself and take up permanent residence. Tell me this, when he tells the people about the haunted room, and they flee from the smell, does he refund their money? I'll just bet ol' Herb forgets all about the cash he's taken off hard-working folk and I'm fairly certain that's still a crime in this world or the next."

Guthrie remained silent as the indignation of this upstart from upstate burning across his face. The motel's sign loomed on the dashboard and Guthrie pulled into the parking lot and wheeled up to the office door. He threw it into park just as Kemmler swung the passenger door open. He eased himself out of the seat and turned to the older cop.

"I'll know more about this case later, tomorrow perhaps."

"Should I come back in a bit to talk more about the case?" Guthrie said.

He was a little shocked by the words leaving his own mouth, he already had a dislike for this man, nearly hated him and here he was asking to come back and talk about the case with him, like a child begging to play baseball with his older brother. He was nearly ashamed of having said anything to the man.

"What?" Kemmler sputtered. "Oh no, don't come back. Something is about to happen – about to change. I can practically smell it on the wind. If I'm right, and I'm certain I am, I will have this case closed in a day or two."

"Right, you are then," Floyd said dismissively. "So... I guess we'll catch up later, then?"

"I would suggest, detective, that you go through your files regarding this case. Perhaps a little more closely, to be certain you haven't missed anything. The smallest detail could make all the difference in the time it takes to solve this case."

Guthrie knew he'd examined every inch of the box that lived on his kitchen table. Every photo, every crumb and scrap of information. He'd seen it all backward and forward time and time again. He could practically recite the reports from memory. His immediate instinct was to tell this young apple polisher from the big city to go fuck

himself but, much to his own surprise, found himself a little hesitant
to do so.

"What will you do?" he said.

Kemmler remained silent and turned toward the concrete stairs
that led to the upper deck of the motel and his room, slamming the
door shut as he went.

"Right-o." Guthrie put the car into drive.

He pulled the car out of the motel parking lot and sat waiting for
traffic before turning down Belmont Avenue. He checked the rear-
view mirror and could see the young detective climbing the stairs to
his room, secretly hoping he would trip and bash his skull in. Or, at
the very least, scrape the shit out of his shins.

"Asshole," Floyd said and pulled out.

BUT KEMMLER DIDN'T TRIP. Instead, he hurried up the stairs and
produced a key attached to a large, plastic fob emblazoned with the
likeness of the winking crescent moon from the motel's sign.
Unencumbered by the bonds of failing electricity, it winked at him in
all its glory. Though, owing to the years of handling by horny
truckers, its letters were worn off, spelling out *Onwin*. The fob still
read number 12, and he opened the door to his room. Kemmler
swung the door open, slowly, knowing that the motion of the door
and the mixing of the outdoor air would churn up a cocktail of odour
that offended his senses more than anything he'd ever smelled.
Charnel house, livestock rendering plant at mid-day in August, paled
compared to the stench that leapt from inside and met him like an
angry landlord looking for rent.

When he felt a decent amount of time had passed between initial
smelling and his getting used to the pungent doorway, he stepped
into the room and closed the door behind him. The sun was
beginning its slow descent to the horizon, and he thought for the
moment he might open the curtains and enjoy the light provided in
the remains of the day but thought that stopping at any point before

he was ready to, was an interruption he wasn't interested in entertaining. He clicked on the lamp above his bed.

Kemmler flipped the strap on the black leather Gladstone bag and dug through its contents until he found what he was looking for. He removed a book – old and worn and looking much too large to fit in the bag it came out of. Next was a sheet of paper filled with names, most of which had a single stroke of pen through them. Apart from that, the paper was unremarkable – a little wrinkled, perhaps complete with a coterie of circles in the margins, the result of unreliable pens. It was a large, leather-bound thing. Perhaps ten inches across and fifteen inches long, the size of an accountant's ledger, but nearly triple the number of pages in such a volume. It was old and well handled and smelled of many years and just as many hands. Written across the front of it, in fading, embossed letters, were the words, The Illustrious rituals, and the Chosen Masters of the Sacred Knights of St. Hubertus.

He leafed through the pages and saw it contained page after page of quasi-religious observances that seemed harmless enough. It reminded him of a handbook his father had from the local mason's lodge. Spooky sounding nonsense words mixed with a handful of Latin phrases that likely meant nothing but whipped the fear of God himself into the untrained ear. The next pages were more of a scrapbook and contained a single group photo of all the members of good standing since the club's inception. In the summer of 1912, according to the first photo.

From what he could tell, they had been a fraternal order since near the beginning of the century and now, nearly 85 years later, it looked like it still existed. The last group photo in the book was from three years ago and the last written entry was from six months ago. That was fine. The Masons, the Elks, and even the Odd Fellows, had been around for longer than Kemmler could remember and were no more dangerous than the accountant's and used tire salesmen that made up their ranks. But they came and went, and their children and neighbour's children refilled their ranks, year after year. These photos, dating from1912, all the way too many of this year, seemed to contain the same people. Image after image all the same people in the same positions and same poses, photo after photo. Aging - yes, as the photos went on but, at such a decelerated rate, as to defy logic. They had gotten older, all of them, but given their apparent age in the original photos to the photos of later years, the majority should have been in wheelchairs and walkers and those that weren't should have been long dead.

There was another peculiarity that Kemmler picked up on. In 85 years, there had only been ten leaders of the organization. If one were to assume that the leader, such as other fraternal organizations, was one of the senior most members, it stood to reason that there should have been more of them. Age alone should have weeded out the old to make way for the new. Popularity, perhaps? Elected to the position at an unheard of tender age to the welcome and praise of all the other members? Not bloody likely. There was something else entirely and Kemmler was certain he knew what it was. He flipped anxiously through the pages of the enormous book, hurrying past the photos and turning pages until he'd nearly reached the end.

He wasn't certain what he was looking for, not really, but he knew when he found it, there would be no doubt as to its importance. And then he saw it. Beginning with the photograph labelled *Summer, 1947*, a name appeared in every photo, right up to the one of three months ago. Along with the name was the image of its owner. A nearly inconspicuous man and the only member of the group that seemed to age with any normalcy. He looked smaller than the others and stood far enough away from the main group it looked as though he didn't really belong with them – let into the photo by some, perceived sense of obligation like being forced to take your little brother along to a pickup football game with your friends from school. Beneath the image, at the end of the list of names of the members in the photograph, was the name of the small, inconvenient man. All the photos from 1947 onward bore identical labels, Save for the last one. At the bottom of the last photo, on the last page of the old book, was hand written *Bob Mifflin, Winterbourne Home.* Kemmler closed the book, and a corrupt smile snaked its way across his face.

22

Floyd aimed the rusty Ford down Gibson Street and pulled away slowly, the anger and embarrassment still burning across his face.

"Little prick," he said to the empty car. "You might be clever. You might even be as brilliant as everybody seems to think you are, but none of that shit matters when you act like a fucking jerk."

He sighed and rolled down the window, hoping a little fresh air across his face might alter his mood somewhat and put his brain back in the direction it sorely needed to be. There were still a bunch of dead kids and nobody, least of all him, seemed to be any closer to finding out who was ripping them up. It had seemed, mercifully that at least there were no more and the group of them were patiently waiting for him to come up with a solution to give them some measure of a peaceful eternity. That all changed with Danny and his God-damned dog finding the Anglin kid. And now, here he was - embarrassed, pissed off, and on the verge of being shown up by a greasy-haired kid from upstate who thought the sun shone out of his ass. Not the best headspace to be in to solve anything, let alone the worst thing that had ever happened in this jerkwater town.

He stuck his head out the window and let the warm summer air blow over him like a dog would. He felt the anger waning and the embarrassment ease and soon it bubbled into laughter at his own stubbornness and stupidity at having the younger man get under his skin. Guthrie figured he would also need a dollop of lubrication to get his brain just about where it needed to be. Relaxed enough to see things that weren't necessarily obvious, but still sharp enough to weed the truth from the spurious chaff, but not relaxed enough to lose sight of the facts and see clues where there were none. It was a microscopic line, and he crossed it often. He was brilliant at the best of times and frighteningly so when he got the ratio of booze and time alone to clues just right. But it would not crack this case of dead kids no matter how drunk or sober or whatever combination of the two he arrived at.

Guthrie toyed with the idea of returning to Butler's for a couple, but his last visit had ended in a man's hospitalization. Though it wasn't remotely his fault, he felt the memory of the incident would still be pretty fresh in the minds of the people on the stools and booths inside the dank, smoky bar. Not to mention that a couple at Butler's had the likelihood of becoming a couple more until it was a couple too many and he was driving blackout drunk and not coming anywhere close to giving peace to the ghosts of five mutilated kids. He opted for the liquor store and the package store next to it for a frozen dinner and a Mars bar for dessert.

"Hey Floyd," the man behind the counter said as he walked through the door of Beckett's liquor mart.

"Hey Sam."

Floyd browsed the shelves absently, looking without actually seeing until he arrived at the shelf he nearly always arrived at. It was whisky he was after, and it was the only thing he'd leave with. Once, a very long time ago, he experimented and left with a bottle of gin. It tasted like perfume and furniture polish, and he decided it was not the drink for him. Vodka made its way into his cart twice, but the lighter fluid flavour and that, regardless of the amount he drank, the fact he almost never woke up with a headache, made him put it back on the shelf. If you're going to drink to get drunk, the blinding headache the next day was proof of a job well done.

He'd also bought a bottle of tequila on a spur-of-the-moment whim, and it was good. Like whisky, there was a bite to it and a warmth that travelled down his throat and burst like a roman candle. As he stood, the full force of the bottle hit him. He was drunk, nearly blackout drunk. Floyd pinballed off the walls on his way to the bathroom, and though he didn't vomit, he wished he would have. He missed the toilet by several feet and slipped in the resulting urine on the floor, cracking his head on the sink. By some miracle, he made it into his bedroom after getting to his feet slowly. In the morning, he awoke in a large, conspicuous puddle of vomit and an even larger circle of soaked in urine. Guthrie burned the sheets and the mattress in his backyard in short order and swore he would never look at the rotten stuff again. Just the sight of the bottle was enough to make the back of his mouth tingle and all the moisture in it run away screaming.

But whisky was his friend - at least to a point. It was a very thin line between enhanced thoughts and synapses firing on all six and raving like a loon about God's toenails and why you just can't get a decent woman anymore, to anyone who got within earshot of you. And he leapt at it frequently. Despite that, the liquor tended to get the gears moving more fluidly and took his brain to places his rational, sober mind often wouldn't go. He grabbed the bottle of White Horse and headed for the counter.

"Shame about all those kids," Sam said casually. "Wasn't another one of them just killed the other day?"

"Yeah," Floyd said dismissively, hoping to avoid any conversation with the man, let alone one about his inability to solve this case.

"And now you coppers just found another one, is that right?"

"Yeah, that's right," Floyd said, doing little to hide his contempt.

"And hadn't you *just* stepped-up patrols and put more cops on the beat in more neighbourhoods?"

"Yes," Guthrie said, the annoyance rising in his voice like bile biting at the back of his throat. "Just what are you getting at, Sam?"

"Well, just that it sure seems like all you coppers are running around, all over the goddam town. Making everyday folks all uptight. It's an awful goddam thing."

"And?"

"And still another kid goes and gets himself killed."

"Yes, I know but–"

"You'd think with these extra coppers running around all over, keeping us safe from all the bad of this world, and each other, of course." He chuckled. "A body might think he'd be safe anywhere in this town."

Guthrie plunked the bottle on the counter. Not hard enough to risk damaging it and ruing the contents, but hard enough that the man behind the counter got the intention of his slamming it.

"Twenty-seven-fifty," Sam said.

Floyd dug through his pockets and wallet both, fumbling and counting until he had arrived at the exact amount in a combination of bills and coins and dumped it, unceremoniously, on the counter.

"You know, with all the armchair detectives in this town, you'd think we wouldn't need a fucking police force," he said and snatched the bottle from the counter.

Floyd got into his car and headed back home, grumbling to himself about know-it-all liquor salesmen the whole way there.

Why were people so opinionated and, in the same vein, completely fucking clueless about the things they believed the most strongly? He didn't need to search for an answer.

If being on the force, dealing with the public all these years had taught him anything, it was this. People, everyday people, the bungled, and the botched from every walk of life, *all* feel they have the proper answers. To everything. Ever. Until it comes down to actually coming down to mucking in with people you've never met and attempting to accomplish something good for everyone, then nobody can be arsed. He opened the front door and stepped cautiously inside. He didn't expect anything to happen to him as he walked in through the front door, but the possibility of his ex-wife swooping in and demanding something outrageous from him, like money or his car or his soul, was still a legitimate concern.

A cursory examination of the apartment's main room told him he was alone - as he was every night since his wife had thrown him out of the house. He headed for the kitchen, opening the only cupboard that still had a properly functioning door, and removed the cleanest dirty glass that was housed within it. Floyd gave a stout twist, spun the cap off the bottle of White Horse, and poured himself a generous serving of the amber hooch. The ripper file lay on the kitchen table, where it always was. It was always waiting for him. Waiting to be picked up and flipped through its folds and photos. Judging him, mocking him for his failure to get any farther in solving it than he had. It had yielded nothing new for him in years, literally, but he reached for it out of habit and flipped the damned thing open.

There was no immediate unifying fact in the images beyond the obvious. They were photographs of dead children spanning seventy plus years. The victims had all been killed in similar manners and, most involved in the case, past and present, felt it was the work of the same hand. Floyd knew it was unlikely that a serial killer could remain active for nearly three quarters of a century, but there was no evidence to suggest otherwise. He took a large brass magnifying glass from out of the box and sat down at the kitchen table, poring slowly over the ghastly images. This was not the first time he'd found himself with a headful of liquor and the pictures laid out in front of him, always hoping his eyes might glean some new tidbit of information that his heart told him was never there.

"This is the same shit it ever was. It's the same shit it was yesterday, and it's the same shit it was the day before. It'll be the same shit tomorrow and the day after that and five fucking years from now. Same as it ever was, same as it ever was, same as it ever was," he said in a half laugh when he thought of the Talking Heads song he mocked. "Letting the days go by," he sang. "The goddamn days are going by all right. Fuck it."

Floyd tossed the file in the table's direction and missed it entirely, scattering the contents of the file folder around the legs. He stood and poured himself another stiff whisky, leaving the bottle just shy of halfway full, and headed toward the bathroom. He figured a hot shower would clear his head and, after a mouthful or two of whatever he could scrounge to eat in the rat's nest he currently occupied, he might see the photos with a fresher head and a more discerning set of eyes. But he had his doubts about the whole goddamned mess would yield anything but the same questions and disappointing results they always had.

He walked by the mess of papers and photos, casually, purposefully, trying to send out a signal to the heap that he didn't care if it ever let go of another clue to him or not. His life would go on. He could sleep with a clear conscience, despite the mutilated bodies of seven dead children. Their pallid eyes staring, accusing him of failing them with nothing more than the desire for clean skin and a clearer head. He wanted to turn his head away, stop seeing them. Even the bleached white backs of the photos brought no relief. Floyd knew what was on the other sides of them, having seen, studied and examined every inch of them for longer than he could remember. He stopped, against his better judgement, and looked at the pile of photos and papers and something suddenly struck him as odd. It wasn't something he could explain, but something was wrong with the lot.

What he saw wasn't new. He'd noticed it a long time ago, maybe even the first time he'd looked at the photos, but something struck him now in a way it had never done before. There were words written on the back bottom of all the photos, handwritten, but Guthrie had always given it a passing glance and moved on, thinking it was the information for the photographer to drum up business. If members of the police force might employ someone who spent the vast majority of the professional life photographing things that would make the hardiest of constitutions puke and run screaming. He picked up two of the photos and then another and another until he's taken them all off the floor. He laid them out on the kitchen table from first victim to last, but with the backs of the photos facing him. They all read the same; *Robert Miflin, Winterbourne.*

All identical. Until the last one. It read *Robert Miflin, Winterbourne Home.*

"Sonofabitch," Guthrie said and emptied the glass of whisky he'd been carrying on his way to the shower.

All these years, he assumed the name was the photographer. Guthrie never thought for a second it could be an addendum to the photograph. Maybe even the name of the killer himself. Whoever had written the name had paid enough attention to the man to know he ended up in the town's only nursing home. That meant something. It meant Guthrie could drink a bit more and go to bed with a hare less guilt eating away at him, because it was something. The minutest of leads was what it was. But it *was* a lead. He would go talk to the old boy in the morning and maybe even catch a killer. If nothing else, he was a living witness to the worst series of crimes the town had ever seen, and he would surely have something in his head to shake an answer loose. If he was lucky, anyway.

23

———————

"**I**'ll apologize for my apartment now. It came with the job, and I don't have company in the normal run of things," Hughie said nervously.

"Oh, I've lived in my fair share of awful places," Michael said. "Some of them were practically holes in the ground.

They climbed the wrought iron staircase that seemed completely out of place on the front of a building, as though it had been a fire escape on the back of some other building and attached to the front of this when no one was looking. Hughie led the way to the door and felt a ball of nervous energy wad itself up in his stomach and wriggle like a dying carp. It wasn't pleasant. But, considering the cause was standing behind him, looking at him with perfect eyes and smiling at him, showing straight, perfect teeth, the principal of Winterbourne High would put up with a river of bile sloshing through his guts if it meant Michael might chew at his ears a little more. In truth, Hughie was hoping the handsome stranger would rip his clothes off and fuck him senseless, but would be happy with a cuddle and a peck on the cheek if it came right down to it.

Not that he ever did. Tidiness was so engrained in Hughie's personality, it caused him to pick up stray bits of paper off the street whenever he saw them, for fear of the street sweepers missing them and leaving a mess in front of his building. Still, he worried about the potential for a mess as the two of them hit the top of the stairs and he fumbled for the keys to open the front door. He was already nearly hard, and he could feel it through his pocket. Hughie lingered for a minute, looking right into the face of the dark-haired man as he finally pulled the keys from his pants pocket. Moving a little closer to Dietrich, fully intending to make another self-deprecating remark, but the other man was already to him, practically on top of him. Without warning, Michael kissed Hughie. Hard. Pushed him against the door. The principal of Winterbourne High, the man who had the power to strike terror in the hearts of junior class men year after year, trembled and, for reasons that escaped him, pulled away from the other man.

"What?" Dietrich whispered through soft kisses along the side of Hughie's neck.

"I haven't–"

"You haven't what?" Michael said.

"I haven't been with anyone else in a very long time and I'm not sure that I–"

"I haven't either. We'll figure it out," he said and nipped at Hughie's ear. "Or we'll just keeping going until we do."

Hughie raised a hand behind his back and turned the handle of the door. The two of them nearly fell inside the doorway, though it didn't break their embrace or dissuade either of them from trying to suck out the other's tonsils out through the mouth. After a cursory glance around the apartment, he pulled away from Michael and moved toward the kitchenette.

"Would you like something to–"

Hughie Koch felt the other man press against him in a withering display of speed, and cut him off mid-sentence, pressing his lips against his. The principal, still a little taken aback by the unfamiliarity of the other man's forwardness, found he was backing away from him again. This served to inflame Michael even more, and he pressed harder into Hughie, moving him backward until they hit the solid top of the counter, and then Dietrich bent him nearly backward over it. The darker haired man put his mouth on the back of Hughie's neck and sunk his teeth in. Not deeply, nor with a harshness that might push the principal away from the counter, but neither was it soft. It was not the playful nips on his ears moments before that made his pulse quicken and the sweat of impassioned expectation gather near the small of his back. There was no mistaking this was every inch the bite he meant it to be. And it drove him over the edge of a cliff he would have leaped off on his own, had the dark-haired stranger not begun slowly lowering him over it.

Hughie's hand moved to his pants and fumbled with the belt, instinctively getting ready to please himself. The other man took the hand and placed it on his own crotch. Their eyes met. His eyes were so hazel, they were nearly yellow and, in the waning sunlight streaming through the filthy lace curtains that covered the kitchen window, they nearly looked like they were glowing. There was something in those eyes Hughie had never seen. It was wild and wanton and corporeal. And it was dangerous. He raised his hand and fumbled with the buttons of his shirt, wanting his skin to be closer to the man. Michael pushed the clumsy hand aside and, in one firm jerk, ripped the grey button down open to the waist. Hughie let out a moan that started at the top of his head and shuddered through him like a fever chill and the other man moved in again.

Michael continued the barrage of soft kisses with enough teeth to keep Hughie's attention along his chest. He glanced around the apartment and saw the battered and worn chesterfield ten feet from where they lay. Koch's hands groped upward again and removed the other man's shirt entirely before leading him to the couch. He followed, silent and willing, and allowed himself to be pushed onto the sofa. The high school principal slithered on top of him, grinding his hips slowly into the other man's crotch until they'd established a kind of rhythm that matched the breaths they were both gasping at. Dietrich moved then to his side slightly and pushed Hughie off, who looked at the dark-haired stranger with a mix of shock and anger at his having stopped. Michael's hand moved to Hughie's waistband,

and penetrated downward, feeling his hardness, and rubbed it slowly, back and forth. Hughie moaned softly and let the other man guide his hand to an open waistband.

They stopped for the moment and a look of uncertainty flushed across the principal's face. It faded quickly as the dark-haired man eased downward to the opening in his trousers.

"Oh!" Hughie moaned. "Oh God, ugnh." And he knew it was about to happen.

Hughie thought Dietrich must have been able to sense his impending climax and grabbed hold of the stiffness at the base, squeezing and then, ever so gently, running his teeth along the head. And that was all it took. Hughie drained into the other man's mouth, pulse after shuddering pulse until there was no more and it left him shivering and breathless. He smiled and slide up to Michael, kissing at the back of his neck and reaching for the fly of his pants.

Dietrich grabbed his hand. "Why don't you make us a drink and we could talk for a bit?"

"Oh," Hughie said, confused by the other man's sudden shyness. "Uh, sure. A drink, yes. I can get us a drink."

Hughie Koch pulled up his pants and disappeared into the kitchen. The room was slightly to the left of the living room, around a load-bearing wall that jutted up in the middle of the room for no other reason than holding up a portion of the room above it. It was lacklustre on a good day, which today was not, and was clearly the most awful place in this awful little apartment. It had a fridge and a stove, both of which worked though the actual putting of food to heat to produce an edible result, was a touch out of his skill set, so he couldn't say for certain if one could cook on it. The fridge, however, did a bang-up job of keeping his leftovers from the Aztec at a constant 40 degrees until they mouldered and mutated and patiently moved their way up the food chain.

"I've got some fairly recent white wine or a decent single malt if you'd like something stronger," Hughie said.

"Let's start with the wine and see where we go from there," Michael said.

Hughie opened the fridge and removed the nearly full bottle of wine. It suddenly dawned on him that a second glass, one that didn't look as though it had spent a part of its life as a vessel for jelly, might be an issue.

"Tell me about yourself," he said as he searched the cupboards for a decent enough glass. "Where do you come from originally?"

"Oh, you don't want to hear that," Michael said. "It's boring. Small-town boy and all that. Besides, I'd much rather talk about you. How did you wind up here?"

"I was guilty of poor taste and fell for the wrong guy. He had powerful friends, and I didn't. One day I was looking at a secure university professorship, the next, somebody offered me the principal's job here. Since nobody was beating down the door to hire me, I took what I could get. I suspect if they ever found out about my lifestyle, they'd tar and feather me. But since, until recently, I seemed to be the only gay man in Winterbourne, I think my secret is fairly safe.

"Well," Michael said. "We all have our secrets, don't we?"

"Oh? Aha!" Hughie's hands found the champagne flute before he saw it. It wasn't a white wine glass per se, but it looked a sight better than a water glass and much less alcoholicky than a jelly jar. "What secrets have you got? You look as though you've never hidden anything in your life."

He poured them each a generous portion and downed most of his own before refilling it and heading out of the kitchen.

Snack, he thought. There was nothing like a nosh after an orgasm that felt like it might blow the top of your head off. Hughie turned back around, set the drinks on the kitchen counter and opened the fridge, praying he had something in it that still resembled food. It chuffed him to see two granny smith apples and a block of well aged cheddar. He cut them up quickly and put them and a handful of soda crackers on a plate.

"You'd be surprised," Michael said from the living room.

"Really? What's the worst thing you've ever done?"

He rounded the load-bearing wall and made it a few steps into the living room. The plate of food smashed to the floor, followed by the wine glasses, sloshing their contents everywhere before exploding into two snowballing piles of razor-sharp shards of broken glass and jagged dust. Michael stood alone in the living room, only it wasn't Michael. It was tall - impossibly tall and were it not for the naturally high ceilings of the apartment, would have had to stoop to fit in the room. It resembled a man, crossed with something awful and hairy and beastly. A dog perhaps, or a wolf, but with much longer, thicker hair. Black as the choking soot at the gates of Hell and long and coarse like the shag that hung from the arms of an orangutan. The thing's face was canine, yes, but kept enough of its original human characteristics that it reminded Hughie of something from an H. G. Wells book. He might have laughed at the comparison were he not terrified enough to piss himself.

"I am cursed for the worst thing I have ever done," the Michael thing said.

"O... oh? What did you do?" Hughie said, doing his best to stop himself from screaming and locking himself in the bathroom.

"I killed a child. I killed a child and then I devoured its entrails," it said through vicious, yellowed fangs.

"Ah... well... I'm certain you must have had good reason to-"

"That's not the worst of it,"

"Really?" Hughie said, surprised at the sudden indignant tone in his voice. "What could be worse than killing a child?"

The thing crossed the room in a single step and stood nose to nose with the now trembling man and ran a long, jagged clawed finger across Hughie's face, gliding it slowly across his lips. He suddenly thought back to the heat and passion they'd shared only a short time ago. He looked into the enormous amber eyes and the animal thing flexed its finger, increasing the pressure and drawing blood from the frightened man's upper lip.

"Killing you," it said.

24

———————

It was big. Massive, by any measure, and was the biggest animal Raisin had ever seen. If he were to say it was a dog, it wouldn't be entirely accurate, though it seemed to share many features with a canine. Its face differed from a dog's, rounder, somehow less angular and elongated. If they forced him to answer, he would have said it was some awful mash-up of a wolf and an ape. Maybe it was bigfoot. But it looked too doggy to be anything like the pictures of bigfoot he'd seen in books in the library. For one, it walked on all fours but looked more like a man imitating the movements of a dog, rather than an actual four-legged creature. Despite the awkward appearance of its movement, it conveyed itself with confidence and strength.

The dog ape let out a growl, low and atavistic that rumbled through her like a thunderclap through an open window. Its eyes narrowed, and it lowered its head. It pushed back on its hind legs, like it was coiling a spring, readying itself to strike.

"Don't move, Raisin," Danny whispered.

She'd forgotten she was there and started a little at him, making herself known.

"Shh," he whispered, never taking his eyes off the thing blocking their path.

It growled again and coiled its legs even tighter. Raisin breathed an audible gasp. It turned from Danny and locked its amber eyes on her. Fear shredded through her, and it wasn't long before a warm liquid ran down her leg. Raisin screamed and turned sharply, darting to get away from the thing. It moved quickly, closing the distance between them in a single bounding step. Raisin could feel its breath on the back of her shoulders as the thing opened its mouth and moved in closer. It stopped, she assumed, for as close as it felt a moment before. She couldn't sense it near her any longer. The girl stopped and turned and saw that it looked as though it were pushing back on itself, and she knew there'd be no outrunning it now. But she tried. She took off at a run, a sprint that she knew she couldn't continue for long.

She stopped and turned. Hoping to see it giving up and turning toward Danny again. She didn't wish him any harm, so much as she thought that if the thing chased him, he had a much greater chance of outrunning it than she did, having done nothing athletic that wasn't mandated or otherwise forced on her. But it didn't turn to the boy. It continued its course, bearing down on her. She closed her eyes out as the fear took her mind. The world went suddenly silent but for the thunderous beating of her heart. Her brain screamed to move, her heartbeat fast enough, hard enough that she felt dizzy and nauseous. She felt the thing's hot breath against her face and knew it was the last thing she would ever feel.

The breath disappeared suddenly, and she opened her eyes to see the thing jerk away suddenly and violently to the right, stumbling and nearly losing its footing as a blur of brown and white coarse, unkempt hair smashed into its shoulder.

"Jack!" Danny screamed happily.

The little dog landed in front of the wolf-ape thing and stood his ground, staring the awful black thing down. Jack dug in and kicked at the dirt with his back legs, preparing to leap at it again if it made a move toward Danny or Raisin. The black-haired thing bared its dingy yellow teeth at the little dog, and the girl was certain she was about to watch her best friend's dog become an appetizer before it moved on to the main course of the two of them. But it didn't eat the dog. It didn't even move toward Jack. The thing let out another growl, but it was different now. Strangled and subdued, sounding nearly dejected. It turned from them and ran off through the trees, followed closely by the little brown and white dog, who snarled and barked as he went.

"Aww shit." Danny sighed and took off after his dog.

"Danny?" Raisin said, not really expecting him to answer. "Danny!" she screamed and ran into the bushes after him.

The girl kept a relative pace with him, or at least with the back of him. Running, or any sort of real physical activity, was never one of Wei Hsin Chan's strongest suits. And neither was dealing with dangerous things. In fact, she would far rather have been watching her father's beard growing or paint drying than to be hauling ass into the forest after something large and dangerous and angry. She liked to read and snack and nap and was certain that, if there were contests for this sort of thing, she could hold her own at the Olympic level.

"Danny, wait!" she called after him, hoping it might slow his pace.

It didn't.

"Shit," she said, and continued after him.

The light filtering through the trees was becoming brighter and Raisin knew they were near to leaving the glade. She knew vaguely where she was, in that it was Winterbourne and in the general area of the old part of town. But beyond that, she was more than a touch lost. She saw a big black shape, followed closely by a small white blur and the back half of Danny, all running at full tilt toward Winterbourne high school. She was a little confused and willing to accept that she had no sense of direction, but the thought of all of them running full tilt after something that big and vicious seemed like a course they couldn't correct even with a road map and a compass.

"Danny!" she said again, as loud as she could. And right then, her body decided that it had run more than it had ever before in the entirety of her fifteen years and had enough sped up propulsion to last it the next fifteen. Her legs buckled at the knees, and she thundered to the ground and watched as her friend disappeared through the undergrowth.

She saw Danny ahead of her, slowly closing the distance between him and the little dog.

"Jack!" she said.

The little dog kept running, trying to chase down the big black thing before it reached its destination. Raisin had enough. Her heart thumped in her chest like a faulty washing machine stuck in a horribly unbalanced spin cycle. Legs burning, lungs aching, and every muscle from the top of her head to the bottoms of her feet screamed out for mercy. One final push, just one desperate last effort, and she'd be beside him when he lay his hand on the little dog's tail. Jack stopped with a yelp and turned around, teeth barred and growling.

"Knock that shit off, Jack," Danny said. He picked Jack up and held him tightly for fear of him bolting after the big thing again.

"Goddammit Jack, stop!"

The dog stopped struggling and zeroed in on the black form heading across the open field to the nearby school. Soon Raisin was watching the figure, too.

"What the f–"

The thing slowed down as it approached the building. It didn't move nervously or attempt to remain inconspicuous. Instead, it stood to its full height, walked slowly and deliberately, nearly sauntering toward the building, and crawled into Winterbourne High School through an open window along the building's foundation.

"Now, where is it going?" Raisin said.

Danny removed Jack's leash from his back pocket and clipped on the little dog's collar. Jack pushed out of Danny's arms and stood with wild eyed abandon.

"C'mon Jack, let's go find out what the hell is going on."

The two of them began walking toward the school, moving slowly at first, hesitant to see where the thing had gone, but as Jack pulled at the leash and practically dragged them to the school, their spirits became buoyed by the dog's confidence.

"Stop!"

Danny turned to see Raisin standing ten feet away from him and the dog.

"Wait," she said through gasping breaths. "Where in the hell do you think you're going?"

"That big thing just went into the school, through a basement window. Jack and I are going to go find it."

"Like hell you are," she said.

"Wait, what?"

"Danny Nesbit, you are not following that thing into the school all by yourself. Jack doesn't count."

Danny rolled his eyes. "Okay. You can come too. I didn't figure you'd want to come."

"I don't want to, and I won't go into the basement, and neither will you."

"How's that?"

"You don't even know what that damned thing is. It could be rabid for all you know. Who knows what it'll do if you corner it in the basement. I think it would likely eat Jack and have you as the main course. Don't be stupid."

"But I–"

"No Danny. Don't do it. I have no desire to go to your fucking funeral. That is, if that thing leaves anything of you to bury."

She looked at him with a mix of fury and genuine panic. Danny met her eyes. Raisin was not the type to just pepper a conversation with random swearing, and that she let fly with a word that her parents would beat her for daring to utter let him know just how determined she was to change his mind.

"Besides," she said. "It's late, and if I don't get home soon, the old man will tear a strip off me a mile wide."

"Oh, okay, go. I'll be fine," he said.

"No," she said flatly. "I am afraid to walk home alone. God only knows what else is out there. I want you to come with me."

Danny looked toward the basement window

"Why do you think thing went into the basement of the school?" Danny said after a time.

"You and Jack scared it, chasing it the way you did. Jack barking at it, you are barking at Jack, and it went to the first place it could find to get away from you. I feel sorry for the poor janitor that finds that thing hiding under a set of stairs."

"Yeah," Danny said absently. "Yeah, that would be scary."

"But?"

"But if it was just trying to get away from me and Jack, why didn't it run sideways or deeper into the woods and hide in the trees somewhere?"

"What is you point?"

"That it headed right for the school, and it sure seemed to know just where that opened window was."

"I think you're imagining things," she said.

THEY WALKED down Parker Street and across Millar's field. Once he had walked her practically to her front door, he thought about the school and finding the awful black hairy thing that was scuttling around in its basement. He even briefly entertained the idea of going back there, but it was getting late. The fosters gave no more than the casualist of shits about his well being. This was true. However, they absolutely needed to know the whereabouts of their young windfall constantly, to keep that money flowing toward them in a steady stream. That fact alone provided endless wonder why that hadn't just locked him into his room years ago, keeping him alive by shoving grilled cheese sandwiches under his door and letting him out once a day to use the bathroom.

Danny ran back down Millar's field, toward Greyhollow road and home. He crossed the street to his backyard and headed into the mudroom, opening the door quickly and quietly and shooting a look at Jack that said any noise that alerted the house and risked Danny having another painful exchange with his foster father might be met with a swift kick up the back of a certain furry ass, though he'd never actually do it. As he left the mud room and walked into the kitchen, Danny's hopes of remaining undiscovered faded like a fart in a hurricane.

"You're late," Randy said.

"Late? For what?"

"For supper, buddy," he said and moved to Danny with an awkward, unsteady gait. Danny stiffened instinctively. Sensing a poorly aimed blow would arrive imminently and collide against some part of his head with the force of a wet mackerel. He was unsure what to do - what to say to the man. The wrong answer would surely earn him a slap from the drunken asshole, but he'd never seen him act like this before, and it threw him off kilter.

The Foster father sounded positively oily, sleazing up to Danny and making certain that the boy was comfortable and happy in his present situation. It was unnerving and downright creepy. And the kid knew in a heartbeat the foster father was up to something. Though, given the drunk's history, giving him the right answer might just have been part of a sick game and earned him a slap, anyway.

"Here, shit down. Shit down," the older man said through whisky numbed lips. "You musht be shtarving."

He pushed a plate toward Danny that contained two perfectly fried eggs and several well-cooked rashers of bacon, hash brown potatoes, and three slices of well toasted rye bread. It was everything he loved to eat. If Danny had to choose one meal to eat for the rest of his life, this was it. A bacon and egg breakfast, in the boy's opinion, was the perfect meal. It contained all the major food groups – well, the important ones anyway - fried pork group, eggs group, bread group, and fried potatoes group. Danny noticed there was also a full glass of chocolate milk beside the plate and suddenly, another food group eased into the running for everything he'd wanted right at that moment. He sat down at the table and tucked in, grabbing a forkful of eggs, ripping the yolk open with the slice of toast in his other hand, and moved the greasy, yellow mess toward his mouth. Stopping just short of actually eating, he realized there was something else to this. The last time his foster parents had made him anything remotely resembling a meal he liked, it was because they knew his placement was up for review and they didn't want to see their beloved cash cow move onto greener pastures. The Fosters were drunken money grubbers and completely transparent. He knew, with all certainty, that they were up to something.

"Your friend, the cop, stopped by," Randy said and attempted to put a drunken arm around him.

"Oh, really?"

"Oh yeah. Left this for you, buddy." He grinned crazily and passed an envelope toward Danny.

It was a white, letter sized envelope that, remarkably, showed no signs of tampering. Across the front of it in flowing, stylish handwriting was written - *Master Daniel Rory Nesbitt.* It was elaborate and formal, and it struck Danny as totally odd. Guthrie used his full name on the envelope. He wasn't even sure Floyd Guthrie even knew his entire name. But then again, the cop writing to him at all was absolutely on a par with the weirdness he'd experienced since starting out this morning. Danny ripped open the short edge of the envelope, revealing the folded slip of a piece of paper inside. He removed it carefully, hesitating a moment before finally unfolding it to see its contents.

It was a handwritten thing and, by the look of it, a practiced hand had written the letter in flowing script using a fountain pen. All the things that Danny was pretty sure Guthrie wasn't. The letters on the page were blocky and angular, in much the same way he thought of the detective. But just the same, there was a flow to it. Rolling, nearly artistic in a way he never thought the old man was capable.

My Dearest Daniel,

It is imperative I see you. Please come to me after the cessation of all your afternoon classes. I will be in the basement janitor's closet at Winterbourne high school.

Your dear friend,
Detective Floyd Robert Guthrie.

A CHILL ROSE through Danny and exited through the top of his head, leaving him cold and confused. He knew two things in that instant, the first that Floyd Guthrie had never laid eyes on this letter, much less written it, and the second, that he'd get his wish to go into the basement of the high school. Only now, the thought of *actually* going down there made him feel a little sick to his stomach.

"Shit," he said and remembered the trouble he was already in.

Guthrie would be there after class to pick him up and take him to the nursing home and, if he mentioned anything about the letter or the thing in the basement, the man would forbid him from going anywhere near it until every cop within a hundred miles of Winterbourne examined it and picked it apart. But, if he could convince Guthrie that he'd already been to see the seniors in the morning, he might let him off the hook after school. Or, he could lie and say he was sick, much too sick to go near anybody as vulnerable as a building full of seniors. But that would mean killing a whole day before heading to the school and might arise suspicion and likely the ire of one or both Fosters. The thought of digging his heels in and telling Floyd he would do anything but go back to that awful place conjured images of a battle of wills with the older man that he had no hope of emerging from as the victor.

Besides, he'd enjoyed the time he spent there - sure the laundry part was about as stomach churning as anything he could imagine, but the old man Don seemed genuine and liked him. Even the staff weren't too hard on him once they saw he was helping people and not just putting in time. And the answer popped into his head like the arm of a mouse trap slamming against the neck of a clueless rodent, hard and fast and final. He'd get up early - really early - and head down to the home by himself. After he'd stayed his time, he'd get the head lady to sign a piece of paper saying he'd been there. He'd give that to Guthrie after school, and when the old boy had left, he'd hightail it into the basement to meet the other Guthrie.

Danny knew his foster father had been hovering behind him, trying desperately to read over his shoulder, but not standing close enough to do it.

"Everything alright?" he said nervously as the boy folded the letter and replaced it in the envelope.

"Fine," Danny said dismissively. "I'm heading up to bed. Early day tomorrow."

"You haven't touched your supper."

Danny grabbed the plate and cup and headed toward the stairs.

"Where the hell are you going with that?" Randy said.

"Oh," Danny said. "I just thought it would be a waste of food not to eat it."

"You will eat it. Your mother went to a lot of trouble to make that for you, and I'll be damned if it goes to waste. Sit yourself on down, pal."

He tried wrapping another sloppy hug around the boy and pointed at the kitchen table. His words seemed clearer, like he'd sobered up some, but the strength of his grip and the tone of his voice said he was a long way from it. Danny walked slowly toward the table, knowing another blow would land on the back of his head if he didn't choose his next moves very carefully. He knew better than to test his foster father's patience when he was in this state - loaded and suspicious. The boy sat and wolfed down the breakfast food, barely tasting it as he cleared the plate. Randy eyeing him suspiciously as he trudged to the dishwasher, shoving his dishes in it, never taking his eyes off the man.

"Heading up to bed now," he mumbled.

Danny snapped his fingers and Jack followed close behind as he walked up the stairs to his room. He closed his door and tossed a piece of bacon he'd palmed to the dog. Jack gulped it up and sat waiting for more.

"That's it," Danny said. "Though if you stay close, there might be more in a minute.

He lay back on his bed as the nausea of having eaten too quickly raced through him. The sweat beaded up on his face as the heat and queasiness rose him.

"Son of a..." he shot back up.

The little dog gave him a confused look.

"I left the letter downstairs," he said.

He knew his foster father would have read it twice by now and would wonder what it all meant. If nothing else, the letter was cryptic enough that he wouldn't know anything apart from where this Guthrie wanted him to go. But that was enough. He pictured the man frantically reading and re-reading, trying to make sense of it all.

RANDY HEWLETT STOOD at the bottom of the stairs, waiting for the boy's door to close before he headed back into the kitchen. He picked up the letter and unfolded it, reading it nervously.

"Shit," Randy said.

He never liked that cop. That fucker was always so busy sticking his nose in other people's business, and now, here he was, demanding to see the kid. If the little brat ever told Guthrie about what happened here behind closed doors, his cash cow would suddenly dry up and he'd likely spend some time as a guest of the state, dancing with hairy, muscular men called Kevin that wanted him to do unspeakable things after lights out. But, if he made it to the school before the boy did, he might explain the whole situation to the cop. Hell, the detective might even recommend him for a second foster child when he learned what an excellent job he was doing with young Danny. And if that didn't work, he'd brain him with a lead pipe and take the boy back home.

"The basement," he said and folded the letter back up.

25

———————

"You haven't touched your supper, Don," the nurse said.

"I'm afraid I'm not feeling very well," the old man said.

"Oh, I could give you something for that," she said.

"No thank-you," he said. "I think I'd just like to go lie down."

Don got up slowly from the table and walked out of the dining room. The chaos and racket made by the other diners still echoing in his ears like a thunderstorm inside a tin can. He rounded the corner and shuffled past the nurse's station at the beginning of the hallway that led to his room and looked to make certain the nurse, plus an orderly, saw him going toward the room. The old man made it a few steps into the hallway, where he dragged one foot behind him pretending to trip, but in doing so, stopped too short and lost his footing for real. He plummeted toward the awful, taupe carpet beneath him and caught hold of the railing that ran the circumference of the entire place.

Dave, the orderly, rushed to him and clapped a pair of meaty hands around the old man's waist, hauling him upward like a sack of apples.

"Come on, old timer," Dave said. "I'll help you back to your room."

"No, no. It's okay. I'm fine."

"Really? You don't look fine." Dave said.

"I am, just tripped over my own feet, is all. I really just want to go to my room and lie down, okay?"

Dave stared silently at the old man and then turned and walked back to the nurse's station.

He smiled at her. "Hey Lorraine, wanna get a beer after work?"

"A beer? With you? Gross," she said.

"Suit yourself," he said, and headed back into the dining room.

Don Pierce heaved a sigh and ambled down the hallway. The nervous adrenaline slowly ebbed away, leaving him feeling worse now than he was just pretending to be. Undaunted, Don made walked slowly back to his bedroom and shut the door.

"Jesus," he said and sat on the bed. "That was a little too thick. The big oaf nearly came back here." He knew from experience that Dave wouldn't come back this way until his next shift and wouldn't be a concern for a while.

The old man opened the drawer on his bedside table, carefully removing the photo album. He'd glanced at the thing twice now, lingering on some of the lurid holiday snaps that were stuck in a clump behind one of the back sleeves, but so far hadn't examined the whole of the damned thing. It drew him to the newspaper clippings and the accompanying photos. So many dead kids and here they were, on full display in the photo album of a man he'd called a friend almost from the beginning. Maybe Old Davey Bulger was right. Maybe Bob *did it, all of it*. Everybody kept secrets, didn't they? His pulse quickened, and his fingertips tingled as he flipped slowly through the remaining pages of the photo album. But there was nothing further. Nothing that aroused any more suspicion or yielded any further evidence of why he had the pictures or what he had to do with the dead kids. Until he arrived at the last page.

Someone had cut a slit in the album's vinyl cover and stuck five photos inside, all about the size of a sheet of paper. On the back of each was a date - the same date, stretching all the way back to 1947. They were group photos of a society or social club. He assumed it from the look of them and the outfits they wore. The lot of them stood in front of an altar of sorts, looking every bit as though someone had carved it from stone. The altar sat atop a heavy stone dais, surrounded by walls of brick. It gave the entire scene a cold appearance. Not one Don would ever associate with any social club he knew of.

The old man recognized some faces in the picture. They had been the big names in Winterbourne. Simon Hall, whose family owned the mill that employed most of the town at one point or another. Beside him, wearing a self-satisfied smile, was Denton Lamont, who ran the freight company that moved a flotilla of barges up and down the Nyegard river. Next to him was a pale wisp of a man that Don knew to be John Rackham, the former chief of police. Most of the townsfolk called him 'Sam Catchem' for his uncanny ability to be a few minutes too late to prevent any actual crime. But never to his face.

Many people with big mouths who liked to make up nicknames had a habit of falling down the stairs of the Winterbourne holding cells several times until they learned that silence really is golden. And good for the health. He recognized a few more, but the years hadn't been as kind to his memory for names as it had been for faces. But something struck him as he examined the photos, so much so that he flipped through them all one by one to make certain he was seeing what he thought he was. There, at the end of the group, sat a man in street clothes, not the uniform that the rest wore and far enough away from the rest that it was obvious he was not one of them. It was a face he would have recognized in the dark. His former roommate and friend, Bob Miflin.

Something struck Don and again, he flipped back through all six pictures. His heart thundered in his chest as the awful truth revealed itself with each successive picture. In front of the group in every picture, each wearing an expression that ranged from uneasy to downright grief stricken, was one of the five slain children. All of them stood in front of Simon Hall, his hands resting stoically on their shoulders. He had no reason for it, but he couldn't help but think that

Hall was the leader of this group. His eyes darted back to the image of his friend.

"What the shit did you get yourself into, you old fool?"

He turned the picture over again and noticed an inscription written in a black pen in the bottom corner of it. 'Winterbourne High', followed by the date and year the photo of the photograph - each one corresponding with the date of the death of each child in the photograph.

"What did you get yourself into?"

A knock at his door broke the near trance he was in, and Don scrambled to gather the photos and the album and stuff them back into his bedside table as the door was creaking slowly open. In walked the head nurse, a thick woman who wore her hair in a bun so tight, Don was certain it must be the reason she was so miserable. Following close behind her was a thin, sallow man with slicked back, greased dark hair that was cut so short on the sides, it appeared he was balding from the ears up.

"Good evening Mr. Mifflin, I am detective sergeant William Kemmler, and I would like to ask you a few questions."

"I'm not Mifflin," Don said and pointed across the room. "He used to be over there. He's dead now."

"I told you; did you think I was lying?" the grouchy nurse said.

Kemmler ignored the nurse's protests. "You'd be Mr. Pierce, then?"

"That's right," Don said, watching the man intently, feeling there was something vaguely familiar about him.

Kemmler wandered, seemingly without purpose. Meandering to the other side of the room and to Don and back again with no immediately obvious purpose until he turned abruptly and spoke again.

"This was his side, I assume?"

"It was."

The cop walked to the bed and, though he couldn't see the man clearly, Don thought the greasy haired detective sniffed the dead man's sheets after smoothing them with his hand. He opened all the drawers on the bedside table and the door to the closet, taking huge gulps of air as he did. There were still a handful of shirts hanging in there and two pairs of pants, nothing of real significance - and nothing that fit Don or appealed to his sense of style. Kemmler took a step back.

"Hello?" Kemmler said.

It was a shoebox, Florsheim specifically, that contained photographs. Hundreds of them. Don glanced nervously at his bedside table. His mind spun. He knew his friend had been involved in the deaths of all those kids. He'd refused to believe it at first, but the photos he'd seen in the album - in the drawer - told an altogether different story. But he didn't see the shoebox, didn't know what it contained, and suddenly felt anxious about what was in it. He looked at the greasy haired man.

Kemmler flipped through the pictures quickly, absently, and turned to the old man.

"Where's the photo album?" Kemmler said.

Don's eyes darted to the drawer, almost automatically, and the second he had, he regretted it. The detective hadn't noticed, much to his relief, and remained focused on the old man's face.

"What?" Don said.

"The photo album, the backs of these pictures are sticky, showing they've recently been removed from an adhesive surface they had been on for some time. An adhesive surface like a photo album. So, do you know where that photo album is? You were his roommate."

Don struggled to think of a quick answer. He could play dumb, but that might cause the cop to tear apart the room, looking for the damned thing. No, there wouldn't be much he could do if the greasy man rummaged through his drawers and closet the way he had next door. He thought he could outright lie and say that Miflin's family had come and taken everything away, but felt that would earn the same result. Kemmler would tear the room apart anyway, to be certain the album wasn't here. And when he found it, Don was, at least, reasonably certain the cop would go from odd and quirky to evil and brutish in a matter of a few minutes.

He acted on the only instinct that didn't have holes big enough to fly a plane through.

"Yes," Don whispered.

"Oh," Kemmler said, doing nothing to disguise the surprise in his voice. "Where is it?"

"Yes," Don said.

"Wait, what?"

"Yes, I really do. I muss. The muss, the muss. The muck and minge and muss is us."

Kemmler looked to the nurse, who returned the look and shrugged her shoulders unapologetically.

"Mr. Pierce, have you seen the photo album?" Kemmler asked, loudly and emphasising every syllable.

"Oh," Don said. "I see alright. I see beside the seaside - beside the sea!"

"Mr. Pierce, have you seen the photo album?" His voice was practically a shout.

"He's not deaf," the nurse said. "He's got dementia, for fuck's sake. It always gets worse for some of them after supper and before bedtime. During the day, you'd never know any different, but as soon as the night comes, they all get weird. Crazy. Like fuckin' werewolves and the moon. Sundowning, they call it."

"And when will this... spell pass?" Kemmler said.

"It might not," the big nurse said. "The man has dementia. It will get progressively worse until it kills him. But not before taking his memories, his speech, his ability to walk and reason, and even make it to the bathroom in time to take a piss."

"What? Really?" Kemmler said, doing little to mask his sarcasm.

"Really."

"Really..." Kemmler half breathed and stuffed his hand into the inside lapel pocket of his jacket. He rooted around inside until his hand hit the object of his search, a business card. "Charming."

He took a silver pen from the same pocket and wrote his name on the flip side of the business card before handing it over to the big orderly.

"If he should come back to the land of the living in the next couple of hours, call me at the-"

"Moonwinks? What room?"

"Yes, the Moonwinks, the number is on the back." Kemmler said flatly.

Kemmler turned to the old man and leaned into him, taking a deep breath that seemed to be forever on the inhale, before moving in close to his ear.

"I can smell you in there. So, you can drop the act. I am going to contact Mifflin's family and sort this out. And when I do, I am coming back here, and I will pick your bones clean before I'm through."

He pushed his nose against the old man's and looked him squarely in the eye, and Don's stomach became a turbid, churning sea. The greasy haired detective's eyes rolled over white, and he wrapped five spindly fingers around a scrawny, sweater clad arm before hissing at the old man again.

"Bet on it."

26

———————

Michael staggered into the bathroom, exhausted and spent, feeling the post orgasmic drain that made him want a snack and a nap above anything else. He flicked the light switch and felt disoriented as it flickered on and off, insubordinately refusing to turn on before finally sprung to life and bathed the bathroom in the vaguely green glow of cheap fluorescent lighting. He knew, instinctively, there would need to be a cleaning. Sanitizing himself and disposing of what was left of Hughie - and of the blood-soaked mess that was the living room of the small apartment. But for now, there was a bathroom and a shower and the need to rinse away the blood and gore and try to process what had happened and what he'd do next.

The water was hot, almost painfully so, but after several minutes of standing beneath it, it was nearly divine and did as much to soothe his aching muscles as it did to clear his chaotic mind. A changeover, as quickly as this one had been, had always left him trying to calm a mind that danced feverishly, never able to settle on a single thought but flapping like a torn flag in a high wind. Michael lowered his head and let the water run over the back of his neck, flowing down in and out of his ears and past his face. Soon, he stood ankle deep in crimson water that circled the shower drain and slowly returned to clear. He added the shower to the running list that began after his head cleared of the things that would need taking care of before he moved on from here. Not the least of which was the late Hughie Koch - or what remained of him, at any rate.

Michael finished up and stood for another silent, peaceful moment in the shower before turning the taps off and stepping out. He looked at himself in the mirror. It wasn't full length, but when he stood far enough away from it, he could see the whole of his body and if blood or flesh remained anywhere on it. The dark-haired man dried himself. He searched the drawers for something to drag through his hair. A grey rat-tailed comb in the right-hand drawer would suffice and, as it moved across the crown of his head, he caught his own eye on the mirror. A vain, malignant smile moved into the corners of his mouth, and he felt the urge to move his hand down and please himself, but the realities of his situation won out. He dropped the comb, wrapped the towel around his waist, and headed to the living room.

He sauntered out. Being careful not to tread in the pool of blood that covered so much of the space. The man was amazed that, with all that had happened previously, the pool remained undisturbed. No footprints were immediately visible, and there was very little splatter anywhere he could see. Michael looked down at the remains of the man he'd been so hopelessly passionate with a few hours before and felt a wry smile pluck at the corners of his mouth, remembering how the man smelled and tasted and how he arched his back a little just before he finally came. And then his smile broadened and spread its way across his face like a snake inching across an empty desert, and he remembered how the man screamed and begged for his life. How the blood gushed into his mouth and Hughie's voice gurgled as he buried his teeth deep into his neck. His hands reached down, and he found himself. And found himself hard.

When he'd finished and showered a second time, he came back into the living room and saw the mess through fresh eyes. He'd have to get rid of the body. That was the easiest of his tasks. There was a massive coal-fired boiler in the basement of Winterbourne high school that would incinerate the principal into a pile of greyish ash and a wisp of memory that few would recall willingly. Nobody would mourn the death of the lone gay man in a town like Winterbourne. There'd be drinks over his death, but no one would be a toast to his memory. But he'd have to clean the apartment and, topo remain completely hidden, he'd need to do it all himself. And then there was the other matter.

There was the ritual to contend with. The killing and eating the entrails of another child. He'd done it more times than he could recall. But he was aging rapidly now beneath the facade he'd chosen. He was weakened, and he knew it. He had to pass on what he knew, continue his bloodline's power over the rest of them. After all, he was the first. Without him, none of them would exist and if he went, so did they all. The boy would do it. Family is everything. Without it, a man has nothing, and the boy would understand that. He had to. Michael looked at the pool of blood and sighed.

He headed into the kitchen, figuring the most likely place to find cleaning supplies in the small apartment would be under the sink. Hughie Koch may have apologized for the state of his apartment, but the place was nearly spotless. Michael's intuition was correct and, in the small cupboard beneath the kitchen sink, he found every cleaning product he could ever imagine needing. There were alcohol-based bleaches, scrubbing powders and creams, along with a wide assortment of brushes and sponges and a generous supply of garbage bags. Everything he could possibly need to clean up the remains of a dead human being.

Michael laughed. "Jesus! It's as if he's already done this once before."

Michael thought, for an instant, about putting clothes on. The risk of becoming covered in blood, made frothy pink by a healthy dose of scrubbing with the power of Mr. Clean, told him that clothes were an exceptionally bad idea considering how much blood there really was beneath the body. He walked back to the bathroom, removed his towel, and headed back into the kitchen. A quick search of the drawers revealed a large butcher knife that would suit his purposes.

Most Hughie's blood was pooling underneath him, so there would be little residual blood coming out as Michael cut him up into more manageable pieces.

Best not to do it here.

He'd take the body of his lover to the bathroom and hack him up in there.

Easier to wash up afterward.

But it wouldn't be easy to get him there. Picking up a body, limp and heavy, off the floor and carrying it to the next room. He closed his eyes slowly, calmly. The lids sliding down like blinds slowly pulling down over a window. He breathed in a deep breath that seemed to go on forever, exhaling it painfully slowly. He followed it with another and then a third and, as he forced a final breath deep into his lungs, he paused and opened his eyes, revealing another amber set beneath. His sinews lengthened and pulled and muscles double in strength as he took to the other form. The form paid for with the blood of six dead children. He grabbed Hughie's body and hoisted it over his shoulder like an empty sleeping bag and bounded into the bathroom, crossing the room in three steps and held the dead man above the tub. A low guttural growl escaped him as he grabbed hold of Hughie's wrist and pulled until it made a loud, sickening snap. Michael moved to the other arm and made similar quick work of the legs.

Michael closed his eyes and took several large, deep breaths again and felt himself shrink and calm as the change washed over him. He opened them again and looked in the mirror above the sink. His eyes had returned to his familiar baby blues. With Hughie's joints completely dislocated, it was now a matter of a few well aimed slices with his butcher knife to get the body into manageable pieces. With a little more effort than he'd counted on, Michael got the entirety of Hughie Koch into three large black garbage bags. He tied them securely closed, left them in the tub, and headed back into the living room. Perhaps the mindless act of scrubbing the blood from the living room might just be Zen enough to steer him toward an answer about how to win the boy over to his side.

The blood was congealing, so dark and crimson it was nearly black in the dull light of the living room. He wrapped a generous portion of paper toweling around his hand and dragged it through the puddle, trying to decrease the volume. The blood was viscous and unyielding, refusing to move as he drew the absorbent paper through it. Michael thought for the moment of leaving the bloody mess in the living room and leaving with the three trash bags. Taking his chances. But leaving it the way it looked now would bring no end to questions as soon as the landlord discovered it. Where was Hughie, what happened up here and how will I get the smell out and who'll pay to have this goddam mess cleaned up? Whether or not it would, the dark-haired man felt that it would eventually find its way back to him.

He dumped most of the lemony fresh cleaning liquid into the centre of the large pool of blood and, after several minutes of anxious pacing and finger tapping on anything he got close enough to, it surprised him to find the whole disgusting affair was fairly easy to wipe up. But even as the last of the blood vanished away and the dirty rags put into the garbage bags to be burned, he was no nearer to the solution in the matter of the boy. He moved back to the bathroom, and in doing so, caught his foot on the corner of an area rug beneath the coffee table. His arms flailed wildly, trying to regain his composure, and came in contact with the picture frames on the wall, sending them crashing to the floor. In piles of tattered photos and heaps of shattered glass. And then he saw it, Hughie's university diploma - his credentials as the principal of Winterbourne high school. Michael looked at the garbage bags and a loathsome smile wriggled its way across his face. The best place to find the kid who was of school age was in school. After he found him, it was a matter of time to convince him of the importance of family, *his* family, and his duty to it. Michael walked into Hughie's bedroom and opened the closet. It might be too late to use the man's skin, but at least his clothes would come of some use.

27

———

Guthrie twisted the cap back on the whisky bottle, a little surprised at his own abstinence. He didn't need to be completely clear-headed to go question an old man about a handful of dead kids, but he would have a better crack at understanding things if he wasn't blind drunk, either. He got into the Ford, said a silent prayer to the gods of internal combustion, and headed down the driveway toward Winterbourne Home. As he rounded the corner of Parker Street and approached the entrance to the nursing home, he caught sight of Kemmler's greasy hair glinting in the setting sunlight and pivoted down a side street to avoid being seen by him. He parked the car and strolled toward the place, stopping at the corner, pressing himself up against the wall of the furniture store and peering around it to see if the young detective from upstate had gone. He had, and Guthrie carried on quickly up the steps of Winterbourne Home and in through the front door.

"Visiting hours are just about over, sir," the receptionist said.

"Oh, I know," Guthrie said. "I just had something important I need to remind my dad about for his doctor's appointment tomorrow."

"If you'd like, you can tell me, and I can make sure he gets the message?"

Guthrie remained silent for a moment, weighing his options.

"No," he said finally. "I think Dad would rather hear it from me."

"Suit yourself," she said. "But you've only got about 15 minutes left. Okay?"

"I'll be back in ten," he said.

Floyd hadn't a clue where to go and thought if he asked where his father's room was, she, at the very least, might think it a touch odd. At the very most, she would know he was completely full of shit and lock the place down. In moments of undue stress, some say that the human mind can astound with feats of intellect. Sadly, this wasn't one of them.

He turned to the receptionist. "Say, where is my dad?"

"Wait, what?"

"My Dad's room, where is my dad's room?"

"You don't know where your father's room is?"

"I hit my head," he said.

"What?" she said.

"What I mean is my sister usually comes because I was in a car accident a while back and I've only recently been able to get back out. The windshield sort of took care of my short-term memory."

Guthrie sighed and looked at her with all the doe eyed innocence he could muster. It wasn't Tolstoy, but he felt it was pretty damn good for being thought up on the spot.

"Oh," she said. "I'm so sorry. What's your father's name again?"

"Robert Mifflin. Bob to his friends."

She clicked the name into the computer on her desk and stared blankly into the screen as the word deceased appeared beside the old man's name.

"Son of a–"

"Is there a problem?" Guthrie said.

"No, nothing they can't sort out upstairs. Room 317. Take the elevator behind you, go to the third floor, and go left once you get there," she said curtly.

"Thanks so much." Floyd smiled and headed toward the elevator.

The music inside the elevator was innocuous and quiet and it was a tune he nearly recognized but not enough to hum more than a few bars and that grated on his nerves, now that the ether of the whisky was wearing away and the world and a huge thumb of a headache pressed in on his skull as the floors ticked up to three. The doors opened, and he stepped off, instinctively looking left and right, though he had serious doubts of anyone lurking in the shadows on his flanks, waiting to spring out at him from within the walls of a nursing home. Feeling safe in any regard, he approached the door, waited to be buzzed in, and walked to the front desk as soon as he was. His smile was broad and friendly, and he looked the girl in the eyes as he flashed it.

"Room 317?"

"Down that hallway." The nurse pointed toward the hallway directly behind the weathered detective. Guthrie got the impression she didn't give a shit either way and, completely trusting her indifference, turned and headed off down the hall, looking for one Bob Mifflin. The door to room 317 was open when Guthrie got there, but only just a crack, and what he could see beyond the crack was darkness.

Sleeping?

Floyd pushed the door open slowly and quietly and saw that the heavy curtains were drawn around the bed to the left. The bed and room to the right were currently unoccupied and looked as though someone had recently cleaned them within an inch of their life. The bed tightly made, the bathroom spotless, and the closets and dressers were all empty and closed. He stepped into the empty side as quietly as he had opened the door and looked around. The drawers of the bedside table contained little, nothing of use, anyway. A few yellowed envelopes and a handful of pictures of Mifflin as a younger man. A quick once over of the closet revealed more of the same.

"Well, I suppose I'll just wait for him to get back then, shall I?" Guthrie said.

"Back from the dead?" an elderly voice called out from behind the curtain encircling the other bed.

"How's that?"

A withered, liver-spotted hand pulled back the curtain that separated the two rooms and an equally withered, liver-spotted old man followed behind it.

"He's dead. Three weeks ago now. I'm amazed they haven't put somebody else in here yet. I hear there's a ten-year waiting list to get into this joint, what with all of us baby boomers going off our nuts and getting all old and decrepit and all. The white tsunami they call it. Don't cotton much with that name, seeing as we were at war with the Japanese once upon a time." Don Pierce said.

"What can you tell me about him?" Guthrie said.

The old man rose and stood in complete silence. An odd look clung to his face like a picture somebody hung crooked.

"What?" Guthrie said, self consciously, feeling very much that the old man's gaze was scrutinizing him. "Have I got a boog hanging?"

"Don't I know you?" Don said.

"I don't think so and, I don't care how drunk you get me, I'm not going home with you."

"Huh?"

"Sorry, our question sounded like a pickup. Never mind. I don't recall ever meeting you before. Why do you ask?" Floyd said with a chuckle.

Don ignored the joke. "What's your name?"

"Floyd. Floyd–" Guthrie said.

"Guthrie. Floyd Guthrie. You'd be Maeve Guthrie's boy?" Don said.

"Yeah, that's right," Floyd said cautiously.

"How is your mother?"

"Dead," Guthrie said flatly.

"Oh," Don said sheepishly. "I'm sorry. We don't always get the news firsthand, and I have been here a while. I'm afraid I'm a little behind on current events."

"Look, could we skip the waltz down memory lane part of this conversation and get right down to it?" Guthrie said.

"Of course, of course. Sorry. What is it you wanted to know?"

"About your roommate."

"You're some kind of cop or something?"

"Yeah," Guthrie said, the frustration bristling through his voice.

"There was already one of you here a while ago, asking a lot of questions," Don said.

"What?"

"Yeah, greasy haired guy. Keller? Himmler? Something like that."

"Kemmler?"

"That's him."

"Jesus, you didn't tell him anything, did you?" Guthrie said.

"No. I didn't like the look of him, all greasy hair and sniffing at everything like some kinda goddam dog. Turned into a bit of a prick as it turns out, so I guess I was right in not trusting him," Don said.

"But you trust me, and you're going to tell me everything, right?"

"Depends on what you want to know."

"I want to know why I have pictures of five dead kids with your roommate's name on them?"

"Huh," Don said and, after a short, uncomfortable pause spent staring at the other man, got up and headed back behind the curtain. "Wait here."

The old man disappeared into his side of the room and returned after a short time carrying the photo album. He sat down on Mifflin's bed and pat the space beside him. Floyd relented and took a seat beside him. Don passed the book to the detective.

"Umm," Guthrie said.

"Don't you see?"

"See what?"

"All those kids, one by one. In the photos. Going all the way back to the first one," Don said.

"No, I don't," Guthrie said.

"What? Oh, wait," the old man said and took the book from the younger man.

He flipped to the last page and removed the photos from the inside of the back cover where it'd been slashed open, handing them to the younger man.

"Jesus Christ, it's all of them. Every god-damned one of them," Guthrie said.

"And that is Bob Mifflin, my former roommate," Don said, pointing to the figure near the corner of the picture.

"How?" Guthrie said, half to himself.

"Hmm?"

"How did they get those kids? How did they keep all of it secret for so long? Didn't any of those kids' parents come looking? Didn't the cops?"

"Nobody gave a shit about those kids. Why would they? Especially back then when it began."

"What do you mean?"

"You don't know, do you?"

"Know what?" Guthrie said, his patience running along a ragged edge, threatening to tear away entirely.

"Once I saw those pictures and all those kids, I tried to figure out just what the hell it had to do with my friend. He'd been a straightforward guy all his life. Worked for WG&E and retired with a full pension. Gold watch and the whole thing. Nothing exciting ever happened to him. Ever. Then I remembered something he told me. That since he was young, he volunteered at St. Margaret's."

"So? Lots of people volunteered at that church. Even my mother did for a while," Guthrie said, not seeing where this was leading.

"Yes, they did. But he didn't. Bob Mifflin volunteered at the *other* St. Margaret's."

"The orphanage?"

"All these kids came from the orphanage. I don't know if you remember where it used to be?"

"Refresh my memory."

"St. Margaret's orphanage and home for wayward mothers stood on the spot of what is now Winterbourne High School. Those photos are all of some club that met in the basement of St. Margaret's. The basement is still part of the school, the boiler and everything is down there still."

"Son of a–"

"You wondered how they got away with it? It's because nobody cared. What's one more dead orphan? One less mouth to feed, that's what. This group of theirs was up to no good if they were killing orphans. I hear there's been another kid found? Was he an orphan?"

Guthrie stood up quickly, so quickly the blood hadn't enough time to make it to his head, and suddenly the room spun.

"What is it?" Don said.

"Danny, I've got to go get Danny."

And the floor rose to meet him.

28

———————

Michael headed out the door of the grubby little apartment, wearing his brand-new suit and his brand-new high school principal disguise, and made his way to the high school. He was tired. Tired and sore and he hadn't slept more than a half an hour stretch before he got back to cleaning the bloody mess that seemed to go on forever. Who could sleep when there was the last of the blood spatter to contend with and bagged bits of high school principal to move to the car for disposal? He hauled the last of them to the rusted-out shit box car that Winterbourne High's Driver's Ed program loaned Hughie Koch and pulled out of the driveway slowly, headed for the school.

It was early enough, just about 5:30 a.m. and the man was optimistic that he wouldn't run into anybody along his way to the school and, if his experiences were to be trusted, he recalled that the far-right window on the most isolated section of the basement's window lock was broken. The glass was smashed some years before by an errant chip, delivered by the school's golf team tryouts, the repair of which had slipped the minds of generations of school janitors. Now it was a crucial part to his plan - there was near to no hope that any door would be open this early in the morning, nor would there be anyone around to let him in.

The early morning air was cool and moist and motionless, and the sun was just teasing its presence along the horizon in ever-growing pools of molten, gold rim corals and shimmering, bubble gum pinks that were doing their best to squeeze in through the faded greys and charcoal shadows that spread out across the horizon. Most of the streets were empty. The bakery trucks and linen delivery services dotting the early morning streets, minding their own business, being the exception. Michael steered the Chrysler compact into the circular driveway that surrounded Winterbourne High like a moat and pulled around the back of the school. He got out, being extra careful not to be seen and, after realizing there was nobody in the school or around it who gave the slightest shit about people wandering around, headed toward the broken window. He passed a heavy steel door with a mesh lined window in the centre of it and, for his own curiosity, his hand found the handle. It was unlocked, and the door swung open as he pushed it. He left it open a crack and returned to the Chrysler and to the bagged remains of Hughie Koch.

He'd reduced the mortal remains of the former principal of Winterbourne High to three well packed plastic trash bags. Michael didn't figure he'd be able to get the bags into the school in one go and going back and forth from the car to the basement, increasing the risk of being seen by someone, would increase exponentially the more he did it. But he realized, with a little *help,* he could make short work of it. His eyes closed, slowly, deliberately, and gulped in three massive breaths, and exhaled, each with a long hiss of whispered words he'd memorized years before. The language and meaning of the words had always escaped him, but it was the result that bore the correct weight of importance.

Michael could feel it nearly instantly. An itch that began at the top of his head and travelled its way slowly downward. He needed to concentrate, to keep control of it. There'd be no end of trouble to come his way if someone happened along midway through a transformation and, strictly speaking, he wasn't about to go all the way with it this time. He needed a little extra muscle to help with the bags, but not the kind that would terrorize the neighbours if they witnessed anything. The man focused, willing the change to stay around his arms and chest and sinews, stretching and thickening them. Muscles plumped and thickened and threatened to tear under the demands of their new shape. The colour of his skin darkened and became blotchy and covered with coarse hair and gave off the aroma of rotted flesh. The well-muscled arms grabbed hold of the bags and Michael hoisted them over his shoulder with ease.

He ducked into the school's basement, descending the stairs quickly and in through the unlocked door. He knew the layout well, having been down there countless times. Even from the days when it was still an orphanage. He reached the bottom and headed left, down a long, narrow corridor that opened into a large room with a massive industrial boiler in the centre. The giant steel tank burned hot enough to dispose of Hughie quickly and there would be little incriminating evidence remaining, though he sensed, that nobody would much miss the fairy of a principal of Winterbourne High, and nobody would kick up much of a stink to find him if he was.

"You're here early," the rough voice said from the darkness.

"I know. I had to do this," Michael said.

"Why didn't you just eat him and be done with it?

"Because, Denton, I'm not a fucking savage."

"Really, Simon?"

The man stepped out of the shadows and revealed himself. Michael's eyes rolled back in their sockets, revealing two pallid orbs. His face lengthened and stretched, to the sounds of sinews ripping and groaning beneath the strain that contorted the man into something no longer human and not quite animal and not quite enough of one or the other to be considered a melding of the two. With blinding speed, he was at the other man's throat, hauling him off the ground and bringing him nose to nose.

"I told you, don't call me Simon," the Michael thing said.

"Sor... sorry... Michael," the other man said out. The steel grip released, and the man dropped to the floor.

He was tall, almost a whole head taller than Michael, though he clearly feared the smaller man. His face was gaunt and grey and the skin that barely covered the skull beneath it was the colour of a corpse, even without the thing revealing its true form lurking beneath.

"What's new, sir?"

"That the principal of this school took excellent care of himself. It was like fucking a calf-skin glove and then dining on milk-fed veal. What have you found out?" Michael said.

"We remain hidden. For now, we are still safe. We have only to find the boy and another child for the ceremony."

"Is that all?" Michael said.

"And that Mifflin did almost nothing to keep the boy hidden," Denton said, his voice taking on an excited tone.

"How do you mean?"

"He's a student at this school. The old fool barely tried to conceal his identity. Changed his surname is all."

Michael smiled, very near to praising the other man when he was cut short.

"There's something else, a bit of a snag - nothing, really. I'm certain it'll be fine," Denton said.

"What?" Michael said through clenched teeth.

"John Rackham is here; he's been nosing around looking for the kid on his own. Already tried to find Mifflin. I imagine it's only a matter of time before he finds his way to the boy."

"Time is running out in any regard. You said the boy is here, at this school?" Michael said.

"He is, yes."

"Then I will bring him to me. Who is going to say no to the school principal? After I find him, it's only a matter of time before I convince him of the importance of staying with his genuine family. Blood is everything in this world. After that, we'll convene and perform the ceremony. He'll have it all then. All my knowledge and skill will be his."

"Yes, sir," Denton said.

"Let Rackham come. Let him challenge. His family was always a step or two away from the breadline. Someone of such low standing could never hope to lead. However, would they inspire the likes of people like us? It would be challenge after challenge until there were none of us left. Anyway, in a few hours, it'll be too late for him to change anything. He can't avoid the ceremony, and when it's over, I'll rip the flesh from his bones with my bare hands."

Denton flashed a reptilian smile at Michael, the smile that sycophantic toadies have always broadcast at powerful men that since the very beginnings of toadiedom.

"And then your family name will live on, your rule will be absolute - even after you are gone!" Denton crowed. "Many years from now, of course."

"What did you say the boy was called now?"

"Nesbitt, sir. Daniel Nesbitt."

29

———————

Danny woke with a start and sat up so quickly, he knocked the still sleeping Jack out of bed. The little dog hit the floor with a thud.

"Shhh," he scolded the barely conscious dog.

Jack gave him a confused look and resumed his position on the bed. His eyes slid closed and soon he was breathing deeply again.

"Wake up, jack," Danny whispered as forcefully as he could manage. "We gotta go."

The little dog cocked his head sleepily.

"C'mon, we gotta get out of here before he wakes up. I smelled his breath when I came in. He's been talking to Tanqueray all night, but it doesn't mean he'll stay passed out all day. So, let's get a move on."

Jack jumped off the bed and turned excitedly on hearing the words, *let's go.*

"Jack!" Danny said. It was as close to a shout as he could manage and still be whispering. He pointed his finger at the dog, who sat obediently, then lay on the floor and avoided eye contact with the boy. Danny crouched in front of him and stroked his head gently.

"He's been acting weird lately. Weirder than usual, so I'm not crazy about leaving you here alone with him. So, I've got to bring you with me. But you can't act like a loon where we're going, okay? Keep your shit together and stick close to me."

The dog cocked his head to the left, and then the right, and back again, as if trying to make out the words the boy spoke.

"If you can behave, I'll make sure you get a treat when we get home," Danny said.

At last, a word Jack knew. He pounced on the boy, knocking him to the bed, and began covering Danny's face in huge, sloppy, wet licks that sent the boy into fits of laughter.

"Stop... st... stop," he said through the giggles. He hugged the little dog and planted an equally sloppy kiss on top of his head before setting him on the floor. Danny dressed quickly and quietly and scooped up the little dog before heading downstairs.

For the age and general run-down shabbiness of his foster parent's house, the stairs were remarkably silent, and a smile snaked its way across the boy's face as he hit the bottom stair, glanced around and headed to the kitchen. Undetected. Passing through the living room, he felt sure now that it was going to be a good day and what he had planned might well go off without a hitch. The streetlights had only recently gone out, and the sun hadn't broken across the horizon yet. What little light the windows allowed in was flat and dull and filtered in through smoke-stained lace curtains. It left the living room half lit in grey, flat tones that made it difficult to discern anything apart from shapes and rough outlines of things.

"You're up early," Randy said in a croaked voice from the darkness.

Danny froze and prayed silently that the words didn't startle Jack enough to growl at the figure on the Barca lounger.

"Oh... I... uh," Danny said.

"School doesn't start until 9:00 last time I looked. Where are you off to?"

A gear clicked over in the back of Danny's mind that opened a small door deep in the recesses of his brain and revealed an answer to him.

"Floyd wanted me to meet him after school, which means he can't take me to the old folks' home to volunteer. I thought I would go early this morning, before school, so I didn't have to miss it." The boy was grinning from ear to ear inside, though his face remained stony and dour, knowing instinctively that anything he did that involved the cop who watched over him, would be taken as gospel truth, lest Guthrie have a handful of words with family services and the foster's cash cow suddenly dried up.

The foster father remained silent. His head had turned toward Danny, who couldn't be sure if the man was staring at him or had passed back out. He turned away from the man and took a step toward the kitchen.

"Wait a minute," his Foster Father said. "Wasn't it the cop made you go to those old fuckers in the first place?"

"Oh." Danny expected this and answered the question so quickly, he practically cut off the man's last word. "No. No, it wasn't Guthrie. It was my principal. Guthrie just said he'd make sure I was really doing it. That's why he said he'd drive."

"Uh-huh," his Foster Father mused.

"Anyway, I really gotta go," Danny said, feeling the thin veil of his ruse was about to be ripped away.

Danny watched Randy stand and step toward him, slow and deliberate. As he neared the doorway, the light streaming in through the big kitchen window illuminated the same clothes wore the night before. The older man leaned into him, pressing an oily, pock-marked nose against his own. His eyes were bloodshot and wild, staring at things with the look of someone who'd been on a bender since Thursday, and now it was time for work Monday morning. It wasn't far from the truth. He looked at Danny and, without warning, his hand flew and connected with the side of the boy's face. Before Danny reacted, another one arrived, leaving him reddened and stinging and angry.

"You're up to something," his foster father breathed, breath stale with liquor in Danny's face. "And when I find out what it is, I'll fucking cripple you. I'll bet that's worth even more money, taking care of a gimp. I'll bet that's worth plenty. Maybe you'll have an accident on the way home from school or maybe you'll be playing in the driveway, and I won't see you and hit you with my car. And there won't be a single fucking thing you can do about it."

Jack let a low, rumbling growl and bared his fangs at the man.

"And the first thing I'm going to do after I see to your future is drown that fucking dog in the river."

The tears burned at the corners of Danny's eyes, and he could feel his legs tremble with the fear and betrayal mixing with adrenaline and atavistic rage.

"Fly... Floyd... Floyd will be mad if I don't get to Winterbourne, sir." Danny's lip quivered, and his chest heaved as he tried desperately to hold back the sobs that threatened to erupt deep within him.

"Sure buddy," his foster father hissed and pawed at the boy's shoulder, never taking his rheumy eyes off Danny's. "I'll see you when you get home."

He stood in the doorway between the living room and kitchen like a gin-soaked golem. Danny turned sideways and tried to squeeze past him. As he made the halfway point between the two rooms, his foster father grabbed the collar of his shirt.

"You make sure you tell that cop how well we're looking out for you here."

Danny kept his head down and pushed through into the kitchen, followed by Jack, who eyed the man suspiciously as he strode past him. Secretly, the boy hoped Randy might take a swipe at the little dog, so he could watch with glee as Jack crushed the man's hand in his jaws. The older man seemed unphased by the dog's contempt and staggered his way back to the living room and the comfort of his Barca lounger.

The boy and his dog headed out the back door and on to Grey Hollow Road. He had two choices from here, two routes to get to Winterbourne home. He could cross Millar's field, cut down across Parker Ave and head west through downtown Winterbourne until he got to the steps at the bottom of the hill. From there, it was the near exhausting trek up the hill to the nursing home. Or he could cut through Winterbourne cemetery - the old cemetery - down past old man Winterbourne's crypt and up the back of the hill to Seonagh's woods and on to the back property of the estate. Going through the cemetery would save him about fifteen minutes, although with it still being as dark as it was, he would run through the place and make it through in record time. He decided instead on the former route. It may have been the longer trip, but it was the safer way to go an infinitely less creepy of a walk.

The guard at the main gate was fast asleep, with his feet propped up on the only clear spot on a desk littered with piles of paper. Danny thought it may force him to rummage quietly around the office and desk, looking for keys or a switch to open the gate, but to his surprise, there was a small paper sign taped to one side of the gate.

DO NOT DISTURB GUARD. GATE UNLOCKED. DELIVERIES AROUND BUILDING TO RIGHT.

Danny smirked at the sign and looked back at the guardhouse. He'd seen his foster father the worse for the drink the next morning, more times than he cared to remember, and he'd experienced the man's wrath when he dared to wake him from a deeply hungover nap. But this fellow in the guard shack seemed to have turned it into an art form, complete with advertising. Danny opened the gate as slow and quiet as a large steel fence door would swing and slipped onto the grounds of Winterbourne Home. He couldn't recall ever being awake this early, early enough that the sun looked as though it was trying to force its way above the horizon and squeezing out pools of light from its side as it did. Danny Nesbitt wondered if everywhere was as quiet this early as it was here.

Nobody paid much attention to him most of his life and usually, it only angered him and make him feel alone and worthless. This morning, however, he was beside himself with glee as he entered the building through the main doors, making his way to the third floor and up to the door of the locked unit without a single person asking so much as his name.

"Shit. The code," Danny said.

A keypad stood between him and the entrance to the locked unit, the place he'd worked yesterday. The head nurse had told him the code and told him to write it down somewhere safe. Which, of course, he hadn't. He was young and felt he had a mind like a steel snare and laughed off the idea of writing four lousy numbers, positive that after only hearing them once, he would remember them. He didn't.

"Well, now what?"

Danny's plan for making it into the basement of Winterbourne High to meet up with the other Guthrie hinged on his getting in to see the head nurse and getting a note from her for the Real Floyd. Without it, there'd be no end of hell for him to pay. He could return downstairs and get the code from someone - the guard, possibly. But that would raise suspicions and likely the hungover man's rage, and then he'd be screwed again. He entertained the idea of punching in random numbers, hoping the four he needed would push through his subconscious into his fingers. The idea was even stupid, just floating around his head, much less put into effect.

The answer came with a loud crash, followed by a metallic clang from around the corner. Danny poked his head out cautiously to see the grey, steel laundry rack being pushed by Evan from the laundry room.

"Hey, barf-bag! You came back!" He smiled.

"The smell wasn't enough to keep me away." Danny beamed at the big laundry man. He liked Evan, although he just called him a barf-bag. Maybe because of it.

"Don't worry," he said. "We can soon fix that. C'mon, you can help me put the laundry away."

Danny watched as the big man punched the code into the keypad 1379. He hoped he'd remember it this time but, if nothing else, he knew he could go to Evan from this point forward if he ever needed help.

"What's with him?" Evan said looking down at Jack who, until now, had been cowering behind Danny.

"I couldn't leave him at home," Danny said nervously, his words coming out in a rapid fire staccato. "He won't be any trouble."

"He was pretty calm last time. Anyway, what the hell do I care?" Evan laughed. "I'm just the guy that does the laundry."

Danny laughed. He was trying a little too hard.

"But if they ask inside, tell them he's with pet therapy," Evan said.

They continued inside the ward and moved room to room, filling closet with various pieces of clothing. Jack followed silently and stuck close to Danny when no one was awake in the room and visited with the ones who were only after they called him over. It was as if he'd done it a thousand times before.

"I don't suppose you could write me a note?" Danny said after a while.

"A note? What, like for your mom or something?" Evan said.

"No, more like a note for school. You know, something saying I was here with you working this morning?"

"Ah," Evan said, and a broad smile pushed across his face. "What's her name?"

"Wait, what?"

"The girl you got into trouble over. What's her name?"

Danny flushed. "It's nothing like that."

He laughed. "Your mouth says no, but your face says yes. You look good in red."

And then, Danny felt for the first time since coming up with the idea that he might actually pull it off.

"So... can you?"

"I guess I could," Evan said. "But I *am* just the guy who does the laundry. Am I allowed?"

"They won't know that you're just the guy who does the laundry. Besides, you're my supervisor."

"Hey, I guess I am. Finish putting this laundry away and I'll see what I can come up with," Evan said.

"Great! Thanks Evan."

He carried on putting away laundry, with Jack following close behind and visiting with the residents until only one room's laundry remained.

D. Pierce. Rm 317

Danny opened the door quietly and crept into the darkened room. The curtain was drawn around the bed and he was glad of it. He liked the old man well enough, but he had a plan this morning. One that might go entirely off the rails if he stopped for a visit or otherwise delineated from it. He tiptoed through the room and motioned for Jack to stay put as he put clothes on hangers and replaced them in the closet, as silently as the little steel triangles would allow. He'd nearly finished when a voice behind spoke, sending bolts of fear stabbing into his back like an arrow buried halfway up the shaft.

"Who left my goddam door open?"

"It's just me, Mr. Pierce," Danny said nervously.

The curtain opened slowly, and the bleary-eyed, balding head of Don Pierce came through the opening.

"Oh, it's you."

His expression softened and the rest of him followed his head past the curtain.

"I was hoping I'd see you again. I seem to remember you said you'd be here all week, but I can't be sure of those kinds of things anymore. But here you are. Good, good! I have a favour to ask you."

"Oh?" Danny said. He couldn't possibly imagine what favour he could do that would be of any use to an old man in a nursing home. "What can I do?"

"Get me the hell out of here."

30

———

"Wait, you want me to what?" Danny said.

"I want you to help me get out of here. Permanently," Don said.

"Are you okay? Do you need me to get the nurse or something?"

"I'm fine," Don said flatly.

"But don't you-"

"Yes, I do. I have dementia, but that isn't what this is. Not yet anyway. But that's why I have to get out of here," Don said.

"I don't think I understand."

Don sighed and walked slowly around his bed.

"I have been in this place for two years. Two years of watching my future hobble past me day after day."

"I don't-"

"Just listen, son, please. You've been here a couple of days now. Tell me what you've seen?"

Danny lowered his head. There had been a few early risers wandering around when he entered the ward. Or more to the point, there were a few people who had likely not slept that night. Or anytime in recent memory from the looks in their eyes. It looked innocent, harmless enough, but he recalled from his last visit the chaos of the dementia ward of Winterbourne Home at mealtime. Elderly men and women crammed into a room too small to accommodate all of them and set at tables with people they hardly knew. Some of them were crying. Some laughed and wandered into the dining room in various states of undress, and continued to wander about the room naked, pausing occasionally to stick scraps of food into their faces, not caring if it came from their designated plates or someone else's. It was loud and disorganized and comical, and Danny thought that trying to meld into the middle of all of it was the toughest thing he'd ever done in his life up to now. It may have been the toughest thing he would ever do. But there was something apart from the chaos. Something he saw that existed in all of them far beyond the crying. Beyond the yelling of tablemates and the food ladies jamming plates in your face and asking if you wanted the chicken or the fish and not staying by the table long enough to hear what your answer was. But beyond those, there was a single, inescapable fact every one of them shared.

They were lost. All of them lost and some, blissfully unaware how lost they were. But there were those unfortunate few, who were still in possession of their faculties at the best of times, sitting at the tables and arguing with the kitchen staff about the inadequate states of their food. Danny felt the worst for them. There was a certain ignorant bliss in the dementia that was well and truly rooted. Some lived in a world of their own creation, some were stuck in the past. Others still were mired in the banality of their working lives, but there was happiness - of a sort in their madness. But the ones that hadn't crossed over the threshold between the real and the surreal, between this world and the next, the ones that wanted the nightmare to end or for death to take them, not caring which came first, these are the ones that Danny truly felt his heart break for. He could leave at the end of each of the days he was there. He got to go home. Maybe the people waiting there didn't give the faintest of shits about him or how he was getting on, but he could come and go as he pleased.

He raised his head slowly and looked at the old man, who continued to stare silently out the window.

"I lose a little bit every day," Don said softly.

"A little bit of what?" Danny said, honestly not understanding what the old man meant.

"Of me." He sighed at the window. "Pieces - small pieces fall away from me every day, and they never, ever come back. Every morning, I start my day with a little less than I was the night before. Every day, I get closer to being one of them, walking aimlessly through the hallway, hoping to remember. Waiting to die."

"But you don't act like them," Danny said. "You don't–" he stopped himself from saying more. Worried that anything he said from this point would only embarrass him and insult the old man.

"They don't lock you away because you don't follow the rules. There's no time off for good behaviour in here. I got shoved in here because my brain started going soft. At first, I fought it. Refused to believe it. That it was really happening to me. I got out of this shithole six times, but I always fucked it up and I'd be back in here in no time. And drugged to the gills."

Danny sat in silence, wanting to reach out to the old man. Even a hand on his shoulder to let him know he wasn't alone in this place, that even in the darkest of times, life wasn't an altogether awful thing. But he couldn't. It was a lie. The boy knew well that life was a series of shitty events meant to wear down your resolve and force you to submit to things you had absolutely no say in or control over and when it had you well and truly down, life really kicked you in the guts.

"There used to be days when I was really sharp, when my mind work be working so well, I was convinced the people here were lying to me. But it wasn't them, it was the disease. The disease lies, tells you what you ant to hear - that they're all out to get you. The staff, your family, the world - all of them. And then things really changed."

"Like what?"

"I can hear my mother's voice. She's been dead nearly forty years, but I can hear her voice just as plainly as I can hear yours. The smell, the smell of the breakfasts she made every Saturday, hangs in the air whenever I wake up. Hell, I can practically taste them. But I can't remember what I take in my coffee anymore. There is a clock in the dining room, but half the time, I don't know what it means. I spent twenty-five minutes yesterday trying to remember what you do with a toothbrush."

"I don't know what to say," Danny said.

"There isn't anything you can say. Have you ever taken a bus, son?" Don said.

"Umm... yeah, sure I have."

"I feel like I've gotten on a bus, but I can't remember why. I look out the window and nothing looks familiar. All the trees and buildings are completely identical and there is nothing familiar that tells me where I should get off. So, I sit back down and wait for something familiar to come by, so I'll know when to get off. Sometimes it takes hours. Sometimes it takes days. One day it won't come by at all and I'll be stuck on that bus with all the other poor bastards who didn't know when to get off."

Danny looked at the old man, saw the fear in his eyes and the sadness he wore around him like a poorly fitting sweater and he decided then that he would help him. However, he could. But life stood up and aimed a kick squarely at his genitals. It wouldn't be that easy.

"Mr. Pierce, I want to help you, really I do, but I'm not sure what I can do. How am I going to get you out of here?"

"That's the simple part," Don said. "You just have to sign me out of here. Once we're off the ward, get me out the front door and I'll take care of the rest."

"I don't know, won't you get into trouble? Won't I?" Danny said.

"My boy, I have escaped from Winterbourne Home six times. I charmed my way out the front door through unsuspecting family members so often, they started sedating me during visiting hours. If anybody asks, you can say you were trying to be nice, and you didn't know I'd run, or you didn't think I was crazy enough to go. Something like that. They'll buy it if it's me. Trust me."

"I don't know. I want to help you, but I–"

"Your Grandfather was my best friend in this place. I know I'm not him, but you'd help him if he asked. Wouldn't you?"

"Well sure, I guess."

Jack, who up to this point had been sitting quietly on the floor between the two of them so quietly that Danny nearly forgot he was there, suddenly hopped on the bed and lay his head in the old man's lap.

"See, even Jack wants to help."

"Get down," Danny said.

But the dog didn't budge.

There was an air of seriousness in Danny's voice that visibly caused the dog some concern, but not enough to make him move. In fact, he wiggled in closer to the old man and doubled his doe eyed efforts to wear down Danny's resolve.

"Oh, for Christ's sake. Fine. Fine Jack, we'll bust him out."

RAISIN CHAN STOOD on the corner of Grey Hollow Road, half a block from her house and Danny's place. She waited for him most mornings. He was mostly late, though never late enough to get them to school after the first bell had rung. Occasionally, once actually, on her birthday, he was early. Early enough that they stopped by Wiederson's Groceteria for fresh donuts on the way to school. Today, however, was not her birthday, and he was well beyond his normal tardiness by about seven minutes. She could feel her heartbeat quicken and the flop sweat bead up on the back of her neck as the seconds became minutes, and the world shifted to high gear and time ripped past her.

If she was late for school, and her father found out about it, and if he learned she was late because of the dirty orphan from down the street, he'd beat her hard enough that she'd sit uncomfortably for the better part of a week. Raisin looked nervously at her watch again. She'd wait another two minutes and nothing more. It would give her just enough time to get to school and still make the opening bell.

The first minute clicked by on her watch, and Danny had not emerged from his house. It'd been so long since she'd walked alone, the prospect of doing so felt odd and vaguely unsettling.

"God damn it Danny," she cursed him and glanced at her watch again. The second minute rolled by, and she couldn't wait any longer.

Raisin hurried down Grey Hollow Road and followed it to Parker Street, moving through downtown quickly and then into the yard of Winterbourne High school, making it before the first bell. She was nearly at the back door when a voice came from behind her.

"Where's your boyfriend?"

It was Baz Schaeffer, football player, dark-haired good-looking kid, well dressed and good looking enough to be completely out of Raisin's league. To say he was attractive to most of the young women at the school would be completely fair. To say he was an arrogant prick because he knew it would have been entirely more accurate. Raising kept her head down and quickened her pace, hoping to reach the double doors and make it into the school before Baz and his cronies moved on her. She knew from a lifetime of being Chinese in a predominantly white school, never to challenge the herd, so she kept her mouth shut and hurried to the door.

She was a handful of feet from the entrance when she felt the sharp sting of impact at the back of her head.

"Hey, you. Fat chink," he said and picked up another clod of dirt. "I said, where is your fucking boyfriend?"

I could answer, she thought. *I should answer. Something snappy and biting. That'd shut them up. But then I'd get something a lot worse than a chunk of dirt up the back of my head. And if the old man finds out I was late because of a boy - three boys who are definitely not even slightly Asian. He'll cripple me before he stops hitting me.*

She ran full tilt and prayed she could make it to the steps before they did. She did. And she pushed her way inside and started off down the hallway toward her class before they caught her.

"You wait until after school, fatty. You'll be sorry you ran."

The bell to begin class clanged out loudly and startled her, and she turned toward the classroom door. Baz took hold of her arm and jammed a finger in her face, wagging as a half-hearted warning to her, while the other two drew their fingers across their eyelids in a mocking imitation of her almond-shaped eyes and cackled off down the hallway, presumably to their own classes. She watched the three of them disappear before entering her own class, a knot tightening itself around in her guts as she took her seat.

"Miss Chan, good of you to join us," the man at the front of the room said.

"Um, the bell just rang, sir."

"Nevertheless, I would hope this is not a behaviour you're inclined to repeat."

He produced a small, folded slip of marigold paper and placed it on her desk. Raisin felt the heat rise in her back and her face went flush. A late slip meant time in the principal's office or worse, a detention after school. Her father would know, without a doubt, and he would hit her. A little at first. But it would change, it would worsen, and all his fears and frustrations would froth over, and he would call her a whore and a fat loser and a failure of a child before it was over. And it wouldn't be over until he was exhausted, and she was sore and in tears. Or worse. Raisin unfolded the paper and felt a small shudder of relief ripple through her.

The yellow paper was not a late slip. Instead, it was a request to come to the office. That was enough to leave her a touch unsettled. But the big hand drawn smiley face at the bottom of the paper said this was likely not to be a punitive visit. In the immediacy, at least, she was safe from her father. Raisin sat at her desk, befuddled. She had never been late, she had never been in trouble, she hadn't so much as ever been called to the office to take a phone call from her father saying one of her relatives had died or the toilet was overflowing, and she needed to come home straight away. Her gaze moved awkwardly from the yellow paper to the black of the slate chalkboard and back again, uncertain what she should do now.

"Miss Chan?" the teacher said, a hint of impatience in the words.
"Sir?"
"Problem?"

"Um... maybe?"

"Yes?"

"Ah, should I go now? To the office, I mean. Should I go to the office now, do you think?"

"I should think you would have left ten minutes ago if I were you," he said.

Raisin stood and stepped toward the door.

"Miss Chan?" the man said.

"Sir?"

"Take your books. You're not likely to be back here."

"Oh, Okay," she said.

She turned back and packed up her books. She could see the others in the room, hear them tittering, and saw them looking at her and looking away before their eyes met. They started with stares and whispers and moved on to open laughter and obscene gestures. It wasn't the first time she'd seen it from them. It wouldn't be the last. She was heavy. She was awkward. And she was Asian. It was as though she wore a sign around her neck that said *Pick on me. I'm different and vulnerable.* She had become so calloused to it that their whispered teasing and barely concealed hands pointing hardly registered with her at all. She slung her backpack and stepped out of the room.

The hallways were empty, save the janitorial staff. Classes being full and properly in session, but Raisin felt she was being watched. Not by many eyes, like the teenaged, judging ones she'd just left, but someone else, something else's eyes, staring at her. Boring holes in her from somewhere deep in the hallway between the classroom where she was and the office where she needed to be. It was unnerving and made her want to turn around and go back into the classroom, but the threat of a school authority telling her father she'd skipped out on a meeting, innocuous or not, was too great a fear for her to ignore and so she pushed through her nerves and headed for the main office. She stopped short of opening the main office door and her eyes whipped quickly to the right of the door. Near the down stairwell, following a blur of black motion. If pressed later, she would swear that she glimpsed the same thick, matted black fur that she and Danny had followed to the school from Seonagh's woods.

Raisin walked toward the stairwell, to the place where she'd seen the dark flash, half expecting to see the big thing sitting at the bottom of the stairs. She didn't and decided it was just a worried mind distracting her. She walked back to the office and pushed the door open.

"Can I help you?" the receptionist said without looking up.

"I was called here," Raisin said.

"What?"

"I was called here," Raisin said again, overemphasising the words.

"You have a slip, I assume?"

The adage about never assuming anything flashed through the girl's mind and nearly escaped her lips, but she thought better of it as another snotty comment from the receptionist seemed the likely result. Raisin handed the slip to the woman and took a step away from the desk.

"This says you're to see principal Koch," she said.

"Um... yes?" Raisin said, confused what she should say.

"Well, he's not here."

"Oh, should I go back to class then?"

"No, he's gone down to the basement with Mr. MacPherson. Something about problems with the boiler down there. He said that anyone who comes to see him until it's fixed will just have to meet him down there," the woman said, sounding entirely put out by the question.

"Oh," Raisin said slowly. "Okay. How do I get to the basement?"

"Do you know the stairwell around the corner from the office door?"

"Yes."

"Go down it."

Again, Raisin bit her tongue, fearing that something insolent might fly off it and get back to her father. She headed toward the door, turned to the left, and walked down the staircase toward the basement. The smell of smouldering, ancient dust and simmering oil and grease rose to meet her as she neared the bottom of the stairs. It was dark. Not too dark to see, but dark enough that unease wriggled in the pit of her stomach like maggots on spoiled meat as she walked slowly toward a grime covered door marker **JANITOR.** It was hot down here. Hot and the basement had a natural dampness that she could feel even at the top of the stairs.

"Dank," she said. "It feels dank down here." She finally understood what the word meant. Raisin reached for the handle but stopped short of opening the door and it suddenly dawned on her how off all of this seemed.

She'd met principal Koch on two occasions, once on her very first day of high school when he presided over a welcome assembly full of nervous freshmen, and the second she was summoned to the office only to discover she'd been mistaken for someone else. Though, being the only daughter of the only Asian family in Winterbourne, she couldn't imagine who he'd mistaken her for. But it struck her how delicate he seemed, despite his height. The man was surprisingly effeminate. Certainly not the type to muck in with the janitor to fix a defective boiler. Maybe he wasn't doing any of the repairing, maybe he was just so overwhelmingly type A, that he had to supervise even the smallest of things to make sure they did them to his satisfaction. It seemed more likely than envisioning him up to his elbows in sweat and hot, black grease.

"Miss Chan, I see you got my message." A voice spoke from the muggy gloom behind her.

Raisin whipped around at the sound of the man's voice, and the maggots stopped squirming in her guts and felt more like a wasp crawling up her leg, slowly and deliberately tickling and pricking her skin ever so slightly as it went. Her knees shook, and she could feel the nervous sweat, driven on by the overwhelming heat of the basement boiler room, soak through the armpits of her shirt.

Raisin couldn't see him. She knew by the voice, she'd heard it more than enough times over the P.A. that it was the principal, but she couldn't see him at all. She looked left and right and behind her and continued to do so, focusing her attention to a particular direction by jutting her head outward and squinting into the near blackness, so that she looked as though she was spinning in a kind of maddened dance recital.

"Sir? Mr. Koch, sir, is that you?" she said.

"Yes, could you come over this way, Miss Chan?" Koch said.

"Which way, sir, I can't see you."

He stepped out of the shadows, tall and thin and sharply dressed in a suit that was tailored to his physique. And there wasn't a speck of grease or dirt near him, let alone actually on him. Raisin backed up as Hughie Koch moved toward her and it seemed to hasten his advance. In a heartbeat, he was practically on top of her, close enough that she could smell his breath. He took several huge gulps of air alongside her face and pulled away from her quickly, heading back to where he came.

"Miss Chan," he said, and the wasp made its way up her leg, past the small of her back, heading north. His voice seemed deeper now, low and deep, like the rumble of far-off thunder.

"Mr. Koch?" she said.

Silence answered her. The principal melded into the shadows once more and her answer came as a cacophony of grunts and growls and low angry guttural sounds.

"Sir," Raisin said. "Sir? If you won't answer, sir, I'm going to go back upstairs."

"Here I am," he said and stepped into her field of vision again.

She held up the yellow slip of paper, thrusting it out to him as though it were a talisman that would keep her safe from whatever was going on down here.

"What have we here?" the principal said.

"Um…" she said, confused at the question. "It's an office slip, sir. You sent it to my home room. Because you wanted to see me?"

"Ah, yes. I remember now," he said.

"Um… did I do something wrong, sir? Did I do something bad that I wasn't aware of?"

A sigh escaped from the shadows, and the man stepped forward again. He was different now. Taller perhaps and thicker, more muscular. The suit that fit him so immaculately moments before now looked stretched to its limits, threatening to tear at the seams and fall away completely.

"Actually, Miss Chan, I didn't want to see you at all," the principal said.

He took in huge gulps of air, sucking and grunting as he did, and he dropped to his knees as though he was going to puke. Raisin felt immediately that she should rush over to him and try to help him, but thought better of it when his head reared up again. But it wasn't him she saw. Instead, it was something else, something changed. Tall and thick and decidedly lupine, but not entirely. There was something about him that was neither human nor beast but stuck somewhere horribly in the middle of the two, ruinous and wrong. His eyes jaundiced yellow and watery, like a face dunked underwater for too long, pallid and waxy and yellowed with decay. His arms seemed lengthened - unnaturally long and thick muscular, hair covered things that came to an end just below the thick and hairy kneecaps in the middle of the thick and hairy legs his body stood above.

"I want to know where your friend Mr. Nesbitt is?" the principal said through massive, yellowed canine teeth.

"Danny? What do you want with him?"

"Well, that's kind of an interesting story." It smiled.

He snapped his fingers and the large, black, hairy thing she and Danny had followed from the culvert stepped from the shadows. Panting and drooling and looking every bit like the awful black dog she thought it was.

"My friend and I have come an awfully long way to find your Danny, and we were thinking, if it wasn't too much trouble, that he might help us with our little problem."

"Oh?"

"Yes, you see, we have this little group, and Danny would fit in perfectly. In fact, you might say it is his destiny to be part of us. The health of the group depends on it," Koch said.

"Oh, so, what did you want me for?" Raisin said, still not entirely certain that it had to do with her.

"Well, two reasons. The first and likely most important is you probably know where young Danny is, yes?" the Koch thing said.

"Well, I don't know where he is right this second, but I can probably figure out where he is or where he's going to end up today."

"Excellent."

"But I still don't see what any of that has to do with me after I get him here," Raisin said.

"Ah," Koch said. "There's the tricky part."

"How is that tricky?"

"Well, we were rather hoping that Danny would help us kill you and then eat your entrails as you lay dying."

He smiled as the large black dog growled and moved on her, pining her to the ground.

"Does that answer your question?"

31

———————

Floyd woke with a start and shot straight up from the couch he'd passed out on, cold sweat streaming down his face and soaking through his grimy undershirt. His hands fumbled, feeling thick and useless, swollen with the booze of the night before, fumbled for his Marlboros and pulled one from the pack with relative ease. They hadn't shaken yet, but he knew the tremors were definitely in the mail. They had already begun as he tried to spark the Bic to life three or four times before the flame ignited and took a meandering path to the cigarette on the way to taking the first, merciful drag.

He was home, on his own filthy couch in his own filthy apartment, but had no actual memory of getting here. It wasn't his first rodeo - or his first fugue state. There were more nights than he could count in recent memory, nights where he'd be hanging off the bar at Butler's, or threatening violence and immediate arrest to anyone that got in his way, only to black out entirely and wake up in his apartment. Usually stinking of the cheapest liquor Butler's offered and soaked in his own piss, wondering who he'd pissed off before pouring himself behind the wheel and hoping that the car still knew its way home. It was reckless and stupid, driving blackout drunk, but he *was* a cop and felt a certain impunity in doing it. Even if he wasn't on the force, there wasn't much beyond being arrested and locked up until he sobered up. That would have stopped him from doing it.

Floyd struggled. Struggled with the shakes that creeped all over him and built in strength with every jerky movement he made, threatening to shake him from the couch and onto the floor in a twitchy mess of addiction and ruined possibility. And he struggled for any small glimpse of the memory of what had got him here. It came to him. Slowly, hesitantly, and painfully, through the fog of spent liquor and forgotten good intentions. But was there liquor? He remembered twisting the cap back on the bottle and vowing to leave off the whisky, as much as he was able, until he got a handle on the deaths of all these kids. There was an old man... Dan... Don. Don Pierce, and he'd pointed him toward an old nun at Winterbourne home who'd told him... well... she'd told him something about someone that seemed incredibly important but was lost in the morning's haze after the night before. It was about the convent, the convent on the other side of town that was also an orphanage back when she was a novitiate.

He remembered the old woman speaking in wandering half truths of the town's elite and their indulgences and the rich old men putting on impressive, silken robes and parading about in the basement of St. Margaret's, keeping the flames of their illicit desires burning brightly in the secret bosom of the Sisters of Perpetual Temperance. And he recalled the awful truth of the orphans in their charge and what they had done to them, time and time again, over so many unchecked years of the orphanage's existence. And where was the orphanage now? He knew this. The answer was so close on the tip of his tongue; it was practically spitting down his throat.

"Convent?" he said to the empty apartment. "Convent? Winterbourne Convent?"

The haze was so thick along the pathways in his brain, and it covered his thoughts in so much self-inflicted muck that it felt as though he were underwater. But he forced his mind forward, heading for a destination that would either get his mind to quiet or overwork it to the point of passing back out. Either way, he'd get some kind of peace.

"Winterbourne Convent? Winterbourne Convent never was Winterbourne Convent. It was always the Sisters of Miserable something or other orphanage until it burnt down. Then it was..." He stopped talking, his thoughts seemingly stalled. Don was lost somewhere in a fog only he could sense, looking for a point of reference. He found it. "Winterbourne High. The Convent turned into Winterbourne High."

And it all came flooding back then. The group of rich, dirty old men taking kids into the basement of that convent and then the high school, and killing them, dumping their bodies all over town. The old lady was demented, yes. But she was clear as a bell about the kids. Names, ages, dates, locations. She knew all of it because she supplied them, brought them like calves fatted for veal. But her dementia kicked itself into high gear. She was certain that they were still doing it. All these years later, the same group of men, save for a couple, bought an unnaturally long life by their willingness to slaughter the youth of Winterbourne. She'd also mentioned that the survival of their group depended on the bringing in of fresh blood. New members to the club, willing to defame themselves and bathe in the blood of the forgotten, rubbish children of Winterbourne.

"The tree of life must be watered by the blood of the innocent," she said.

"Oh... um... yes?" Guthrie said.

"Yes. And lo, the scion shall feast on the offal and gain life everlasting," she said.

"The righteous scion." Guthrie chuckled. He was certain the old gal had slipped well back into her dementia now. "And what's that?"

"It is he, or she, I think Elanor Blanchey did it for a while in the thirties, who would lead us all. Lead us from the darkness into the light of eternity."

"Oh, I see. I think I have enough here, Mrs. Fitzgerald."

"It would be a child. Standing on the threshold of adulthood, but not yet crossed over. A child alone in the world through no fault of their own with nothing to gain and no fear of losing everything. He must come willingly. He must eat of the organs freely and of his own accord. Only then will he appease the great and lonely one." She was practically whispering.

The memories crowded in then, forcing their way in and overwhelming his hungover brain. The old woman told him of entire families tied to this secret society, nearly since the beginning of the town. All the big names of the town had their fingers dipped in the blood of these dead kids. Except one. Strangely enough, the only name the old nun hadn't mentioned was old man Winterbourne, the industrialist who'd shamed and bullied the town into giving him whatever he wanted - including renaming the place after him. *Jesus,* Guthrie thought. *If somebody as rich as that miserable old loony couldn't get into this club, just how rich did you have to be? Or how fucking crazy?*

He remembered the other cop, Kemmler, and that he'd been there to Winterbourne home already, sniffing around and intimidating the old man. Don had remained tight-lipped about anything he knew. Guthrie was sure of that. But the nun. The old nun had probably told him everything. Told about the meetings and the sacrifices and the basement of the high school. Squawked about the ceremonies and needing new blood. Floyd knew that he'd need to get to the high school before long. Sooner rather than later, or there'd likely be another dead kid.

"A child alone with nothing to gain and no fear of losing anything," he said out loud. And it hit him, like a bolt from a crossbow, fired point blank through the centre of his forehead. "Danny!"

But it all went south from there.

The shakes hit him, full and hard and unrelenting. The tremors beginning in his hands and racing up his arms and, by the time it registered in his brain that they were shaking, they had moved on to another part of his body, compounding the insult and betrayal perpetuated by years of slavery to a cold amber liquid. The shakes hit his stomach, the awful vinegar and chyme-soaked queasiness that came from too much booze and too little non-fried food over too long of a time. The perspiration that beaded up on his neck and quickly soaked through his undershirt was cold and likely more scotch than sweat. He felt his knees tremble, threatening to give way if he didn't sit down.

Guthrie made his way to the kitchen in a stumbling, near roll to the wooden chair sitting at the table. The sickly tingling in the pit of his stomach had moved south, and he knew, from experience, if he tried to do anything apart from sitting down for a minute and keeping a clear path to the toilet, he'd shit himself in the middle of his apartment. He made it and sat in the chair. The coolness of the wood felt good against his back and the calmed his mind from spinning around just how awful he felt. The bottle of White Horse sat on the table. Lid gone and contents nearly the same. The man could have a drink. He was an adult, he could have a drink whenever he wanted to and also, he could do it with a clear conscience. The man was his own person.

The trouble with being your own man is there isn't anyone you can sling your bullshit onto that'll believe it. He was his own man, sure, but he was also a blackout drunk who had recently drunk so much that he had little memory of even getting to his apartment and was now so sick from the drink he wasn't sure if he'd ever be well enough to go help his friend at the high school, He could take a drink any time he wanted to. It was 7:30 in the morning, but he was an adult, and he could take a drink anytime he wanted to.

"Fuck-you," he said to the bottle and pushed back from the table.

A shower, he thought. *I'll have a shower and something to eat. It'll straighten me out enough to get over there. Shit, maybe a few jumping jacks for good measure. Don't they say exercise can get you over the hump of a hangover?* He could have a drink anytime he wanted. He was a grown man. But there were things to do and sitting here wallowing in a gargantuan hangover, near to shitting his pants. He could have a drink anytime. But he wouldn't. Guthrie stood up, full of resolve, and headed toward the kitchen cupboard. There were boxes of cereal in there. He could eat one without too much risk of it coming back up right away. What he really wanted was a plate of bacon and eggs from the Aztec, but he knew that would ask for trouble and shit smeared trousers, attempting to make it to the other side of town with nothing in the bottom of his stomach but vinegar-soaked good intentions.

The cereal bar was dry and mealy and nearly as delicious as strawberry flavoured baby food. He swallowed hard and felt it hit the bottom of his gut like a stone. He made his way to the bathroom, praying the stone would stay put and not start hurling itself about, as stomach stones do. The light flickered and came to life. Flickered again and died and after several painful, buzzing minutes, flickered to life again and blazed in all its sickly, blue-white glory. He turned the knob for the shower and waited an eternity for the water to run from rust, to piss coloured to clear, and stepped beneath the flow of it. It was good. It was glorious, and he let it run across his face and down his chest, taking a hefty portion of the hangover with it.

When he was certain he was near enough to sober, he turned the tap off. Floyd took the least offensive smelling towel from the back of the bathroom door and remembered it had been months since he'd last done the laundry. He headed to his bedroom to get dressed, passed the kitchen table as he walked by, looked at the bottle as he walked by, felt like the horse on the label was staring at him as he walked by. If he wanted, he could have a drink anytime. He was a grown man. But he wouldn't, not now.

The landlord must have gotten the light fixtures on sale as the bedroom light worked with nearly the same efficiency as the bathroom one did. When the light finally gave in and turned on, Floyd rummaged through his dresser and found, to his surprise, a clean pair of socks and drawers. There were several pairs of pants in the closet that weren't completely geometric with wrinkles and one shirt that wasn't yellow at the neck and armpits with sweat stains. The tie was an afterthought, and if it matched his outfit, all the better. He'd just finished tying it when he heard the old woman's voice in his head.

"A child alone... a child alone..."

Floyd walked back out into the kitchen and stopped at the kitchen table. He was a grown man; he could drink any time he wanted. Guthrie stood paralysed, staring at the bottle, and wandered into his mind. Back to a rain-soaked night a while back when he was the first on the scene of a car accident. Two adults lay dead inside the mangled pretzel of steel along the side of Highway 9 and a little boy, peppered with teardrops of broken windshield and flecked with the blood of the other occupants of the car.

"A child alone."

"I don't know what to do," the child said to Guthrie. "It's all gone now, all gone now."

Guthrie's hands shook, and he turned toward the door of his apartment, heading out the door. He turned back toward the kitchen and saw Danny, standing on the other side of the table, covered in glass again, bleeding, and so very lost.

"It's all gone now, all gone now."

He grabbed the bottle, put it to his mouth, and upended it. He was a grown man, and he could drink any time he wanted to.

"Fuck," Guthrie said and threw the empty White Horse bottle across the room.

32

<hr>

"This won't work," Danny said, looking around nervously. "Somebody's gonna stop us and then we're both screwed."

"It'll work, you watch. Nobody's going to say a word to either of us," Don said.

The old man sat in a wheelchair, with Danny pushing him. Strictly speaking, he didn't need to be in it. He could walk perfectly well, if not a little more slowly than he used to. They decided the chair would make a quick exit from the building a thousand times easier. It also gave the pair of them the ability to run from anybody who got a little too close to stopping them. The boy folded up the walker he used normally and hung it carefully between the handles of the wheelchair like the frame of a backpack. Danny had imagined he might make it off the ward before a curious nurse or orderly stopped the pair of them to find out where he was taking this old man. Nobody so much as looked at them sideways as they made it to the locked door that led into the main hallway.

"Shit," Danny said.

"What?"

"The code."

"What?"

"The code to get out of this place. I can't remember the goddam code."

The colour suddenly drained away from the old man's face.

"Well now, what?" he said to the boy.

He was a clever kid, in most situations, but he stood staring at the small black control panel, unable to organize a single thought. What would they do now? Asking someone for help was out of the question and he doubted Dave from the laundry room would be along this time to help him out. He looked over at the nurse's desk. Nobody seemed to pay any attention to him and the old man. At least there was that. He was looking at the nurse's desk when the thumping sound from beside him broke his concentration.

Don Pierce was out of his wheelchair and pulling on the door as hard as he could. The door made an ugly, wooden thud as it gave ever so slightly against the electric locks that held it in place, though remaining firmly locked. The old man continued pulling at it, as though repeated effort might get the door open and let them out. It was not an unusual occurrence, people trying to rip the door off its hinges. It was an occurrence, however, that always drew the attention of the orderlies and nurses.

Danny looked back at the nurse's desk and saw the head of the woman sitting there turn toward them.

"Shit," Danny said. "Shit, shit and double shit."

The old man continued to pull on the door and the door continued to thump and clatter every time he did.

"Come on," Danny said. "Come on, we've gotta get away from the door."

He looked back at the desk and saw the nurse speaking to an orderly and pointing toward him and the old man.

"Shit, shit, shit, shit, shit," Danny fretted. "We've gotta move. Now!"

Don turned back to the door and began reefing on it again, getting the same thunderous result.

The boy looked over his shoulder toward the desk and saw the nurse had gone back to whatever she had been doing before Don began rattling the door on its moorings. The orderly, however, was nowhere to be seen. *Probably gone back to whatever he was doing,* Danny thought. He relaxed a little and felt if he could just concentrate a little harder now that the commotion didn't seem to get a response, that he'd remember the code in time.

"Going out, are we?" the big man in white said.

"Oh... we're just... that is we're going to... I'm just taking grandad..." he said.

"A bit early for that, isn't it?"

"Grandad is a little sharper in the mornings these days. If I wait until the afternoon, I'm never sure who I'll be taking for a walk, you know what I mean?"

The orderly moved closer to the door, nearly between the boy and the old man, and looked closely into Don's face.

"Yeah, I sure do. We lost my momma to it a few years back. The dementia don't care. It don't care who you are or what you do. It sneaks in and steals everything you are," he said, and Danny could see the corners of his eyes glisten.

He was a large man, thick and muscular, with a neck that looked bigger than Danny's waist. The raw emotion that seemed to pour out of him seemed completely out of place.

"Grandad used to coach my baseball team," Danny said and motioned toward the old man.

Don continued to fiddle with the door, pulling and thumping and not getting any farther than he had the previous times.

"Well, you fellas enjoy your walk," the orderly said and continued to stand almost between the two of them. Close enough to the door that Danny would have to manoeuvre around him.

Don yanked on the door again and looked at the larger man. "That's really odd," he said. "I can't seem to get this door open. Very odd."

And a memory slammed its way into Danny's head like a gun shot.

"Odd! It's so odd!" he said.

He pushed his way past the thick necked man and put his hand on the keypad. He punched in 1379, the code to get out, all odd numbers.

"Let's go, Grandad," Danny said and pushed the wheelchair through the open door.

"It's not the only thing that's odd," the orderly said and turned back toward the ward.

Danny and Don boarded the elevator and remained silent as it descended to the lobby. The doors chimed open, and they walked slowly out of the car, scanning the lobby to be certain they were still in the clear. They were and made their way to the front door. From there, it was a few steps through the automatic doors and out into the fresh, free air of an early fall morning. Not cold, but crisp enough to remind you of seasonal inevitability.

"Are you able to walk down the stairs? There are an awful lot of them," Danny said to the old man.

"I don't think so. My knees are for shit. But they paved the driveway all the way to the street. Just wheel me down that way and then I'll take it from there," Don said.

"Oh, okay." They walked to the left of the main entrance to Winterbourne Home and stood looking down to the street below. Between them, a newly paved black tarmac driveway extending some hundred and fifty feet downwards in a gradual arc, ending on the back end of Parker Street.

"Jesus, are you sure about this?" Danny said, looking down the hill, a huge knot of uneasiness tightening in the pit of his stomach.

"It'll be fine," Don said. "Just go slow."

Danny moved the wheelchair into place at the top of the hill, leaning slightly backward to slow the forward momentum as they moved further down. It was going well for the first leg of it, and he thought they'd make it down to Parker Street without a problem.

"So, what are you going to do once we get to the–"

The words stopped dead and so did he. The back wheels of the chair came to rest, momentarily, on a long, thin tree branch laying across the driveway. It was enough to break Danny's stride and trip him up. He lurched forward and tried to grip tighter on the wheelchair and, in doing so, pushed it forward, farther away from him and travelling faster now.

"No!"

He was back up nearly instantly, but it wasn't enough. The chair - and the old man sitting in it - were barrelling toward the bottom of the hill and the steady flow of traffic along Parker Street.

"No!" Danny took off in a run after the chair.

The old man in the chair was gaining speed now, moving so much faster than Danny thought a wheelchair could travel. The boy couldn't see Don's face, but his head didn't appear to be turning frantically or anything. Danny thought he might have blacked out. He pushed himself, running as hard and as fast as he could run and tried to catch the aging juggernaut, closing the distance almost enough to grab hold of the chair, when the last curve of the long driveway appeared, and the chair continued on straight. It hit the grass that lined the drive and stopped dead, launching the old man ten feet forward, where he came to rest in a crumbled heap against one of the big box elders that lined the property.

"Don!" Danny ran to the old man.

He had visions of the old man laying there dead, a gruesome wound across his head and gushing blood all over the perfectly manicured grass as his skin greyed and he sputtered and choked on his last words, spitting curses at Danny and blaming him for getting him into this. He stopped running, afraid to go over - fearing it was true and the old man really was gone. *But what if he isn't?* It occurred to him then that Don could well have survived the jolt from the wheelchair and the collision with the tree, but he could now lie in a heap as his life ebbed away while Danny stood there slack jawed. Whatever his condition, dead or alive, it wasn't about to change while Danny stood there slack jawed and apprehensive. He crept nervously to the body on the lawn and bent down to turn him over. A sound erupted from the old man, and Danny blanched in complete terror.

The laughter bubbled up from the old man like a warm spring and a broad, fat smile spread across his face like an old friend, long estranged and recently returned to the betterment of all. He rolled over, still convulsing with laughter, and tried to sit up. When he couldn't, he stuck out a hand to the boy, asking for help. Danny pulled him up into a sitting position and leaned him against the box elder he'd come to a rest against.

"Are you alright?" Danny said.

"That was great! Most fun I've had I years. I'm better than alright. I'm fucking great!" Don said.

Around the crash site, were most of the contents of the old man's pockets, shaken out of him as he rolled and tumbled to a rest against the big box elder. A comb, a handful of coins and three small ceramic figurines - the kind that came from well meaning boxes of tea bags and tended to multiply despite never buying more boxes of tea bags. A little closer to the old man, lay a tall, orange plastic pill bottle. The cap had come off in the accident and spilled the bottle's contents out a little where it came to rest. The pills were oblong, Tic-Tac shaped and yellow. Danny knew what they were by sight. The Foster Father had an ample supply of them to ease him through a back injury he never actually had. He always thought it was funny that the Foster Father's back only ever seemed to flare up on the weekends when the gin ran out or he had been fighting with the Foster Mother. But why did this old man have so many of the rotten things?

"Give me those now," Don said, sticking his hand out to Danny.

"What have you got them for?"

"You just never mind that now and give me back my medicine. I need it."

"You got an injury?" Danny said.

"I got plenty. Give me them."

Danny scooped up the yellow tablets, put them back in the bottle, and handed them back to Don after he secured the cap. The old man grabbed them and held the bottle close to his chest, not as a junkie holds his stash, God knows Danny had met enough people like that through the Fosters, rather he held it like a pilgrim clings to a bible in an unholy land. As though the pill bottle was a holy relic, sanctified and consecrated, and, just possessing it, made his life safe again.

"That's an awful lot of pills," Danny said. "Should you even be out here if you need that many pills in a day?"

"Can we just drop this? Come help me up and let's get out of here before they come down here looking for us."

But Danny couldn't let it go.

"What time do you want me to bring you back?"

"You don't have to. I'll be alright."

He helped the old man up and, when he was certain he was safe, he went back up the hill to where the wheelchair had stopped. He came back down to Don and helped him to sit. The old man still clutched the bottle like it was a holy relic. Danny pulled the brake lever forward on the right wheel of the chair and then the left. Then he walked around the chair and crouched so he would be eye to eye with the old man.

"I know what you're doing, and I won't let you. You can give me the pills, or I can take them away from you."

"You can try," Don said and pushed himself up into the chair.

"Why?"

"Why what?"

"Why would you want to take all those pills?"

"Are you kidding me? Are you fucking kidding me? Do you know where I live?" Don said, the ire rising in his voice.

"Of course, I kn–"

"You don't know shit about shit. I live in a madhouse. A rat trap with yellow stained sheets and shit covered walls. I live in pissy carpets in hallways that don't go anywhere. A room with a view that I will never see from the other side of the glass again. I live in a dining room that sounds like the inside of a beehive, with food, overcooked and brown, flavourless and soft, trying to remember the taste of a good steak or a malted milkshake and a cheeseburger tasted like."

His voice trembled.

"I'm sorry, I–"

"Look, Danny, I don't have a lot of time left."

"Wait, what? Are you dying?"

"Yeah. But no, not soon. I have dementia. It's why I got locked up in there. Every day, I can feel a little bit more of me fall away and disappear. For the last three months, I have been saving these pills. I wanted to be sure there was enough, that there would be no chance of me waking up or somebody finding me and bringing me back. I knew I couldn't do it inside. I knew I had to get out. When I met you and Jack, I seized my chance. I'm sorry I did it to you, but I can't, Danny. I can't go back in there and watch myself fall apart. I can't be one of them," Don said.

Danny knew what he meant by *them*. They were the demented of Winterbourne. Confused and angry and sad and crying and raging and fighting and lingering in a life most of them would just as soon not live anymore.

"But you promised," Danny said.

"What?"

"You promised to tell me everything you knew about my grandfather and my parents, and you haven't told me shit. I won't let you do yourself in, not yet."

Don considered this for the moment and conceded. He had given his word to the boy.

"Fine. Get me to the High School and I'll tell you everything I know about what went on there and what your family had to do with it," Don said.

"Okay." Danny smiled. He hadn't prevented the end, so much as slowed its progress a little, but for now, that was enough.

"But after I've helped you, you will promise to help me. If I can't manage all these pills on my own, you will help me take them. Deal?"

Danny remained silent, contemplating what the man had just asked him. He bet that, when it came right down to it, the old man did not have the stones to go through with it. What would be the harm in agreeing to help an old man who really had no intention of doing himself in?

"Deal," Danny said, and the pair shook hands.

33

Guthrie pulled the beat-up Ford into the parking lot of Winterbourne High and parked in the spot furthest away from the door. It was cold and damp and late August was quickly giving way to September and the mornings held a chill that previewed the weather that was to come. Floyd had put on a tweed sport coat, and it had been warm enough yesterday, but today, this morning, he wished he'd pulled an overcoat on top of the entire outfit. He blew out a few quick breaths. It wasn't cold enough to see his breath yet, but the air told him it wouldn't be long. Two, maybe three weeks before he could see it hanging in the air like fog. He closed the door to the Ford and pulled the lapels of his jacket up around his neck, and headed toward the front door of the school.

The door was locked up tight, and why wouldn't it be? It was just after 6:30 in the morning and the only people Floyd imagined were currently here were the janitors, getting ready to keep the place clean and puke free for the rest of the school day. He went back toward his car when a flash of movement registered in the corner of his eye. His head snapped toward the movement and focused on the man attached to it. It was Randy, Danny's Foster Father, headed into the basement of the school.

"What the fuck?"

It was the excuse he needed to stay out of the car. He followed quickly and quietly around the back of the school and, as he watched the grubby man enter, pursued him into the basement of the school. It was hot here. Hot and dry and stinking of grease that was probably older than he was, mixed with the odd stink of burnt dust that came along with firing the boilers for the first time after a long, hot summer. It was dark and desolate down here. Nobody hanging around the bottom of the stairs and standing in the shadows. Nobody that he could see, anyway. Which begged the question, where had the prick Danny lived with gone? Guthrie was only a few feet behind him, right until he entered the basement door. He hung back a little before entering, to give the weaselly bastard a chance to get a little beyond the door before he entered it. But he was nowhere near here now. There was no sign he'd ever been there.

Guthrie dug in his pockets, looking for something that might help him navigate the place, and came up with a half empty cigarette lighter. He hadn't smoked now in more years than he had the filthy habit and chuckled a little, trying to recall the last time he wore this particular tweed sport coat, marvelling that it didn't smell any worse than it did. He flicked the Bic and followed the partially illuminated path it provided, which wasn't more than a foot or two in front of him. The further along he moved with the lighter blazing a trail in front of him, the hotter his hand became and the more he realized it wasn't dark enough to actually need the damned thing. He let go of the plunger and stuffed it back into the side pocket it came out of.

The air was dank and stale, making it difficult for him to breathe, making it difficult for him to breathe, hangover notwithstanding, and he thought of turning back for the moment. But he knew Danny would end up here and even if there was nothing going on down here, Randy was now down here and if he got a hold of the boy down here, dark and secluded as it was, there was no telling what he'd do. Guthrie gave himself a smack across the face. Not hard, but forceful enough to chase away the remaining cobwebs from his mind. It was answered with a scream that, for the briefest of moments, Guthrie couldn't be sure whether it came from him or not. His hand flew again and a third time. When no more screams came back to him, Floyd gave his head a final shake and stood up to his full height. Thinking a little more clearly now, he proceeded down the hallway, walking toward the smell of the boiler.

The hallway came to a T with a door in the centre. He tried the door and was surprised to find it unlocked. Floyd opened the door slowly and groped along the inside wall for a light switch. He found it and suddenly the room lit up like a high mass. In a heartbeat, he wished he hadn't bothered. Laying a crumpled heap, in an ever-widening pool of blood, was Danny's foster father Randy Hewlett. His neck was so severely broken, it had practically turned his head the other way around. Guthrie moved quickly to him and took his wrist, checking for a pulse he knew couldn't possibly be there. It was then he saw how bad the man's wounds were. The jagged gash that encompassed the length of his throat was a fatal injury in its own right, but for good measure, someone had crushed his chest in and ripped open, spilling his organs liberally beneath him.

"You earned this," he said to the dead man.

Danny had mentioned that his foster parents were no picnic to live with, but Guthrie never suspected they would be stupid enough to physically abuse the boy. Until they did. Danny showed up with bruises on his arms one Monday and refused to talk about how he'd gotten them, beyond saying he'd fallen. And these were just the bruises Guthrie could see. After that, he showed up at the fosters house and assured them that if the boy showed up with anymore bruises, he would take a personal interest in inflicting bruises on the both of them. They both swore it was an accident and it would never happen again, but Guthrie knew it was a lie.

"Yeah, you really earned this, asshole," he said.

There was somebody standing behind him now. Guthrie had heard nothing and there was no change in the smell or the feeling of the air or anything else that might have tipped him off, but there *was* somebody standing behind him. He was certain of it and stood slowly, turning back toward the door. Floyd hated being right. It wasn't somebody, not exactly. It was humanoid in that it stood on two legs and had two pendulous arms dangling at its sides, but beyond that, it was something freakish and twisted. More a nightmare on feet than a man standing behind him.

It was at least two heads taller than he was and its face was nearly devoid of any visible flesh, as though someone had plopped the skull of a wolf atop a body that wasn't its own. Around its shoulders, hugging to the base of the skull and extending downward to the middle of its back, was a glorious mane of thick, soft looking black fur. Its ribs were visible beneath olive skin that was stretched so thin it was nearly translucent. The arms were long and sinewy and ended in elongated, black clawed fingers. It stood atop two muscular legs that bent in the opposite direction of a man's leg. The knee joint bent away from it, the way a dog's leg would.

It reached out with one of its leathery arms and placed a clawed hand on his shoulder. The grip was powerful, crushing, and meant to be precisely that. Guthrie felt that if the thing wanted to do him harm, there would be very little he could do to prevent it. The wolf thing pulled him closer and leaned into him. Floyd could smell its breath; it was hot and fetid and reminded him of a rendering plant.

"You'd better come with me," the thing said and strong armed him toward the door.

Guthrie was a little startled that the thing was capable of communication, let alone able to form complete sentences.

"And if I don't?"

The thing tightened its grip on his shoulder, burying its claws deep into the flesh below his collarbone, and Guthrie felt the awful pressure and the strength left his legs. He dropped to his knees, and the thing turned him to the rumpled corpse on the floor. The thing pushed his face closer to the dead man and jammed a finger toward him.

"He didn't come with me," it said with a growl.

And the whole world went black for Floyd Guthrie.

"Hey, is that Butler's?" Don said as they rolled by the town's only bar. "God, I haven't been inside there in ages. Do you think we have time to stop for a quick one?"

"It's just after seven in the morning," Danny said.

"So, that's no?"

"That's no."

"Shit." He sighed. "A last drink would have been nice."

"Can we talk about something else?"

"Sure," Don said. "What's so important at this school that we need to get there straight away?"

Danny figured he had little to lose at this point by telling the old man the truth, and so he did. All of it. From finding the dead boy while he and jack were out walking, to the black thing in the forest by the drainage culvert that chased him and Raisin, to following it to the school and then getting the cryptic message from Floyd Guthrie.

"Floyd Guthrie? I was talking to him yesterday. I told him about the other weirdo cop that came to Winterbourne asking a lot of questions," Don said.

"Questions about what?"

"About your grandad, mostly. About who he hung around with and about some people in that photo album."

"And?"

"And any of the photos he'd be interested in were already out of the album, hidden under my mattress."

"Well, that's good, I guess," Danny said.

"But he didn't stop there. He kept on with the questions."

"Questions about what?" Danny said.

"Questions about Bob's family and specifically, about..." his voice trailed off, and the colour drained from his face.

"About what?"

"Now that I think about it, they were questions about you."

"Wait, what?" Danny said.

"Yeah, asking if Bob had any grandkids and how old they were where they went to school. That kinda shit."

"What did you tell him?"

"Nothing really, I didn't know yet. I mean, I didn't put two and two together about you. I guessed mostly. I said I *thought* Bob had grandkids and that they would probably be about your age. And that if they were of an age, they'd likely go to Winterbourne high. I guess he heard what he needed to. He left after that."

"And what did you tell Guthrie?"

"Floyd? Not much else. He didn't ask about you, mostly about the other cop and what he was up to. They were both bound and determined to get to the high school this morning," Don said.

"Well, there's that anyway," Danny said.

"There's what?"

"That big dog or wolf or whatever the hell it was went into the basement of the high school. If it's still there, it'll be hungry and trapped and pissed off. If Guthrie shows up, he'll have a gun."

"Well, there's that anyway," Don said.

They carried on in an awkward silence, walking along Parker Street until it intersected with Berwick Street and the high school came into view.

"There are stairs into the basement. Do you think you can get down them?" Danny said to the old man.

"I should be able to. I've rested enough now," Don said confidently. "If I can't keep up with you, leave me and I'll catch up with you."

"Okay," Danny said.

He pushed the wheelchair from the effortless movement of the concrete driveway onto the rough, uneven grass and found it nearly impossible to get the old man over to the stairs. He was nearly out of breath by the time they made it.

"Jesus, that was rough."

"I suppose I could have walked," Don said.

The old man stood at the top of the sun-bleached concrete stairs to the basement. They were steep, much steeper than he thought they'd be, and a monstrous wave of vertigo crashed over him, dizzying him and forcing him to take a seat on the top step.

"Holy shit!" He gulped and closed his eyes. "I can't do it. The height is making me dizzy. I could fall and break a hip. Where would I be then? You go on, I'll catch up."

"Are you sure? I could help you down."

"I'm sure. I'll get down there in my own time and then I'll come find you."

"Alright," Danny said. "Be careful up here. See you soon. Jack, you wait here with him."

The little dog, who had been silent up to now, gave a small grumble of protest and took up a seat beside the old man. Danny descended the stairs and disappeared through the basement door, only to re-emerge a second later and march back up the stairs to the old man.

"Nice try," Danny said.

"What?" Don said, feigning as much innocence as he could muster.

"Give me the pill bottle if you're not coming with me."

"What?"

"The bottle filled with all the Percocet. Give it to me."

The old man let go a heavy sigh, stood and walked to the bottom of the staircase, turned and looked up at Danny.

"You coming or what?"

34

Guthrie's eyes fluttered like an over wound window blind and slowly rolled open. His head pounded. The thing hit him solidly enough that the blow knocked him out cold. But he had no memory of it. He recalled it tried to rip his shoulder off, but it hadn't laid a hand on him otherwise. How he got in this shape seemed completely unimportant now. What mattered now, however, was he remained trapped in the basement of Winterbourne High School and, somewhere in this sweaty, musty gloom, so did Danny Nesbitt. And he needed to get him and get the hell out of here. And he needed to get him and get the hell out of here.

It wasn't as dark in there. There were torches in sconces along the walls that bathed the room in a dull orange glow. He looked around and could see that, for now, he was alone in the room. The big dog thing was gone. There was a small stone dais in the centre of the room, on top of which was a large stone X and attached to it was a girl. Her head hung forward and her long hair obscured her eyes. Floyd couldn't say for sure if she was living or dead.

He stood quickly, much quicker than his heart had reckoned he would, and the delay of enough blood getting to his head made the room spin. He feared he would black out again, but lowered his head and took several deep breaths to clear it. The fog lifted, and he made his way over to the girl.

"Hey," he whispered as loud as he could. "Hey there, you okay?"

Floyd reached out and put a hand on her face. She was still warm and appeared to be breathing.

"Hey," he said again and gave her cheek a light slap. "Are you okay?"

She lifted her head and tried to force her eyes open. She gave a little start when she finally saw him.

"No!" she shouted. "Get away from me.

"Shhh! I don't want that big goddam dog coming back in. Pretty sure we're both screwed if that happens," Guthrie said.

"I want to get out of here," she cried. "I want to go home."

"I'm gonna try to get us out of here, honey. Let me get you off that thing first."

He looked at the bonds holding her in place. Tight chains wrapped around her wrists and ankles, locked to themselves and a large, rusty chain around her waist, locked to the stone cross. All secured together with large, rusty, barrel shaped padlocks.

"Shit," Guthrie said.

"What, what is it?" the girl said.

"What's your name?"

"Raisin," she said.

"Wait, what?"

"Raisin," she said again. "Long story."

"Okay, Raisin, we have a problem. You're attached to this cross with three really large, really thick padlocks and without a key or a saw or something, I can't get you off of it."

She said nothing, just stared at him in silent hopelessness and Guthrie could see the huge tears well up in the corners of her eyes.

"But I will not give up. I passed a janitor's closet a little way back, and I'm going to go back to it and see if there is a hacksaw or something to get you off that. Okay?"

She nodded. Tears streamed down her face.

"I'm not leaving you," he said. "I'm just going to look for something to get you down."

He looked into her face, searching for some sign she understood and that there was still some hope in her situation. He saw a glimmer, if only for a second. The hope faded, quickly replaced by the look of naked fear. He turned to the doorway and saw the large, black dog thing coming through the doorway, followed by a dark-haired man in a well tailored suit.

"Excellent," the man said. "You two have already met. Now, if Danny would hurry and get here, we can all be one happy family.

THE OLD MAN opened the basement door and turned back to Danny.

"So?"

"Wait, what?"

"Oh. I guess I'm not as bad off as all that," Don said. "But you really seemed like you were enjoying pushing me around in that thing."

Danny could feel the anger pulsate behind his eyes, like a kettle just before the boil. He stopped dead and crouched, sucked in huge breaths as he did.

"You okay?" Don said.

Danny raised a solitary finger and stared at the old man with a look that blended rage and betrayed exasperation in equal measure. Jack didn't hesitate to notice the boy's closeness to the ground and took it as an opportunity to add his two cents to the current situation and did so. He leapt down from the concrete abutment and licked the boy's face like there was a smoked sausage hidden just below the skin. Rage burns fierce, but it never burns long and within moments, the flames gave way to giggles and soon the boy was roiling on his back with a dog on his chest and laughter bubbling up from deep inside him. It felt good to laugh again, like he hadn't done it in years, and it was enough to turn his attitude around and follow the old man into the basement.

"Jack, you stay here," Danny said, and motioned for the little the dog to stay back.

He gave a little whine and tried to push himself forward.

"No, for real Jack, stay here," Danny said.

"You know, his vision is better than ours. And so are his hearing and his smell."

"And?"

"And if there really is anything down there, he will probably know about it long before we will. Might be safer if we brought him along," Don said.

Danny eyed the dog. He had told him to stay because the thought of anything happening to him while they were down there drove nausea through his belly like a punch. But the old man was right. Danny's senses were massively high when compared to the octogenarian he travelled with, but they paled compared to the little dog's own.

"This is a terrible idea," Danny said.

"He'll be alright. He's a hell of a lot quicker than we are and I'll bet he's pretty good in a scrap," Don said.

Danny recalled Jack had once gone toe to toe with the next-door neighbour's Pitbull and scared him so badly, the dog shit itself on their front porch.

"Fine," he said.

Danny couldn't be certain, though he felt sure he knew that with all certainty, he knew it was impossible, but if asked later, he would swear the dog was smiling.

"Alright, let's go."

The three of them entered the basement through the door at the bottom of the stairs and the stink of the place blew up into their faces like a slap.

"What the hell is-"

"Can you smell that?"

"Yeah, it's awful. Like old ladies rolling in a campfire. What the hell *is* it?" Danny said.

"Lavender," he said after a time. "And sage. Meant to purify and consecrate. There is somebody around here, and they are definitely up to some witchy shit."

Danny stared at the old man in stunned silence and before the question that was practically choking him worked its way past his lips, he spoke again.

"My wife was into all that Wicca crap when it first came into style. We used to be meat and potatoes. Work nine to five, home for dinner by six, maybe a cocktail or two - three or four on the weekend - and then in bed by ten at the latest. On a good night we were in bed by ten, but stayed awake and fooled around 'til eleven. But then she picked up a book in the supermarket, just a little thing on a rack while she was waiting to pay, that said she could win friends, influence people and heal the world all through the practice of Wicca. Mostly, it was harmless. Thanking the goddess at supper time and saying shit to the four corners. But there was also cleansing and purifying. Christ, you could eat off me for all the cleansing she did around me. Burnt a ton of sage and lavender all over the house. I'll never forget the smell of it, always reminds me of her when I smell it now. If that shit is burning down here, something is about to happen."

"Like what?" Danny said.

"The wife told me you burn that shit to start, to clean the slate. If they're burning it down here, it means they're clearing the way for big magic."

"Big magic?"

"Yeah, that's what the wife called it. Cleans the place out, makes room for new stuff," Don said.

"You don't mean real magic, right?" Danny said, fearing the old man's dementia had caught up with him.

"Of course not. There is no such thing. The wife tried all that shit for years and all we ever got was a smelly house and a cat that refused to leave the bathroom," Don said flatly.

Danny sighed and turned back down the hallway.

"The problem is, whoever is down here with us *does* believe it's real and that's liable to make them wanna do just about anything to make sure it happens," Don said.

They carried on in silence for a while, coming to the end of a long hallway and faced a door in the centre of the wall.

"Probably the janitor's office," Danny said.

"Probably should check it out," Don said.

Danny reached for the door handle and Jack let go a deep, atavistic growl before moving between the boy and the door.

"Move Jack."

But he didn't. Instead, the little dog curled himself into a ball and lay down at Danny's feet, growling and grumbling all the while.

"Jack, move."

"That's one stubborn dog," Don said.

"You have no idea," Danny said.

He reached out a foot and pushed the dog aside, amid grumbling protests, which finally gave way to Jack getting up and moving beside him, watching the door intently. Danny turned the handle on the door and dragged it toward him.

Immediately in front of him lay the janitor's body. Bloody and broken and looking as though somebody had folded him in half and stuffed his body into a wooden box before being dumping him here.

"Jesus," Danny said.

"Did you know him?" Don said, pushing in behind the boy.

"Mr. MacPherson, the janitor."

The old man leaned a little closer to the body, taking in the pile of gored flesh that was formerly the janitor of Winterbourne high. "Jesus! Who could do that to a man?"

"Umm... actually, we could."

The voice came out of the darkness beside them, but it didn't stay there. The sound of heavy footfalls coming toward them rang out and in minutes, detective William Kemmler stood in front of the two of them, accompanied by the large black wolf thing that Danny had followed from the drainage pond.

"You?" Don said.

"Yes, me," Kemmler said.

"But you're a cop."

"That's right, and you're a doddering old fool that was given an opportunity to be something, something better than this slow, circling the drain you call a life but, like everything, every other choice you've had, you blew it."

"I blew nothing," the old man said. "Never in my life. I didn't exactly come out on top all the time, but I did alright for me and mine."

"Oh?" Kemmler said, and an awful grin peeled its way across his thin lips. "How're the kids? Been by for a visit lately?"

Don lowered his head and fell silent.

Danny looked at the old man, then back at the man with the short, greasy black hair. "Why are you arguing with him? You don't need to explain anything to this asshole."

"And you!" Kemmler turned to the boy. "You'd be Danny I bet."

"That's right."

"Well, you're just in time. You're the guest of honour at the little party I'm throwing."

"How's that? I'm not going anywhere," Danny said, and turned to leave.

"Oh. You'll want to come to this party," Kemmler said and reached out, grabbing hold of the boy's arm.

"Let go of me!"

A sound erupted from just below Danny's knee, low and rumbling. Like thunder wrapped in cotton. He felt the familiar heat and taut shoulder muscles of his little dog. But he didn't feel it for long. In a flash, Jack had left his side and was mid air, bound for Kemmler's arm. A meaty clout from the wolf thing stopped him abruptly.

"Kill that goddam dog!" Kemmler said.

The wolf thing reached down with surprising speed and scooped up the little dog, staring directly into its face and tightening its grip as the horrid teeth in its horrid mouth moved closer to the dog's throat. The little dog struggled and tried to get away from the thing's constrictor grip and lifted his head up defiantly. It was little use and quickly, the little dog went limp.

"Jack!" Danny said and pulled against Kemmler's equally powerful grip.

The little dog remained drooped over, limp as a jellied eel, and motionless as the wolf thing opened its mouth impossible wide and pushed the little dog's form toward it.

"No!" he said and felt another arm clamp around his wrist. "Jack!" The little dog remained motionless, and he was certain that his best friend was about to become a hot lunch.

Without warning, the little dog sat bolt upright and missed the wolf thing's ravening jaws by inches before clamping his own jaws firmly onto the hairy bastard's ear. It let out a pained yelp and dropped the little dog, who landed on his feet and stood his ground, waiting for round two.

"Go Jack! Get out of here. Go!"

The dog took off out the door and disappeared into the darkness.

"Let go of him," Don said.

"Or what? You'll get lost down here and wander aimlessly until somebody comes to find you, or death comes for you? Sit down, old man. Your time here has come and gone. Just like your usefulness," Kemmler said.

Don opened his mouth to speak, but the words wouldn't come out.

"I'll just bet she went to the ca... to the ca... to the car key car stairs bolt," he said finally.

"Yes." Kemmler smirked, confused at the old man's reply. "I imagine she did."

He snapped his fingers and the wolf thing stood to attention, watching his every move.

"Bring him," he said and shoved the boy toward him. The gangly black thing took hold of Danny and laid a meaty fist along the boy's jaw, knocking him out. He hoisted him up to one shoulder like a sack of potatoes and turned to the old man, holding out his free arm.

"Leave him," Kemmler said. "He's no worry to us," and stepped over him. "Or use."

35

Danny's eyes rolled back into his head so far, he was certain there were colour spots inside his skull. He tried to prop himself up on elbows, but his head swam, and he was sitting in total darkness, or his eyes remained completely closed. There was a strong smell in the room, must and years of neglect left the place acrid and dirty, and it hung in the air like an awful perfume. But there was something else, beyond the dirt and the smell of wet dogs. It was smoke, but unlike the smoke of a campfire with its pleasing, slightly burnt hot dog smell, instead there was something vaguely chemical about the smell. It reminded him of the foster father pouring kerosene on a pile of leaves and garbage in their backyard, to burn through it more quickly and get back to the bottle he'd left alone in the house.

His head was pounding, and his jaw was sore, but if he was ever going to get out of here, he would have to open his eyes some time. Now seemed as good a time as any. He found just doing that required an effort that told him he had just been taking, opening his eyes for granted up to this point. They cracked open and creaked up like a rusty garage door until they were, more or less, open all the way and now that they were, he wished he could take it back and close them tight again.

They were in a large room somewhere in the basement of Winterbourne high school. Danny guessed it was somewhere under the gym - it was the biggest room in the school, so it stood to reason that his room, as large as it was, must be beneath it. The glow of backyard tiki torches in metal sconces along the walls bathed the room in pools of orange yellow light and cast shadows that seemed to breathe as they danced with the flickering of the flames. At the end of the room, he guessed about fifteen feet from where the hairy thing threw him to the floor, was a large stone dais that rose a few feet from the floor, at the front of which stood a large stone lectern with an intricate carving of a flayed man - muscular and venous and appearing to be wearing his own skin as a stole around his shoulders. Behind the podium, massive and dominating the centre of the dais, was a large x-shaped stone cross. It was imposing and overwhelming and strapped to it was a very unconscious Raisin Chan.

Whatever fog still swirled inside Danny's head blew away the second he saw her, and his mind cleared at the sight of his friend trussed up like some awful Sunday School prank.

"Raisin!"

She remained still, head lolling forward and hand and legs limp. Were she not tied to the cross, she would have dropped to the floor in a heap, like an old laundry bag.

"Raisin! Raisin Chan!" he said to her again, and she stirred. Her head lowered again, raised slightly and fell forward under the immense weight of whatever got her hung up on a cross in the first place. She struggled to open her eyes and lost the fight. They closed again as quickly as they had opened, and she went limp again.

"Wei-Xin!" Danny said at her. "You get up now! Do you think fat lazy girls get married and do well? No, fat lazy girls shame their parents with every step they take. You get your lazy ass up now and stop bringing shame on your poor mother!" Danny had heard Raisin's old man scream the words at her so many times that he could recite them from memory. They made the girl mad, and he knew it. Maybe just mad enough to wake her up.

Raisin's head lifted again, eyes fighting to stay open and mouth gulping at the air, trying to clear the fog from her brain.

"Hey!"

Her eyes struggled to focus, and her head turned to the sound of the voice. Soon the two reconciled, and she focused in on his face and managed a sleepy smile.

"Hey, what time is it?" she said dreamily.

"What?" Danny said, slightly perplexed by her response.

He drew himself up from the floor slowly, taking a knee on his way to standing to full height. The dizziness brought on by the crack on the jaw that knocked him cold still lingered behind his eyes. He made his way to the stone dais and Raisin trussed up on the stone cross. She had dozed off again.

"Hey," he said, and gave the unconscious girl a shove. "Wake up."

She remained motionless and Danny was losing hope that, even if he got her off the cross, that she'd be able to get out of here on her own if he didn't do something drastic. He let a slap fly that connected with the side of her face. The crack of skin on skin rang out like thunder and the girl's eyes shot open, rimmed with anger and confusion.

"Ow! What the fuck, Danny?"

"Are you awake now?" he said and raised his hand a second time.

"Yes, I'm awake, I've been- hey, what are you doing here?" She said.

"Looking for you, dumbass. What do you think I'm doing?" He untied the heavy leather thongs holding her onto the stone x.

"No, you've got to get out of here," she said.

"Wait, what? That's gratitude," he said, almost feigning insult in his voice.

"You don't understand. They brought me down here because they knew you'd come looking for me down here eventually," she said.

"I didn't even know you were down here. I came down here

looking for the thing we followed from the culvert. Wait a minute." He stopped untying her. "Who brought you down here?"

"We did," a voice behind him said.

Danny turned to the voice and saw Kemmler and the gangly black dog thing standing alongside him. The greasy haired man wore a long black robe now, silken and shimmering in the torchlight, looking like stars in a cloudless night sky.

"You see," Kemmler said. "I knew that if I brought her down here, you *would* eventually follow. The fact that you came down here on your own was just a coincidental bonus."

"So," Danny said. "Here I am. You don't need Raisin anymore. Let her go."

Kemmler smiled. "Well, that's not entirely accurate.".

Danny stared at the man in the black robe, burning inside to slap the widening grin off his face.

"What do you need her for? It's me you want."

Kemmler sighed. "You really don't know what this is about, do you? Didn't your parents prepare you for any of this?"

"My parents?" Danny was puzzled. "My parents have been dead almost ten years. What could they possibly have to do with any of this?"

"Oh dear," Kemmler said. "It might be easier just to show you than to explain it. Alright everyone, you can come out now."

From the darkness behind the dais, a second tall, gangly dog like thing emerged. Then a second and a third and then there were many of them, ten or fifteen, all standing on the dais and all with their attention trained on him.

"What the f-"

"A little overwhelming, isn't it?"

"What's going on here?" Danny said.

"If you would?" Kemmler said to one of the dog things.

It stood and grasped its top and bottom jaws, pulling in opposite directions until it had peeled the long dog skin off itself and revealed a very naked, slightly slime covered human man standing there in its place. One by one, all the people on the dais followed suit until the whole thing was crowded with naked, mucous covered men and women.

"What the hell are you people?"

"A sort of members-only club," Kemmler said.

An old woman stepped forward and wagged a finger at Kemmler. "Stop wasting time with all of this jabber-boxing," Danny recognized her from Winterbourne home and wondered how she'd gotten here so easily on her own. She seemed all but helpless there and hopelessly deranged. "Tell him what he has to do and let's get on with it."

"Wait, what? What do I have to do?" Danny said.

"Well, yes. A very long time ago, a promise was made, and you were meant for us, and now it is time for you to honour that promise. A promise made by your parents, I might add," Kemmler said.

"I know nothing about it. What did they promise you?"

Kemmler sighed and followed it up with a deep sucking breath. "A very long time ago, three men were out hunting deer. They had not seen a single buck or doe all day and had all but given up and were heading back to their cabin when they came upon a man lying naked in the snow. He was so cold he was near to freezing and so they brought him home with them, set him in front of the fire and warmed him with brandy and soup and warm bread. Soon, he came around and told them all something incredible. He was the last of his kind and he was well over one hundred and fifty years old and, for a small price, he could show them how they could live on and on. Nearly forever."

"What? This sounds like a shitty fairy tale. These three men, did they believe what the man was telling them?" Danny said.

"Of course not," Kemmler said in answer. "They weren't stupid. This wasn't once upon a time. It was just after the first war. People were a little more naïve than they are now, but in some ways, they were a lot smarter. They had a lot more common sense, and they immediately thought the man was crazy."

"But that didn't matter, did it?"

"You're smart Danny. Your whole family was smart, and that's why they promised you. No, to answer your question, it didn't matter. At least not to one of the three. He asked the man how it was possible, how he too could live as long as the naked man said he had lived."

"And?" Danny said impatiently.

"And the man told him. He said that he was what some of the Natives around here called a skin walker - a shapeshifter and he could change his form at will to almost anything he chose. Though his preferred form was a black wolf that walked like a man or crawled on all fours as fast as any animal ever did. The stranger told the man that he would teach him how to change their skin and it would bring them near immortality, but it came at an unbelievable price."

"What price? What wouldn't be worth living forever?" Danny said.

"Would you take immortality over the cleanliness of your soul?"

"What do you mean?"

"Would you cast aside everything you believed your whole life, everything you'd been told is wrong? Could you... would you do *anything* to achieve what the man offered you?"

"Like what? My life has been fairly shitty up to this point, so there wouldn't be much I wouldn't do to change things around here," Danny said.

Kemmler lowered his head and raised it back up again as an ugly, uncomfortable grin spread its way across his face. "I was hoping you'd say that. You see, the man told the stranger how the magic worked and there were two things he would have to do to keep it working. "

"Oh, just two things?" Danny said snidely, his patience for make-believe wearing dangerously thin. "And what are the two things? Does he have to sell his soul to the Devil and rub baby fat all over himself?"

"No, nothing so fanciful. First, the stranger told the man that his youth and power would last so long as he found fresh blood. Every decade, there must be a child who comes freely to the group to learn all the secrets and rituals so that one day, he or she might become the leader and protector over all of them," the greasy haired man said with a laugh.

"What's the second thing?"

"The child must eat the entrails of a freshly killed child of the same age," Kemmler said as though he'd just ordered a sandwich and asked for extra mayo.

"And I suppose this first kid has to kill the second one?"

Kemmler looked toward the ceiling and rubbed his chin in thought. "I don't think that's in the rules, no. But if it turned out that way, I don't think there's anything against it either. But you needn't worry about it. We've got somebody to help you out with the killing part of it."

"Wait, what?"

"Bring him out this way," Kemmler said to the lone remaining dog thing, who disappeared out the only door into the big room and re-entered shortly after, pushing Floyd Guthrie ahead of him.

"You sonofabitch!" Guthrie spat at Kemmler, then he caught sight of Danny. "Are you alright?"

They'd cuffed Guthrie's hands behind his back and stripped him down to just a t-shirt and his dress pants. The dog thing pushed him closer to the dais and turned him around to face Kemmler. Danny could see Guthrie's service revolver still tucked in its holster attached to the back of his belt. Though, with the cop's hands bound up, it may as well have been laying across the room.

"Your friend Floyd has graciously volunteered to help us out with our ceremony today."

"You told me if I did what you told me, you'd let Danny go," Guthrie said.

"Ah detective, the booze must be wearing off, is it? What I said to you was that if you took part, that is, filled a necessary role in the whelping, that I would release Danny."

"So, you'd better keep your end of the fucking bargain."

"Indeed, I will, Floyd. I will release Danny from your world, and he will walk to ours and embrace his destiny with open arms."

"Excuse me?" Danny said.

"Yes, Danny, your parents wanted this for you. In fact, it may be the very reason they created you in the first place. They conceived you to take up the leadership of the Brotherhood of St. Bartholomew."

"How do you know what my parents wanted for me?"

"Because they were members of this brotherhood with excellent standing. In fact, most of your immediate family were members at one point. Mother, father and grandfather. Though he died with the shame of betrayal hovering around his bloated corpse like so many flies."

"Well, that's a lie already. My grandfather died in a nursing home a little while ago. The old man you bullied away from me was his roommate and was with him the day he died. There was no shame, there was no brotherhood. There was a broken-down old man whose mind wasn't his anymore. He was scared and tired of fighting and then he died. Simple as that," Danny said.

"Yes, well, that is an *excellent* whitewashed version of what happened and, if you'll indulged me a moment or two, I insist I shed the light of the lord's own truth on this fairy tale you've been labouring under. When your grandfather came to us, he was still a young man, but his soul was already well and truly broken. His wife had recently succumbed to cancer, leaving him alone to care for a young child. Your mother. We promised him a long life, filled with triumphs and riches if he was willing to work hard enough to get them. He would apprentice himself to one of us and do as they asked until he was worthy enough to become a full-blooded member, but only *if* he was prepared to make the supreme sacrifice. To offer one of his own children. Since his wife was already gone and his prospects of finding another were less than promising, we settled on the gift of a grandchild. You," Kemmler said.

Danny's mouth dropped open in disbelief.

"Things were going well, according to all divine plans, until your mother got wind of what her father had promised. She and her fool of a husband took you and headed away from Winterbourne. Your grandfather was not a powerful man. We barely had to torture him before he told us everything we wanted to know, where your parents had gone, whether they hid you with someone or were stupid enough to bring you along for the ride. Guess what the answer was? After that, it was a few well-placed knocks with another car, and they went careening into a guardrail just above the Nyegard river. With them out of the way and the old man under our control, it was a matter of scooping you up and starting your training to take over."

"But?" Danny said.

"Ah, but then that awful cop friend of your showed up. He was the first on the scene, as I recall, and he insisted on taking care of you until you found somewhere suitable to live. We had hoped for the orphanage, in which case the good sisters would have delivered you to us that very night, but it wasn't to be. You ended up with a couple who are little more than a six pack away from skid row."

"But now you've found me," Danny said.

"Yes, we have, and all will be right soon."

He motioned to the thing standing behind the cop, who pushed him forward, toward Raisin Chan, still firmly tethered to the cross. Kemmler produced a long, slender knife with a curved silver blade and moved around behind Guthrie's back. He slit the black zip ties that had clenched Floyd's hands in place, but not before taking the holster and pistol from the cop's belt and levelling it at him.

"You may proceed," Kemmler said.

"Wait!" Danny said. "What are you doing?"

"We must spill blood for the magic to take hold. It's how it works, Danny. She is of your age. We must sacrifice her."

"No!"

"We've already set the wheels in motion. The man in the woods was perfectly clear about this sort of thing. Once you've accepted the responsibility, you have to carry it out. The blood must flow or there will be dire consequences." He passed the knife slowly to Guthrie, never taking his eyes from the detective's.

"Like?"

"A painful reckoning for all the unnatural things that we are. We who have stolen time for so very, very long. The spilling of the blood seals the pact and eating the entrails brings a certain curative effect. To break faith with the ancestors would cause all the diseases you've avoided and healed with the magic to come roaring back, I should think."

Danny looked at the man with the greasy hair and then at Floyd, who looked at the dagger in his hand and turned his attention to Kemmler.

"No," Kemmler said and fired a single shot into the cop's left foot. The bullet destroyed Guthrie's third toe. A severe enough wound to get his attention and, more importantly, his obedience, but not near anything vital enough to worry about killing him. "Now, if you could just get on with it."

Guthrie limped to the trussed-up girl and held the knife to her throat.

"Wait!" Danny said and walked over to them. "It should be me. I'm her best friend. If anybody should do it, it should be me."

Kemmler sighed. "Fine."

Danny took the knife from Guthrie and raised it to his friend's throat. Her eyes were watery with tears.

"Wait," Danny said.

"Oh, for fu-yes? What is it? Is it too much to ask for someone to kill this fucking girl?"

"You said they promised me?" Danny said.

"Yes. Your parents promised you to us the day you were born. That, when you reached an appropriate age, you would lead us all into a new dawn," Kemmler said.

"But you said the child had to come of his or her own free will. I didn't."

"Yes, we thought about that. It's a bit of a loophole. Your parents speak for you until you are, legally speaking, an adult. It turns out that in the supernatural world, the same sort of thing applies. They promised you then, and you are bound now."

"That's not fair!" Danny said.

"No." Kemmler flashed a satisfied smile. "No, it isn't."

"So, I'm stuck with you assholes, no matter what I do?"

"Looks like," he said and smacked the big revolver across the back of Guthrie's head, dropping him like a stone. "In case he decided to be a hero. Now, if you don't want to suffer an agonizing death with the rest of us, you might take that knife and—"

The door to the big room flew open and slammed against the adjoining wall with a thud. Through it walked a grey-haired old man and a small dog, both of which looked as though they had been through a clothes wringer at least twice before being thrown into a corner.

"Put that goddamned knife down," Don Pierce said.

36

The old man moved surprisingly quickly to the interior of the room and stood his ground there, intending to make a stand and get the boy the hell out of there. How he intended to do it remained a bit of a mystery and the greasy-haired man pointing a pistol at him did little to buoy any courage that he might have been feeling to that point. Fortunately, there was a small, but massively tenacious dog that came in through the door with him and didn't wait to consider a plan he may or may not have had. Jack leaped at the greasy-haired man in the black robe, catching him entirely off guard and sending him back first toward the ground. The force of the impact with the floor jolted the pistol from his hand and knocked the sense from him. At least long enough for the old man to pick up the gun and stand over him, joining the dog in glowering down at him as he motioned for Danny.

"Come here kid," Don said.

"We need to get Raisin off that thing," Danny said.

"Keys, now," Don said.

KEMMLER SAT up and thrust a hand into his pocket and removed it again with a group of keys attached to a small silver ring. He tossed it toward Danny, the jangle of which immediately got the dog's attention. Enough that it caused him to run over to where the keys had fallen. It was the breathing room that Kemmler needed. He sprung at the old man and knocked him flat, pushing the wind from his lungs and taking the pistol out of his hands. He walked to Danny and pointed the revolver at his head.

"Pick up the knife," he said and drove the cold steel against his head. "Please."

Danny took up the knife and gripped it tightly, eyeing the greasy-haired detective with murderous intent.

"Try it," Kemmler said. "I'm begging you. You might get to me. Might even stick the knife into me. But in a heartbeat afterward, all of them would get entirely more beastly and chew through you and your friends like overdone beef. Now, if you could just, you know?" He motioned toward the terror stricken Raisin Chan.

Danny sighed and relaxed his grip on the knife. He was over a barrel and he knew it. Guthrie was still out cold and with Kemmler having a hold of his service revolver, what difference would it make if he was awake? Floyd Guthrie was a lot of things, but a serious contender for proficiency at boxing was likely not one of them. He swallowed hard and walked over to his friend.

"No," Danny said, and dropped the knife.

"What?"

"I said no. All of you might go through a bunch of shit if I don't do it, but what do I care?"

"Not listening? Typical for someone your age. I said you were bound to us by your parents. Once they swore a blood oath that we could have you after you reached an age, you became ours. Danny Nesbitt became one of us. You will suffer the same awful fate as we will if you don't fulfil the ritual. One of us, one of us. We accept you, one of us, young man. Like it or not. Flourish or burn with us, your choice."

"Fine," Danny said.

"What?"

"Fine, I said. But not her. Somebody else. I'll do it, but get somebody else, somebody I don't know."

He dropped the knife and folded his arms across his chest.

"Very well," Kemmler said and walked to him.

"Really?" Danny said.

Kemmler picked up the knife and sidestepped Danny, moving behind him and standing face to face with the semi-conscious girl on the stone cross.

"No," he said calmly. "Not really." And drew the knife across the girl's throat.

Raisin's eyes snapped open, filled with a mix of fear and betrayal, searching the room for something to say this was just an awful dream and soon she'd be waking up in her bed. She opened her mouth to speak but found no words left her. The best she could manage was a choked, frothy gurgle.

"No!" Danny rushed to her and put his hands up to her neck, trying to staunch the flow of blood. It was a losing battle. He looked up to her eyes, hoping there might be some measure of peace in them as her life slipped away, but there was only panic and the terrified realization that she was about to die.

"It'll be fine." Danny's voice shook as the tears bit at the corners of his eyes. "It'll be fine. We'll get you to the hospital and they'll patch you up and you'll be back at school in no time."

But she was already fading. Her skin greyed, and her eyelids drooped as the blood gushed from the wound, taking her life with it.

"Don't you go! Don't you go and leave me, Raisin. I'm going to fix this. I'm going to fix all of this. I just need a big bandage or something. Can somebody get me a fucking bandage? Somebody get me a bandage!" he said.

But he couldn't stop the blood flowing out with his hands any more than he could have held the tide with a teaspoon, no matter how many bandages. He looked into her eyes with pleading in his own.

"Don't you leave me, don't you fucking leave me! Please, Raisin. Please!"

She met his eyes, forcing her own open one more time and, after forcing a whisper over failing lips, she was gone.

Danny dropped to his knees, wracked with sobs. Jack walked slowly to him and licked his face. The boy took hold of the dog and hugged him within an inch of his life. The little dog, for his part, let him until he couldn't take the confinement a second longer. He wriggled free of Danny's grip and walked toward the greasy haired man. The dog seemed to sigh and sat back on his haunches, begging to scratch his ear. First lightly and quickly, and then slowly and deliberately. Digging at the side of its head as though a massive tick was feasting on its hide, somewhere deep beneath the fur.

Kemmler moved toward Danny, but Jack sat up and growled at the detective.

"I just killed his girlfriend," he said to the little dog. "I won't have a bit of a problem shooting you."

He cocked the pistol and levelled it at the dog. Jack continued to dig fiercely at his ear until it dropped to the floor.

"What the f-"

Jack dug more. Scratching and scraping, deeper and harder and soon, a great crevice opened across the top of his head. The little dog lowered its face, staring at the ground, and brought one of his paws up, snagging the back of his head until the crevice split open entirely. He groped at a piece of the ragged flesh and pulled it downward while pushing up with his muscular back legs. A face emerged from the torn flesh, followed by a head and a neck. A few grunts and barks and shoulders and a chest pushed their way forward. In short order the rest of him followed and stood up, kicking away the skin of the little dog which was little more than furry underpants at this point.

"What the f-" Kemmler said again, and it was as much as he got out.

The man that was formerly Danny's dog, leapt at the greasy

haired detective with a blind fury and caught him mid chest, knocking him to the floor and sending the revolver flying toward the boy. He landed on top of the detective and rained blow after blow after blow on him. Kemmler raised his hands to stop the onslaught, but a few well-timed shots from the other man landed on his chin and soon he was out cold. But the attack didn't stop. The man continued raining blows on the unconscious cop until he was sure the man wasn't going anywhere. Only then did he stand up and back away from the bloody, prostrate figure.

"Who the hell are you?" Danny said.

"Danny, I'm your-ughnh!"

Kemmler leaped off the floor and was on the man in an instant. Only, it wasn't Kemmler anymore, not entirely. He was mid transformation from the rat-faced-greasy haired detective to one of the shaggy haired, gangly dog-like things that Danny had chased from the drainage culvert. It flattened the man and repaid him for the assault with a flurry of blows of his own.

"Now," the Kemmler thing said.

The figures standing on the dais, who, until now, had remained silent and still, ripped at their flesh, revealing the doglike things beneath. Soon they were all savage and ravening forms moving into a circle around the two struggling men-beasts. The Kemmler thing took the upper hand and the two figures thundered to the ground in a cloud of dust and sweat and blood. He put his hands around the other man's throat and squeezed for all he was worth. After losing consciousness, the man reverted to his old appearance. Kemmler released his grip and stood back as the little dog lay there in the centre of the circle, looking for all intents like he'd gone to sleep.

"Rip this fucking dog to pieces," he said to the assembled beasts.

One of the larger dog things moved to the centre of the circle and it bent to get Jack and bared its lethal fangs. The wispy hairs that danced along the top of the dog's head were practically in its mouth when an odd mix of confusion and disappointment flashed in its right eye as the left one burst out of its face. It fell to the floor in a heap.

"Get the fuck away from that... dog? Wait, all this is about the goddam dog? Alright, nobody is doing anything else until I find out what the hell is going on here," Guthrie said.

He waved the gun at the assembled things, making certain they knew he would shoot the next one that moved.

"Well," Don said. "It looks like this is some kind of cult and these... people are a part of it. They want Danny to-"

The Kemmler thing leaped forward and tackled the old man.

"Danny, take this," Floyd said and handed Danny the revolver. "If anything moves, kill it."

He jumped on the back of the Kemmler thing and began beating for all he was worth. The old man struggled to keep the black, hairy thing from ripping his throat out, but it was a losing battle and soon he was far too tired to hold it back anymore. He let go and closed his eyes, waiting for the sickening crunch of canine teeth around his neck. His eyes looked at the cop on the thing's back and smiled.

"Hey, old man, not that time yet, don't you check out on me," Guthrie said.

Floyd grabbed hold of Kemmler's long ears and yanked his head backward. He had nearly bent his head backward when he felt the claws of the other things grabbing at him, trying to pull him off their leader. Guthrie struggled, trying to remain upright and on top of the greasy-haired detective, but there were too many of them. The cop went down. Soon the hands were all over him and he was praying he would black out before the worst of the ripping and tearing began. A single shot rang out.

"Let them up, both of them," Danny said.

The things moved away from Guthrie and the older man, and the Kemmler thing stood and faced all three of them.

"By my count, you've got four shots left. You might get one of them off - maybe even two of them and if you're lucky, you might just kill me with them. But the second I fall, they'll tear you and your friends and your precious little dog to ribbons. Why not just drop the gun and take your place alongside us? The way your parents intended."

Danny lowered the gun and walked over to his fallen dog. He crouched low beside him and stroked the soft fur on his ears, hoping for a sign that Jack was still a going concern. When he saw his chest rise and fall several times in succession, he breathed a sigh of relief that at least the little dog was alive. He turned and moved toward the dais, looking at the blanched and bloody corpse that was his best friend, and turned back to the assembled group of people.

"It's the only way Danny," Kemmler said. "You have no other choice. You are bound to us. Come here, son." He stretched out his arms to embrace the boy.

Danny looked at the bloodied faces of Guthrie and Don Pierce and saw the defeat in their eyes. He knew the second he fired the gun, the dog things would be all over the pair of them. Or worse, he'd agree to join them, and they'd force him to kill the two men. He lowered his head and sighed. Kemmler was right. There really was no choice at all.

"No other choice," Danny said. He raised the gun and fired.

The bullet ripped through the side of his head, taking fragments of his skull and spraying blood and bits of brain with it. His body stiffened instantly, and he hit the ground like a broken ironing board, the blood spurting out of his head like a gruesome fountain. His legs kicked out, straightened and kicked out again. And he was gone.

"No!" Kemmler said.

But it was too late. The cataclysm had already begun, and the assembled group of skin-walkers were falling victim to it quicker than any of them could have known. Most of them took a few steps before withering up and falling away like leaves from an autumn maple tree. Kemmler was not as lucky as the rest. The skin of his face sloughed off in huge chunks, falling to the ground with the sound of rotting fruit. The blood and exposed muscles that remained sizzled and curled up like burnt strips of bacon and dropped off. He screamed and writhed and tried to make it stop and, after what seemed an eternity, there was little left of him but a few bits of rancid flesh hanging off a mangled skeleton. They were gone, all of them, and the brotherhood of St. Bartholomew with them.

"Are you alright?" Guthrie said.

"Never mind me, go get the boy," Don said.

Guthrie crouched down and took Danny in his arms. His head lolled freely like a rag doll and the man pulled him to his chest. The cop's tears poured down his face, streaking his cheeks and splashing liberally on Danny's blood-stained face. The boy wasn't sick. The boy wasn't sleeping. The boy was dead.

"Come on, Floyd," Don said. "Let's get him out of here. I'll get the dog."

They walked out in silence and made it to Guthrie's shitty green Ford.

"I'll take care of Danny," Guthrie said. "I'll take him to the hospital and make sure he gets a proper burial."

"That would be good," Don said, unsure of what else he should say.

"Can you take care of his dog?"

"I'm not really sure I can. They don't allow dogs at Winterbourne.

"I think I can pull a few strings."

"That'd be lovely, Floyd. I think everyone would like Jack."

They remained silent all the way back to Winterbourne home. Floyd pulled the Ford up to the front gate and put it in park.

"Say, listen Floyd, if you ever need to–" Don said.

"I know, I know. I'll be around," Guthrie said.

37

D on Pierce sat in his room on the third floor of Winterbourne home and stroked the fur behind Jack's ears. It was the little dog's favourite place to be scratched. Jack allowed the scratching until his back leg shook involuntarily.

"We've got to get ready soon," he said to Jack. "It's Monday, Floyd's coming today to take us to lunch."

IT HAD BEEN six months since the basement of the school, and Floyd Guthrie had done his best to take the old man and the dog to lunch every Monday, the way he would for Danny. Occasionally, the bottle got the better of him, but mostly he was there, like clockwork. They would eat at the Cedar Rail, the shitty little take out joint on the other side of town that hadn't changed their fry grease since the late sixties, but Don never ate much anyway, though Jack had developed a healthy addiction to foot long hot dogs and onion rings. Their conversation would start off innocently enough, weather, current events, and each other's health, but would inevitably delineate to what they'd been through, as all people with common trauma do.

"How long before they open the school again?" Don said.

"Not long now. I told my bosses that the mess left behind when all those things died was a huge rat infestation and they all but condemned the place while they pumped enough poison in there to level the city. The basement is likely just about clear by now."

"Do you think there are more of those *things*?"

"I don't think so," Guthrie said flatly. "Kemmler was pretty clear about what they were up against and what would happen if Danny didn't go through with it. Once the kid… you know, did what he did, I figure he broke the chain, and it all came crashing down."

"I hope so," Don said. "I'd hate for one of them things to come looking for you and start chewing on your ass while me and Jack ain't around."

"You two plan on going somewhere?"

"Well, no, but we won't be around forever, you know?"

Guthrie laughed. "Shut up." He started the shitty green Ford.

They told one another the same stupid jokes they had told every Monday for the last six months and laughed just as genuinely and joyously as they had the very first time, each man truly enjoying the other's company. They pulled up to Winterbourne Home.

"Help me get out. My knees are awful stiff these days," Don said.

Guthrie got out and came around to the other side of the car and helped the old man get to his feet. Don leaned forward and gave the detective an awkward hug.

"Thanks Floyd," he said, and the tears welled in the corners of his eyes.

"For what?" Guthrie said.

"For giving a shit."

"Get going, old man. I'll see you next week," Guthrie said, choking back his own tears.

Don and Jack made their way into Winterbourne home, stopping occasionally to visit with the wheelchair bound old ladies who roamed the halls and never tired of showering the little dog with hugs and ear rubs and the odd stolen biscuit or scrap of meat from the previous meal of the day. They made it back to their room and

Jack Jumped up on the bed, waiting for Don to snuggle in beside him, knowing full well this was the usual time when the old man would take his nap.

"You know," Don said. "The one thing I could never figure out? How all of those awful things burnt up and flaked away, or whatever happened to them, after poor Danny killed himself. Yet, you're still here, aren't you, Bob?"

The little dog looked at the old man and cocked his head, looking every bit like the old man had just asked him if he wanted food.

"I know it's you, Bob Mifflin, so you don't have to hide from me anymore. Fact is, I miss you, old bastard, and I wish you would just knock this shit off and come back in here with me."

Don hugged the little dog and lay down on the bed.

"I know it's you, Bob. And I know that you know I know it's you,"

He rubbed the little dog behind the ears, which was as comforting to him as it was Jack, and soon, Don Pierce was fast asleep. Jack wandered up beside the old man and tucked in beside him, snuggling up as tightly as he could.

"I told you to leave my goddam shirts alone," the little dog said and licked the old man's face.

ABOUT THE AUTHOR

S. A. Baker is a health care worker and recovering professional musician who spent eleven years touring around North America and despite popular opinion, he really does know how to smile.

From early on, he excelled at telling stories and won several local writing awards before being bitten by the rod and roll bug.

He currently lives in a small town in Ontario with his wife and two children and two of the dumbest cats that have ever drawn breath. When not writing, Mr. Baker plays bagpipes competitively (no, really) and thinks about learning to fly fish. Sleeping Dogs is his 5th story in the ever growing Winterbourne omnibus.

ALSO BY S. A. BAKER

Winterbourne

Faun Song

Somewhere Beyond the Fire

Not a Hope in Hel

Wisdom from the Fuzzy Blue Chair